INNOCENT INTENTIONS

ELLIE HALLARON

Cover design by Ellie Hallaron

ISBN: 979-8-9990397-0-5

First edition, 2025

Innocent Intentions

Book One of the Syndicate Series

For rights, permissions, or inquiries, contact:

EllieHallaron.Author@gmail.com

To my Circle of Trust, if it weren't for your encouragement and support, Innocent Intentions, and all the others to come, would still be sitting in my mind. Thank you. I love you guys.

And to all the lovely ladies wasting away on your couches with your romance novels waiting for a sexy, rich mafia-man to kidnap you, obsess over you, and serve you coffee in bed every morning, I wrote Matthias just for you.

Content Warning

This is a dark romance intended for mature audiences. It contains themes that some readers may find triggering, including kidnapping, murder, violence, attempted sexual assault, and blurred lines between protection and possession. The heroine runs her mouth, refuses to behave, and has no idea how to back down, even when she's losing. The morally gray anti-hero never planned for love but will burn the world to keep hers.

This is not a safe romance, but it is a satisfying one.

If you like luxury you never asked for, desire you never expected, and intimacy you can't stop craving...

Let me introduce you to Matthias Montclair.

Prologue
Matthias

"Mr. Montclair!" a deep voice calls from over my shoulder.

I turn to see Senator Prescott approaching. He's an older, lanky man with gray hair obviously combed over to hide his balding, wire-framed glasses perched on his long nose, and enough wrinkles to expose his age. Even with his above average height, I tower over him at six foot four inches.

"I was hoping to catch you. You've been popular tonight. Then again, you always have people lining up for your attention."

Oh God, not another one. When will this night end?

I force a laugh. "That does seem to be the case. How can I help you, Senator?"

"I wanted to discuss your newest piece of tech. I've heard rumors it's quite the advancement," he says, eyes filled with thinly veiled greed.

This is how my life goes as the CEO of Syndicate Enterprise, one of the biggest private defense and security companies in the nation. People always want something from me. They weasel their way into my life. It happens everywhere, especially at these damn galas.

"Now Senator, this is a party. Why don't we set up a call on Monday to discuss business? I wouldn't want to keep you from your wife." I glance over his shoulder and suppress a grin at the sight of his inebriated wife blatantly flirting with a much younger man.

With that, I shake his hand and walk away.

I have no more patience for pleasantries. My usual charisma has been depleted. It was a long day at the office, closing out an even longer week at the office. The last thing I want to be doing on a Saturday night is entertain the social elite of Boston. These charity galas are merely façades, excuses for the self-important to shmooze one another.

But as the face of Syndicate Enterprise, I have to make an appearance and don my own mask. My role in the family demands it. Although it has its inconveniences, like wasting my weekend at an event I couldn't care less about, we all knew I was the best man for the job.

With my charming, approachable demeanor and ability to dominate a boardroom, not to mention my insanely good looks that have women desperate for me, I exude power. People trust a good face and easy smile. It's not all an act; I do enjoy the finer things in life.

My older brother, Dominic, was born to be the head of the Syndicate. No one dares defy Dom. His men respect him, and his enemies fear him. He's cold. Calculating. Which makes him perfect to rule our criminal empire. So, he took over when our father stepped down. That, and he's bossy as fuck. *Maybe a good lay will loosen him up and melt that frigid heart of his.* Hell, maybe I'll pay a woman to keep him company. Not that he'd appreciate it. He'd probably shoot me for the thoughtful gesture.

Roman, our younger brother, would be a disaster running the legal side of our operations. He doesn't have the patience or composure for boardrooms and galas. He's better with his... fists. And weapons. No one can resist spilling secrets once Roman gets involved. Anyone who crosses us faces his wrath. He definitely has some anger issues. He's honestly a little terrifying, but that makes him the perfect enforcer for the Syndicate.

Sebastian, the youngest, is far too intelligent to waste his talents at events like this. Not that I'm not intelligent, I am. He's just a genius, not that I'd ever admit it to him; he'd enjoy that far too much. Bash can do things with computers that shouldn't be possible. It's actually terrifying how little privacy people have. He's the brain behind everything, both legal and otherwise. But don't be fooled, he can be just as lethal as the rest of us.

Which leaves me, Matthias Montclair, as the CEO of Syndicate Enterprises. I love what I do. And I'm damn good at it. There's a reason the Montclair name is now synonymous with security and defense instead of crime.

When our father passed down the organization, we decided to clean up our reputation and start working in the light as well. We built Syndicate Enterprises as a way to legitimize ourselves, and it's now a multibillion-dollar empire. This company is my baby, and I've nurtured and shaped her into the powerhouse she is today.

Which is why I'm here. While my brothers prowl around the underbelly of the city, I play the role of polished businessman.

I check my watch: *eight thirty p.m.*

How is it so early?

I promised myself I would stay until the auction ended. Which takes place in an hour and a half.

I excuse myself from yet another mind-numbing conversation in search of some food, or better yet, booze. I don't normally drink at these events, preferring to keep a clear head, but tonight, I need something strong to get through the next, I check my watch: *eight thirty-seven p.m.,* hour and twenty-three minutes.

At the bar, I order a whiskey neat. The first sip sends a soothing burn down my throat. It warms my body, easing some of the tension. I take a few deep breaths trying to summon patience.

It's not working.

So, I take another sip. Then another. Until finally, I feel like I can survive until ten p.m.

I check my watch again: *eight fifty-five p.m.*

Only one more hour of this nonsense. I can handle that.

"There you are, darling! I've been looking all over for you," a shrill voice chirps.

I turn around to see a blonde in a tight dress approaching.

Fuck. I forgot I brought a date.

I had thought that if I at least had a woman to go home with, it'd make the evening more bearable.

I couldn't have been more wrong.

Just the sound of her voice annoys me. I'm in no mood for this.

"Adrienne." I address her with a grin. It's not her fault she grates on my nerves. It's just been a long week. Maybe a good lay will help me relieve the stress.

She must be thinking the same thing because she curls up to my side and thrusts out her fake tits. She shoots me a salacious grin, but it does nothing for me. She just seems too eager.

She's one of my regulars. We've had our fun, but I'm bored. Maybe I just miss the chase. Women throw themselves at me. There's no challenge anymore. Maybe I might even want more than just sex. I'm getting older. Fuck, I'm thirty-four. It could be time I settle down.

Or maybe I'm just tired. I'll be better tomorrow once I'm rested up.

"Let's see if there's anyone else I need to talk to before I go," I say, more to myself than to her.

My California king consumes my thoughts. Silk sheets and warmth wait for me at home.

She must misinterpret my disinterest in the party as interest in her, because she leans in and whispers in my ear, "Or we could find a closet. You're looking a little tense. I can help with that." She shoots me a wink.

I hold back a shudder. I could not be any less interested in sex with her right now.

"Not now. I still have a few people I need to catch." I let her down gently.

"Are you sure? I'll let you do anything you want." She pouts her lips in a way that she must think is sexy but makes her look like a toddler throwing a tantrum.

"We're not hooking up in a supply closet at a gala with business associates around." I'm losing my patience.

"Fine. Come find me when you're ready to leave."

"I'm going home alone tonight. I can get you a cab if you need."

I'm still a gentleman after all. I'll make sure she has a ride home, but knowing her, she'll probably try to find another rich man's bed to get into tonight. *Not my problem.*

"Don't bother!" She huffs and storms away.

I assumed correctly. Good luck to the man she sinks her claws into for the night. I really need to end things with her.

At least that's settled. I check my watch: *nine twenty-three p.m.* Good enough; I'm heading home. My patience has run dry, and my bed's siren song is too seductive to ignore.

...

As I pull into my driveway, my phone rings.

Dom.

If he's calling when he thinks I'm at a business gala, it must be serious.

"Dom, what is it?" I ask, too exhausted for greetings. Every second that delays me from my bed isn't worth my energy.

"The Bratva is up to no good. I'm not sure what, but something doesn't feel right." His tone is hard.

Dom's good at what he does. If he has a feeling something is amiss, then we take that seriously. He's rarely wrong.

"What makes you say that?"

"They're getting bolder and seem to have more money to throw around, but I don't know where it's coming from. Keep an eye out on the legal side of things. Let me know if you hear anything."

He hangs up before I can respond.

As I get ready for bed, a strange sense of anticipation settles over me. Something is coming. I don't know what, but I can feel it. And for the first time in a while, I'm excited.

I'm ready for something new.

Chapter 1
Margot

THUD!

My forehead smacks on my desk. I'm so done with this. I cannot figure out what's going on with these shipments.

I'm trying to balance last month's records for the northern ports. At least I was, until I found a discrepancy.

At first, I only noticed one shipment. Nothing major, just a few crates, but the pay was astronomical. That was the first red flag.

I did some digging but couldn't find the detailed invoice. There's no record of what was in the crates, where they came from... nothing. So, I got curious.

I started searching for similar shipments and found pay stubs for the same amount, deposited every other Saturday for the last few months from the same company: Koschei Group.

I investigated the company. *You googled the company.* I couldn't find anything. Nothing. No website, no social media, no advertisements.

Alarms blare in my head. Something sketchy is definitely going on.

The only thing I found were legends about Koschei the Deathless in Russian folklore, a sorcerer who torments people, hiding his soul in a needle, which he then locks inside a series of objects, like Russian nesting dolls.

As long as the needle remains intact, he can't be killed. In most stories, he kidnaps a princess and forces her to marry him, only for a hero to destroy his horcrux-needle and set the princess free.

Creepy.

I never considered the possibility that Northern Hemisphere Cargo could be involved in something illegal. Being an international shipping company operating out of the Boston Harbor ports, it'd be a good way to smuggle things.

How am I just realizing this?

But there really isn't much crime out here, so I don't know who would be using the ports like that.

I've been working for NHC since I graduated college four years ago. It's been fine. I'm a financial analyst in the Boston branch, working mostly from home. My hybrid schedule is perfect, because it lets me lounge in my pajamas all day. I only go in for important meetings.

Honestly, I feel a little guilty for not noticing the Koschei Group's orders earlier. But, in my defense, my job doesn't always get my full, undivided attention. One of the consequences of working from home is, well, not always working.

I have a little less motivation to actually give a full eight hours to staring at numbers. I may sleep in a little, and go on my daily coffee run, and then there's the occasional nap.

I'm more invested in my side gig: audiobook narrator.

It started as a hobby, but I've really gotten into it.

I heard someone say that people either view their job as just a job, others as a career, or, if they're lucky, as a calling. My Northern Hemisphere Cargo position falls in the just-a-job category. I didn't know there were people whose jobs aren't a chore, but recording audiobooks proved me wrong. It brings me a level of joy that could only be summarized as a calling.

My addiction to a good love story inspired me to start narrating audiobooks. I read over one hundred and fifty books in a single year and realized many of my favorites didn't have audiobooks. I researched, reached out to authors, bought some equipment, and the rest is history.

Despite my love for romance stories, real life romance hasn't seemed to be in the cards for me. I'm twenty-six and still haven't been in a serious relationship.

My dad thinks I'm going to be a spinster. He constantly reminds me that I'll never meet someone from my couch. My mom, on the other hand, keeps trying to set me up with her friends' sons, none of whom I've been remotely interested in. It never goes well, and I fear it'll eventually ruin her friendships.

It's honestly a relief that they're traveling now. Since retiring, they've been roaming the world together. They never got to explore and are making the most of it now. I do miss having them in the city, but I'm happy for them.

To be fair, they aren't entirely wrong.

I don't put much effort into dating. Another problem with being hybrid is that I don't leave the house every day. Which is why my coffee runs are so important. *As if you're going to meet someone on a coffee run.*

It's not that I don't want to have love. I really do. I've even tried online dating, but none of the guys on the apps compare to my beloved men-written-by-women.

So, for now, I'm sticking to my books and movies from the comfort of my couch.

Which is where I currently am, staring at my computer, deliberating on how to proceed with the whole Koschei Group situation.

Actually, this is above my pay grade. I'll let my boss handle it.

I draft an email to Ronald explaining my findings. I attach screenshots of the payment records, dates, and amounts, and tell him I can't find a public record of the company. I even add that I think something illegal may be going on and offer to report it to the authorities.

After hitting send, I glance at the clock: *five p.m.* Officially the weekend.

I shut down my laptop. I watch my work phone die, but since it's Friday, I don't bother plugging it in. I'll do that Sunday night.

I have a strict rule of not working outside of work hours. It's bad for the soul.

I check my audiobook email and smile when I see a new author reaching out about recording her book. I'm excited to read it. I message her back, letting her know I'm interested.

I'm still not making enough money to quit my day job, but every book is getting me closer.

One day, I'll be able to leave finance behind and narrate full time. *I'm sure that'll be the day you also have a happily ever after with your dream man.*

For now, I'll stick to dreaming.

Chapter 2
Margot

My alarm goes off. *For the fifth time.*

With a groan, I finally drag myself out of bed. One day, I'll wake up to a hot man bringing me coffee in bed every morning.

Keep dreaming.

I shuffle through my morning routine. Brush teeth, wash face, fix hair. Then head to the kitchen and set up the coffee maker, desperate for my caffeine fix.

BEEP!

I follow the noise to my desk in confusion. It came from my work phone, which I plugged in last night before bed.

Ronald.

Fuck. Why is my boss texting me?

I open the message. He wants to meet at a coffee shop near the office at nine a.m. I check my watch. Double fuck. It's eight thirty a.m.

I throw on random clothes, grab my bag, and rush out the door.

...

On my way to the coffee shop, I skim through my work phone and feel my stomach sink. Three emails. Four texts. Seventeen missed calls. All from Ronald.

What the actual fuck?

The first email came minutes after I sent my report on Friday, asking me to call him immediately. Each gets progressively more serious.

Yeah, I definitely stumbled onto something serious.

...

By the time I get to the café, it's five past nine. There's no sign of Ronald.

Weird. He hates tardiness.

Lucky me. I have time for a caramel macchiato. *Looks like you have your priorities in order.*

I step in line, scrolling through my phone, until I look up.

And nearly forget how to breathe.

The man in front of me has the best ass I've ever seen. I mean, he could be a baseball player with glutes like that. And if his ass wasn't enough, the rest of him sure as hell is.

At around six foot four with his broad as hell structure, he obviously *enjoys* the gym. And I'm enjoying the effects of him enjoying the gym. His custom-tailored navy-blue suit hugs every muscular inch of him. His short, dark hair falls just messily enough to look good.

I know it's soft. I just know it is. My fingers twitch with the need to run through it. I can't seem to look away.

Then he speaks.

"A large, black coffee, please."

I swear to God, my *entire body* tingles. His smooth voice exudes confidence. The deep timbre feels like an earthquake in my bones.

I instinctively step forward, drawn to him before my brain catches up.

This man is doing things to me that I've never experienced, and I haven't even seen his face. This is ridiculous.

He pulls his card out to pay, but just as he hands it over, his phone rings.

"Roman," he answers, voice clipped.

The man, Roman, on the other end says something I can't make out. Then he turns to the cashier. "Cancel the order. I have to go."

And just like that, he's gone.

I don't even catch his face. Just his scent. His clean, masculine, expensive scent. I shudder.

Jesus, Margot. Get a grip.

"Miss?"

I blink. The barista stares at me like I have two heads.

"Um... sorry. What was that?"

She sighs, looking exasperated. To be fair, I'd also be annoyed if I had to deal with sleep-deprived caffeine addicts all morning.

"Are you with him?" She holds up a matte black credit card. "He left this."

The card looks expensive. Stiff black, probably made of metal.

He's obviously rich.

"Yes," I say before I can think about it. "I'll take it to him."

This will be my good deed of the day. I'll give him his card then come back for my meeting.

And if he wants to thank me with a kiss, that's his prerogative.

That's likely.

I ignore my inner fiend's sarcasm and snatch the card from her. I hurry outside, hoping to catch him.

Glancing down, I check the name.

Matthias Montclair.

Chapter 3
Matthias

I listen to Roman talk as I rush out of the café, irritation bubbling under the surface. I've been waiting for his update, but did it really have to come right before I got my coffee?

One of our men caught a Bratva member snooping around our territory last night. He was propositioning men outside one of the nightclubs. They know they're not allowed in our territory. The consequences can be deadly. Before Roman kills him, we need to know what he was up to.

Even though I run the legal side of the family, I still stay in the loop about what's happening on the other side. We try to keep the two worlds separate, but inevitable crossover occurs. It's better for us to all stay informed.

"The man is a low-level soldier," Roman says. "I could tell based off his tattoos. He claims he didn't know he was on our turf."

I take a sharp turn down an alley to make the conversation private. Another turn, and I'm behind a brick building, leaning against the wall.

"Is he lying?"

"Yeah. The Bratva may be inept, but they make sure every recruit knows where the boundaries are."

"You sure?"

"Let's just say, I used some very persuasive methods to get the truth out of him." I can hear Roman's grin at that, the sick bastard. No doubt those methods were bloody.

I sigh. "Spare me the details of the torture. I trust your methods. Did he tell you what he was selling? New blow?"

"That's where it gets weird. He claims he doesn't know."

I straighten. "What the fuck do you mean, 'he doesn't know'? He's obviously lying. Threaten to cut his tongue out if he doesn't start using it to tell the truth."

"I don't think he is, man." Roman sounds just as confused as I feel. "He claims he was told to lure men behind some clubs and send them to Bratva-owned clubs on their side of town."

That doesn't sit right. "Are you sure it's not drugs?" Their product is garbage, cut with rat poison, bleach, and fentanyl. I don't know how they have any clients left with how many their drugs kill. "I don't want that shit killing people in our city."

"I really don't think it's drugs." Roman exhales sharply. "I'll push him for more information."

"Did you question the men outside the club?"

"Too drunk or high to remember anything."

I grind my jaw. "Fuck. Are you going to kill him, or let him crawl back to Viktor with a message?"

"Not my call. Gotta see what Dom says."

"Fine. If any more come into our territory, we need to know if it's shoot-on-sight or bring them in for questioning. Keep me updated."

I don't usually get my hands dirty, but if I do, I need to know the rules of engagement.

"Will do," Roman says, then hangs up.

And I hear a crash.

Chapter 4
Margot

I rush out of the café, determined to catch him. At first, I don't see him, but then... there! About fifty feet away, turning down an alley.

I quicken my pace and follow him.

This alley looks sketchy as hell. What is a man like him doing sneaking around back here?

He takes another turn behind the building. I follow.

I'm about to shout his name. Should I call him Matthias or Mr. Montclair? But then I hear him talking.

He's still on the phone. Maybe I should wait for him to finish. It must be important if he canceled his coffee order. It takes a lot for me to give up coffee... like doing a good deed... *for a sexy man.*

"Spare me the details of the torture. I trust your methods. Did he tell you what he was selling? New blow?" That smooth, sexy voice graces me again.

I'm getting goose bumps just hearing it. My body's visceral reaction to this man is ridiculous. I haven't even seen his face.

For all I know, he could have a face only a mother could love. *Doubtful.* There's no way this voice and ass belong to a man who isn't attractive. I can hear his confidence in his voice. Only a sexy man sounds like that. I need to see the face that matches that voice.

Then his words register.

I freeze midstride.

Excuse me, what did he just say?

I don't even have time to process it before he speaks again.

"What the fuck do you mean, 'he doesn't know'? He's obviously lying. Threaten to cut his tongue out if he doesn't start using it to tell the truth."

My breath catches, and I start rethinking my decision to follow a stranger into a dark alleyway where no one from the street can hear or see us. The theme song for Dumb Ways to Die starts playing in my head. *Not the time for this, Margot.*

"Are you sure it's not drugs? I don't want that shit killing people in our city."

Oh my God. This is bad. This is really bad.

Should I report this? What even is the protocol when you accidentally eavesdrop on crime? Not just any crime, *torture.*

I try to weigh my options. Do I stay and listen so I can file a report? Do I sneak away before I become the next cautionary tale?

I really like my tongue. I would very much like to keep it. I need it to talk. To narrate my audiobooks. To sing. Even though my voice is horrid, my shower concerts bring me great happiness. Losing my tongue would be a tragedy.

"Fuck. Are you going to kill him, or let him crawl back to Viktor with a message?"

My stomach plummets.

Is this premediated murder? Oh my God, I need to call the cops. They can save this guy, whoever he is, from this Roman guy's torture... and intent to murder. Is that what it's called? I don't know the legal jargon!

"Fine. If any more come into our territory, we need to know if it's shoot-on-sight or bring them in for questioning. Keep me updated."

I back up. Slowly. Quietly. I don't turn my back on this man. I want to be ready if he attacks me. Not that there's much I could do against this god of a man. His suit can't hide his muscular build–

CRASH!

Time slows.

It takes me a second too long to realize *I* was the one who made the noise.

Oh my God. I backed into a dumpster. Oh my actual God. Of all the fucking times to be clumsy.

I look up, right into his eyes.

Before I can even blink, he's on me.

I gasp as my back slams into the brick wall. His arms cage me in, one on either side of my head. He's crouched just enough to be eye level with me.

"Who are you?"

His voice sounds even harsher than it did a few seconds ago, and he sounded pretty damn scary then.

But I'm not paying attention. Not to his tone, not to his words. Because, *holy shit,* his eyes.

Light brown, flecked with gold. They're mesmerizing. And his lashes, they're thick, dark, and ridiculously long.

Not fair.

He lets out a grunt of annoyance. Which draws my gaze to his mouth. His full, pink lips. I bet they're soft. My tongue darts out, wetting mine. I start to lean forward, needing to feel them.

"Who are you?" He repeats, his voice sharp as a knife.

I freeze mid-lean.

Oh, right. The part where he might kill me. That's where we are right now.

My cheeks start blazing. Definitely out of fear. Not embarrassment from being caught ogling him. *Sure, and also not from being held up by such a hot man.*

My inner tramp needs to calm the hell down.

"Hello?" He gives me a little shake.

That does it. I blink, snapping back to reality.

"I'm Margot." I blurt before I can think better of it. *Great. Give the potential murderer your name. Brilliant.*

He exhales sharply. "Okay, Margot. Why were you following me?"

I fumble in my pocket, pull out his credit card, and hold it up.

"Oh! You forgot your card at the coffee shop, so I was bringing it to you. It was my good deed of the day. But then I heard..." I trail off.

No way am I admitting I just overheard all of that. I like my tongue. I would like to keep it where it belongs. In my mouth.

"I left my card." He says slowly as if realizing it for the first time.

"Yes."

"And you followed me, a stranger, into an alley... to return it?"

"As I said, it was my good deed of the day." I repeat, flushing further. Why does doing a good deed make me even more embarrassed in front of this man?

He sighs, pinching the bridge of his nose before looking up at the sky, "What am I going to do with you?"

I don't get a chance to respond, because an accented voice calls from the darkness. "Come out. We found you. You have nowhere to go."

"Help!" I scream over his shoulder, hoping the man will hear me.

Mr. Montclair curses, and slaps a palm over my mouth, but it's too late.

"We will tell Viktor we have eyes on the target. He will be happy when we deliver."

Target? Nowhere to go? Deliver?

What the actual fuck?

Mr. Montclair moves. His hand leaves my mouth as he reaches under his jacket. When it reemerges, I see a gun.

Movement in front of me breaks my spiral.

Oh my God. Why does this sexy hunk have a gun?

He puts a finger over his lips. A silent order: stay quiet.

Fat fucking chance.

"Help! We're over here!" I scream.

Laugher echoes in response.

Then I see them. The men. And all hope evaporates.

These men look downright creepy. This was a very bad plan. Follow a stranger into an alley. Then not learn from that mistake and get two more strangers to come kill me. And these two aren't even hot. If I'm going to be murdered in this dark alley, I'm voting that Mr. Montclair, the sexy one, will be the one to do it.

Mr. Montclair turns, pressing me against the wall with his back, shielding me.

"Who the fuck are you?" He demands.

"We are here to get you. Come with me." One of the Russian men says. He's looking right at me, even as he talks to Mr. Montclair. I'm so fucking glad they're not here for me. They're terrifying.

"No one is going anywhere. Who sent you?"

"Viktor. Now let us get what we came for."

"No."

There's a rapid exchange in Russian between the two goons.

Then, gunfire.

I duck, screaming.

But within seconds, silence descends. I heard five shots fire. I can see where bullets hit the wall mere inches from us.

I peer around Mr. Montclair's arm. The two Russians are on the ground.

A bullet hole between both of their eyes.

And that's when I really start screaming.

Chapter 5
Matthias

The woman, Margot, starts screaming again. I whirl around and pin her against the wall, caging her between my arms.

She's shaking. She's hysterical... or pretending to be.

I can't tell if it's an act. Did I just kill two Bratva men in front of an innocent civilian... or did I just kill her accomplices?

They were here to take me, which is fucking ridiculous if they thought the two of them were enough. But the real question is, why does Viktor want me?

"You... you... killed... dead..." She stammers, eyes wide with shock.

This girl is either a really good actress, or I just severely fucked up.

"Calm down. Take a deep breath. They were going to kill us if I didn't kill them. It was self-defense." I keep my voice steady, trying to calm her. If she *is* Bratva, she's probably laughing on the inside right now.

Once her breathing evens out, I start questioning her.

"Are you with them?" I demand.

Her eyes bug out, and she looks at me as if *I've* lost *my* damn mind.

"No! Of course not! Why the hell would I be with them?" she snaps, completely baffled.

"You called them over. And you expect me to believe you and they were following me for separate reasons."

"I have absolutely no idea what you're talking about." She glares at me. "You left your card. I was bringing it to you as a *good deed.* Then you *attacked* me. Then you *attacked* those men. Then you *killed* those men. And now you're blaming *me?*" She huffs. "It's the twenty-first century, Mr. Montclair. We left victim-blaming behind in the twentieth century. Get with the program."

Then she has the gall to roll her eyes at me. As if she didn't just witness me kill two men.

I'm stunned silent for a full minute.

Who the hell is this spitfire?

"Fine, let's say you're telling the truth—"

"I am!" she interrupts, like it's the most obvious thing in the world.

I narrow my eyes. Who the hell is this girl?

"—then what happened once you followed me? Why didn't you give me my card?"

"I... you... phone... Roman... call."

I smirk. *Gotcha.*

"You heard my phone call with Roman?"

Her face blanches. "Absolutely not! I didn't hear anything! I swear I have no idea what you're talking about! I didn't hear you talk to Roman about killing someone! I swear I don't know anything! I didn't hear anything!"

She's spiraling. I can see the moment she realizes she's incriminated herself, because she panics.

"I won't tell anyone anything, Mr. Montclair! I don't even know anything! I mean, what you and Roman do is your business. I'll mind my business, you'll mind yours, and you definitely don't have to worry about me!" She's hysterical again. "Please let me keep my tongue!"

I blink.

What the fuck is she talking about?

The more she scrambles to assure me she didn't hear anything, the more convinced I am that she did.

I go over the conversation with Roman in my mind.

Shit.

She heard too much.

Hell, she just named Roman and me. *How does she know who I am?* I'm not sure I'm buying the credit card story. But she doesn't look Russian, or Italian, or even like she's ever committed a crime, but the best spies blend in.

"How do you know my name?" My tone stays even and cold.

Her eyes dart to her hand, still holding the Amex. "It's on your card. I read it when I was leaving the shop." She thrusts the card up like it's evidence.

I snatch it from her hand and slide it into my pocket. I don't give her an inch of space to escape. My arm comes back up, keeping her trapped.

What the fuck am I going to do with you?

I can't let her go.

Best-case scenario? She's just an innocent bystander who witnessed way too much. Worst-case scenario? She's with the Bratva, and the moment I drop my guard, she'll come at me.

But I'm starting to suspect she's telling the truth. Viktor would have to be a moron to send her to get me. Unless he sent her to seduce me.

If I can't let her go, that only leaves one option.

I have to take her.

But where? And for how long?

I just need enough time to think. We can't linger in this alley. Someone might find us. She hasn't fought me yet, but I know it's coming.

She looks like a fighter.

The thought has my dick twitching.

Not the time or place, Matthias Junior.

I take my first real look at her.

She's short, maybe five foot four at most. Thick, curly light brown hair that looks too soft not to touch flows around her shoulders. I have to stop myself from picking up a piece. Big brown eyes. Fair skin, with a blush creeping up her face and neck. And fucking freckles. *Stunning.*

And her lips? Plump. Rosy. Perfect for biting.

I let my gaze drop and nearly groan. *Fuck.*

She's in a sweatshirt and those tight, athletic, spandex pants that chicks wear. They look absolutely provocative on her. I need to see her ass in them. I know it'll be sinful.

She's all curves. Soft. Plush. She's small enough that I can toss her around, but thick enough that I won't have to worry about breaking her.

An image flashed through my mind of me, throwing her onto my bed, gripping her hips, pounding into her until she's screaming my name.

"You could let me go," she says sweetly. "I promise I won't say anything about anything."

The fantasy vanishes.

After months of not being interested in any women, why is this the time Matthias Junior decides to make an appearance?

It's this woman. She's downright stunning.

I drag my gaze back to her. She looks up at me with those big eyes full of hope.

Once I process what she said, I have to hold back a laugh. It's cute she thinks she has a chance of getting away from me.

"That's not going to happen, sweetheart. I need you to come with me."

I give her my signature grin. The one that's gotten me plenty of women.

She smiles back. "Oh, that's quite alright. I think I'll just go back and get my coffee. I'm supposed to meet my boss. He's probably looking for me."

She says it so sweetly, so innocently, that if I didn't catch the slight edge to her stare, I'd believe her.

Maybe her boss is waiting for her, but he's getting stood up today.

"Let's go. You're coming with me." This time, it's a command.

It must set her off because before I know it, she's pushing me, trying to escape.

She shoves at my chest, but she's not nearly strong enough to make me budge. Even through my button-up, her hands scorch me.

I grab her wrists with one hand and pin them against the brick above her head. She starts struggling in full earnest, shimmying around, trying to break free.

With every move, she rubs against me, her tits pressing into my chest. She doesn't seem to notice.

But Matthias Junior sure as hell does.

This should *not* be making me hard.

I'm not some sick fuck that gets off on forcing women. Every woman I've been with has wanted me. Has practically begged for my cock.

I step aside just in time, dodging a knee aimed straight for my balls.

See, I knew she was a fighter.

I can't stop my grin.

"No! You can't take me! I won't go with you! You're a killer!" she yells. "Let go of me, you sick bastard!"

Luckily, the street is far enough away and the traffic too loud for anyone to hear her. But we need to get moving before someone steps out of the building.

She stomps on my foot hard.

Fucking hell. She just crushed my genuine leather loafers.

I bite back a curse, but she's already gearing up to do it again.

"That's enough!" I say exasperatedly.

I grab her waist and throw her over my shoulder.

My muscles protest at the sudden movement. "Not warmed up for this shit." I grunt.

She *scoffs*. "Seriously? If I'm too heavy for you, then just let me go."

I laugh at that. "Spitfire, I could bench double your weight. You're not even close to heavy. Plus, I like some meat on my women."

To prove my point, I *pat* her ass.

She inhales sharply, caught off guard. If she were in front of me right now, she'd see just how much I like her jiggly body.

"No! Someone! Help me!" she screams.

I shift her slightly so she can see my gun in my waistband.

"If anyone comes over and tries to help you, I will shoot them." My deadly voice leaves no room for doubt. "You know I'll do it. You just saw me do it to these two. Do you want more blood on your hands?"

I channel Roman, making sure I sound as merciless as possible.

"And I'll cut out your tongue," I add just because that part of the conversation really seemed to stick with her.

She freezes.

A few beats of silence pass before she mutters through gritted teeth, "Fine. Can I at least walk? This is uncomfortable."

Her voice strains. My shoulder digging into her stomach must be making it hard to breathe.

Letting her walk makes this a whole lot easier for me. Dragging a screaming, flailing woman to my car would have been a pain in the ass. But I'm not going to let her know that.

"Yes, but only if you promise to behave." My sharp tone makes it sound like a concession, not a favor. "If you try to run, I will shoot you. If you so much as cause one person to look our way, I will shoot them. It's their life in your hands. Do you understand me?"

She nods stiffly.

I nudge her and she takes the cue to start walking.

She behaves the few blocks to my car. Besides the tear stains down her cheeks, she looks normal enough. To anyone watching, we just look like a couple having a fight.

I like the sound of that.

Us, a *couple.*

Her, as *mine.*

Just the thought of having a claim to this spitfire makes me hard. The thought of her as mine makes something dark and possessive curl in my chest.

What the hell am I thinking?

This is *not* a date.

We are *not* a couple.

She is a *witness.* I *have* to take her.

But a small part of me is excited to have her.

Chapter 6
Margot

We sit in silence as he navigates traffic.

I'm too busy trying to figure out how to escape to care about where we're going. Jumping out of a moving car is out of the question. I'm far too clumsy to come through unscathed. I know they say your survival rate drastically drops once you get to a secondary location, but there's just no way in hell I'm jumping.

If I can figure out where we're going, then I can make a plan. *Think, Margot.*

I still have my phone. He never took it. Rookie mistake. Very inept of him as a kidnapper.

Oh. Maybe he is a rookie. Maybe this is his first kidnapping.

Am I his first victim? How special. Honestly, it's an honor to be chosen. My first time as a captive. His first time as a captor.

Aw. How romantic.

Wait. If he's new at this, that means he'll mess up again. He already messed up by leaving me with my phone. I just need to know where we're going.

"Where are we going?" The question pops out before I can stop it.

Not very sleuth of me. *Damn it.*

It takes him a moment to answer, like he doesn't know.

"We're going to my place." He finally says with a smile, looking pleased with himself.

His place?

"And where is your place?" I force my voice to stay light, hoping he'll just tell me and make my grand escape much easier.

My current plan? Feign compliance until I'm alone. Then order an Uber home.

"Nice try." He chuckles.

Double damn it.

"How long will we be there, Matty?" I try a nickname, hoping to appeal to his emotional side. I heard that's what they do when negotiating with criminals. Maybe if he trusts me, he'll let me go, with my tongue intact.

"Don't call me that." He snaps; his voice sharp with frustration.

Okay. Duly noted.

Let's try again.

"Alright. So, what should I call you?"

"Nothing. You shouldn't know my name. Admitting you do makes me less likely to let you go."

I blink.

Well, that's not promising.

"I don't know your name." I lie.

He knows I'm lying.

I know he knows I'm lying.

 But I have to try.

"You've called me by my name multiple times." His voice is dry. "Just call me Matthias."

He sounds annoyed. Sorry, Matty. If you wanted an easy afternoon, maybe you should've just *not* kidnapped a random, innocent girl. You know, after *murdering* two people in front of her.

Like damn, Matty. It's before noon on a Monday and you've already killed two men and kidnapped me. I hate to see how the rest of your week looks.

"Okay. So, Matthias." I exaggerate his name just to be annoying, "How long will we be at your place?"

"I don't know. I need to figure it out."

That doesn't sound comforting. I need to go home.

"Could we make a pit stop at my house on the way there?"

"No."

"Please? I really need to go. I'll even come back with you."

"No."

"Please?"

He sighs. "What do you need?"

"I need to check on Benny!"

He slowly turns his head from the street to glare at me.

His entire body tenses. "Who the fuck is *Benny*?" He seethes the name.

Excuse me?

I stare back, completely baffled. "Benny is my puppy."

He relaxes.

Okay, wow. That was a *reaction.*

"He needs to be let out and fed. He probably needs a walk as well. He's not used to being alone for long. I don't leave the house much."

Way to sound like a loser, Margot.

Not that I care what he thinks. *Liar.*

"Who names their dog, Benny?"

"I do!" I say smugly. "He's named after Benjamin Barry. He's Benjamin Barry Peterson."

Matthias stares at me blankly. "Who?"

"Benjamin Barry?" I repeat. Nothing. "Benny Boo Boo?" Nothing. "Andie Anderson, How To girl." I say in my best high-pitched voice.

Still nothing.

I gape at him. "*How to Lose a Guy in 10 Days*? Classic rom-com? Kate Hudson? Matthew McConaughey? He needs a girl to fall in love with him, she needs a guy to dump her."

"I have literally no idea what you're saying."

I groan. "How have you not seen *How to Lose a Guy in 10 Days*? It's a classic!"

Not seeing *How to Lose a Guy in 10 Days* might be a bigger sin than kidnapping.

Well, maybe not bigger than double homicide though.

But close.

"It's only one of the best movies ever." I fold my arms across my chest. "You should definitely watch it."

"Sure." He says flatly.

I sigh in defeat. You can bring a horse to water...

"I'm not really into chick flicks." He says like that's any defense against this grave sin.

"Figures. I bet you're into action movies. Thrillers. Serial killer documentaries. Oh, wait! I bet 'Taken' is your favorite movie." I shoot him a pointed look.

"Huh?" He sounds confused.

"Because, you know." I gesture at him then myself. "You're kidnapping me."

"I'm not kidnapping you!" He sounds exasperated.

I arch a brow. "No? Then what would you call you taking me against my will?"

He pauses.

"Think of it as... a vacation"

I gape at him. "A vacation?"

"Yeah. An adventure. A break from your normal life."

Is he serious?

"Speaking of my normal life, can we go get Benny, please?"

"No."

"My puppy needs me!" I whine, trying to emphasize how important this is.

Matty grabs his phone and makes a call. It connects to the car through Bluetooth.

"Hey, boss. What's up?" A man's voice answers.

"I need you to stop by–" He turns to look at me. "What's your address?"

This is my chance.

"Help! I'm being kidnapped! Call the cops!"

I shout the words as fast as I can before Matthias ends the call.

The voice on the other end coughs awkwardly. "Uh... boss?"

"Don't question me. Do as you're told." He tells the guy on the phone.

His eyes lock onto mine, his voice drops lower, deadly serious. "And you. Don't pull that shit again."

My stomach turns.

"He won't go against me. Neither will anyone at my house. Nor anyone else you come across." His voice is measured, even, like he's stating cold, hard facts. "These are my men. They only listen to me."

And then he says it.

"If you keep this shit up, I'll take it out on Benny. Do you understand?"

My blood runs cold.

I feel like I've been punched in the chest.

Not my poor Benny.

I won't let anyone hurt him.

Up until this point, although knowing I was being kidnapped by a murderer, it didn't feel real.

Yes, I saw him shoot those men, but I was detached, like a scene from a movie. Maybe because those men were shooting at us, and against my better judgment, I believe him when he said it was us or them. Maybe because I've been in shock.

Or maybe it's because his face and body almost make you forget you're not here willingly.

But this? This makes it real.

Not my sweet baby.

Matthias threatens my puppy.

And suddenly, everything crashes down.

"Answer me. Do you understand?" His voice is razor-sharp.

"Yes." Mine comes out barely a whisper.

"Good. Now, what is your address? Rocco here will go pick him up."

I can't answer immediately. I'm still stuck on the whole hurting-Benny-thing.

"If you don't give me your address, I can't send someone to get him." Matthias sighs. "He won't be let out or fed. Do you want that to happen?"

That snaps me out of it.

"No. My address is 6215 Goodwood Ave." My voice is tight, my throat closing up.

Then without thinking, I turn to the speaker. "Rocco, please be gentle with him. He's just a puppy."

That was a mistake.

"Don't talk to Rocco!" Matthias snaps.

I flinch.

His eyes flash, a dark warning behind them. He turns back to the phone. "Rocco, you catch that? Get the dog and bring him to my place."

"Yes, sir."

Matthias hangs up.

The second he does, he turns to me. His head tilts slightly, calculating.

"Never speak directly to my men."

I freeze.

"They don't get to hear your voice." His tone takes a deadly turn, emphasized by how quiet it is. "That's only for me."

Something inside me twists. I don't know if it's fear, revulsion, or something else entirely.

"And never disobey me in front of them." His voice dips even lower. "You won't like the consequence."

And then.

"Neither will Benny"

Something inside me snaps.

The sob punches out of me before I can stop it.

And then another.

And another.

Before I know it, I'm crying hard. Uncontrollably. Big, fat, ugly tears. My body shakes and my breaths come in ragged gasps.

"Today has been the worst fucking day."

I break.

"First, my boss rushes me to a meeting about the stupid discrepancy. This Koschei Group is making my life a living hell. Then, I have to abandon my coffee at home in my rush. Then, my good deed! I try to return some asshole's credit card, and what happens? HE MURDERS TWO MEN AND KIDNAPS ME! In what fucking world does that happen? My good intentions lead to me being taken, Liam Neeson style"

I sob harder.

"And now, now you're threatening my puppy. Benny didn't do anything wrong! *I* didn't do anything wrong! I was just trying to be nice! And now I'm in this fucking car, with a fucking murderer. AND I NEVER EVEN GOT MY COFFEE!"

I completely break down.

I hold my face in my hands as my entire body convulses with sobs. Tears stream down my cheeks. I don't even bother wiping them away.

I'm just done.

Then I feel it.

A tentative pat on my back.

Oh. My. God.

Matthias is patting my back.

Matthias the kidnapper. The murderer. The psycho.

Comforting me.

Matthias the hottie.

"Hey, it's going to be okay. As long as you follow my directions, nothing will happen to Benny. I have a big yard he can play in while we figure this out."

His tone is soft. Cautious.

I guess he's not used to hysterical girls. But it's his fault I'm this way. If he didn't want to deal with a sobbing wreck of a girl, then he shouldn't have kidnapped me. I refuse to feel sorry for him. But at least now I know he has a heart. Even a psychotic murderer needs one.

Oh my God. I'm letting a murderer comfort me. *A hot murderer with a soothing voice.* But a murderer nonetheless. A murderer who is currently kidnapping me and is the reason I'm a wreck.

The realization snaps me out of it.

"GET OFF OF ME!" I shriek as I shrug him off.

He hesitates, like he doesn't quite understand what just happened. But then, he just nods and goes back to driving.

We sit in silence once more.

I couldn't say if it's been minutes or hours when he finally speaks again.

"We're here." His voice is quiet.

I exhale shakily, only just managing to pull myself together. The car slows, pulling through a massive wrought-iron gate guarded by armed men.

I glance out the window.

My jaw drops.

This isn't a house. It's a *castle*. I've never seen a bigger home.

It's breathtaking, all warm stone, with a grand entrance, towering columns, and intricate balconies that look straight out of a historical romance.

The front garden alone is bigger than my entire backyard and full of fountains, sculpted hedges, and bushes trimmed to perfection.

It's beautiful. Elegant.

I've never given much thought to my dream home, but now that I've seen this?

This is it.

And for a brief second, a thought flickers through my mind.

What if I stayed?

What if I never leave?

I get lost in that daydream.

Chapter 7
Matthias

Margot is in such a state of awe that she doesn't notice we've parked. Not until I'm opening her door.

She mumbles a *thanks* as I help her climb out, still entranced by the house.

I glance at my home, trying to see it through her eyes.

It's a multimillion-dollar estate, sprawling and imposing. The moment I saw it, I knew it was the one.

Kind of like the girl next to me.

Where the fuck did that thought come from?

I shove the thought deep down. I need to get it together. She is my captive. She is here against her will. She's not mine to keep.

But I want to.

I grit my teeth.

Shut the fuck up, Matthias.

I lead her inside, and the moment we step through the door, she lets out a sharp, audible gasp.

I don't blame her.

The white marble floors reflect the sunlight streaming in from the massive windows, bathing the grand foyer in warmth. A sweeping staircase commands the center of the room, rising elegantly to the second floor.

She barely breathes as she takes it all in.

But I can't let her get too comfortable.

I hesitate only a second before deciding: she's staying in my room.

Fuck it. I've already taken her. Keeping her in my room is just... practical.

Only so I can keep an eye on her through the night.

Nothing more.

I lead her up the stairs and down the hallway to the master bedroom.

"Where are we going?" She asks, her voice tinged with curiosity.

"My room." I can't keep the smirk out of my voice.

She stiffens instantly. "Why? You're out of your damn mind if you think I'm sleeping with you after you've kidnapped me!"

Her anger is fierce, but there's a hitch in her voice.

Interesting. Is she as affected by me as I am by her?

No, don't go there, Matthias.

I shake off the thought.

"You're staying here where I can watch you." My firm voice stops her in her tracks. "There will be a guard stationed outside your door. Don't even bother trying to leave."

She crosses her arms, glaring at me.

I continue, unfazed. "The windows are too high up. You'll only succeed in injuring yourself if you try to escape through them. And if you do manage to get out, my men outside will shoot you." I pause. "And don't forget, I have Benny."

I make myself sound threatening. It doesn't come naturally.

My default setting with the ladies is charming. Suave.

This? This is different.

But she needs to believe it.

The truth? No one will shoot her. No one will even touch her.

She's mine to touch.

And Benny? He's completely safe. I don't hurt animals. But she doesn't need to know that.

I shut the bedroom door behind her.

Once I finish briefing my men with clear instructions, don't touch her and don't let her leave, I head downstairs to my office.

I need to update my brothers.

I call Dom. As the head, he needs to know.

He picks up on the second ring.

"Dom, two Bratva men attacked me in an alley downtown. I took them both out. You need to send a cleanup crew."

"What the fuck?" Dom sounds just as confused as I am. "Why the hell would they come after you? We've been at peace with them for over a year."

"I don't know. It doesn't make sense."

"Give me the rundown."

I relay the situation to him but leave out one small detail: Margot.

She wasn't involved. She was just an innocent bystander. At least that's what I've decided.

I'm leaving her out to save Dom the trouble of questioning her.

And because I don't want her involved in the Syndicate at all.

She's too sweet.

Well, not exactly *sweet.*

More like *spicy.*

My spitfire.

"Is that everything?" Dom demands.

"That about sums it up."

Except the sexy woman locked in my bedroom.

"I'm going to look into this. Try to avoid alleys. Good thing you had your gun." He says it sarcastically.

I roll my eyes. "Fuck off. Dad drilled that into all of us: 'Never leave without a weapon.'" I try to mimic Dad's gruff voice. "Let me know if you find anything."

"Of course."

And with that, he ends the call.

Now that that's taken care of...

Time to do some research on my spitfire.

Chapter 8

Margot

I can't believe he locked me in this room.

I can't believe he locked me in *his* room.

He's insane if he thinks I'd actually sleep with him after he kidnapped me.

Is he though? You seem awfully aware of how sexy he is.

Although, when I brought it up, he didn't seem remotely interested. Why would he? He's so far out of my league, it's not even funny. He's NHL level. And I'm... a high school team. Not even a good one. Like, a Division III team.

But that's just fine. I wouldn't give in to him even if he wanted me. No matter how sexy he is.

Sure.

BRRINGG!

My phone buzzes, interrupting my spiral.

Shit.

I grab it as fast as I can, not even checking the caller ID, just praying the guard outside my door didn't hear.

"Hey, Margot, it's Ronald. You didn't show up to our meeting. We need to talk about this, but not over the phone."

My boss.

Before I can even decide if I should ask for help or to just hang up and call 911, the door slams open.

I freeze.

A tall man runs in, eyes scanning the room. The second he spots my phone, he snatches it from my hand and ends the call. He's gone before I can even process what happened.

Well, there goes my escape plan.

I take a moment to look around.

There's an obnoxiously large bed, easily big enough for six of me. No one needs this much bed.

The frame, along with all the furniture, is dark wood. The bedding is navy, and the headboard has way too many pillows for a single man.

Either he had an interior decorator, or there's a woman in his life.

Oh my God.

What if I'm locked in his wife's bedroom?

I will murder him if I'm stuck here while his poor, unsuspecting wife wonders where he is.

I try to think if he was wearing a wedding band, but my mind comes up blank. Probably because I was a little distracted by the whole double murder.

And by his jawline.

I shake that thought away and focus.

The walls are a soft cream, trimmed with crown molding. Two beautiful sconces hang above the nightstands, casting a warm glow. At the foot of the bed sits a bench seat, and beneath it all is the softest rug I've ever felt.

I take a step towards the beautiful armoire facing the bed and open it.

Empty.

I move on to the three doors.

The first door: Closet.

More like small boutique.

It's insanely organized, everything color-coded, meticulously folded, and arranged by category. But no women's clothing.

Okay, so no wife.

The sense of relief I feel has nothing to do with him being single and everything to do with the fact that I'm not locked in another woman's room.

Keep lying to yourself.

The second door: Balcony.

I step outside.

He wasn't lying. A fall from this high would leave me seriously injured. Or dead. The breathtaking view shows the acres of land behind his house. The greenery stretches for miles.

Benny's going to love playing out there.

The thought soothes me.

The third door: Bathroom.

If I thought the closet was excessive, this?

This is insanity.

The double vanity is immaculate. Two sinks, but only one has products around it. A massive tub sits against the wall. It's big enough to comfortably fit Benny. The shower stall has glass so clear, I can see the plethora of showerheads mounted on the ceiling and walls.

Who needs that many showerheads? How does someone even use them all at the same time?

Unless... he's hosting orgies.

I cringe. I know some people are into that, and no judgement, but I am not one of those people. I pray I'm not catching anything from standing in here.

I quickly walk out.

By the time I make my way back to the bedroom, exhaustion hits me.

On top of not getting my coffee, I also missed my nap.

Oh, and being kidnapped is rather taxing.

After a little debate as to whether I should trust the possible orgy bed, my exhaustion overwhelms me.

I lay on top of the pristine covers, not wanting to contaminate the sheets with my dirty alley clothes.

Even though I hate Matty, I have to admit...

He has great taste.

Chapter 9
Matthias

I call Sebastian, hoping to catch him before Dom fills him in on my little mishap.

"Hey man, I need a favor." I keep my voice light and casual. Like I'm not hiding a kidnapped woman in my bedroom.

Bash has always had a sharp moral compass, or at least as much as you can in our profession. I thought I did too, but one look at her and, well... While Roman would probably find the situation hilarious, Bash?

Bash might tell Mom.

And I do not need *that* problem right now.

Since I only have Margot's first name and address, there's not much I can dig up on my own. I need Bash's skills.

"Yeah, what's up?" He sounds upbeat.

"How much information can you get me on someone if I only give you a first name and home address?"

Bash scoffs. "Don't insult me. Who's the target?"

"Margot. 6215 Goodwood Ave."

"On it. Who is she? Is she involved with something? Does Dom know?"

"Don't tell Dom!" The words come out too fast.

Bash goes silent for a second. "Matthias, what's going on? Is this a woman you're seeing?"

"Don't worry about it. Just get me the information."

There's a knock on my door.

"Come in."

In walks Ryan, the guard stationed outside Margot's door.

Before I can put Sebastian on hold, Ryan starts talking.

"Boss, I heard a noise from the bedroom, so I went in and found her on her phone. She was answering a call when I apprehended–"

"Stop! Stop speaking!" I shout frantically. "Bash, I'm going to put you on hold." I hear him start to protest before I press the button.

I turn to Ryan. "What happened?"

He pales. "I heard some noise coming out of the bedroom, so I walked in. I saw her talking on the phone. She was receiving a call. I took the phone before she could say anything. Here." He hands me a phone in a light blue case.

At first, I'm proud of him. Then his words register, and I'm furious.

"You walked into my bedroom. Where she was. Alone. Without permission. Then forcibly apprehended her phone?" I try to stay calm, but by the end of the sentence, I'm bellowing.

"Sir, I thought you wouldn't want her calling for help. I apologize." His voice wavers. He's afraid. Good, he should be afraid.

I stare at him for a long, tense second.

Then I take the phone and clench my jaw.

"Go back to guarding her door. Do not walk in again. If you hear anything, call me." I dismiss him. Looking at him any longer will just piss me off more.

Ryan nods stiffly and rushes out.

I exhale, trying to cool the anger simmering in my chest.

How dare he touch her.

How dare he manhandle her.

How dare he walk into my bedroom where she is alone. Where she could have been indecent.

I shake the thought off and focus on the phone in my hand. It's locked, of course.

I take Bash off hold. "Hey, sorry about that. One of my men needed something." I keep my tone carefree, as though I didn't just consider murdering my own security.

"What the hell is going on Matthias? Why is one of your men taking a girl's phone? Who is Margot Peterson?"

I blink. *Margot Peterson.*

I like it. It fits her.

But Margot Montclair will sound so much better.

"Don't worry about it." I dismiss it quickly. "Tell me what you found."

"No. Tell me what's going on."

I sigh. "Bash, trust me. You know me. I would never hurt a woman. Everything is fine. Just tell me what you've found."

Bash hesitates. "Fine. Give me another hour, and I'll send you a file."

I smirk. He trusts me. He always has.

"Thanks. Oh, also, how do you get into a phone with a password?"

Bash walks me through a code that'll unlock all phones, which is very concerning information to know exists.

A call interrupts me before I can dig through her phone.

It's Rocco, the guy picking up Benny.

"What is it?" I snap.

"I'm having a problem with the dog, sir. He won't come with me."

I roll my eyes. "He's a puppy. Just pick him up."

"I don't think he is. He's huge." Rocco hesitates. "Sir, you don't understand. He has to be over 200lbs."

I pause.

She has a massive guard dog?

I like that. I like that she has something looking after her.

"Is he attacking you?"

"No. He's just lying there. Didn't even look up when I walked in." He deadpans. "This is the worst guard dog I've ever seen."

I pinch the bridge of my nose. Of course. Of course she would have a lazy guard dog.

"Lure him out with some food. Make it quick."

She has zero survival instincts.

She followed a stranger into a dark alley. Then she stayed after overhearing a murder being planned.

Really, it's her fault I had to take her. How else was I supposed to handle the situation?

Maybe by not kidnapping her.

I ignore that thought.

...

I smell him before I see him.

The door opens, and in strolls a giant English mastiff.

Benny.

He doesn't even look for Margot.

What a terrible guard dog.

"Where should we put his stuff?" Rocco asks, carrying an absurdly large, well-used dog bed and a bag of toys. "There's more in the car. I just grabbed everything."

I glance at Benny. I don't trust this *puppy* in my office. He's eyeing my desktop cords.

"Put him in a downstairs bedroom." I don't want dog slobber on my furniture. And I'm certain if he found my pantry, he'd clear it out in under ten minutes.

Rocco nods and leaves.

Benny stares at me.

"Looks like it's just you and me."

His eyes narrow.

Finally, some concern about Margot. It only took him four hours. We're going to have to work on that.

He starts walking around the desk, eyeing me.

"No. Stay."

He ignores me.

"Stay." My voice sharpens.

He doesn't even blink.

Of course, Margot's dog is just as disobedient as her.

When he reaches me, he rests his head on my lap.

And then.

Puppy dog eyes.

I stare at him.

"No."

His eyes widen.

"No."

His lip quivers.

"Fuck. Fine." I rub his head.

He sighs. Actually sighs.

"No one hears about this. Got it?"

He leans into my leg.

If only his owner were this easy to please.

After a few minutes, he settles at my feet, sighing like he's had a long day. As if he's the one dealing with a fiery woman and a potential war.

I'll admit, he's a sweet dog. Useless as a guard dog, but at least he's big enough to be intimidating.

I glance down, reaching to pet him again, and freeze.

There are wet slobber streaks on my Italian slacks.

I exhale slowly. "Did you seriously just drool on me?"

Benny blinks. Unbothered.

I narrow my eyes. "You little–"

He tilts his head at me, and my annoyance evaporates.

I sigh. "Fine. You're not an asshole."

I give him another scratch behind the ears. A silent apology for my completely justified insult.

He leans into my touch, his massive body pressing into my legs.

Jesus. He's been here five minutes, and I'm already whipped.

I shake my head.

"Welcome to your new home, Benny Boo Boo."

Chapter 10
Margot

I don't know how much time has passed, but when I glance outside, the sun has set. I don't even remember closing my eyes, but I feel shockingly well-rested. Even over the covers, this has to be the comfiest bed I've ever slept in.

But now that my brain is functioning again, one thing is painfully clear. I feel disgusting in my alley-murder-outfit.

Before I can talk myself out of it, I make my decision. I'm taking a shower.

I march into his absurdly organized closet and start picking out clothes.

A pair of gray sweatpants. *Picture him in those.*

A black t-shirt that's soft, perfectly broken in.

A pair of socks.

And... boxer briefs.

I hesitate, staring at them for a long moment.

Screw it. I inspect them thoroughly, even sniffing to make sure they're clean. When they pass my stringent hygiene test, I scoop them up.

If he didn't want me borrowing his clothes, he shouldn't have kidnapped me. So, that's on him.

Actions have consequences, Matty.

I head to the luxury spa paradise. I mean bathroom.

It takes me several failed attempts to figure out the wall-mounted showerhead from hell. When the water finally heats to a perfect near scalding temperature, I let it run for a few extra minutes. To wash off any potential orgy residue.

Because God only knows who or what has been in this shower.

Once I step in, it's heaven. I scrub myself down with his ridiculously expensive soaps, inhaling that fresh, crisp scent that smells like him.

I hate how much I like it.

Before I get out, I wash my own clothes and hang them to dry. Because I have standards.

I dry myself off with a towel and pull on my borrowed outfit.

The boxer briefs fit embarrassingly well. The soft, loose t-shirt goes mid-thigh. I forego my bra; that thing needed a wash more than my girls need to be perky. The sweatpants are ridiculously long. I have to fold them four times at the ankle to keep from tripping.

At this point, I'm playing dress-up in my kidnapper's closet. But that's his problem, not mine.

I rummage through his cabinet, looking for necessities.

Wide-tooth comb? Found it.

Toothbrush? Jackpot.

I get to work on my hair, cursing the lack of proper curl-drying tools, then brush my teeth like I'm preparing for battle.

By the time I'm done, I look like a completely different person.

I'm not exactly here of my own volition, but at least I'm clean and comfy.

Back in the absurdly lavish bedroom, I flop onto the bed.

My mind wanders. Who is this man? Who is Matthias Montclair? He's obviously rich. And involved in something illegal. But he doesn't feel like he's in a gang. He's too... put together.

I've lived in Boston my whole life. There aren't gangs here. I laugh at the absurd thought.

Maybe Roman was in Chicago during the call. I know they have sketchy shit going on there.

My thoughts spiral until a knock on the door startles me.

The door swings open and in steps an older woman.

She's short with gray hair and kind eyes.

My heart leaps. Surely this woman will help me.

"I'm here against my will." I blurt out, my voice full of desperation. "Can you please call the cops?"

She smiles kindly, and my stomach drops.

"I'm sorry, honey. If Matthias has you here, it's for a good reason." Her voice is gentle, like her not helping me escape is for my own benefit. "He's a good man. Very sensible. Unlike his brothers."

I blink. "Excuse me?"

Her expression softens. "I'm just here to bring you dinner."

That's when I notice the tray she's holding. And the mouthwatering smell coming from it. My traitorous stomach betrays me with an embarrassingly loud growl. I'm not one to miss a meal, and seeing as I've missed all three today, I can't deny my hunger.

I debate not eating it, just out of principle, but my stomach grumbles again.

I consider the risk of the food. Realistically, what use would he have drugging me if he already has me locked up?

Zero.

And really, I don't think this woman would be involved in anything nefarious.

"Thank you." I mumble.

She gives me a warm smile then leaves.

I peek at the plate.

Meatloaf, mashed potatoes, and vegetables. Figures he'd eat healthily.

The first bite is so good, I lose all self-control. I inhale the rest in record time. I might not be happy here, but damn it, at least I'm well-fed.

By the time I finish eating, my eyelids droop. Despite my nap, exhaustion pulls me under.

I brush my teeth again because I'm not a heathen and crawl back into bed.

Tomorrow, I'll come up with a plan.

I will not spend another night here willingly.

Chapter 11
Matthias

After what feels like hours but is actually only thirty-seven minutes, my computer chimes, notifying me of an email from Bash.

I open it instantly, holding my breath. If she's a spy for the Bratva, I'm going to be pissed. *And disappointed.*

Full Name: Margot Anne Peterson

Age: 26

Employment: Financial Analyst

Company: Northern Hemisphere Cargo

Education: Boston University

Major: Finance

The document goes on. It includes background on her family and friends, even Benny's medical record.

She lives alone, works hybrid, and doesn't go out much except for coffee and the occasional meeting.

I already knew that from her phone. Perfect for kidnapping. No one will notice she's gone.

I don't see any evidence of a man in her life. How convenient. *It would have been a pain in the ass to have to go kill someone for touching what's mine.*

Stop it Matthias, she's not yours... *yet.*

I keep scrolling until something catches my eye. A pen name.

Why the fuck does she have an alias? My chest tightens. Is she hiding something? Is she a spy?

Bash is one step ahead of me.

Not a spy.

Something far more surprising: an audiobook narrator.

My mind flashes to her voice. That smooth, sultry sound. I'd pay to listen to her read to me.

I download the audiobook app that publishes her work. She's recorded four books. It looks like her career started a year ago. How prolific of her.

I click on her most recent release. Many of the comments are about Chapter Thirty. Curiosity gets the best of me. I buy the book, and I skip straight to Chapter Thirty.

Her voice comes through the speaker. Low. Sensual. Tempting.

"He looks at me, his eyes full of hunger. 'Get on your knees, baby.'

Too overcome with need, I obey immediately."

I freeze.

My body goes rigid.

What the fuck?

Her voice is breathy. Needy.

"He pulls his long, hard cock out of his pants. I can see the beads of precum collecting at the tip."

I shift in my seat.

"I subconsciously lick my lips. His arousal doesn't compare to my own. I can feel it dripping down my thighs. I want to take his cock in my mouth and worship it."

Oh my fuck.

My jaw clenches.

I adjust myself, already painfully hard.

"I open wide, and he shoves his cock in until it hits the back of my throat. I sputter and feel spit dribble down my chin."

Fucking hell.

This is what sweet Margot narrates? This explicit, filthy fantasy? I don't know what I was expecting, but it wasn't this.

"'Relax your throat. I'm going to fuck this dirty mouth.'

I do as he says and let him go deep. I can't help moaning around his length. I feel myself flood. I wouldn't be surprised if there was a puddle on the floor beneath me."

I'm so hard it hurts. Before I can stop myself, I'm undoing my belt and pulling out my cock. I stroke myself, matching the rhythm of her raspy, sinful voice.

"He abruptly pulls out. 'On your hands and knees. I'm giving my girl what she wants. You've been bad and don't deserve my cock, but I want to cum in that tight pussy.'"

She moans.

I bite back a groan, pumping faster. This is her. This is Margot.

"He slams into me in one thrust. He doesn't start slow. No, his thrusts are fast and hard. He slaps my ass, and I clench around him. The spanking only adds to the pleasure.

'Thank you. Thank you. Thank you.' I chant with each thrust."

I hold back, gripping the base of my cock. I won't let myself come until she does. In my mind, it's not some fictional scene anymore. It's her.

On all fours. Jiggling. Begging me. Begging for me.

"'Please, sir. I can't hold it. Please let me come'"

Her voice quivers. I can hear the desperation in it. I swallow hard, my hand tightening around my length. I picture her lips parted, eyes wide with need.

"'Come. Now!' He commands and pinches my clit."

She screams.

"MARGOT!"

I yell her name as I come, my release spilling hot and fast over my fist. I can't hear anything. I'm seeing stars.

I've never come this hard in my life.

I unload into my fist, but there's so much, some spills on my pants. It doesn't matter; Benny already slobbered on them. Thankfully we put him in his room earlier. But I don't think even his presence could have stopped me from jerking off to her voice.

The audiobook keeps playing, rolling into the next chapter. I barely register it, until I hear another voice.

A *man's* voice.

My blood boils. Who the fuck is he? Who the fuck is reading these filthy scenes with her? My hands clench into fists. He's a dead man. There's no way you can sit next to her, hearing her moan like that, and not be thinking about her.

And the listeners! Any pervert can download these books and jerk off to her voice.

Like I just did.

But it's different for me. Because Margot is mine. She may not know it yet, but she is.

She's done with these audiobooks. She doesn't need the money anymore. I have more than enough to support us and our kids. I'll get Bash to take them all down.

But first, I need to buy every single one. Looks like I have a new soundtrack while I work.

...

Later that night, I creep into my bedroom. The sconces cast a soft glow over the mop of light brown curls that spread across my pillow. She's sleeping on her stomach, her curvy body swallowed by my bed.

My chest tightens. I never noticed how empty this room was until now. The room feels warmer and cozier with her in it.

I showered in one of the guest rooms, not wanting to wake her.

While brushing me teeth in our bathroom, I freeze mid-scrub, toothbrush in my mouth. There, hanging neatly on the towel rack, are her clothes from today.

If her clothes are out here, then... is she naked in my bed?

The thought slams into me like a freight train. Margot. Naked. Between my sheets. Waiting for me.

I go rock hard in an instant, my body ignoring the fact that I got off less than an hour ago to the sound of her voice.

I don't even put the toothbrush down, just bite down on it as I slip into our bedroom quiet as a predator.

My pulse pounds in my ears as I reach the bed. Slowly, carefully, I pull the comforter down...

Black fabric.

For a split second, disappointment flares. Then my brain catches up.

I know this shirt. It's mine.

Heat floods my veins, overtaking any hint of frustration. She's wearing *my* clothes.

And just like that, I decide she will never sleep in anything else again. Not unless she's naked. She can always sleep naked.

That thought alone has me holding back a groan.

I turn back to the bathroom and force myself to finish brushing my teeth. But my gaze catches on the pile of clothes. On one article of clothing in particular.

Black lace.

Before I even register the movement, I've crossed the room and they're in my hand.

She's in my bed. After using my shower. Smelling like my soaps. Wearing my clothes. *With no panties.*

I swear under my breath, my body tightening to the point of pain.

I know how much of a fucking freak this makes me, but I don't care

I bring the lace up to my nose and inhale. Clean, fresh soap, *and her.*

Margot.

My gut clenches.

It takes every ounce of restraint I didn't even know I possessed, to put the panties back. To walk away.

I climb into bed, my skin burning, my body screaming. I drag her against me and lock her in my arms. She sighs in her sleep and molds into me. I match my breathing to hers.

It's the only thing that calms me.

The last thought in my head before sleep finally takes me is:

Margot Peterson isn't going anywhere.

Chapter 12
Margot

There's a comforting weight on top of me, and an intoxicating scent surrounds me. I inhale deeply, sinking in, letting it lull me back to sleep.

Until a breath of air brushes the back of my head.

Then, the weight rises slightly in an inhale, hold, then exhale.

Oh my God.

Matty!

Everything slams back into place. The café. The credit card. The phone call. The *murders*. The *kidnapping*.

My eyes fly open.

The weight, it's Matty. Sleeping on top of me. Not spooning me. No. He's smothering me. Covering me like a damn starfish.

I'm lying on my stomach, facing away from him. Some of his chest lies on the mattress, but since he's a fucking giant, the rest sprawls across my back. One massive arm drapes over my shoulder, onto my pillow. His right leg covers mine, the rest tangles around me.

Too close. Way too close. I need to get out of here.

Just one more minute.

No!

I shift, trying to wiggle free, but the slight movement earns me a low, rough groan.

I freeze.

That's when I feel it.

The hard, thick bulge pressing against my ass.

He. Is. Huge.

Panic, or something far more dangerous, races through me. I try to slip out again, but I must shimmy against his... situation... because this time, not only does he groan, but he grinds into me.

I go completely still.

Then he does it again.

My body betrays me. My breath catches. My thighs squeeze together. His thrusts are slow, powerful, needy.

Another groan rumbles through him, a deep, wrecked sound, and my entire body lights up.

Shit. *Shit.*

I shove at him, throwing every ounce of strength into it.

He doesn't budge.

"Ugh, get off me!" I snap, desperate to escape before I do something reckless, like lean into him.

Don't act like your boxer briefs aren't soaked. Shut it! How else am I supposed to react when I wake up to a giant, sexy man humping me? *You're on his side of the bed. You sought him out.*

Matty stirs. His voice is low, disoriented, drenched in sleep. "Huh?"

"You are on top of me! Get Off!" I demand, fighting the breathiness in my voice.

"Give me a minute, sweetheart." His weight shifts, more of it settling onto me. "You're too soft."

Soft? How dare he!

"Get off, you bastard! Now!"

He exhales, completely unbothered. "Shh. It's too early for this."

Too early? The sunlight streaming through the window says otherwise.

"I swear, if you don't get off me right now–" I cut myself off. I have no leverage. No threat to make.

Finally, finally, he moves, shifting lazily as he gets up against the headboard, the sheets still covering his torso.

I should be relieved. Instead, my body misses the warmth.

Which is ridiculous. How can I miss my kidnapper's warmth?

I scramble to my side of the bed, putting as much distance between us as possible, but I make the mistake of looking at him.

Big mistake.

His dark hair is an absolute mess. Then he stretches, arms overhead, muscles flexing, and the comforter slides down his chest.

Good. Fucking. God.

His abs. His pecs. His cut, chiseled everything. My tongue flicks out to wet my lips. I hate myself for it.

A low chuckle rumbles from him. "Sweetheart, if you keep looking at me like you're going to pounce, I won't be able to hold myself back."

I meet his gaze. It's dark. Hungry. Dangerous.

My entire body flushes red. "Fuck off. You know you're hot."

His smirk deepens. "Don't worry, spitfire. I'm holding myself back too. Seeing you in my clothes, no bra, knowing that sweet pussy is bare against my pants..."

My breath catches.

He's watching me, devouring me with his eyes, the sleepiness long gone.

Then his words register.

Oh my God. He knows.

He must have seen my panties in the bathroom.

My brain scrambles. What pair was I wearing? Were they lacey? Or granny panty? Dear God, please tell me they were sexy.

Beneath my embarrassment is giddy, reckless satisfaction.

Because Matthias Montclair wants me. Wants me badly. And the way he looks right now, like he's barely restraining himself from demolishing me, is thrilling.

Please do.

No. No! I need to shut this down.

I clear my throat. "So... what's there for a captive to do on Day One?" I leap out of bed, desperate to create space.

His smirk turns amused. "Changing the subject?"

Yes.

His gaze sweeps over me, slowly and thoroughly. Head to toe, and back up again. The fire in his eyes ignites.

"Fuck." He rakes a hand through his hair, exhaling sharply. "Don't ever stop wearing my clothes." His jaw tightens. "Unless you're wearing nothing."

He adjusts himself beneath the sheets.

My eyes drop before I can stop them.

Holy hell. I was right. He's huge.

I bite my lip.

His entire body tenses.

"Fuck it."

He lunges.

I yelp, barely escaping, sprinting into the bathroom and slamming the door shut.

A low, dark laugh rumbles from the other side. "I'll let you go this time, sweetheart. But I'm going to have you soon. I know you're going to taste so sweet. You can run, but you won't get far."

My pulse races out of control.

I press my back against the door and inhale sharply. Since I'm already in here, I might as well get ready for the day.

By the time I've brushed my teeth and washed my face, his footsteps retreat.

I tiptoe into the closet in my now-dry panties. Black and sexy. Not that it matters. I don't care what he thinks.

Liar.

I might as well wear his comfy clothes. He kidnapped me. He can deal with me stealing his wardrobe.

I grab a pair of black sweatpants that cinch at the ankles and a worn navy T-shirt tucked under an oversized sweatshirt.

The sweatshirt falls just above my knee. Shockingly, it isn't tight around my hips. *I'm keeping this one.*

As I'm throwing my hair up in a messy bun, a knock sounds at the door.

Here we go.

Chapter 13
Margot

Matty walks in.

"I brought you coffee." He holds out the mug like a peace offering. "I wasn't sure how you take yours, so I put cream and sugar in it. If you don't like it, we have more downstairs. There are a few machines that I think also make coffee, but I don't know how to use them. You can ask Dotty. She'll make some for you. She was busy, and I didn't want to be the reason you go two days without coffee."

He throws me a wink. A fucking wink.

That can't be right. My captor cannot be sweet.

Wait... Dotty? Who the hell is Dotty?

"I won't be the other woman," I mutter under my breath before I can stop myself.

His brows furrow. "What?"

"Who's Dotty?" I snap, my jaw clenched.

He stares for a second, before answering. "Dotty is the head of house. She's in charge of cleaning, cooking, and whatnot."

Oh.

I'm *too* relieved. Not that it matters. It doesn't.

"She's also old enough to be a grandmother." His lips twitch. "So, how do you take your coffee? I'll get it right tomorrow."

"Caramel macchiato. Wait." My stomach drops. "Tomorrow? You're keeping me here another night?"

He winces. "I haven't figured out what to do with you yet."

I gape at him. "Excuse me? I'm leaving immediately!"

I storm towards the door, but he blocks my path, his broad frame unmovable.

"Move."

"You know I can't let you go. Just hang tight."

Hang tight?

My voice rises. "What am I supposed to do all day? I will find a way to leave."

Before he can respond, a bark cuts through the air.

Benny.

My heart lurches. "Where is he? Bring me to him now! If you hurt a hair on his head, I'll kill you."

Matty's expression darkens. "I'll take you to him. But if you cause any trouble, it's Benny who'll pay."

Tears sting my eyes. I nod. I won't let anything happen to Benny.

Matty leads me out of the room, down a series of hallways, and finally down a grand staircase.

I'll never remember how to get back to our room.

His room. Not *our* room.

He's out of his damn mind if he thinks I'll spend another night in bed with him.

We enter a bedroom and my gaze locks onto the dog bed.

Benny.

Curled up, content, on a nicer bed than the one at home. A pile of new toys sit beside him.

I freeze.

Did this man buy my puppy a new bed and toys?

I sprint across the room, launching myself onto Benny. He lazily licks my face as I frantically check him over, searching for injuries. He's okay. He's more than okay. I bury my face in his fur, pressing kisses to his head.

"I missed you, Boo Boo. I'll never leave you alone for that long again. I'm so sorry, Benny. I love you."

Benny stares at me. Not traumatized. Not upset.

He looks... content.

Like he enjoys being here.

I glance at Matty. He's leaning against the door, arms crossed, watching us with an unreadable expression.

Almost adoring.

That can't be right. He wouldn't care about me reuniting with my puppy.

When our eyes meet, his tone is calm, businesslike. "I need to get some work done. You can roam around but stay inside. I'll have Dotty give you a tour."

He turns to leave.

"Wait!" My voice rushes out. "Benny needs to go outside. He likes walks. He can't stay cooped up all day."

Matty looks at Benny, skeptically. "He doesn't seem like the high-energy type."

I double down. "He needs to run around."

I pull out the big guns, channeling Benny's puppy eyes.

I see the exact moment Matty caves.

"I'll have a guard let him out every hour."

I fake a lip tremble, a Benny classic. "No. I want to take him out."

Matty exhales sharply. "Fine. But a guard will be glued to your side the entire time. Anything else?"

I shake my head.

He turns and disappears down the hall.

I collapse beside Benny, and whisper, "How did we get here?"

...

I find the kitchen after about fifteen minutes of wandering. I'm going to need a map with the size of this place.

I tried to get Benny to come with me, but he refused to leave his new kingdom of treats and toys.

A warm, aged voice greets me. "Hello, dear. I was wondering when I'd see you."

Dotty.

She reminds me so much of my Nana, I can't even be mad at her.

"Here. Eat this." She sets a plate of eggs, bacon, and toast in front of me, her tone leaving no room for argument.

I sit down and start eating. It's delicious.

The kitchen is bright and pristine, all sleek appliances and a marble island at the center. The fridge is restaurant-sized. It smells amazing.

"I wasn't sure what you liked, so I made something simple. You'll tell me your favorites for my future menus."

I swallow my bite. "Oh, I don't plan on staying long."

"Nonsense." Dotty waves me off. "My sweet Matthias has never brought a girl home. Now that he has, we're not going to let her go. He's spent too much time working and not enough on finding a wife."

I nearly choke.

"We're not together."

She smiles knowingly. "You'll see soon enough."

She's planning our wedding. I can feel it.

Nope. No. Absolutely not!

Dotty takes my empty plate and claps her hands. "Now, time for your tour."

"I–"

"You should get to know your new home."

"Not my home."

She ignores me. "I'm so proud of Matthias. He built all this from nothing. Unlike his brothers." She tuts. "They take after their father."

I go still.

"Brothers?" I ask carefully.

Dotty nods. "There are four of them. Matthias is the second-born. Dominic is the eldest. The poor man is far too serious. He should've run the company with Matthias, but instead, he chose the *Syndicate*. Then there's Roman. He's close behind Matthias. That troubled boy needs to sort through his anger issues. And seek the Lord's forgiveness for his offenses. And finally, Sebastian. The baby. His brilliance is wasted on *that life*." Her voice turns wistful. "Evelyn didn't raise them for that. Their father, Damien, left them a dark legacy. Only my sweet Matthias chose to work in the light."

My blood turns to ice.

Roman.

Roman, the psychopath torturing and potentially murdering someone, is Matty's brother.

Syndicate. Offenses. Dark legacy.

What the hell did I get dragged into?

I force a blank expression. "What's the Syndicate?"

Dotty freezes.

She plasters on a too-bright smile. "Let's continue the tour"

I barely hear the rest.

Who is this man holding me captive?

How much danger am I in?

Chapter 14
Matthias

I try to drag my eyes away from my monitor, but it's impossible.

Margot's image consumes my screen.

The security feed from Benny's room takes up the rightmost display, capturing her in all her beauty.

She's giggling, laughing, playing with that damn dog, and the sound alone pulls a genuine smile from me. She looks so carefree. I want her to be that way with me. I want her to look at me the way she looks at Benny, sweetly, affectionately, and completely open.

Am I seriously fucking jealous of a dog right now?

My jaw tightens.

I recall the feel of her against me this morning. So warm, soft, mine.

If she had kept wiggling another thirty seconds, I would've come in my pants like a fucking teenager.

That's when I decided, I'm going to wake up on top of her every morning. For the rest of our lives.

And then when she got out of bed, drowning in my clothes, bare under them, her pussy pressed against my pants... I was even harder than I was the night before.

She was adorable, scrambling to change the subject, trying to distract me from what we both knew was happening. But the second she bit that plush, fucking perfect bottom lip, I lost it.

That's my lip.

Mine to bite.

If she had hesitated for one more second, I would've had her pinned to the mattress.

I shiver at the thought of everything we could've done.

She's becoming an addiction.

I can't go minutes without thinking of her. I need her in my sight. Not just to get my fix, but also to keep her safe.

I know no one is after her, but the second the world realizes she's mine, they'll try. Enemies of the Syndicate will see her as leverage. A weakness.

They don't understand.

Margot Peterson isn't my weakness. She's my fucking priority.

Mine to keep. Mine to protect. Mine.

As long as she's with me, nothing touches her.

Which means I need to focus. On anything but her.

I drag my gaze back to my work, scanning the same paragraph I've been trying to read for the past half-hour. It's a document on our new prototype. Bash's project. I should be interested.

I'm not.

I try again. First sentence.

Before I even register a word, my eyes flick back to the right monitor.

Margot's losing a tug-a-war battle with Benny, her tiny frame no match for a dog his size. I smirk. She doesn't stand a chance. *What's the biggest dog she could take? A toy poodle?*

I laugh, shaking my head.

My girl is not built for combat.

Not with those soft curves. That full, plush body.

Her belly. Her thighs. Her heavy tits. Her juicy, round ass.

All of it jiggling while I pound into her, her breath hitching, panting for me.

Begging.

A shiver rolls through me. My cock twitches.

PING!

The email notification jerks me back to reality.

Jesus Christ. This is getting ridiculous.

I hover the mouse over the camera feed tab close button, then hesitate. I minimize the window instead. At least this way, she's still there.

I go back to the document and continue onward.

I pick up my phone to play music. Maybe some background noise will help. Anything to keep me from spiraling into thoughts of Margot.

The screen lights up.

I freeze.

'The Line of Want and Need.'

The audiobook. Narrated by Margot Peterson.

This is stupid. Ridiculous. What am I even doing?

I start it from the beginning and hit play.

"Chapter One."

Her voice fills the room. Smooth, sweet, and tempting.

If I listen to the book, I can focus. I can work. Right?

Bullshit.

...

The next time I glance out my office window, the sun has set.

Shit.

I hope I didn't miss dinner. I want to eat with Margot. Help her settle in. Wear down those defenses.

I check my phone.

Chapter Twenty-Six.

I'm hours into the book. I got too wrapped up. I'm not a romance guy. Hell, I can't remember the last time I read something that wasn't for self-improvement. Probably in high school.

But Margot's voice?

I could listen to her forever.

And I intend to.

I haven't gotten to another naughty scene, which is probably for the best. I wouldn't have been able to focus. Not when the sound of her voice alone has me hard.

My stomach growls loud enough to echo.

I call Dotty.

"I'll be having dinner with Margot tonight."

She lights up. She tells me how wonderful Margot is. How she fits in perfectly. How she adores her. How I should keep her.

Oh, I intend to.

I listen, pretending I don't already know Margot's every move of the day. No one needs to know how much she means to me. I don't even understand the hold she has on me.

Dotty rambles on. I skim Margot's file, soaking in every detail, committing everything to memory.

Then, business.

"Have Margot in the dining room in an hour and a half."

That gives me just enough time to workout and shower, as long as I don't idle.

I stand, eager.
Eager to see my girl.

Chapter 15
Margot

I'm playing with Benny when Dotty appears at the door.

"Are you ready for dinner, dear?" It's framed as less like a question and more as a command.

I sigh. "I'm guessing I don't have a choice."

She laughs, shaking her head. "Come with me to the dining room."

"Why can't I just eat in the kitchen? I had breakfast and lunch in there?"

"Matthias wants you to join him for supper. He specifically requested eggplant parmesan, which is odd. He usually has meat or seafood with every meal. But I found a good recipe, and I think it'll be great."

I freeze.

Eggplant parmesan? That's my favorite.

Does he know that?

No. That's impossible.

But then why would he request a meal he never eats?

I shake the thought away. He doesn't know. He wouldn't care. It's just a coincidence.

I force myself to focus as Dotty carries on about the homemade red sauce, fresh tomatoes from the garden, and hand-baked breadcrumbs. Normally, I'd be impressed, but my brain is stuck on why the hell Matty is making me eat with him.

I haven't seen him all day. He hasn't had any interest in me since he dropped me off with Benny.

Why now?

But before I can figure it out, we're in the dining room.

The first thing I notice is the table. It's massive, solid mahogany, intricate detailing, surrounded by ten chairs, but could easily fit more.

The second thing I notice?

The place settings.

One at the head of the table. The other right next to it.

Absolutely not.

Before I can second-guess myself, I grab my setting and haul it to the opposite head of the table.

Dotty gasps. "Oh, dear. I don't think you should do that. Matthias specifically instructed me to seat you next to him."

Fat fucking chance.

"I'm sure he won't care." I say casually, dropping into my new seat.

Dotty mutters something about *"obstinate girl"* under her breath as she disappears into the kitchen.

I barely have time to adjust before the door swings open.

Matty enters with a wide smile, until he sees me.

He stops mid-stride.

"I thought I told Dotty to set you at my side," he says, confused.

"She did." I confirm, not wanting Dotty in trouble.

Understanding dawns on him. His smile vanishes.

"Why did you move?" His voice dips lower.

I avoid eye contact. "I didn't see the need to be that close." My cheeks burn. It's a dead giveaway.

He goes silent.

I risk a glance up, only to find him grinning. Then he laughs.

"And why don't we need to be close?" He leans forward, eyes gleaming. "Are you scared of how much you want me?"

I roll my eyes. "Keep dreaming, Matty. I'm not into you."

His smirk deepens. "Didn't seem that way this morning, sweetheart."

I turn red. He's talking about when I checked him out. When I practically devoured him with my eyes.

"And don't call me Matty." His voice shifts into something sharper and commanding.

Oh, he hates that.

Perfect.

Dotty saves me by walking in with our food.

"Here you go, dears. Eggplant parmesan with garlic bread." She sets them down and heads out.

I mutter my thanks, relieved for the distraction. Matty, however, is not distracted.

Instead of taking his seat at the other end of the table, he slowly picks up his plate.

Fuck. Fuck. Fuck.

"What are you doing?" I ask as suspicion overwhelms me.

He ignores me.

Balancing his plate, utensils, and glass with ease, he walks straight to my side of the table. He sets his place directly next to mine. Then, finally, he looks at me, grinning like the Cheshire Cat.

"I have trouble hearing across the room," he says smoothly. "It's better for me to be close to you."

I narrow my eyes. "You're lying."

He doesn't even pretend to deny it. He just smiles wider with an evil gleam in his eyes. He settles in like he owns the place. Which, technically, he does.

I grip my fork. "You don't seem like the kind of man to give up the head of the table."

"Oh, sweetheart," His voice drops to something slow, teasing. "My seating arrangement doesn't change my position in this relationship." He takes a bite, swallows. "In and out of the bedroom. I will always be in charge."

I scoff. "We don't have a relationship, and you certainly aren't in charge of me."

"That's where you're wrong." He sets his fork down, completely composed. "Your obedience will be rewarded. Your defiance will be punished."

Heat floods my veins.

"Fuck you," I snap, pushing back my chair, but his hand clamps down on my shoulder. I shiver. Betrayed by my own body. "This is why I knew sitting next to you was a bad idea."

"Sit down and eat." His grip stays firm. "It won't be as good when it gets cold, and Dotty made this just for you."

My stomach betrays me next, by letting out a loud growl.

His smirk deepens.

Damn it.

I grab my fork and stab a bite.

The moment the food hits my tongue, I melt. It's perfect. Cheesy, saucy, crispy in all the right places. A soft, involuntary moan escapes me. I close my eyes, savoring it. I take another bite. Another moan.

Something shifts.

I open my eyes.

Matty freezes, fork suspended midair. His hungry gaze is locked on my mouth. Full of a barely leashed intensity. Then he groans. Low. Rough. Wrecked.

I replay the last few seconds. The moaning. The lip licking.

Oh. My. God.

I turn scarlet.

I cut off my next moan midway, trying to act normal.

Matty exhales sharply, shaking his head.

But his eyes stay dark.

Chapter 16
Matthias

I've never been jealous of *pasta* before.

I've never wanted to *be* pasta before.

But here I am. Losing my goddamn mind.

Margot makes the most obscene, sinful, wreck-me noises while eating her damn dinner. Moaning. Sighing. Like she's being fucked senseless, not eating eggplant parmesan. My cock is so damn hard, I could split a two-by-four.

If this is how she reacts to food, I'm going to make sure she never eats another meal without me. It's sweet torture. Hearing those noises of pleasure, but not to being the one to cause them.

And then she licks her lip, and I almost come in my pants. *That's my lip to lick.* I should be cleaning the sauce from her mouth. I should be the one making her moan like that.

Was she sent to this earth to drive me insane?

I see the moment it clicks for her; what she's doing to me. And unlike the women that normally surround me, who would use this to seduce me, she stills. She turns bright red, mortified. It's adorable. Her flushed cheeks, the rosy tint creeping down her neck. I want to see how far down that blush extends. But what gets me the most? The way she ducks her head. She's not doing this on purpose. She's not trying to seduce me.

And yet, she is.

Despite her embarrassment, I can see a flicker of something else. Excitement. She likes the effect she has on me. If I were a betting man, I'd put money on some of that flush being from arousal. She's enjoying this. Even if she won't admit it.

Two can play this game.

I keep eating with my right hand and place my left on her thigh just above her knee.

The contact electrifies me. Even through the barrier of her sweatpants, her warmth seeps into my palm, shooting straight to my dick.

Margot nearly falls out of her chair.

I grip her leg tighter, steadying her. I lean in, my lips brushing her ear. "Careful, sweetheart. We wouldn't want you getting hurt."

Her breath hitches.

She's reacting to me. To my presence. To my touch.

I sit back and motion to her plate. "Sweetheart, keep eating. Your food's going to get cold, and Dotty made it just for you." I pause. "If I have to tell you again, you're getting punished."

She gasps.

Her thighs clench.

Interesting.

My sweet girl might not be as innocent as she pretends.

I let her get back into the rhythm of eating before I inch my hand higher.

She freezes.

I grunt a silent remind. She forces herself to move, shoving another bite into her mouth.

I start massaging her thigh.

She keeps eating, but now her breathing comes in quick, uneven pants.

I slide my hand higher.

Inches. Mere inches from where I want to be. I can feel her heat. Even through the sweatpants, her body calls to me.

My cock is aching, throbbing, demanding. My grip on her leg tightens. Not to tease her, but because my own need overwhelms me.

I started touching her to drive her mad. To make her suffer like I'm suffering.

It's backfiring. The blood in my head is roaring. I can't hear anything else. Can't think of anything else. *I need her.*

And I can see I'm affecting her just as much. She's completely red. Her chest rises and falls with quick, uneven breaths. Her thighs press together, trapping my hand between them. Inches from her sweet, wet, perfect heat.

I lean in, dropping my voice to a rough whisper. "I'm seconds away from bending you over this table and fucking you, sweetheart." Her breath catches. "Just say the word." I nip her earlobe, in a sinful promise.

She shudders. Not just a tremble, her entire body reacts.

For a split second, she leans in.

Not away. In.

Then, like she realizes what she's doing, she jerks back, eyes wild.

"I can't–" The words are a breathy whisper, barely there.

Then, before I can blink, she bolts.

She jumps up from her chair and sprints out the door.

I sit there, stunned.

What the fuck just happened?

I've never had a woman literally run away from sex with me. Is there something wrong with me?

Impossible. I'm irresistible.
So, what the fuck is wrong with this girl?

Chapter 17
Margot

I'm sprinting down the hallway, taking random turns. By some miracle, I find the stairs and fly up them, moving faster than I knew I could. By the time I reach the master bedroom, I'm out of breath.

Huh. I made it to the bedroom. Guess I paid more attention during the tour than I thought.

Fuck. I'm in the bedroom. And Matty will be here any second.

I know I can't outrun him, but I had to get out of there. If I stayed a second longer, I would've begged him to follow through on his promise. To bend me over the table and fuck me on it.

My stomach tightens.

He kidnapped me! I cannot be having these feelings towards him. Who the hell lusts after their kidnapper? A crazy person! Oh, maybe I have Stockholm Syndrome. *Or maybe he's hot as hell and sexy as sin.*

The door slams open.

Matty crosses the room in a blur. Before I can react, I'm pinned against the wall. His body cages me in, hands firm and unyielding. His jaw tightens, nostrils flaring, eyes burning with something dark. No teasing, no smirks. Just pure, unfiltered rage.

"Why did you run?" His voice lowers to a dangerous level.

I look away. "You were scaring me." *Lie.*

"Bullshit." His grip tightens. "You were trembling with need. I could feel your heat."

"I don't want you." I whisper. *Another lie.*

He doesn't buy it. "Look me in the eyes and say that." His fingers pinch my chin and tilt my head until our eyes lock. He leans in so closely, his breath teases my lips.

I swallow hard.

"Who the hell would want their captor?" I deflect.

"Who the hell would want their captive?" His eyes darken.

I gulp.

"We're both fucked up in this situation. That doesn't change the facts. I want you. You want me. Stop denying it." His voice drops lower.

I try to deny it, but the words don't come.

"Just say the words, and we'll be explosive. I already know you'll be the best I've ever had," he murmurs, his eyes dropping from mine to my lips, then back up. "And I'd make it just as good for you."

No. My head is spinning. He's wrong.

His voice is pure gravel when he growls, "I can smell your arousal."

I shake my head, denying it.

"So, if I dip my hand in those lacy panties, they won't be soaked?"

Damn him. I look away. "No."

It's a lie. A terrible, obvious, pathetic lie. He knows it. I know he knows it. He knows I know he knows it. But it's all I have. The only defense I can cling to. My only sense of sanity in this nightmare.

Not a nightmare. A dream. Your fantasy. What you've always wanted. A man this crazy about you.

No. I don't want him. I can't.

Maybe if I tell myself a few more times, I'll believe it.

"Fine." His hand slowly, sensually slides down my body.

His fingers tease my waistband before crawling inside.

I could tell him to stop. I should. But the words don't come.

His fingers find my soaked slit, and he hisses a breath. I clench my thighs, as he strokes through my wetness. A moan escapes.

His fingers tease my clit in slow, deliberate circles. Pleasure sparks up my spine. Then he stops, and pulls his hand away.

Denial rips through me. I tilt my hips forward, trying to chase his fingers, but his other hand pins me to the wall.

I whimper. His eyes burn into me. Dark. Starving. He's not just turned on. He's possessed. Obsessed.

"Tell me you want me." He demands.

I know if I do, if I give him even an inch, he'll make me feel things I've never felt before. He'll ruin me. And yet, I shake my head.

I can't form the words to deny him. But I can't give in. He's my captor. He's involved in something dark. He's a murderer. A monster. I should be terrified. *But you aren't.* I can't sleep with him. *But you can. It'd be so easy to give in.*

"I can feel how much you want me." His rough voice reveals his own arousal.

I shake my head again.

"You're soaking my fingers, spitfire." He contradicts me.

I look away, my defenses cracking.

"I can feel what I do to you. Feel what you do to me. Feel the pull you have over me." He thrust against me, groaning. Once. Twice. Three times. Heat floods my core. He grips my face with his hand not occupied in my panties, forcing my gaze back to his.

"Fuck, sweetheart. We'd be so good together." His voice is sin incarnate.

I shut my eyes.

No. No. No.

He exhales sharply. "Fine. If you won't admit it now, so be it." His tone shifts to something dangerous and smug.

"But know this. When you want me. When you *need* me, I won't take you until you beg for it."

My stomach flips.

"Until you need me so badly you debase yourself for it."

He nips my jaw.

"Then I'll punish you for denying me. Only then will I take you."

His ruthless claim on me snaps me back into reality.

"That will never happen." I seethe the words, my hands clenching into fists. "I will never bow to you. I will never beg. I am not yours."

His smirk infuriates me.

"Soon enough, you'll see."

He pulls his hand from my panties. Lifts his fingers to his mouth. And sucks them clean. Slowly. Loudly. Filthily. His tongue swirls around them. His lips enclose them.

I can't breathe.

He pulls his fingers out with a loud pop and paints my lips with them.

"Mine." He growls.

Something inside me snaps.

I spit in his face.

Instant regret.

It lands on his cheek. His eyes widen. A deadly silence passes over us. Slowly, he wipes it away, never breaking eye contact.

I can feel his palpable anger in the air.

"That'll add to your punishment."

Then he turns and storms out.

I exhale shakily.

What the fuck have I gotten myself into?

...

Once I realize he's not coming back, I take a shower.

The warm water does nothing to relieve the ache between my thighs. The ache he put there. It takes everything in me not to relieve it, but I can't risk him hearing. He can't know how wrecked he left me.

He's already felt your wetness. Pretty sure he knows.

I scrub my skin harder than necessary, as if I can erase what just happened. Erase him.

It doesn't work.

After cleaning my panties and bra, I hang them up to dry and wrap myself in a towel before raiding his closet again. I pull on another pair of his boxer briefs, a long-sleeve t-shirt, and his sweats. Layer after layer. I cover myself from head to toe, as if it'll make a difference.

But I know the truth. No amount of clothing could stop him.

Once I crawl into bed, I eye his obnoxious amount of throw pillows. Fuck it. I build a wall between us. A thick, sturdy, clear divide.

I can't wake up under him again. I can't let myself crawl to his side. I need distance.

But as I drift into sleep, one thought claws at me, relentlessly and undeniably.

I don't know if I'm strong enough to resist him much longer.

Chapter 18
Matthias

I've been in my office for over an hour, but I can still smell her arousal on my fingers. Despite the empty tumbler in my hand, I can still taste her sweetness.

I reach to refill my whiskey but stop. I need to keep a clear head to form a plan.

At first, I was angry. Not about the spitting, which will be punished, but at her refusal to admit she wants me. Who is she to deny us? Why does it matter how we met? There's a pull between us that she can't ignore; I sure as hell won't.

But I meant what I said. I won't force her. Even if I know she wants it. And I won't be the one begging. I just need to get her to the point where she can't resist anymore.

My cock hardens at the thought of her on her knees, eyes full of need, begging. Begging for my touch. For my cock. For a pleasure we both know only I can bring her.

But what will win her over?

I've never had to work for a girl. Never *wanted* to. Never *needed* to. None of them were worth more than a quick fuck. But Margot... She's different.

I don't just want her body. I want her. Her brain, her sass, her fire.

I need her.

She won't be won over by money or shiny things. It's one of the things I appreciate about her. She craves freedom. I need her to choose to be here. Or at least, think she's chosen. She doesn't realize she's never leaving me. She was mine the second she stepped into my bed, wearing my clothes, smelling like my soaps.

When she chooses to stay, she chooses me.

I thought my way to her was through her body, but that didn't work.

So, what does she love?

Benny.

It's ridiculous, but I find myself making my way to the dog's room. Maybe he has some insight for me.

I settle next to Benny's oversized, expensive dog bed and run my fingers through his fur. He rests his massive head on my lap. *At least someone likes me.*

"Hey, buddy. I need your help." His eyes flick up. "How do I win Margot over? You know her better than anyone."

He lets out a bored sigh.

This damn dog.

"I know she wants me. She's just too stubborn to admit it. She's too caught up in the whole kidnapping and killing thing to see how good we'd be together."

Benny lets out a sharp bark mocking me.

I stop petting him. *See if I'll put up with that.*

"Stop mocking me, Benjamin. You know damn well I couldn't leave her there after what she saw. And it's not like she's suffering here. She's living better than she did at home."

I use his full name. You can't scold a dog named Benny with a straight face. It's ridiculous.

That's when I remember she named him after a guy from a rom-com.

My brows furrow. Why the hell did she do that?

Then it hits me.

She narrates romance novels. She spends hours in those worlds. She loses herself in them.

I snort. No fucking way.

Romance? Love? *That's* the key?

That's fiction. Women don't need pretty words or gentle touches, they just want... *me*. I don't need to convince them.

But Margot's different.

She loves romance. Craves it.

If that's what she wants, if that's what'll win her over, then that's what I'll give her.

I'll be her knight in shining armor. I'll be the perfect gentleman.

I need to take a step back physically and pull her in emotionally. And when she finally trusts me, when she finally believes me, she'll never want to leave.

I glance at Benny, ready to share my revelation, but he looks away, done with the conversation.

Fine. But at least now, I have a plan.

When he lets out a soft whine, I turn to see him holding his rope toy, with big, sad puppy eyes locked on me.

I sigh and grab the other end. "This isn't going to be as easy as with Margot. I'm a lot stronger than she is."

Benny yanks so hard the rope flies out of my hand. This fucking cheater.

"That time didn't count. Rematch."

He glares at me, as if *I'm* the one cheating.

Fine. No more going easy.

I brace myself and tug back, my muscles burning. This dog's strength is impressive, but I still win. We start again. Then again.

After several more rounds, I tap out, my arms sore as hell. I started switching arms after the fourth round, telling myself this counts as a workout.

"Sorry, buddy. It's time for me to join Margot in bed."

Benny flops onto his bed, exhausted. I smirk, satisfied. I toss him a few treats and make my way out.

The dog is growing on me.

...

After a quick shower in the gym to wash away the sweat, slobber, and dog smell on me, I head to our bedroom.

Walking in, the first thing I notice is the pillow wall.

She built a fort between us.

I can't stop the smile spreading across my face. She's adorable. If she thinks a pile of feathers is going to keep me from sleeping on top of her, she's delusional.

Now that I've had a taste, I won't spend another night not touching her.

I slip into bed. Knowing she's a deep sleeper, I carefully lift her over the pillow wall and curl on top of her.

She melts into me.

My soft, stubborn girl.

My spitfire.

She's mine.

Nothing, especially not a pile of pillows, will ever come between us.

Chapter 19

Margot

For the second morning in a row, I wake to a warm, heavy weight on me. It only takes me a minute to realize it's Matty. Again.

I glance at my pillow wall. It's shredded. Destroyed. Pointless. Why does my body betray me in my sleep? *Or does it give in to what you truly want?*

Despite the warmth, the comfort he provides, I move to push him off me.

He doesn't budge.

I scowl. If brute force won't work, fine. Time to get dirty.

I wiggle my right arm free and slam my elbow into his ribs. "What the fuck!"

He jerks upright, grabbing his side. His rough voice betrays his pain, and for a second, guilt stabs me. Did I hurt him?

Why do I even care?

Because you like him.

I shake the thought away and slip out of bed, bolting for the bathroom before he fully wakes up. After last night, I'm not putting myself in a position where I have to refuse him.

Because, if I'm honest with myself? I'm not sure I can.

I go through the same routine. Brush teeth. Wash face. Change.

By the time I peek out, Matty's gone. Good.

I sprint to the closet, and yank open drawers, grabbing another pair of sweatpants. He's running low. I need to ask Dotty to do a load. What will I even wear when he runs out?

You could wear nothing He'd love that.

Fully dressed, I step out of the closet, and nearly scream.

Matty stands at the entrance.

"You scared the crap out of me! I didn't even hear you come in."

He grins. *Grins.* Like we're normal. Like last night never happened. Like he didn't have his hand in my panties, didn't claim me, didn't promise I'd beg for him.

Does he have short-term memory loss?

He holds something out. "A caramel macchiato. Dotty showed me how to make it."

I stare at the mug. He brought me coffee?

He just smiles, sweetly and innocently.

My brain short-circuits. What in the fuck is happening right now?

"I thought you didn't know how to use the other coffee machines."

His smirk deepens. "An old dog can always learn new tricks with the right incentive."

I gawk at him.

Is he *flirting?*

I feign ignorance, grab the coffee, and take a sip, then instantly regret it. A moan slips out before I can stop it.

Fuck.

My eyes shoot to his. Direct eye contact.

But he doesn't react. No smug smirk. No shift in posture. Nothing.

What the fuck?

"Is it up to your standard?" He asks, still all sunshine and rainbows.

My brain is breaking.

Last night he was feral, completely losing control over me. Now, he's acting like we're roommates.

I glance down and am relieved to see the outline of his hard cock. Not that I was looking. Not that I care. *You care.*

I flick my gaze back up. He's still smiling. Like nothing is out of the ordinary.

I narrow my eyes. "It's good."

And damn it, it is good. Just how I like it.

His smile brightens. "Perfect! I'll be in my office if you need anything. Let Dotty know what you want for dinner. She can cook just about anything but give her enough time to gather ingredients. Looking forward to tonight."

Then he *kisses my forehead.*

His eyes stay on me a beat longer than necessary before he turns and walks out.

I stand there, stunned. If it weren't for the coffee in my hand, I'd think I hallucinated the whole thing.

…

I'm still thinking about our weird exchange this morning when Benny barrels into me, nearly knocking me over.

"Jesus, Benny! Be gentle!"

He nudges me again, whining.

I sigh, running a hand down his head. "I'm sorry. I know I've been distracted. Matty just has me all messed up."

His ears perk.

I huff a laugh. "Last night, he was all over me. He couldn't control himself. It was the hottest thing I've ever experienced, and he didn't even touch me. Well... besides..." I shake my head. *Not the point.* "It took everything in me to resist him. I don't know how much longer I can keep it up. But then this morning, he was completely unaffected. It makes me wonder if it was all in my head. Maybe I imagined his interest."

Benny tilts his head.

I scowl. "It's not that I want him to want me. I just don't like the whiplash. I want consistency."

He stares at me judgingly.

I groan. "Fine! Yes, I want him. But he's my captor! I'm here against my will! What kind of tramp gives in this fast? It's only been two days!"

He rolls his eyes. This damn diva.

I glare at him. "You don't get it. Is this even real? He only wants me because I'm the only girl around. I want to know he'd choose me. In a room full of women, I still want to be his choice."

The words fall out before I realize I feel them.

Benny tilts his head again. *'Has he given you any indication he'd choose you?'*

I hesitate. Matty's words from last night echo in my head.

"You're mine."

I shift uncomfortably. "Okay, yes, he's made comments about me being 'his'. But that should be infuriating. No man owns me. I'm not his."

'But you want to be.'

Benny stares at me knowingly.

"Fine. I wouldn't mind being taken care of. Not having to worry about things. And his body... Jesus. Our chemistry is undeniable. I know it'd be incredible. He'd ruin all other men for me." I scrub my hands over my face. "This is just my inner tramp talking. I swear her voice has taken over my thoughts."

Benny doesn't look convinced. He's telling me to give Matty a chance.

Would it really be so bad?

No. I can't let myself think like that.

"We're not talking about this anymore." I shake my head. "He needs to think I don't want him."

Benny tilts his head, calling me on my bullshit.

I try again. "He threatens you if I don't behave. He's a bad man. You should be scared of him."

Benny rolls his eyes and turns his back to me.

He's not scared. Not even a little.

And for some reason, neither am I.

Matty doesn't seem like a bad man at all.

Chapter 20
Matthias

I see Margot talking to Benny on the screen in the corner of my eye, and I can't stop myself from turning the volume up. Curiosity gets the best of me.

"...I'm sorry. I know I've been distracted. Matty just has me all messed up."

Damn *Matty*. I've always hated the nickname. It's too childish, too soft. But when *she* says it? *I love it.* I love that she has a name for me no one else does. I love that she says it to get under my skin. *It's exactly where I want her.*

I would handcuff her to me if I thought I could get away with it.

Sweetheart, what do you mean I have you all messed up? Am I driving you as crazy as you are me?

"Last night, he was all over me. He couldn't control himself. It was the hottest thing I've ever experienced,"

Me too, sweet girl. Leaving the room was one of the hardest things I've ever had to do. But if I'd stayed another second, I would have been on my knees begging.

And I don't get on my knees for anyone.

"and he didn't even touch me. Well... besides..."

Oh, sweetheart, I definitely touched you. The taste of your sweetness is branded in my memory. Next time, I'm taking from the source.

"It took everything in me to resist him. I don't know how much longer I can keep it up."

Hopefully not much longer. You will be on your knees for me, sweetheart.

"But then this morning, he was completely unaffected. It makes me wonder if it was all in my head. Maybe I imagined his interest."

What?

I grip the edge of my desk. She thinks I don't want her?

Sweet girl, it took everything in me to hold myself back this morning. That mask of indifference? Only decades of boardroom experience made that possible. But I couldn't hide my reaction to her moan. She saw my cock straining against my slacks. Was that not proof enough?

Maybe my plan to back off isn't the best. I can't have her doubting my attraction. I need to find a balance. To show her I want her without being the one to initiate. She will be the one begging.

She keeps talking, interrupting my thoughts.

"It's not that I want him to want me. I just don't like the whiplash. I want consistency."

I can give you consistency, sweetheart. I can give you everything.

"Fine! Yes, I want him. But he's my captor! I'm here against my will! What kind of tramp does it make me to give in this fast? It's only been two days!"

Tramp?

Fuck no. No one calls my sweetheart a tramp. Not even herself.

"You don't get it. Is this even real? He only wants me because I'm the only girl around."

My jaw clenches. Is that what she thinks? That I only want her because she's here?

Absolutely not.

I could leave this house right now and get any woman I want. But I don't want any of them. The thought of touching another woman makes my stomach turn.

"I want to know he'd choose me. In a room full of women, I'd want to be his choice."

She doesn't have to compete with anyone. She is the competition. It's not even close.

I need to up my game. I can't have my girl doubting herself. Doubting us.

Despite her protests, she's mine. But she doesn't realize I'm hers just as much.

She owns me.

"Okay, yes, he's made comments about me being 'his'."

Yeah, sweetheart. Because you are.

"But that should be infuriating. No man owns me. I'm not his."

Spitfire, get used to it. You *are* mine. There's no escape.

"Fine. I wouldn't mind being taken care of. Not having to worry about things."

My sweet girl, I will always take care of you. You will never have to stress over anything again.

"And his body... Jesus. Our chemistry is undeniable. I know it'd be incredible."

Spitfire, you have no idea.

"He'd ruin all other men for me."

Yes. Yes, I would. And no other man will ever touch you again.

The thought of another man's hands on *my Margot* has me seeing red.

"This is just my inner tramp talking. I swear her voice has taken over my thoughts."

Stop. Calling. Yourself. A. Tramp.

I'm going to punish her for that.

"We're not talking about this anymore."

That's okay, you've given me more than enough. You're closer to breaking than I thought.

"He threatens you if I don't behave. He's a bad man. You should be scared of him."

That has to stop.

She loves that dog. As long as I'm holding Benny against her, she'll never give in to me. Plus, Benny and I bonded last night. The way he rolls his eyes at her tells me he's on my side.

...

New plan: I need to embed myself in her life. She needs to depend on me. I want to be her stability, her comfort.

I'll be her constant.

She won't even realize what's happening until it's too late.

We'll start small. Making her coffee in the mornings. Eating dinner together in the evenings. Going to bed at the same time. I'll build routines with her until she can't even remember what life without me felt like.

I'll find ways to get close to her. Until I'm in every corner of her world, until she needs me as much as I need her.

No matter how long it takes.

Chapter 21
Margot

This time, when Dotty gets me for dinner, I'm ready.

Or at least I think I am. Until I step into the dining room and see my place set next to his.

So, we're doing this again.

I grab my plate and move it to the other head of the table. Distance. I need distance. Dotty sighs in disappointment. She can get over it.

I don't know which Matty I'll get tonight. The seducer or the friend.

The seducer? He melts my brain with smooth words and heated touches. I'm struggling to keep denying him.

The friend? He confuses me. He feels like a trap luring me in with a false sense of security, only to attack.

Neither one is safe.

I take my seat and force myself to breathe. I took a yoga class once, but I quit immediately. I remember they taught deep breathing for relaxation.

I try to do it, but I sound like I'm wheezing. After a few more seconds of that, I give up.

Matty walks in a few minutes later, smiling.

A real smile.

And it does something dangerous to his face. It softens him. Makes him look younger. Warmer. More welcoming.

Like he's not a kidnapper. Like he's just a man.

His strides don't falter when he sees where I'm sitting. He sighs, amused.

"I see you moved again. My stubborn girl."

I'm getting Friendly Matty.

I can do this.

Can you?

Like last night, he grabs his setting and moves it to my right. I blush, remembering what he whispered last night. What he threatened to do to me on this table.

He doesn't seem to notice. He sets up his place and, before I can react, leans over and kisses the top of my head.

What was that?

I freeze. I don't have time to process it before Dotty comes in with our plates. The salmon smells amazing. Another one of my favorites.

"Tell me about your day?"

I blink.

It's not a demand. It's a question.

What universe is this?

"Sweetheart, will you talk to me? What were you and Benny up to today? Anything fun?" His gentle voice and open expression confuse me even further.

I hesitate. Is this some game?

"Oh, um, we went for a walk around the courtyard." I clear my throat. "It was...nice?"

It comes as a question, not because it wasn't nice, but because I still don't know what the hell is happening.

"That's good. Am I correct in assuming a guard was with you?"

I flash a grin. We made the guard fetch the balls Benny lost interest in.

"Yes, he was with us."

"Good. Remember, don't leave the walls of this house without a guard." His tone is calm, but firm. Like it's non-negotiable.

It can't be about me. Maybe he just doesn't want his landscaping ruined. Or maybe he wants his captive contained.

Or maybe he wants to keep you safe.

Safe from what?

I nod and take a bite of salmon. This time, I make a conscious effort not to moan. It's delicicus, but salmon is the meal, not me.

You wish you were his meal. His mouth between your legs.

I clench my thighs, irritated. Not now, tramp.

I need to get him talking.

"How was your day?" It comes out awkwardly. I still don't know how to act around this version of Matty.

"It was productive. I had multiple meetings and was able to sign some important contracts."

"Do you always work from home?"

I don't think he's left the house once since I got here. But he wears slacks and a button-up every day, like he's going somewhere.

"Only when I have a beautiful woman in the house." He winks.

Why is he being so playful?

He called you beautiful.

I blush.

Damn it.

"So, what do you do?"

"I'm the founder and CEO of Syndicate Enterprise. It's a multibillion-dollar security and defense company. We handle physical weaponry and cyber security for the private sector and government."

Syndicate Enterprise. Dotty mentioned it. What does that have to do with criminals? Are they arming bad people?

I don't understand.

"That's nice. You're the founder. What made you start your company?"

His face lights up. His excitement is almost... cute.

And I hate myself for thinking that.

I let him talk. Half-listening. Half-distracted by the fact that I still don't understand what's happening.

"Enough about me." He tilts his head. "Is there anything you need to enjoy your stay?" He says it so casually. As if this truly is the *vacation* he claimed, and not a kidnapping. As if I'm a guest.

"Can I have my phone back?" It's out of my mouth before I think. *Stupid. He's not going to just hand it over.*

He's silent. Long enough I start to think he won't answer.

Then, "If you behave and earn my trust, you can have it back."

I blink.

He'd... actually give it back?

Of course, I wouldn't be able to call for help. But I could at least have my kindle app.

That's better than nothing.

Dinner ends, and I make my way to the door. Footsteps echo behind me. I turn to find him trailing.

"Why are you following me?"

His brows furrow like he's confused by the question.

"I'm going upstairs to our bedroom."

"*Your* bedroom." I correct.

He chuckles. "You'll come around soon enough."

I snort. No, I won't.

He holds out his hand. I take it instinctively. It's warm, steady, and sends a shiver up my arm.

And I hate that I don't pull away.

When we get to *his* bedroom, we both head to the bathroom. We brush our teeth and wash our faces in a comfortable silence.

Comfortable. That should worry me.

I go to his closet, grab a pair of sweats and boxer briefs, and change behind the closed door. Panties in hand, I return to the bathroom to wash them in the sink.

A low growl rumbles from next to me.

I glance up and find Matty staring.

Not at me.

At the black lace in my hand.

His gaze is scalding. It drops from the lace to my pantiless body beneath his sweatpants. His stare consumes me so thoroughly, I wonder if he can see through the layers. Lust radiates off him.

There's the Seducer Matty I know. *And love.*

A thrill shoots through me at finally getting a reaction I pretend not to notice his obvious erection and keep scrubbing.

As if you're not just as wet from his lust.

I use his distraction to ask him something that's been bothering me.

"If you're not going to let me go, can you at least bring me some of my clothes from home?"

"No."

He doesn't even look up, his eyes still locked on my body.

I huff. "Matty, I need more panties. And I'm sick of wearing your sweats." I don't even care that I'm whining.

"Just don't wear any panties. And I like you in my clothes." His voice is gruff.

I roll my eyes and change tactics.

"I need panties. Do you really want me walking around your men bare?"

His lethal gaze shoots to mine.

I knew it. Possessive bastard. What a brute.

As if all your book boyfriends aren't possessive as hell. That only makes him hotter.

His jaw locks.

"No one gets to see what's mine. And no one gets to be around you with that sweet pussy bare except me. I'll have new panties for you tomorrow."

I bite my lip to hide my smirk. Predictable.

But insanely hot.

"And some clothes?" I push. "I'd rather not walk around looking like a prisoner."

He exhales sharply. I can tell he doesn't want to give in.

"I'll get you some clothes. But only for the day. You wear my clothes to bed or nothing." His eyes narrow. "Don't argue."

Victory.

I huff dramatically and storm out. I settle onto my side of the bed, debating whether to build another pillow wall. Before I decide, I hear rustling. I glance up, and instantly regret it.

Matty is undressing.

First, his shoes.

Then, his shirt.

His belt.

His slacks slide down his legs, pooling at his feet.

Until he's left in nothing but tight boxer briefs.

I forget how to breathe.

He's all muscle, all power. Perfectly sculped, every inch carved from stone. And when he turns, when he walks into the closet and shoves his boxers down…

I suck in a sharp breath.

His ass is magnificent. Sculpted. Muscular. *Bitable.*

He pulls on a fresh pair of boxers, completely unaware of my internal crisis, and heads toward the bed.

A chill runs down my spine. *It's not fear. It's lust.*

"What are you doing?" I squeak out.

He stops mid-step. His brows furrow. "Getting ready for bed?"

"Why are you naked?"

He looks down at himself, confused. "I'm not naked. I'm in my boxers."

"You're practically naked."

He shrugs. "I always sleep like this. Clothes make me too hot."

"You can't get in here like that."

His lips twitch. "I've slept in my boxers next to you the past two night."

I freeze, realization dawning.

"But I didn't know."

"Now you do."

That doesn't make it okay.

I glare at him. He has the audacity to look amused.

"We just haven't gone to bed together yet," he adds smoothly. "But that's going to change."

"What?" I barely breathe the word.

He just smirks.

Fine. I'm not playing this game. I turn my back to him and scoot as far to the edge of the mattress as humanly possible. Not that it'll do any good. By morning, I already know where I'll be.

If this is how it's going to be from now on...

I don't stand a chance.

Chapter 22
Matthias

After a pleasant morning of waking Margot up with coffee in bed, I sit in my office getting some work done. Or at least, trying to. My focus is better than yesterday, but my mind still drifts to her far too often.

I can't help smiling at the memory of her annoyance when she woke up on my side of the bed again.

Like clockwork.

I, of course, dragged her to my side as soon as her breathing evened out. Yes, I did stay awake just to do it. No, I don't regret it. There will be no more cold nights without her in my arms. Staying up just to watch her fall asleep isn't a hardship. It's a privilege.

I woke up before her but stayed on top of her for a while basking in her warmth. Enjoying how small she feels beneath me.

Eventually, I got up to make her coffee. And like Pavlov's dogs, she woke up as soon as the smell hit her nose.

Her cheeks were rosy from sleep, her hair a wild mess. It's the most docile I've ever seen her. I wanted to gather her in my arms and never let go.

For once, she wasn't biting at me or pushing me away. She was just soft. Open. Unburdened.

Mine.

The sight of me shirtless and holding coffee brought a dreamy smile to her face. The absence of a shirt may not have been accidental. All's fair in love and war, right?

But the spell broke when I sat on the edge of the bed. She realized where she was and huffed. She tried to move back to her side without spilling her coffee. It was adorable.

She doesn't suspect that I'm the reason she wakes up on my side. I have no intention of correcting her. If she thinks it's her subconscious pulling her toward me, then soon enough, the rest of her will follow suit.

Movement catches my eye and my gaze flicks to the security feed.

I have it minimized to the corner of my monitor. I've improved. I only check every five minutes now instead of every minute. It's better like this. More manageable.

Having her out of my sight creates a new stressor. If too much time passes, I get heartburn.

But there she is.

Playing fetch with Benny. Or trying to. Which is going about as well as you'd expect with her lazy dog.

If she throws the ball further than fifty feet, Benny flops to the ground and starts chewing a stick instead. Then Rob, one of the few guards I trust enough to watch her, has to run to get the ball. Like a damn dog. Except the actual damn dog won't do it.

I should be annoyed.

Instead, I'm entertained.

I suspect Margot does it on purpose. Making the guard run laps just for her amusement. A little act of defiance. My spitfire.

Her rebellious streak is one of the things I love most about her. She's so full of fight. So alive.

I was bored before I took her.

But now?

Every second has been exciting. She awakened something in me that's long been at rest.

I don't want to smother her fire.

I just want to tame it.

My cock stirs at the thought.

Taming her.

Breaking her down, just to build her back up into mine.

Being the only one to have her obedience.

Being the only one to have her submission.

She thinks she wants control. Thinks she doesn't want to belong to me. She's wrong. I see how much she needs me. How much she craves me, even if she won't admit it yet. She'll feel free when she doesn't have to think for herself anymore.

She's mine. And I always take care of my things. She's just too stubborn to give in.

For now.

I pick up my phone and dial Bash.

"Hey Matthias, what's up?" he answers, cheerful as always.

Sebastian's always been the happiest of us. The youngest. The one we sheltered the most. Even though he's seen violence and has done what needed to be done, he still has his joie de vivre. It's why I have to tread lightly.

Bash might be loyal to the family, but I'm not sure he'd approve of what I'm doing. Not yet.

"Not much going on. What about you?"

"I have a date tonight." I can hear his smirk.

I grin at his excitement. He's turning into quite a bit of a player, taking after yours truly.

My grin instantly drops. The comparison makes my stomach turn. The thought of touching another woman disgusts me. I don't even want to think about it. I feel the need to burn the thought off my skin. It feels like bugs crawling under my flesh.

There's only Margot.

There will only ever be Margot.

I force a chuckle. "That's great, Bash. Have fun. Make sure to wrap it. Mom would kill you if you got some hookup pregnant."

Pregnant.

Pregnant Margot.

Margot. With my baby.

Babies that look like her.

Slow down. I have to get her to like me before we can start naming babies.

"Shut up, man," he groans.

I chuckle but shift gears. "I have a question for you."

"Shoot."

"If I wanted to stop someone from sending texts and calls on their phone, how would I do that?" I aim for nonchalance.

"That's easy."

Bash walks me through each step. I take notes.

Perfect.

Before I hang up, he pauses. "Is this about Margot Peterson?"

I freeze. I must be silent for too long, because he continues.

"Matthias, I don't know what you're up to, but I won't help you hurt a woman."

There's conviction in his voice.

I exhale. "Relax, Sebastian. You know I'd never hurt a woman. Plus, Mom would kill me if I ever did."

He quiets.

Then, "Alright. I'll let you go."

He doesn't sound fully convinced.

That's fine. I don't need his approval.

All I need is Margot.

The call ends.

I open my desk drawer and pick up her phone. The light blue case is delicate like her. I follow Bash's steps. Then, I add my number: *Matty.*

I try to call myself. It rings on her end, but my phone never receives a call.

Perfect.

I go to put the phone away, then pause.

I open her contacts. And delete every male name that isn't family. There aren't many, but enough to make me wonder. *How many of these men have had what's mine?*

Maybe I'll need to pay a few visits. Just to be sure.

All I know is this:

No one touches her again.

Chapter 23
Margot

The days start to blur together. A routine has formed. One I didn't agree to, didn't plan on, but somehow have fallen into anyway.

Every morning, I wake up on Matty's side of the bed.

Some mornings, I wake to coffee in bed. He makes it exactly the way I like it.

Other mornings, I wake to the weight of him on me, pressing me into the mattress, solid and immovable. His warmth lulls me into a sense of comfort that's getting harder to fight. Those mornings, I feel his arousal pressing against me, and I try desperately to ignore the wetness that follows.

It's been a constant battle. A war between my body and my mind.

With lingering touches, scalding stares, and far-from-innocent comments, he knows exactly what he's doing to me. And I'm starting to fall into them.

At this point, the only thing keeping me grounded is my pride. I refuse to beg a man for pleasure.

But his touch would make the bruises to your ego so worth it.

It's getting harder to quiet the wanton voice in my head.

Because you agree.

After coffee, we part ways. I go downstairs and join Dotty in the kitchen for breakfast. I've come to appreciate her. Yes, she idolizes Matty, but it's because she loves him. And I can't fault her for that.

I've stopped probing for information on the brothers. What's the use?

While I eat, Matty works. Some days he works from home. Other days, he leaves for the office, wherever that is. Even though when he works from home I don't see him much, the house still feels emptier when he's gone.

Occasionally, he'll join me for lunch. I usually eat outside on the terrace. The weather has been too nice to waste.

Benny enjoys it too. We go on at least one walk a day. We play outside until we're exhausted. Then we wander around the house, exploring new rooms.

The library is my favorite place. It contains a full wall of books, the classic rolling ladder, and a fireplace I can't wait to use in the winter. It's the kind of place I could get lost in and forget the real world.

The house has a home theater full of big reclining seats, which have enough room for Benny to take up an entire chair. It also has a fully stocked snack bar, a massive screen, surround sound, and every streaming platform imaginable.

There's a gym that I don't frequent. Sweating isn't my thing. However, Matty sure enjoys it. Every afternoon, he leaves covered in sweat.

On my favorite days, he's shirtless.

I'm not proud of how much I enjoy those days.

In the evenings, Dotty collects me for dinner. It's always delicious, but the best part is the company.

Matty genuinely cares about my day. He asks what I've been up to. He tells me about his business successes and shortcomings.

And every evening, the same little ritual unfolds.

My place is set next to him. I move. He follows.

I don't even do it to get away from him anymore. Now, it's a game. Our inside joke. And I love it.

He hasn't come onto me as boldly as he did that first dinner, but he does touch me every chance he gets.

Tucking my hair behind my ear. Kissing my forehead. Holding my hand. Resting a palm on my thigh. Whispering in my ear. Nibbling my lobe. Knocking shoulders. Brushing thighs.

And I'm not fooling anyone.

My breath catching in my throat. Sharp inhales. Full-body shivers. Goosebumps down my arms. Wiggling in the chair. Clenching thighs. Sighs. Gasps. Moans.

I know he notices.

But he never takes it further. He's the perfect gentleman.

It's hell.

I tell myself it's what I want.

But I can't deny the disappointment each time he pulls back. The problem is, it's not just physical anymore.

I miss him throughout the day. I count down the hours until dinner. I look forward to his jokes. I even plan ways to make him smile. It isn't difficult. He seems happy around me.

And that realization terrifies me.

Some evenings, we go our separate ways. Others, we take Benny on a walk around the property. Occasionally, I'll read in the den while he works on his laptop. Those are my favorite.

We always get ready for bed together.

I don't know how I'm always ready for bed when he is.

You stay up until he's ready.

We brush our teeth and wash our faces in synchrony. He still only wears his boxer briefs to bed, something I've had to get used to.

You love it.

I, thankfully, now have panties, but don't wear them at night to conserve them, leaving me in his boxers as well.

Bullshit. You have several pairs, and Dotty does your laundry at your request. You don't wear them because he told you not to, you obedient girl.

I also have my own clothes now, but I don't have any sleepwear, which is why I continue to wear his sweats to bed.

So now you can't wear yoga pants and T-shirts to bed?

Every night, I go to sleep on my side of the bed.

And every morning, I wake up on his.

My body knows what it wants.

And it's starting to convince my mind.

Chapter 24

Matthias

I can see my plan working. Margot's accepting me. Accepting our life here. She doesn't see the shift in herself, but I do.

My spitfire hesitates longer each morning before pushing me off. She leans into my touches now. She even seeks me out during the day and greets me with smiles so bright, they warm my goddamn heart.

There's no more animosity in her eyes when they land on me. Sometimes, if I look close enough, I swear there's something else. Something softer. Something closer to a tenderness I don't deserve, but I'll take it anyway.

It happens in the small moments. When we're laughing. When I compliment her. When she watches me treat Benny sweetly.

She's forgetting life outside of these walls. She doesn't realize it yet, but I do. She's comfortable here. She has everything she could ever want.

And that's by design.

Dotty's observing her in person. I observe her on my cameras.

Anytime she mentions she wants something, it appears.

A new book? Sitting in the library by morning.

A favorite snack? Stocked in the kitchen by the next day.

A softer blanket? One shows up in the movie room that evening.

She hasn't noticed. Or maybe she's choosing not to.

With every day that passes, I can feel her defenses crumbling. Soon, she'll abandon the farce altogether. Soon she'll give in to me. Give in to us.

I'm looking forward to that day.

Margot's not the only one affected. I'm not immune to our newfound relationship.

I used to love my work. Now, I count down the minutes until I see her. I used to focus. Now, I'm distracted by thoughts of her, which are only relieved by watching her on my security feed. I never used to work from home. Now, I only leave for mandatory meetings. My office at work has been all but abandoned. Everything has been transferred to the one here.

Even my brothers have noticed. All three have reached out separately. My mother is concerned I'm depressed. She couldn't be more wrong. I'm the happiest I've ever been.

Margot's the best part of my day. Waking up on top of her grounds me. Ending the day with our nighttime routine gives me something I never thought I'd crave: a domestic life.

A life with Margot as my wife.

Every moment I spend with her brings me closer to the edge.

And now?

I fear I'm at risk of falling for her.

It's not about her silence. It hasn't been for a long time.

I'm not sure it ever truly was.

It's not even about her body, as much of a temptation as it is.

It's her.

Margot.

All of her.

I need her to be mine. In every way a woman can belong to a man.

Margot will be Mrs. Matthias Montclair.

Chapter 25

Matthias

We're enjoying a pleasant dinner, until Margot suddenly jerks upright in her chair.

I freeze.

"What's wrong?" My voice betrays my panic. My heart slams against my ribs. My chair scrapes against the floor as I shoot to my feet.

I'm on her in seconds, hands gripping her arms, checking for injuries.

"Are you hurt?" My hands skim her body, searching for blood, bruises, anything.

She swats me away. Then to my complete horror, she starts giggling.

Giggling.

The giggles turn into full-blown laughter. She's clutching her stomach, shaking.

Is she going into hysterics?

What the fuck is happening?

"Sweetheart," I say carefully, trying to keep the desperation out of my voice. "Tell me what's wrong."

She wipes a tear from her cheek, still laughing. *A fucking tear.*

"I'm so sorry, Matty," she gasps between giggles. "I didn't mean to scare you."

My entire body deflates. "Sweet girl, you just took years off of my life." And gave me a minor heart attack. I should call Dr. Richard, the Syndicate doctor, and have an EKG done.

She giggles again.

Now that I'm not in a state of all-consuming panic, I can appreciate the sound. Her laughter is angelic. Addicting. I'll never get enough.

Then she says something that stops my heart for the second time tonight.

"I'm sorry, babe."

Babe.

She called me *babe.*

First, Matty. Always Matty.

Once, in the alley, Mr. Montclair. *I wouldn't mind hearing that one again.*

But now, *babe.*

She didn't even notice. It slipped out naturally.

But I noticed.

It's the closest thing to affection I've gotten so far. And it feels euphoric.

She suddenly brightens, like a lightbulb went off in her head.

"Let's watch a movie!"

I blink, still stuck on the *babe* thing.

"Huh?"

"A movie! That was my idea! We have the theater, and I've watched some things in there. I thought it'd be fun. I think it's

Friday, so I figured you didn't have work. But if you do, that's totally okay. And I get it if you don't want to–"

"That sounds great, sweetheart," I cut in, smiling.

She talks so fast when she's excited. It's adorable.

But something bothers me.

She was nervous to ask.

I frown. *Why?*

Are we not at a point where she should feel comfortable inviting me to do things? I need to do better.

Then it clicks.

Dinner and a movie.

Is my sweet girl asking me out on a date?

I feel lightheaded.

Or she just wants to watch a movie.

Nope. I reject that idea.

She could always watch a movie alone. She's inviting me to join her.

That makes this a date. Or at least, in my book it does.

Her smile widens. "What do you want to watch?"

She's bouncing in her seat, and I can't remember ever feeling this happy.

"How about the one Benny's named after?"

Her face lights up.

"*How To Lose a Guy In 10 Days*! That's one of my favorites. You're going to love it."

She's already skipping out of the room, the rest of her dinner forgotten.

...

An hour later, I regret everything.

"*This* is the asshole you named Benny after?" I grumble, dumbfounded.

Margot sighs. "Yes. He's so dreamy."

I scowl at the screen.

Dreamy?

I'm way hotter. She cannot seriously think this jackass has better abs than I do. She wakes up against my chest every morning. What the fuck?

Before I can fume further, she gasps and starts explaining the plot to me. I'm following along, but I let her talk anyways. Because she's adorable when she's passionate.

And I'd listen to her ramble about anything.

Then the music starts.

And my entire world shifts.

Margot starts singing along.

No, not just singing.

Performing.

She's bouncing in her seat, grinding her hips, *like she's riding my cock.*

She lifts her shirt, seductive as sin.

I think my brain short circuits.

If it moves an inch higher, I'll come in my pants.

Then, the music stops.

Margot sits back down like nothing happened.

I stare.

Still hard as steel.

Still struggling to process what the hell just happened.

I discretely adjust myself. I've never seen anything sexier.

The movie continues, but my eyes keep drifting to her. She's engrossed. She mouths the words, knowing the movie by heart. Her lips part slightly when the male lead takes control with a kiss. She leans forwards, captivated. A faint blush dusts her cheeks. She wants a man to take control. I already knew that. But seeing it play out on her face?

I clench my fists.

One day, I'll give her that. And she'll never want for anything, because I'll give her everything.

She yawns and I smile. She's trying so hard to stay awake. I don't think she just wants to finish the movie. She wants to see my reactions. She's been watching me, sneaking glances when she thinks I don't notice. I exaggerated a few reactions for her sake. I don't think I've ever been so charmed by a person before. I want to give her the world.

By the time they leave the city, she's asleep. I lift her effortlessly and settle her on top of me. The sigh I let out is pure relief. Finally, I can touch her again.

I let the movie play. Not because I care about it, but because I know she'll ask me about the ending tomorrow. And I want to have an answer to make her happy.

The movie makes me think of her family. She's close to her parents, but they've been traveling for months. When was the last time she saw them? Spoke to them? Their lack of cell service made keeping her here more convenient, but I bet she misses them.

She should meet my family. My mother will welcome her immediately. Hell, Mom will probably start planning our wedding before dinner's over.

That might actually be a good idea.

By the time the credits roll I already know what I'll tell Margot.

I enjoyed the movie. Because she does. Because anything she loves, I love.

I carry her to our bed and tuck her into my side. For a moment, I debate stripping her down. She's been in these clothes all day, and I don't want her uncomfortable. But I decide against it.

We're not there yet.

But we will be soon.

Chapter 26
Margot

I wake up in our bed. On his side, of course.

I don't even remember getting ready for bed. As a matter of fact, I don't remember the end of the movie. Did I fall asleep?

I must have.

Does that mean Matty carried me to bed?

I don't know how to feel about that.

Excited? Cared for? Butterflies in your stomach?

Before I can dwell, I start to get up, only to realize Matty isn't here.

That's... strange. He's always here when I wake up.

Not strange, disappointing.

But before I can process that feeling, the door swings open, and in walks Matty. The rich aroma of coffee follows him, filling the air.

His easy smile relaxes his features.

"Good morning, sweetheart. I come bearing gifts."

That's when I notice he's holding something blue.

My phone.

I freeze.

I figured he'd forgotten or decided against giving it back.

A real smile takes over my face. The kind I don't have to think about.

"Are you really giving me my phone back?" I ask, excitement creeping into my tone.

"Yes, sweet girl. I think you've earned it. There are a few *safety measures* in place. But besides that, you're free to do whatever you want with it."

"Thank you!"

I launch myself into his arms, wrapping around him in pure, unfiltered joy.

He freezes.

And suddenly, I regret it.

I've never initiated contact before. Maybe I've been reading the signals wrong. Maybe there weren't any signals. Has it all been in my head?

I start to pull back, but his arms tighten around me.

"Don't you dare let go." His voice is low. Gravelly. His grip unrelenting. "I just don't want to spill scalding coffee on you."

A moment passes, and I feel it. His deep, long inhale.

Did he just sniff me?

And why does that make the butterflies in my stomach flutter?

Because you love him being obsessed with you.

I loosen my grip slightly, prepared to step away, but he doesn't let me go. Instead, he pulls me tighter.

"Just a little longer." He murmurs.

I giggle.

Giggle.

This man has me giggling. Who even am I?

Eventually, we break apart before my coffee can get cold. Matty lingers for another moment before brushing a kiss on top of my head. Then he excuses himself, mentioning he'll be in his home office all day and to come to him if I need anything.

And just like that, I'm alone with my phone.

...

I'm sitting in the kitchen with Dotty, sipping coffee, scrolling through my inbox. I have hundreds of unread emails. Most of them are junk. I'm sorting through them, deleting those and reading the important ones, when one catches my attention.

An audiobook contract.

Oh my God.

I completely forgot.

My stomach plummets. The author I agreed to narrate for has emailed several times. The most recent one was yesterday, reminding me of the deadline in four weeks.

I need to start *yesterday*.

Thankfully, she assumes I've been busy recording, which explains my silence.

If I back out of this project, it'll ruin my reputation in the romance audiobook community. I love narrating these books. If I could do it full-time, I would. And I refuse to let her down.

"Dear girl, what has you white as a ghost?" Dotty asks, concerned.

I don't answer. I fly out of my chair.

I don't even take a moment to form a plan to convince Matty to let me go home and grab my equipment. I can't waste time.

"Where are you going?" Dotty's startled.

"I need to talk to Matty!"

I don't wait for a response, letting the door swing shut behind me.

I burst into Matty's office without knocking.

At the sight of me, his brows snap together. He rushes to his feet and makes his way over.

"I have to go. I'll call you back later." He hangs up mid-conversation. He doesn't even give the other person time to respond. I should feel bad. That was probably an important call. But I don't care.

"I'm sorry." I blurt. "I should've knocked."

"You never need to knock." His voice is steady, but his eyes scan me for signs of distress. "What's wrong?"

He tilts my chin up, forcing eye contact. His massive hands completely engulf my face. My brain stutters.

"I need to go to my house." I rush out. "I promise I'll come right back."

"No."

There's no hesitation. No room for argument. Because he doesn't trust me.

He gave you your phone back. And you haven't even tried calling for help.

Why haven't I? Any sane person would have. Right?

You don't want to leave.

The thought startles me. That can't be true. It must be Stockholm Syndrome, right?

"What do you need?" Matty asks. "I can send one of my men to get it."

A blush crawls up my neck.

I like narrating romance novels. I really enjoy it. And I'm proud of my success. But I don't want to tell him. There's a reason I use a pen name. If he knows, he'll have questions. And if he listens? Oh God. I go over my last project in my head. There are way too many *spicy* scenes. That cannot happen.

"I have to be the one to get it." I try to reason.

His eyes narrow. "Why?"

"It's... private."

He tilts his head. "I had Dotty get you feminine hygiene products when you first arrived. If that's what you need, she can grab more for you."

I blink. "You... you thought of that for me?"

He nods, completely casual.

I don't know why that makes my heart race.

A man making sure you have tampons and pads. A man paying attention. It's attractive.

Is that weird?

No. It's thoughtful.

But I shake my head. "It's not that."

"Then what is it?" His voice is gentler now. "Margot, you can tell me anything."

I inhale. Okay. Here we go.

"I narrate audiobooks. I need to collect my equipment."

A beat.

Then, "I know."

I frown. "What do you mean, you know?"

"I just finished your last one. You're very talented."

Oh my God.

My face goes up in flames.

"They've gotten me through quite a few *situations*." He adds, smirking.

I stare at him.

Then, it hits me.

Oh. My. God.

He's been getting off to my narrations. *To me.*

I'm redder than a fire engine. This is beyond embarrassing.

But I can't stop the images flooding my mind. Images of him gripping his cock, stroking himself, listening to me voice erotic scenes. Does he picture me in them?

To my horror, the image has heat pooling between my thighs. I cannot find that hot. It's embarrassing.

Babe, he's getting off to only your voice, filled with fantasies of you. That's such a compliment.

I shove the thought away.

"Oh... Well... Umm." I clear my throat, struggling to regain control. "Can you get one of your men to gather my equipment? I have a recording due in a few weeks, and I need to start working on it now."

I can't even look at him.

"No."

My gaze shoots to his in confusion. "No?"

He meets my eyes evenly. "You're not recording anymore."

I stare at him. "Excuse me?"

He doesn't waver. "You're never narrating scenes like that with another guy again. And not to mention listeners. Do you know how many perverts out there would get off just hearing my sweet girl's voice?" His expression darkens. "No one else gets to hear you like that. I'm working on getting the ones you've already recorded taken down."

My stomach drops.

There's no room for argument in his tone.

Well too damn bad! I'm arguing anyways.

"First off," I snap, "in dual narrations, I record all the female points of view, and the male narrator does his. We send the files, and they put the chapters together. I've never even met my male counterparts. And second, these books are a form of art. People listen for the story, not to get off on it. No pervert is sitting through fifteen hours of romance books just for forty minutes of sex scenes."

I keep my tone calm and even. I'm proud of how steady my voice is. Until he shatters it.

"I did." His voice is unapologetic, smug, like this is the most obvious thing in the world. "I listened to hear your sexy voice. It's the hottest thing I've ever heard. I'm hard *right now* just remembering it."

My eyes drop before I can stop them, and sure enough, he's painfully erect.

My breath hitches.

I rip my gaze back up, furious with him, furious with myself.

"Then *you're* the fucking pervert! You can't stop me!" I raise my voice.

Ok, so the calm tone didn't last long.

The second the words leave my mouth, his entire demeanor changes.

His expression hardens.

I see it. The exact moment his patience evaporates. It happens right around the time I call him a pervert.

No kidding.

Well, he is one, getting off to my books.

You love the fact that he finds pleasure in your smutty narrations. You're dripping.

Shut. Up.

His voice drops lower, sharp as a knife. "Actually, I can. You're not getting the equipment." His tone makes it clear the conversation is over.

Something inside me snaps.

"Who the fuck do you think you are?" I shout.

He doesn't hesitate.

"I'm *your* Matty."

The way he says it sends a shiver down my spine.

Your Matty.

Not Matthias.

Not your captor.

Not the man who kidnapped you and turned your life upside down.

But Matty.

My Matty.

Mine.

"You're mine," he continues, his voice dark. "And no other man gets to hear your sweet voice so seductive." His tone isn't loud, isn't yelling. It's low and lethal. A promise and a threat all in one.

"Ugh! Fuck you, you psychopath!"

I shove both hands against his chest, but it's pointless. He doesn't even stumble.

But his grip on me tightens.

"Not yet, spitfire," he murmurs, voice thick with conviction. "Soon."

I do the only thing I know will set him off.

I spit in his face.

The moment it lands, everything shifts.

One hand snaps to my throat. His huge palm nearly encircles my entire neck. His grip is firm, unyielding. It's not painful, not yet. It's a warning, a declaration, a display of control. A reminder that he can do whatever he wants to me.

You're even wetter than before.

His other hand wipes the saliva off his cheek, slowly and deliberately.

When his eyes lift back to mine, they're black with rage.

He's so close, our noses nearly brushing, his breath warm against my lips.

Even now, even with his fingers wrapped around my throat, even when he could cut off my air or snap my neck in an instant, I'm not afraid.

Maybe I should be.

But no matter how furious he gets, I don't think Matty would ever hurt me.

At least not outside of the bedroom. You'd love that.

His lips part. His unhinged expression exposes the level insanity I've driven to. Then...

RING!

The sound shatters the moment.

His jaw clenches, muscles tight as steel. He doesn't release my throat immediately. His hand stays there for a second longer, like he wants me to feel his power as long as possible. Then, with one final squeeze, he lets me go.

I stumble back, breathless.

His free hand fishes his phone from his pocket. He checks the caller ID, mutters a curse, then locks eyes with me again.

"Get out of here." His voice is gritted, dangerous.

I don't move.

His gaze darkens.

"Know that this behavior will not go unpunished."

A shiver runs through me.

"I have to take this call," he continues, his expression murderous. "But we'll finish this later."

There's a promise in his tone.

I storm out, his words ringing in my ears.

But even as I throw the door open, as I stomp away, as I try to collect myself, a single thought lingers.

Did I push his buttons on purpose?

And if I did...

Why?

Chapter 27
Matthias

"What?" It comes out far harsher than Roman deserves.

"Dude, what crawled up your ass and died?"

I ignore him. "What do you need?"

"I wanted to give you a heads-up. There's been more movement by the ports. The Russians are becoming a bigger problem than we anticipated. They have too much money floating around. They're growing in numbers. More men from the motherland are popping up. Bash is having a hard time keeping track of everything. Dom's getting restless. We may need your help. I don't know what the hell you've been up to at your house, but you need to get your act together. Something's not right." Roman's voice is calm, but I hear the levity in it. This is serious.

But my mind isn't on the ports.

It's on *her.*

My constant distraction.

"I'll be on the lookout. Keep me posted."

"Good. Talk to you later." Roman hangs up before I can tell him *not* to talk to me later.

I have a spitfire to punish.

...

After hours of work, I finally power off my desktop and sit back, replaying this morning in my head.

How did a day that started so good turn to shit so quickly?

I love waking up my sweet girl with coffee almost as much as waking up on top of her. She always stirs when she smells it. She's adorable when she groggily reaches for it, too sleepy to guard her reactions. Too sleepy to stop herself from checking me out.

Then, seeing her light up when I gave her phone back...

For a second, I almost felt like an asshole for taking it in the first place.

Almost.

I did what I had to do.

But the highlight of my day was our hug.

She initiated contact.

She wrapped her arms around *me.*

She wanted me.

And she didn't even realize what she'd done. Her body acted on instinct. And her instinct was to go to me.

Holding her felt like holding the sun. I never wanted to let go.

Then she burst into my office, pale and frantic, and my heart fucking stopped. I was across the room in seconds.

Fear consumed me.

I hated it.

I hated that she has the power to make me feel that kind of panic.

When I realized what she was asking for, I was confused. Why would she want to do something that could open her up to perverts? I have more than enough money to support her. She doesn't need to work. She doesn't need to expose herself to disgusting men who would jerk off to her voice.

But she refused to see reason.

And when she spit in my face, I saw red.

Our first fight.

That's a milestone.

Her fiery temper made me just as angry as it did hard. I wanted to pin her to my desk and fuck the attitude out of her.

I didn't. But I wanted to.

I can't let her see that kind of weakness in me.

So, I leaned into the anger instead.

As much as her fire turns me on, I can't let her disrespect me. I've been too lenient. She needs a reminder of who's in charge. She needs to be punished.

The thought makes my cock throb.

But now that I've had a few hours to cool off, I realize I may have been too harsh. I stand by my decision. No perverts get to listen to my girl's voice. But narrating clearly means something to her.

Maybe I can find a way to make it work.

Maybe I can get Bash to track who listens to her audiobooks?

They can listen.

But I'll know who they are.

And if I ever find out one of them is getting off to her?

I'll handle him.

Hearing that she doesn't record those scenes with another man helps. I would have put a stop immediately. That changes things.

So, I'll think on it.

But first, I need to apologize.

And remind my sweet girl that no matter how hard she fights me...

She's already mine.

Chapter 28
Margot

It's been hours since our fight, but I'm still fuming.

Who the hell does he think he is telling me I can't record my books?

It's ridiculous. And over what? Possessiveness and jealousy?

A man who's possessive and jealous, the horror.

My inner fiend's sarcasm is infuriating right now.

Because you know I'm right.

I'm not backing down. I will be recording my audiobooks. Maybe I can convince him.

...

After playing outside with Benny to calm down, I'm gross and sweaty. I need a shower. And now that I finally have my phone, I can listen to music while I'm in there. These silent showers have been brutal.

I sort through my playlist, landing on *Angry Girl Revenge Anthems.*

Perfect.

I'm just stepping into the shower when I hear rustling in our bedroom.

Matty.

I guess he's back from the gym. He can find another shower to use.

I turn up the volume and sing along, letting the rage-fueled lyrics pour from me.

I'm not going to let this go easily.

My audiobooks mean too much to me.

By song six, I'm scream-singing.

Then I hear knocking.

Matty's voice booms over the music.

"For the love of God, turn that shit off!"

He sounds like he's losing his mind.

Good.

Just to spite him, I turn the volume up and sing louder.

"I swear, Margot. Turn. It. Off!"

He's pissed.

Fuck him.

I crank the volume all the way up. Full blast. And I scream the lyrics, pouring every ounce of rage into it. Let him seethe. Let him lose his mind.

Then... *BANG.*

The bathroom door slams open. It swings so hard it smacks against the wall before rebounding toward him. He marches forward before it can hit him.

I didn't think to lock the door. I figured he heard the shower. I figured he'd respect that boundary.

How naïve of me.

Through the fogged glass, I see him. He's wearing the same white button-up and slacks from earlier. So, no working out the anger in the gym, I guess. Lucky me.

He storms forward and rips open the shower door, so hard I'm surprised it's still attached.

His nostrils flare. His chest rises and falls with uncontrolled fury. There's murder in his eyes. And smoke pouring from his ears. Or maybe that's just the steam from the shower.

Even furious, the sight of him has my body betraying me.

My nipples harden.

My core tightens.

Dampness that has nothing to do with the water collects at my core.

"You're about to learn your place."

Shivers tingle my spine.

I am absolutely fucked.

Chapter 29
Matthias

I see the moment fear seeps in her eyes.

She's never truly been afraid of me before. Both times she spit on my face, she was furious, not scared. Even when I kidnapped her, even when I killed those men, she didn't look at me like this.

I didn't think I was capable of scaring this girl.

But now?

Now, she's scared.

Good. She should be afraid.

My intentions to apologize evaporated at her blatant sass, at her defiance in the face of a simple request to turn off that God-awful noise she calls music.

She needs to be taught a lesson. It's long overdue.

But anger takes a backseat to something much more wicked when I register her state of undress.

Being fully clothed while she's naked perfectly symbolizes my power in our relationship.

My cock hardens instantly, and I haven't even looked down yet.

I take in her face first. Water droplets cling to her skin, falling down her body in slow streams, the ones beneath her eyes remind me of tears.

She'll have real tears soon. Tears of pleasure.

My gaze follows the path of the water down her neck. That delicate, dainty neck, so small my hand nearly circled it earlier.

Down her chest, flushed from the heat of her shower.

Then I see them.

Her breasts.

Full, heavy, tipped with dusky rose nipples so tight, they beg for my mouth. Whether it's from the open shower stall or from my presence, I don't know.

I pray it's the latter.

The need to touch her, taste her, bite her, overwhelms me.

Precum leaks from my tip.

I force my eyes lower, only because I know what I'll find.

Her soft belly. I can already imagine the way it would move if I took her from above. The thought alone is nearly enough to break my restraint.

And then, paradise.

I inhale sharply, instinctively.

She found the razors. She's bare. I wouldn't care if she wasn't. Margot could be covered in hair, and I'd still be brought to my knees. But now, there's nothing between me and the most beautiful sight I've ever seen.

And I know the difference between shower water and slick arousal.

Her thighs glisten with arousal. I haven't even touched her, and she's already wet for me.

At the sound of my inhale, she snaps out of her trance and scrambles to cover herself. Her right arm crosses over her perfect breasts while her left hand drops over her core, blocking my view.

I knock her hands away.

"Never hide your body from me." It's a growl. A command. One she will obey.

She hesitates, still fighting me.

I narrow my eyes.

She huffs but lowers her arms.

"Good girl." I murmur.

Her blush deepens, spreading across her chest.

I take my time now, admiring the rest of her.

Those hips. Wide, made for my hands. Made for me to hold while I thrust into her.

My fingers twitch as I force myself not to grab her.

Her thick thighs. The ones that will wrap around my waist and keep me locked inside her.

She squeezes them together, rubbing them, trying to relieve the ache. Trying to hide her arousal.

That won't do.

I step into the shower, fully clothed, letting the hot water flow freely over me. Her eyes widen as the distance between us closes. Every step I take forward, she matches with one backwards, until she's pressed up against the wall. I trap her with arms on either side of her head.

I wedge my leg between hers, forcing them apart.

Heat. Slickness.

Even through my slacks, I can feel how wet she is. I don't bother swallowing my groan.

"You only get pleasure from me."

She needs to understand.

I can't stop myself. I reach forward and grab her breast. It's heavier than I expected. It's so full, it spills from my hand, too much to contain.

I roll her nipple between my finger, twisting until she gasps. The sound more beautiful than I imagined.

Her eyes flutter closed.

I pinch harder.

She yelps.

"Eyes on me." I reprimand.

She blinks up, breathless. She doesn't realize it yet, but she's learning. There are rules, and there are consequences. From now on, she will obey.

I shift my grip, moving from her breast down to the softness of her stomach. She tenses and bows her head.

I swat the outside of her thigh.

"Eyes on me." I growl.

She looks up again.

"I won't have you embarrassed by your body. You're the sexiest woman I've ever seen. This soft belly showcases your womanhood. Feel what you do to me."

I grab her hand and press her palm against my cock.

Her breath hitches. She tightens her grip, testing, feeling. I thrust into her hand, letting her know exactly how badly I need her.

She's transfixed.

I release her wrist and let my hand drift lower.

She swallows hard.

I move my thigh, spreading her legs further.

She's soaked for me.

I stroke my fingers through her folds, collecting wetness. I tease her clit, rubbing lazy circles, drawing out her pleasure. She lets out a beautiful mess of moans.

Her hips start to move, chasing my touch.

I swat her thigh again.

She moans louder.

Interesting. My girl likes being spanked.

"Stay still."

She huffs but obeys.

I go back to her slit, rubbing slow, deliberate strokes.

She shudders, her thighs trembling.

I tease her entrance, dipping just the tip of my finger inside before pulling out. Again, and again. Every time, I push a little deeper.

She whines in frustration.

"Tell me to stop, and I will." I murmur. "But I think you want this just as much as I do."

She opens her mouth to deny it.

I cut her off.

"I can smell your arousal. I can feel it. It's soaking through my slacks. Don't bother lying to me."

She flushes. Her skin, already pink from the heat, turns a deeper shade.

Breathtakingly beautiful.

I thrust a finger inside her.

She gasps, clenching around me.

I start to move, slow at first, then faster, falling into a rhythm.

She's close.

Her hand flattens against the wall, as if bracing for impact.

Good girl.

I lean into her, my lips brushing her ear.

"If you come without my permission, you won't come for a month."

She freezes. Shock and desperation evident in her expression.

I smirk. She doesn't realize it yet, but I do.

She's mine now. Completely.

And she will obey. Because she wants to. Because she needs to.

This is going to be fun.

Chapter 30
Margot

He can't be serious.

I search his eyes for a joke but find none. The taunting smirk on his face reigniting my anger. The nerve of him to think he has that kind of control over me.

But he does. You want to listen to him. You want to please him.

Shut. Up.

"You can't do that." I snap, but my voice betrays me in how weak and breathy it sounds. Because I know he can. As much as I deny it, I already am his. The moment I let him touch me, I signed the dotted line. I just don't know what the fine print entails.

"Are you willing to risk it?" His eyebrow arches.

Why is he so damn hot when he's so damn infuriating?

I freeze, but he doesn't.

He fingers continue their relentless assault, fucking me with his slow, deliberate strokes. His thumb never ceases its torment against my clit. My thoughts are scattered. My body trembles against the tile as pleasure overtakes my ability to fight.

I clutch the wall for balance, knowing if I squirm, he'll spank my thigh again. The twisted part of me, *the part that liked it,* wants to disobey. But I know each slap will only be harder.

Matty brings me close to the edge effortlessly. My vision blurs, stars dancing across my periphery as my pleasure crests.

And then he stops.

His hand retracts completely.

A strangled noise escapes my throat. I barely have time to protest before he drops to his knees.

Matty kneels for me.

The man who never kneels for anyone.

He throws one of my legs over his shoulder, baring me to him. His mouth is so close to where I need him. My breath stutters.

He inhales deeply, groaning like a man savoring the scent of his next meal. "Delicious."

He leans forward. And licks me.

Once. Then again. His tongue drags through my folds in slow, teasing strokes until I'm shuddering against the wall.

Just as my muscles relax, he *bites* my clit.

"Fuck." I curse, but it comes out as a moan.

The pain only amplifies the pleasure.

Matty groans, the vibration shooting through me as he sucks my swollen flesh into his mouth. At the same time, he thrusts two fingers inside me, curling them against a spot that makes my brain white out.

I don't even realize I'm moving, grinding against his face, chasing more, desperate for relief, until he yanks his hand away.

A sharp slap lands on my thigh, directly over the same burning spot.

I moan.

Shit.

"Stop moving." His voice is guttural, wrecked with need.

I bite my lip and force myself still, but he knows now. Knows I like it.

His fingers return, sliding into me again. His tongue works in tandem with his hand. My nerves sing as my body coils tighter and tighter, and I know I won't last long.

I glance down and *fuck.*

His white button-up clings to his chest, drenched from the shower. But that's not what has my breath catching.

Matty is stroking himself.

His big, veined hand is wrapped around his cock, pumping in time with the way he fucks me with his mouth.

Holy fuck.

I've never had a man want to go down on me before, much less get off on it. He's falling apart from my pleasure. *From me.*

My orgasm starts to slam into me before I can stop it.

But he stops first.

I whimper. So close, so desperate for one more second of friction, but he's already pulling away.

"If you want to come, you'll ask nicely." His voice is maddeningly calm.

I shake my head, panting. "I won't beg."

He's out of his fucking mind if he thinks I'm begging him for an orgasm.

"Is that so?" His smirk presses against my clit, sending shockwaves of pleasure through me.

I can hold out. I can win this. I can.

Then he starts again. Torturing me. Pulling me back to the edge.

Then he stops.

Again.

And again.

And again.

I meet his eyes, refusing to cave.

Matthias only chuckles and doubles his efforts.

Twenty seconds later, I break.

"Please, Matthias." My voice is ruined. Tears spill from my lashes. I'm trembling, shaking, aching. "I'm begging you. Please let me come."

His fingers don't stop. His tongue doesn't stop. But he pulls back, just enough to whisper, "It's *Matty*. Only ever Matty to you."

He spanks the same fucking spot of my thigh. The sharp sting makes me gasp.

I don't hesitate this time.

"Please, Matty." My voice cracks. "Please, I need it."

He groans, but instead of letting me fall, he pulls away completely.

And then he says the worst thing I've ever heard.

"*Only good girls get to come.*"

My stomach drops.

"What?" My breath catches as I try to understand what he's saying.

His expression turns to cruel amusement. "Only good girls get to come." He strokes his fingers through my soaked folds teasingly. "Have you been a good girl?"

"Yes," I gasp. "I have! I begged. I called you the right name. I held back. I haven't come–"

He tuts, shaking his head. "No, sweetheart. You've been a bad girl. You've fought me. Disrespected me. Disobeyed me. You spat on me. *Twice.* I told you that you'd be punished."

He flicks my clit.

"*This is for me, not you.*" He goes back to his assault, and I see his hand jerkily stroking his cock.

Realization slams into me.

This is my punishment.

He made me beg to have me concede. To break down my ego. To prove me wrong.

And it turned him on.

My begging, my surrender, my obedience turned him on.

Fuck him.

I'm going to come anyways. He can't control my orgasms for a month.

But I'm wrong.

Matty brings me to the edge over and over and over, until my body is wrecked with unsatisfied pleasure. Until I hate how badly I need him.

By the time he finally stops, I don't know if I'm relieved or devastated.

Matty rises to his full height, his body towering over mine. His face glistens with my arousal.

He looks sinful.

I barely register the feel of his cock brushing against my belly until I glance down and see him stroking himself furiously.

I reach out, my fingers brushing his length.

He hisses.

Encouraged, I reach lower, tentatively cup his balls.

His head falls back instantly, his mouth parting in a silent curse.

"Fuck, Margot," he rasps, his voice desperate. "Grip them tighter."

I obey, tightening my hold. My thumb rolls over them, testing.

The noise he makes is animalistic, so raw it sends a shockwave down my spine.

I react instinctively. My fingers clenching tighter.

That completely undoes him.

His entire body shudders as he comes apart.

Thick ropes of his release coat my stomach, my chest, my breasts. Marking me, claiming me. His cock twitches in my hand before he releases himself from my grasp, stroking the last of his release onto my mound.

There's so much of him. My formerly clean body is now covered in him.

But I don't move. I don't wipe it away.

Because he's staring at me like I'm a masterpiece.

He's the artist.

And I'm his canvas.

His gaze is almost reverent.

His eyes darken and his pupils blow wide. He drags his fingers through the mess, swirling his seed across my skin. Spreading it.

I shudder.

He pinches my nipples, hard.

A needy moan rips from my throat. Even the slightest touch lights me up. My body remains on edge, still desperate for the orgasm I now accept will never come.

His fingers sliding up my neck and curl around my jaw. He pinches my cheeks together, forcing my gaze to his.

His voice is pure command. Pure ownership.

"Taste yourself on me."

The words are my only warning before his mouth claims mine. His tongue pushes past my lips, stroking, devouring, conquering me.

I respond immediately.

The kiss is rough and consuming. He's not kissing me. He's reminding me he's in charge.

Tasting myself should be repulsive. But from his lips, I crave it. I taste sweet, like fruit.

He bites my lower lip before pulling away. It's over too soon.

I barely have time to catch my breath before he drags two fingers though the release frosting my skin. He scoops some up, then raises his fingers to my lips.

"Open."

I obey instinctively. Because I never want to be denied my pleasure again.

The taste is salty, musky, unmistakably him.

He watches intently as I lick his fingers clean, sucking softly before he pulls them free with a wet pop.

His breath catches as our eyes meet.

The moment stretches, electric. Charged.

We're thinking the same thing.

The next thing I suck will be his cock.

His smirk is dark, satisfied. He drags more of his release across my lip, feeding me every last drop.

He doesn't stop until there's nothing left. And when I've swallowed it all, he nods in approval.

Something inside me thrums with pride.

He notices.

He always notices.

"How do we taste combined?" He asks, genuinely curious.

I swallow, my cheeks flaming.

"Sweet and salty," I whisper. "Fruity but manly."

He smiles softly. "Good girl."

My stomach tightens. Heat rushed through me at the words, at the approval I didn't even realize I wanted. Needed.

He chuckles knowingly.

I blush harder.

He grabs *my* loofah and pours a generous amount of *his* soap on it.

"If we're washing my cum off of you," he murmurs, "you're using my soap. You're smelling like me. One way or another."

His tone is dark, dissatisfied. Like he hates that he can't leave his mark on me permanently.

He washes every inch of me, making sure I'm just as clean as before he broke into my shower.

I return the favor, cleaning him just as thoroughly.

And somehow, it's more intimate than everything we just did.

When we step out of the shower, I realize my *Angry Girl Revenge Anthem* is still playing.

It didn't serve its purpose. I didn't stay angry.

But it still feels like a small victory that it was blasting while he came.

...

Dinner passes in a blur.

I'm too distracted to be good company. Matty carries the conversation easily, barely phased.

There's no lingering anger from earlier. And yet, I can still feel the ache between my legs. I still feel his words, his control, his denial. And I can't help but think...

Maybe I deserve it.

For what I did.

I didn't think he'd actually follow through on punishing me. But now that he has, I can't help but feel that I got off easily.

We get ready for bed in a comfortable silence.

When Matty joins me, he pulls me onto his side and tucks me against him. I guess he already knows I'd end up there, so why bother waiting?

His warmth envelops me. His breathing is steady. Even.

And right as sleep starts to pull me under, I hear him murmur, "Goodnight, my sweet girl."

It's soft and gentle.

He presses a kiss to the back of my head.

I pretend to be asleep, because I don't know how to respond to this side of him.

We've crossed a line into a territory I don't know how to navigate.

And the worst part?

The part that makes my stomach twist?

I can't help but feel he's been right all along.

I am his.

And worst of all...

I love it.

Chapter 31

Matthias

Waking up on top of Margot feels sweeter than usual. I lingered, savoring her warmth. The soft rise and fall of her chest, the way her body molds against mine. It's enough to make me consider staying in bed all day.

But work waits for no one, and if I don't leave now, I'll spend the morning buried in her.

Still, I can't fight my good mood.

When I walk in the kitchen to make our coffees, Dotty stares at me like I've grown a second head. She eyes me for all of two seconds before asking, "What's gotten into you?"

I smirk, unable to suppress the satisfaction curling in my chest. "Just had a good night."

Dotty gives me a once-over. Then, to my absolute horror, she mutters under her breath, "I'm sure it wasn't just a good night of *sleep.*"

I nearly choke on my coffee.

Dotty has been like a second mother to me my entire life, and never, not once, has she ever said anything remotely crude.

The mere suggestion of her thinking about my sex life is enough to make me want to throw myself into traffic.

Taking my silence as unwitting confirmation, she continues.

"Finally winning over that girl."

I huff a laugh. If only she knew *how* I won her over.

"She's a good girl."

I smirk. Dotty doesn't know just how untrue that is. But that'll change. Margot will be a very good girl for me from now on if she wants to avoid another lesson like last night.

Dotty isn't finished though.

"You're lucky she's giving you a shot after how you got her here," she says, leveling me with a pointed glare. "Don't screw it up."

What the hell?

Since when does she favor Margot? I've always been Dotty's favorite. How did Margot even win her over?

I frown but keep my voice even. "I won't, Dotty." My tone comes out steadier than I expect. "She's not like the other girls. She's it for me."

The moment I say it, I know it's true.

Margot's the only woman for me.

Dotty seems satisfied. "Good. Now go bring her that coffee." She waves me out of the kitchen like I'm a meddling child.

I blink. *Did I just get kicked out of my own kitchen?*

Dotty and I always have our morning conversations. She's never shooed me away before.

By the time I reach our bedroom, I've already forgotten about Dotty. My focus shifts entirely to Margot.

I'm not sure how she'll react after last night.

At dinner, she was docile. She let me pull her against me in bed without protest. But that doesn't mean she isn't still angry about the audiobook thing. Or even the orgasm denial.

Or maybe, just maybe, she feels the same way I do. That last night brought us closer.

I'm hoping it's the latter.

When the smell of coffee reaches her, she stirs. She slowly sits up, her hair a tangled mess.

Fuck, she's beautiful.

"Morning." She mutters, her voice hoarse and sleepy.

My lips twitch. She's too cute.

"Good morning, sweetheart." I hold up the mug. "I brought you something."

Her eyes light up, as if this isn't our daily routine.

My chest tightens.

Does she not realize I'll bring her coffee every morning for the rest of our lives?

I settle on the bed beside her, still treading lightly.

"I've got some work to do," I tell her, "but I have time for lunch." I don't actually have the time, but I'll make some for her.

She nods sleepily, still rubbing the drowsiness from her eyes. I hold the coffee just out of sight. The first sip will jolt her awake.

"I was also thinking we could watch another movie after dinner." I add, keeping my tone casual. "How does that sound?"

She lets out a sleepy "Mhmm. Sounds good."

I smirk. She has no idea what just she agreed to.

But that doesn't matter.

In my book, this is our second date.

I press a kiss to her forehead, then hand over the coffee.

Walking out of our bedroom, I feel lighter than I have in weeks.

If I'd known the key to Margot's obedience was between her legs, I would've had her long before now.

But I'm not going to give her a reason to regret last night. Tonight, she's going to learn exactly how I treat her when she's a good girl.

And I'm not going to fuck it up.

Chapter 32
Margot

It's been a good morning.

Benny and I have been hanging out in the library. Besides taking him out to potty a few times, we haven't been playing outside because the weather looks questionable.

By questionable, you mean that the sun is out, and you don't want to risk sweating before your lunch date.

It's not a date.

You want it to be.

I roll my eyes. I should be upset about yesterday, but the anger just isn't there. I'll bring up the audiobook at lunch, and hopefully, he'll see reason.

I feel like we both let our guards down yesterday. I'm excited to see where we go from here.

Maybe this time, he'll let you come.

I shake off the thought and stand, smoothing my dress. I'm usually fine waiting for lunch on the terrace, but today, I don't want to wait.

I make my way towards his office but stop cold when the front door swings open.

That's... strange.

Normally, the guards use the side entrance.

Curiosity and something dark coil in my stomach. Something feels off.

I duck under the staircase, pressing into the shadows, and watch through a banister.

A man steps inside.

The scariest man I've ever seen.

His brown hair is buzzed close to the scalp. His eyes are so dark, they're nearly black. His nose is crooked from multiple breaks. The plethora of scars on his face scream violence.

He's built like a war machine. Matty is big, but this man? This man is huge. And he's covered in blood. Not a little. A lot. Bright red splattered across his arms, T-shirt, and jeans.

My stomach churns. I want to believe it's not blood, but what else could it be?

What is a man like this doing in Matty's house? And why does he have a key?

He strolls in like he owns the place, tossing his keys on the entrance table without care.

"Matthias!" His voice booms, deep and gravelly. "Come out, pretty boy. You have a visitor." He practically sings the words, but they're laced with mockery.

Then he laughs.

A laugh so dark, so sinister, it chills my blood.

A door opens down the hall, Matty's office. His footsteps approach. Matty can't see me. But I can see him. And I can hear his tone.

"Fuck, Roman." Matty sounds frustrated. Panicked. "What are you doing here? You can't just show up uninvited."

Roman.

Roman, the *torturer.*

Roman, the *killer.*

Roman, the *brother.*

The realization slams into me.

Of course. They look so similar.

The same sharp jawline. The same cocky, confident stance. The same deadly aura.

"Well, when you turn me down every invite to spend time with your brother, I have to come to you." His voice darkens. "Plus, we have some things we need to discuss."

Matty sighs. "In my office. Not here."

He turns, and Roman follows.

They stalk back down the hallway. I hold my breath until the door clicks shut behind them.

I don't move.

I can't move.

My whole body is trembling.

How could I be so stupid?

How could I forget why I was brought here?

Matty *kidnapped* me to *silence* me.

I witnessed a crime.

A double murder!

And now I'm hiding under a staircase, watching Roman stroll in, dripping in blood, laughing like it means nothing.

It doesn't mean nothing.

It means he hurt someone. Or killed someone!

I tried to justify it before by telling myself it was self-defense in the alley.

But Roman was torturing that man. And possibly killing him.

That's not self-defense.

How could I be so blind?

You were blinded by smooth words and a sexy body.

I bite down a gasp.

I should run.

I should go back to the library and pretend I didn't see anything.

Instead, I creep forward. My back presses against the wall. I shouldn't do this. I should walk away.

Instead, I press my ear against the door.

"You can't just show up here unannounced." Matty's irritation is evident in his sharp tone. "Give me a heads-up next time."

"You've never had a problem with it before." Roman sounds bored. "And you've stopped leaving your house. You even missed family dinners. Mom's worried. But the rest of us? We're pissed. What the fuck is going on with you?"

Matty's reply is icy.

"Drop it. I'll come to the next one. Don't show up here without letting me know. Now what's wrong?"

Roman exhales. "It's the fucking Bratva. It's always the fucking Bratva. We caught three more sneaking onto our territory last night. Same as before. Talking to men outside the clubs. I came from questioning them."

"I can fucking tell. You couldn't clean up before coming to my home? You're covered in blood." Matty, *no, Matthias, he can't be Matty anymore,* sounds annoyed. But not shocked.

"They wouldn't talk. After some *convincing,* one finally broke. I gave that one an easy death." My stomach lurches. He doesn't sound remorseful, just annoyed. "He told me they have new product on the market. Something we can't compete with. He wouldn't tell me what." Roman sounds furious.

The sound scares me. I don't want to be in the same house as Roman when he's angry. I don't want to be in the same house as him at all.

At least Matthias isn't torturing and killing people, right? Doesn't that make it better?

No. I let a man related to this psychopath go down on me then come on me. I let a murderer do that. There's no making that better.

You don't know anything for sure. Don't jump to any conclusions.

Matthias hums. "Okay. We already knew this. What do you want from me?"

"We're starting to collect them more frequently. These aren't the first ones I've caught. If they keep growing in numbers, you're going to need to start helping out."

I hold my breath.

Please say no. Please, Matty, say no.

"You know I'll always do what I have to for the Syndicate."

No.

No, no, no.

"Even though I'm on the legal side, I can still get my hands dirty."

Then, he laughs.

A cold, unsettling chuckle. Dripping with malice.

I've never heard Matthias sound so evil. So villainous.

It shatters me.

I have to get out of here.

It's Matty. Are you sure you can't overlook this?

No.

I don't know this man.

I don't want to know him.

I feel sick that I ever let him touch me.

I need to leave.

And never look back.

Chapter 33
Margot

"Benny, get up! We have to go." I whisper frantically, heart pounding.

But this damn dog won't listen. He just stares at me, stubborn and unmoving, as if he knows. As if he can sense that this isn't just another walk, this is an escape.

His big, brown eyes glare like he's saying, '*No.*'

Damn it.

I grab a bag of treats and shake them. The sound coaxes him up, but he lets out a loud, dramatic huff.

"Shhh! You're going to get us caught."

At least he isn't a barker.

We slip out the side door and into the garage. My gaze flicks to the key rack.

Sports car? Too obvious.

Then I spot it: a Mercedes SUV.

Perfect.

I unlock it and open the back door, bribing Benny with a few more treats, until he finally jumps in. *Minutes.* I just wasted minutes. Minutes I don't have.

Matthias will notice we're gone soon. It's already been ten minutes since I overheard *that.*

I climb into the driver's seat and plug my home address into my phone GPS. Thirty-minute ETA.

I'll drive home. Grab the emergency cash from my mattress. It's only three thousand dollars, but it'll get me out of the state. I'll swap this car for mine. I have a fake ID from college. It won't hold up under serious scrutiny, but it'll buy me time. I need a new identity. A legitimate one.

Where the hell do you even find someone who knows how to make fake IDs?

I'll figure it out later. Right now, I need to focus on getting past the gate. The gate guard doesn't look familiar. *Good.*

I roll down the window, schooling my expression into irritation, not fear.

"I need to get Mr. Montclair's dog to vet. It's urgent."

The guard's brows furrow. "I didn't know he had a dog."

I force my lips into a sneer.

"He obviously does. And he cares about him a lot. The dog is sick and needs medical attention immediately. Mr. Montclair won't be happy with you if you delay us."

His eyes flick to the backseat where Benny is lying down obediently. Bless him.

A beat passes.

Then the gate opens.

I floor it.

I made it out.

I made it out.

Chapter 34
Matthias

RING!

I let the call ring through, irritated beyond belief. Roman's unannounced visit has already thrown off my day. I need to get this conversation over with so I can have lunch with my sweet girl.

This delay pisses me off.

His presence pisses me off.

Not because he's here, but because Margot could've seen him.

I don't care if he knows about her. Hell, I want the whole fucking world to know she's mine. But not yet. Not before I've solidified our relationship.

I'm almost certain she won't run anymore, but Roman showing up, *covered in blood*, strutting in my house like a fucking animal? That could spook her. Thank God, I intercepted him at the door.

My phone rings again.

I clench my jaw and pick up, ready to snap. "What?"

The guard at the front gate clears his throat. "Uh, hey boss. Just wanted to verify the maid taking your dog to the vet."

Silence.

The words don't register at first.

Maid? Dog? Vet?

"What did you just say?" My voice is calm. Too calm.

"The girl, uh, she rolled up in your Mercedes. Said she needed to bring your dog to the vet. He was in the backseat. She said it was urgent, so I let them through. But something felt off, so I wanted to confirm with you."

Buzzing.

That's all I hear.

A slow, creeping static buzzes in my head.

"You let her go?"

My voice is even. Controlled.

I already know the answer.

I already know what's happening.

But I need to hear it.

"Yes? She said the dog was sick. And, uh, she seemed in a hurry, but..."

I don't hear the rest, because he let her go.

He let her go.

It can't be Margot.

She wouldn't run.

She wouldn't.

She was excited about our lunch this morning. I know she wasn't upset anymore.

She wouldn't leave.

But as much as I tell myself that, I know the truth.

I take a deep breath. "When?"

"Uh... about three minutes ago."

The guard sounds nervous now.

He should be.

I end the call.

I turn. Walk out the door.

Roman falls into step beside me. "Where the fuck are you going?"

"She left." The voice isn't mine. It isn't me who she left. "Why would she leave?"

She was happy.

She was mine.

Why the fuck would she leave?

Roman stiffens. "Hold it together, dude. Who–"

"Margot! MARGOT!"

I shove open the door to the only room that will prove me wrong.

It's empty.

No Benny.

No Margot.

She's gone.

Dread curdles in my stomach.

Then, it ignites into fury.

Who the fuck does she think she is, leaving me?

She doesn't get to leave.

She doesn't get to fucking leave.

She's mine.

I thought we were past this.

I thought she understood.

I sprint to the garage, and sure enough, my Mercedes is gone.

I grab the keys to a BMW SUV. I'll need the extra space to put Benny in the back when I bring her home.

And she is coming home.

I get in and open my tracker app. She's on her way to her house.

Of course.

Of fucking course.

I clench the wheel so tightly my knuckles turn white.

The passenger door opens and Roman slides in.

"What the fuck do you think you're doing?" I growl.

"I'm coming with you."

"No. Fuck off. Get out."

"No."

"Fine. Just stay quiet." I exhale sharply. I don't have time for this. I gun the engine and tear down the driveway.

Roman laughs. "So, this is her, huh? The reason you haven't left your house?"

I grit my teeth. "Shut the fuck up."

"Seems like an awful lot of effort for just some girl."

I don't answer.

I can't.

Not when my pulse is roaring.

Not when I'm seething.

Not when I'm already planning what I'll do when I catch her.

He shakes his head, laughing. "Damn. She's really got you fucked up, huh?"

I slam the gas harder. "I let you come. Now shut the fuck up."

My thoughts are racing.

Why did she leave? Did she seriously run because of a fucking audiobook? She wouldn't take Benny if she was just getting her equipment. She's not just running an errand. *She's trying to leave me.*

The thought rips through my chest.

No.

No, no, no.

She wouldn't.

She wouldn't.

She's mine.
I will find her.
And when I do–
She will never run again.

Chapter 35
Margot

For thirty minutes, my mind races.

Big city or small town? Do I dye my hair? Cut it? Can you report an adult missing? What do I pack?

I need a plan. I need to think.

But all too soon, I pull into my driveway.

The first thing I see is a black van parked in front of my house. I don't think anything of it. Just a neighbor using my spot.

I stare at my house.

It's not fancy. It's old. Small.

But it's mine.

Or... *it was.*

I exhale sharply, pushing away the emotions creeping up my throat. There's no time for tears.

Benny lets out a sharp, aggressive bark.

I snap back to reality, rubbing my eyes. There's no time to cry. No time to grieve.

I leave the car running and step out. No one's going to steal my car the five minutes I'm inside.

I reach the potted plant by my front door, which is now dead and brittle, lift it and grab the spare key. I slide it into the lock and turn the handle.

The door swings open.

It shouldn't.

It should be locked.

I step inside, and everything stops.

My world tilts.

My furniture is flipped over. My decorations are shattered. My cabinets are hanging off their hinges. There are holes in my fucking walls.

I can't breathe.

I can't think.

Did someone break in? What happened?

Then realization slams into me.

Matthias. His men. They did this.

What little was left of my heart shatters completely.

I walk to my bedroom, carefully dodging the mess, when I hear footsteps.

Heavy, male footsteps.

Fuck! How did he find me so quickly?

I whip around, heart hammering. My eyes scan for a weapon, but I left my emergency bat by the front door.

A man appears at the entrance of my bedroom. A man I don't recognize.

"I found you."

This isn't one of Matty's men.

None of them look at me like this.

None of them send such fear through me.

And none of them have Russian accents.

"Get out of my house!" I try to sound strong, but my voice wavers.

"Margot Peterson," he says smoothly. "We have been looking for you for a long time. My boss wants to talk to you. Come with me."

"Oh, no thank you. I'm in a hurry, so if you'll excuse me, please?" I try to squeeze past him, but he lifts an arm, blocking my exit.

"That was not a question. You will come with us." Then he shouts something in Russian.

Two more men barrel in. I thought Roman was scary, but these men are something else entirely. Not only terrifying, but downright disgusting.

Unkempt. Rotting teeth. Greasy hair. Reeking of sweat.

I try to bolt, but Toothless grabs me.

"Where do you think you are going, shlyukha?" He leans in, breath so foul it churns my stomach.

"Let me go!" I thrash, twisting and jerking wildly. My elbow flies back, catching his ribs. He grunts but doesn't let go. I drive my foot down onto his instep, grinding my heel into the soft spot in his foot. He howls, his grip loosing just enough for me to rip free.

I make it one step into the living room, then I'm tackled.

Sweaty slams me down, pinning me beneath his disgusting weight.

I fight with everything in me. My nails dig into his face, dragging across the skin, leaving deep scratches that make him hiss.

Toothless grabs my wrists and slams them on the floor, forcing my arms above my head. I kick my legs, twisting and bucking under Sweaty, trying to throw him off. He barely budges.

"The boss will not care if we break in the bitch before we take her, no?"

Malicious laughter surrounds me. My stomach twists violently. Bile burns my throat.

No, no, no.

My panic surges, but so does my fight. I slam my head forward, trying to bash his nose. I jerk my arms, my legs, everything. A crazed, primal scream tears from me.

But their grip is too strong. My fight does no good.

Sweaty yanks at my shirt. The fabric tears exposing my bra. Cold air rushes over my exposed skin. His fingers hook into my waistband, and he yanks my pants down.

I try to kick, but Sweaty sits on my knees, restricting my movement. I try to free my arms, but Toothless only tightens his grip.

I let out one last scream. One last plea.

Then accept defeat.

I squeeze my eyes shut, trying to block it out. Trying to go somewhere else.

I let my mind drift.

It's going to be okay, sweet girl.

Chapter 36
Matthias

I pull into her driveway four minutes after she did. I pushed the speed limit the entire way, knowing every second counts.

I park behind a black van and throw my car into park. The second I step out, I hear it. Loud, furious barking.

I freeze.

Benny.

He's clawing at the window of my Mercedes, throwing his entire weight against the door, teeth bared, growling like a rabid animal.

But not at me.

At the house.

Something is wrong.

A pressure clamps around my chest, squeezing my lungs. My feet move before my brain can catch up.

I hear Roman coming up behind me.

"What's wrong? What–" He's cut off by a sound that'll haunt me forever, a scream cutting through the air.

Margot's scream.

The anger evaporates as everything inside me shatters.

I'm running. Roman's at my heels, yanking out two guns and tossing one into my waiting hand.

Fear like I've never experienced consumes me.

Because the next sound is worse than her scream. So much worse.

Silence.

Her screams are cut off.

My heart slams against my ribs, my ears are ringing so loudly I can't hear myself breathe.

I break down the front door, gun raised, ready to kill.

Then I see her.

My Margot.

On the floor.

Her shirt torn, leaving her bra exposed. Leggings shoved so low I can't see where they begin.

A man pins her down, holding her wrists above her head. Another sits on her legs, pulling at her panties.

The third stands nearby, watching. Waiting.

Margot is gone. Her eyes are clenched shut. She's facing the door, but she doesn't see me. She isn't looking. She isn't moving. She isn't fighting.

She's given up.

My spitfire is out of fight. They took her fight from her.

I can't breathe.

A bullet tears through the head of the man on her legs before I even realize I pulled the trigger. His body jerks, then collapses on top of her.

On top of Margot.

I almost fucking vomit.

Roman's shots go off. Two more bodies hit the ground.

I don't know if they're dead. I don't care.

Roman moves past me, gripping one of the men by the collar. "Go to her," he mutters gently in a tone I've never heard from him before.

A tone that tells me just how bad this is.

I don't remember moving. One second, I'm frozen. The next, I'm shoving the dead bastard off her, nearly breaking at the sight of blood smeared across her skin.

I know it's not hers. But it doesn't matter.

Margot. My Margot. *Covered in blood.*

She's limp. Her arms stay where he pinned them, like she's still trapped there. Her breathing is slow and weak.

She's not here.

She doesn't even flinch when I touch her, gently pulling her pants back into place, trying to close her torn shirt.

Nothing.

I failed her.

I failed her.

I let her run. Right into this.

I wasn't there to protect her.

I lift her into my arms and hold her so tightly I think I might crush her, but I can't help it. She's small, fragile, breakable in a way I never want to see again.

She should be cursing me out. Kicking. Fighting.

But there's nothing.

I feel like I'm holding a mannequin.

I squeeze my eyes shut. I can't let her see how wrecked I am.

"Margot, sweetheart. My sweet girl. Are you in there?" My voice breaks.

Nothing.

I swallow back the terror ripping through me, and try again, rocking her gently. "Please, sweetheart. Open your eyes for me."

I press my lips to her forehead, a gentle kiss.

My body sags when she finally stirs.

Her lashes flutter. Her gaze lifts. And when her eyes meet mine, I shatter all over again.

She isn't *there*.

No fire. No smartass remarks. No Margot.

Just emptiness.

I can't handle it.

"Sweetheart, please." I whisper.

She blinks. Slowly. Like she's waking up from a nightmare.

I run a trembling hand through her curls. I don't know what else to do. I just can't let her go.

"It's going to be okay, sweetheart," I whisper against her forehead. A promise. A vow. "I'm here. You're safe now."

Her entire body shakes.

And then she breaks.

Sobs rip through her, full body tremors as she clings to me. Like I'm the only thing keeping her grounded.

I squeeze back tighter than I should. Tighter than she probably wants.

But I can't let go.

I press my lips to her temple, murmuring over and over, "You're safe. I've got you. I've got you."

She sobs against my chest, shaking, so small in my arms.

I don't know how long I hold her.

I just know I'll never let her go again.

Chapter 37
Matthias

I don't know how much time passes. It could be minutes or hours. All I know is that eventually, she stops shaking. The sobs fade to shallow breaths. Her body sags against mine, spent.

But she's still not here.

Her eyes are open, but they don't hold the fire I love. They don't hold anything. Just blank, hollow torment.

A rustling sound behind us makes her flinch. She tenses, eyes darting toward the noise. Before she can turn, I grab her chin, forcing her to look at me.

"Don't look, sweetheart," I murmur. "You don't need to see this."

Because if she does, she'll see him. The bastard who had his hands on her. Dead. And she'll see the other two, bloodied but alive.

I don't want her to have those images in her nightmares. She's already been through enough.

Roman moves past us, dragging one of the men by his collar. He hauls them out of the house, one by one, shoving their limp bodies in the SUV. When he comes back, he's carrying a towel and a sweatshirt, one of mine from the car.

Margot flinches at the sight of him. Her breathing hitches, and she presses deeper into my chest for protection.

She flinches.

Margot's never been afraid. Her fear crushes me.

This isn't my spitfire.

Roman freezes. He doesn't move any closer, just crouches at a distance, and sets the clothes beside us.

"It's okay, Margot," he says softly. "I'm Roman, Matthias's brother. I'm not going to hurt you." He gestures to the sweatshirt. "I just wanted to give you something warm to wear. You don't need to be in that anymore."

I don't know this Roman. This caring Roman. But I'm grateful for him.

Margot doesn't respond. Doesn't move.

Then, slowly, she looks down at herself. At the blood smeared across her skin. At the torn fabric clinging to her. And reality sinks in.

Before she can spiral, I gently lift her chin again. "Remember, eyes on me, sweet girl."

She obeys, blinking up at me like she's trying to process everything.

"I'm going to take care of you."

She nods, just barely, but it's enough to make my chest ache.

I grab the towel and begin wiping away the blood. Roman disappears into the house and returns with a wet cloth and a first aid kit before stepping back, giving us space. I clean her off the best I can, each wipe over her skin making me sicker. Then I slip the sweatshirt over her head and pull her hands through the sleeves.

I hate having to ask this next question, but I have to. I need to know.

"Sweetheart," my voice is raw, barely audible. "Did they... did they touch you anywhere else? Did they hurt you?"

I'm praying to every higher power that I arrived in time. That she didn't endure anything worse than what I saw.

She swallows hard. Then, wordlessly, she lifts her wrists.

Bruises.

Dark, ugly, large bruises mar her delicate skin. Purple, what was once so beautifully pale.

Rage fills me so suddenly, my vision blurs. My grip tightens around her fingers.

I will make them pay.

I press a kiss to the inside of her wrist. A silent promise. She doesn't say anything. She doesn't have to.

When she's as ready as can be, I scoop her up and carry her outside.

The second I open the passenger door, Benny launches himself out of the car. He's all over her, sniffing every inch of her body, whining, circling, protecting. He stops at her wrists and licks them, his way of trying to make her better.

For the first time since I found her, I see a flicker of something real.

A small, weak smile.

It's barely visible, but it's there.

My heart finally starts beating again.

I place her in the seat and round the car. I take a deep breath before getting into the driver's seat. My hands grip the wheel, but I don't move.

I need a second. A second to force air into my lungs. To swallow back the rage, the guilt, the unbearable weight of knowing I almost lost her.

I need a clear head to drive her home. I won't ever put her in danger.

The drive back is silent. Both of us trying to cope with what happened. But the whole way, my hand is on her thigh. Benny lays his head in her lap. She rests a hand on his head.

She'll get through this. She's Margot. She's strong.

It won't be easy. But I'll be there. Every second. Every step.

Because I'm never leaving her side again.

Chapter 38
Margot

I don't process anything from the drive home.

I don't process anything at all.

Matty opens the passenger door, unbuckles my seatbelt, and picks me up. I don't protest. I don't tell him I can walk.

Because I can't.

Benny whines at the loss of contact, and the moment I'm out the car, he's right there, pressed into Matty's legs, glued to my side like he's afraid I'll disappear.

Petting him in the car kept me grounded. That, and Matty's hand on my thigh. Though I think he needed the connection just as much as I did.

He carries me upstairs, through our bedroom, and into the bathroom.

He sets me on the floor beside the tub and turns on the water, adjusting the temperature, testing it, and adjusting again until he deems it acceptable.

He hesitates before leaving, stepping into the bedroom. I hear him telling Benny he needs to stay before the door clicks shut.

He's only gone for seconds.

But when he returns, the look on his face... it's like he's been away for hours. Like he couldn't breathe without me in sight.

I know how he feels. I can't be alone right now. I need him too.

He looks at me for permission, and I nod.

He gently undresses me.

I sigh, relieved to be rid of the clothes. They feel wrong. Dirty. Contaminated. I never want to see them again.

He lifts me into the water. It's hot, but not enough to burn. The tub is so deep, the water rises to my collarbones. I'm engulfed in warmth, but I can't relax. My eyes stay locked on the pile of discarded fabric.

"Can we throw them away?" My voice is barely there, raw and quiet. "Those clothes. I don't want them. They feel dirty."

Matty exhales in relief. "Of course, sweetheart. You never have to see them again. We can do whatever you want." His voice is patient. Gentle.

I look at him for the first time since he found me.

His eyes are haunted, like he's seen his own demons and barely survived. Lines of worry mar his face, aging him decades. He's pale and tinted green.

And he's shaking. It's a small tremor. Almost unnoticeable. I don't think he even realizes.

I reach out, my fingers closing around his hands. I hold them still, steadying the tremor.

He freezes. His breath hitches.

"They were shaking." I whisper. My voice cracks.

"I didn't realize." He speaks just as softly. Then firmer. "And sweetheart, you can always touch me. There doesn't need to be a reason. I'm yours."

I'm yours.

The words settle deep. He's told me I'm his, but not that he's mine. There's something different about it. Something that stitches together a little of what was broken.

I nod and slowly pull my hands away.

He fills a cup and wets my hair carefully, like I'll shatter under his touch. He pours my shampoo into his palms and massages it into my scalp for a few minutes. It's calming and relaxing. After a few minutes, he rinses it out in slow strokes.

Then he reaches for the conditioner, ready to smooth it over my scalp.

"Just on the ends," I correct softly.

His brows furrow. "Why?"

"Conditioner doesn't go on your scalp." I explain. "It'll make your hair greasy."

He nods and adjusts. He runs his fingers through my ends, working through the knots well after they're gone. He keeps going, over and over, like he's soothing himself just as much as me.

I let him.

Then he lathers a loofah with soap and starts washing me, light strokes over my arms. Too soft. Too gentle.

"Harder, please," I whisper, voice thin.

His hands still. I look into his eyes, and he understands.

He scrubs harder, making sure to cover every inch of me. With every swipe of the loofah, every pass over my skin, it feels like some of the horror washes away. Not all of it. Not what lingers inside. But enough.

When he rinses the soap off, I can breathe again.

And when he's done, I finally feel clean.

Chapter 39
Margot

After soaking in the bath, Matty brings me some sweats, as well as a pair of his boxer briefs and a pair of my panties to choose from.

I choose the boxers.

Because I need his comfort. Because I need the familiarity. Because I need to follow his ridiculous rules.

Because I need him.

He doesn't say anything about it. Doesn't read into it.

None of it has been sexual. Even with his hands on me, washing me, dressing me, there was no sexual current. But it was intimate.

And that's what I needed. Comfort. Tenderness. Not passion, not heat. Just him taking care of me.

I lie on top of him in our bed. He's stroking my back, calmingly. Every so often, he presses a kiss to my hair. Nothing rushed. Nothing forced. Just Matty, grounding me, holding me together when I feel like I could still break apart.

I don't know where I'd be if it weren't for him.

Don't think of that.

I press my cheek against his chest, listening to the slow, steady beat of his heart.

You're here now. In his arms. He saved you. He protected you. And now he's taking care of you.

You are his, but he's also yours.

You can think of it tomorrow. Today, just breathe.

I let my eyes drift shut.

...

I must fall asleep, because when I open my eyes, the room is dark.

Matty's voice is soft as his hand brushes my cheek.

"I'm sorry, sweetheart," he murmurs, lightly shaking me. "I don't want to wake you, but do you think you can eat something? You haven't had anything since breakfast."

There's so much concern in his voice. So much care. And as much as I want to ease it, I can't. The thought of food makes my stomach twist.

"I'm not hungry," I whisper, my voice thick with exhaustion. "I'm sorry."

Matty immediately shakes his head. "No, sweetheart. It's okay. We're going at your pace." He presses a kiss to my temple. "I just don't want you to be uncomfortable."

His warmth surrounds me, protecting me.

I let myself sink back into him. Into the comfort of his arms. Into the safety I only feel with him.

And this time, when I close my eyes, I sleep dreamlessly.

Chapter 40
Matthias

I can't sleep.

Every time I close my eyes, I see her pinned down and helpless.

It plays on a loop, each second more agonizing than the last. If this is what it's doing to me, I can't even begin to imagine what my brave girl must be going through.

I look down at her. She's curled into me, warm and soft. She's been tossing and turning, but at least she's sleeping. At least she's safe.

My phone lights up.

Roman.

They're awake.

The men who touched my sweet girl. The scum who dared to lay a hand on her. They're tied up in the warehouse, waiting.

I text him back.

'Hold off. They're mine'

I don't want to leave Margot, but I have no choice. I need answers. I don't understand why the Bratva would be at her house. No one knows about us. It doesn't make sense.

And I need to make them suffer. They made my girl hurt. They will beg for death before I'm through with them.

I ease out from under her and put a pillow in my place. She whimpers in protest, and my chest tightens.

"I'm sorry, sweetheart." I whisper. "I promise I'll be back before you wake up."

I kiss her forehead, then slip out of the room.

I make a pit stop.

"Benny." My voice is low and commanding.

His head snaps up, instantly ready.

"I need you to watch Margot. Don't let her out of your sight."

Benny understands. He jumps up immediately and follows me to the bedroom. He sniffs her, checking for himself that she's okay. Then, without hesitation, he plants himself between her and the door, waiting for me to set up his bed.

I do as I'm told.

Once I'm sure Margot is protected, I head out.

I have guards stationed at the top of the stairs and surrounding the house. No one gets up here without my say. It's shoot on sight. I'm not taking any chances.

...

I walk into the warehouse and see both men tied to metal chairs. As promised, Roman hasn't touched them yet. They're shirtless, wrist and ankles cut from the tight rope binding them. They're stripped bare for maximum exposure.

Roman leans against the wall like this is routine. I guess for him, it is.

"How is she?" he asks, his voice steady but serious.

"Sleeping. Barely. Let's make this quick. I don't want her waking up alone."

He nods. Then, without warning, he picks up a bucket and sloshes cold water over them. They jolt awake, sputtering and coughing.

"We're going to have a conversation," Roman begins coolly. "You'll answer every question. Lie? You suffer. Refuse? You suffer. Give us what we need? Maybe we let you go. Understand?"

It's a lie. They'll die for what they did to Margot.

The one on the right, the older one, laughs. It's wet and phlegmy, a smoker's rasp. "We are not scared of you. When my boss finds us, you will be the ones screaming."

Roman's smile is nefarious. "I'm not scared of Viktor. He fears me."

Their smirks vanish. Their Pakhan's name wasn't supposed to come out of our mouths.

"Viktor fears no one, you fools." The other, *the one who held Margot down,* says, but his voice falters.

"Zatknis, durak," The older one hisses.

Roman moves so fast, it's a blur. A knife slams into the older one's hand. A scream rips through the warehouse.

"English only," Roman orders.

"Who the fuck are you?" The dumb one mutters, eyes darting around the room as if it'll give him answers.

Roman steps forward. "Roman Montclair. This is my brother, Matthias. We want to know why you were after Margot Peterson." Roman's smile is sinister.

They pale instantly.

That's the power of his name.

The younger one visibly shrinks back. Even the leader looks like he's swallowed glass.

"We will not betray the Bratva," the older one says, voice steady despite the knife sticking from his hand. "We will die before we talk."

I walk over to the table of weapons and quietly survey my options.

"Why were you at Margot Peterson's house?" Roman asks the younger one.

"I won't tell you shit," he mutters, but it's empty.

Roman drives a knife into his hand.

Unlike his partner, he doesn't stay calm. He cries.

Pathetic.

"What kind of man breaks down at a little pain?" I mutter under my breath.

"Answer the question," Roman demands.

"Why do you care about some fat bitch?" the younger one hisses.

My blood turns to fire.

Get it together. Stay in control.

"It would do you well to watch your mouth," I grind out.

"You couldn't keep your slut at home. She would have been so good."

Red. My vision reddens blindingly.

I move slowly. Calmly. I pick up a tin of gasoline and slide a matchbox into my pocket.

He's still talking. He doesn't know I've already decided he's going to die violently.

"Her screams made me hard. Her wrists were soft. I was waiting for my turn when you interrupted."

He stops talking when he sees me approaching.

Fear registers in his eyes. Finally.

He realizes I'm not like Roman. I don't do this because I have to. It's not my job. I'm here because I want to. Because he hurt my Margot.

I silently start pouring the gasoline over his head. Chest. Groin.

He starts screaming before the match is even lit.

Begging.

I don't say a word as I let it soak.

Then I answer his earlier question.

"She's my everything."

I light the match, and flick it on him.

He ignites.

And I stand there.

Watching.

Reveling.

His screams fill the warehouse, echoing off the walls.

I don't look away.

I don't blink.

I want to remember the way he sounds. I want to remember the dance of the flames. I want to remember what happens to people who hurt my Margot.

Eventually, his cries stop. He slumps forward, a charred carcass.

Roman calmly walks over, grabs a hose, and douses the remains.

"You ready to talk now?"

The older one stares at the corpse of his comrade, horror etched into every line of his face. Then he meets my eyes, and for the first time, he's truly afraid.

"If I talk, you put a bullet between my eyes. No more pain."

I nod. "Deal."

He swallows. "We watched Margot Peterson's house for weeks. Our orders were to bring her in. She knows too much. We do not know if she went to the authorities. We need to question her. Then silence her."

Silence her.

I keep my expression passive while my world crumbles at the suggestion. At the image of my sweet girl silenced forever.

Roman raises a brow. "Has she been targeted before?"

"Yes. The first team never reported back. Viktor assumes she took them out then vanished. But we go to her house randomly to make sure."

I stiffen.

The alley. The men. What if they weren't after me?

"She was the target," I whisper.

He nods then closes his eyes.

Roman doesn't hesitate. One bullet flies between his eyes.

"Why the fuck did you shoot him?" I snap. "He might've known more."

"He told us everything he knew," Roman replies. "You wanted to get back to your girl. Go home."

I don't like it. But he's right.

"Thanks for today," I mutter.

"It's what I do. For the Syndicate. And for my family." With the way he says family, I know he means Margot too.

I nod. "She's it."

"What does she know?" he asks. "She's not capable of making men disappear."

"I don't know. But I'll find out. When she's ready."

"You're going to have to tell Dom."

"Not yet. I'll figure this out first."

I'm halfway to the door when Roman calls after me, "Take a shower. You smell like burnt flesh, you sick fuck. And you owe me a new pair of jeans."

"Fuck off."

"That stench doesn't come out of clothes. And I had to sit through that shit. You owe me."

I roll my eyes. "You have millions in the bank. Spend a little. The dark look isn't in style anymore."

Roman grins. "Dark works for me. Gets the ladies."

I don't bother responding. I leave, already knowing one thing.

The Bratva will never get their hands on my Margot.

Chapter 41
Margot

I wake up to the smell of coffee. Matty sits on the edge of our bed holding a mug. A smile breaks out on my lips at the sight of him.

I sit up, ready to accept the liquid elixir of happiness.

"Good morning, sweetheart." He presses a kiss on my forehead and hands me the cup. His touch is warm and steady. But when I look at his face, I notice the bags under his eyes. The paleness of his complexion. The sadness lingering there.

A pang of concern hits me. Did he not sleep? Is he getting sick?

Then yesterday's events come crashing back to me.

I'd forgotten, but it sweeps over me like a tidal wave. A hollow ache settles in my chest, but there's no fear. Not with Matty here. Not when I know he won't let anything happen to me.

He saved me.

"Hey, sweet girl. How are you feeling?" His gentle voice matches his expression.

I know he's not asking about my body. He's asking how I'm doing emotionally. He's genuinely worried about me.

"I'm still a little shaken, but I feel safe with you. It didn't get too far, and I'm just... I'm grateful you came for me. And Roman too." I pause, exhaling slowly. "I think yesterday hit me so hard because of what could've happened. But now that I've had time to process it, I'm doing better." I give him an encouraging smile, even if my hands tremble around the mug.

Matty shakes his head. "No, sweetheart. Stuff did happen. Even though it didn't go further, you still have a right to be upset. What you went through was traumatic. I'm sorry I didn't find you sooner."

His voice is so sincere, his words so grounding, that my eyes sting with tears.

His expression crumbles. He takes the coffee from my hands and pulls me into his chest, murmuring soft reassurances against my hair.

"I'm not crying because of yesterday. I'm crying because of you. Your patience. Your support. It means everything to me."

He studies me, searching for deception, but he won't find it. When he finally believes me, his features soften. But his next words come cautiously.

"Sweetheart, I hate to ask you this. And if you're not ready, we can talk later. But I need to know, so I can keep you safe. Can you talk about what happened?"

I nod, understanding. He deserves to know. I've dragged him into something. But the problem is... I don't know what. I don't have answers.

"I'll tell you everything, but I don't even know what happened," I admit. "I'm sorry."

"It's okay, sweetheart." He takes my hand, his thumb tracing slow circles over my skin. "Start from when you got to your house. Tell me everything."

So, I do. I recount every moment I remember. Matty grips my hand, squeezing tightly at every hesitation, every painful detail. His expression twists with every word. By the time I finish, he looks devastated.

"Thank you, sweetheart. You did so well. This is helpful."

"It's *not* helpful at all. I don't understand anything." Frustration seeps into my voice. "Who were those men? Why were they after me? They *knew* my name."

Matty exhales, jaw clenching. "What do you know about the Bratva?"

"The what?"

"The Bratva. The Russian criminal organization."

I stare at him. *Criminal organization?* "I don't know anything about it. What does that even mean? Why are you asking me this?"

"Because the Bratva is after you. That's who those men were. Do you know why they'd want you?"

My stomach lurches. "The Russian mafia was after *me*? Why?"

"They think you know something about their operations. They're worried you went to the authorities. They wanted to question you about what you know and who you told. What do they think you know, sweetheart?"

I open my mouth in confusion, but then realization slams into me.

"Oh my God. Oh my God! I was right. Oh my God!" My stomach drops. "No, this can't be. That's ridiculous. I was just doing my job."

Matty straightens, suddenly on high alert. "Margot, what do you know?"

"The day you took me I was supposed to meet with my boss about a discrepancy I found in our bookkeeping." My voice shakes. "I work for Northern Hemisphere Cargo. There was a company, the Koschei Group. They paid a huge amount of money for small shipments. I checked the invoices, but all I found was the name. Nothing else. There wasn't even payment information. It made no sense. I looked into them, but nothing came up. No company website, no records. It felt off. So, I emailed my boss, said I'd be willing to talk to authorities if needed. That morning, I was meeting him at the coffee shop." I hesitate. "Then you happened."

Matty doesn't speak for a moment, absorbing it all. His fingers tap against his thigh in a calculated rhythm, piecing things together. "Did you talk to the authorities?"

"No. I turned off my work phone over the weekend, then woke up to a ton of missed calls from my boss. When I got here, he called again, asking to meet. But before I could answer, one of the guards grabbed my phone and ended the call. I haven't heard from him since." I swallow hard. "That has to be it, right? I stumbled onto something I wasn't supposed to? Koschei... it's a *Russian* legend."

"Yes, sweetheart." His voice is grim. "That's what they were after."

"I'm so sorry I got you involved. This is my mess. I–" I stop mid-sentence, his words echoing in my head. "Wait, what do you mean, '*it aligns with what they said?*' When did you talk to them? How did you know the Bratva was after me? How do you even know what the Bratva is?"

Matty stills. Then, carefully, "Roman and I interrogated the men who attacked you. After some... *encouragement*... they told us they were sent to bring you in."

My stomach plummets. "Encouragement? You mean torture?"

He doesn't answer.

Then an even more alarming thought slams into me.

"Oh my God. You *killed* another man. The one on top of me. Oh my God. This time it wasn't self-defense! You really are a murderer!"

I jolt back, scrambling away, but the sheets tangle around my legs. Matty moves instantly, pinning me down.

He straddles my hips, trapping my wrists above my head. His hold isn't cruel, but it is firm. Controlling. Unyielding.

"Stop fighting me, Margot. Let me explain."

My pulse hammers. I should be afraid. I should be terrified. But I'm not. Because it's Matty. Because I don't want to run. Because he's already saved me once.

"Listen to me. He was hurting you. I will never apologize for protecting you." His voice is dark and certain. A lethal promise. "I will *always* choose you. I will *always* protect you. Do you understand?"

I exhale shakily. "Thank you for saving me."

His eyes darken. "I *will* always save you. You are mine."

Chapter 42
Matthias

I see the moment my words settle. The second she stops fighting. The exact breath she accepts this. I see it in her eyes.

What I don't expect, what I never expected, is for her to close the distance between us and press her lips to mine.

I react instantly. Possessively.

Her lips are soft and warm. A lush invitation.

This kiss is nothing like our first. That was hard, rough, and desperate. That was me taking. Me dominating.

But this... This is something else. It's gentle, sensual, unhurried. This isn't about control. This is about her.

She wants this.

She wants *me*.

I feel the surrender in every delicate brush of her lips against mine, in the way her body melts into mine. This isn't fear. This isn't force. This is trust. This is forgiveness.

She shifts against me, struggling against my grip on her wrists. I let go.

Immediately, she wraps her arms around my neck, using them to hold her herself up.

That won't do. She will never have to support herself. I will always hold her up. I will always take care of her.

I slide my arm around her back, my hand finding the nape of her neck, fingers spanning her delicate throat. I pull her in, molding her body to mine, making sure she feels every inch of me.

Then she moves.

A slow, shattering roll of her hips. A teasing grind of heat against me. A firestorm in a single motion.

I groan, deep and rough against her lips.

Fuck.

Even through the layers of fabric, I can feel her warmth. I can feel the intoxicating friction between us. I pin her hips to the bed, and push against her, chasing every bit of pleasure I can get from the pressure.

She frees her legs from the sheets and wraps them around my waist, pulling me into her. A soft moan leaves her lips, vibrating against my own, as I press exactly where she needs me.

I tear my mouth from hers, trailing feather-light kisses down the column of her throat. She arches, silently begging for more. Her beautiful moans fill the air. I find a spot behind her ear, and when I suck, tremors run through her, and she lets out the most enticing whimper.

I make a mental note of the spot.

We pull apart only when air is a necessity, but it's still far too soon. If I had my way, we'd always be touching, always be connected.

And all I can think is...

She started this.

She made her move.

She gave in.

She's been mine since the moment I took her, but now?
Now, she's sealed it.
She just signed her life over to me.
And she will never escape.

Chapter 43
Margot

I'm panting, lost in the feeling.

If I had known it would be so electric, so consuming, I would've given in sooner. My mind floats away, caught in the haze of what we just did.

Until he breaks the spell.

"Why did you leave?" His voice is rough, still thick with remnants of what just happened between us.

It takes me a moment to register the words, but when I do, reality slams back into me.

Roman. His conversation. The truth I tried to forget.

Matty is a bad man.

A killer.

A killer for you.

But he's killed others too. People who had nothing to do with me.

I try to pull away, but he doesn't let me. With his grip pinning my hips and his body caging me in, there's nowhere to go. I unwind my legs from around him, drop my arms from around his neck, and shove at his chest.

It's useless. He barely budges.

Although, a grunt of irritation escapes him. "Don't make me pin you down again."

I keep pushing.

He follows through on his threat. With one hand, he captures my wrists, securing them above my head. His other grips my chin, tilting my face towards his.

"Tell me why you left. Everything was going so well, then suddenly you run." His tone is firm, unwavering. "I need to know why."

I grit my teeth and swallow down my defiance. I want to fight. I want to lie. But I know I won't.

You've never been able to disobey him.

"Because you're a criminal. A psychopath. *A murderer.*" My voice is raw, sharp with fury. "You and your sick brothers. You're all fucked up and should be in jail! That's why you took me in the first place. But I'm too much of a tramp to remember that. I let myself get sucked in. I let myself forget. I think with my pussy when I'm around you. But not anymore! I won't fall for it again. I'm getting away the first chance I get. I'll never give in!"

I scream the words in his face. My chest heaves as my pulse beats like a wild drum.

His nostrils flare. His voice is deadly serious when he speaks. "Do not talk to me that way. You will respect me. And do not ever speak about yourself like that. You will respect what's mine. And you. Are. Mine."

His words hit like a slap. His control coils around me, tightly and suffocatingly.

Then, his voice dips lower, darker. "Maybe I'd believe you, if I couldn't feel your peaked nipples pressed against my chest. If I couldn't smell your arousal."

I freeze as shame crawls up my spine.

"I bet *my* boxers that you're wearing are soaked through with your juices. Let's check."

His hand leaves my chin, and trails down my body with excruciating slowness. When he reaches my breast, he pinches my nipples hard.

I gasp as a traitorous moan slips free. He mocks me with his cocky grin.

His fingers dip beneath the waistband of his boxers I'm wearing. I already know what he'll find.

When his fingers stroke between my folds, he hums in satisfaction. He circles my clit teasingly, until my hips shift forward chasing the pleasure.

Then he pulls away.

I whimper at the loss, but I don't have time to dwell on it, because he shows me his fingers.

His fingers that are glistening with my arousal.

He smirks. "Hmm. Seems I was right. Now, open up."

He drags his coated finger over my lips, pressing on them until I obey and they part.

Even when fuming at him, you still listen, like a good little girl.

I take his fingers in my mouth and suck them clean. Tasting myself on them.

Victory flares in his eyes. He pulls his fingers free with a soft *pop*, then murmurs, "My good, little slut. Always ready for me. Obeying my every word. You submit so beautifully. Without a fight."

He's mocking me.

He's wrong.

He's not wrong. Just because you rebel, doesn't mean you disobey.

Fury ignites in my veins, hot and blinding. Before I can second-guess it, I do the only thing I can think of.

I spit in his face.

Matty stills. For one charged second, everything stops. Then, slowly, dangerously, his lips curl into a wicked grin.

He slowly wipes my spit from his cheek with the same fingers that were in my mouth moments ago. And then, he smears the saliva back over my lips.

I glare at him, refusing to give him the satisfaction of a reaction.

"Such a bad girl," he murmurs, eyes glistening with delight "That just added to your punishment. And it was already going to be hell for leaving me."

His cock is still hard against me. He's excited. He grinds against me, reinforcing the truth of his words.

"Now, tell me what made you run. Yesterday morning, you were excited for our date. By midday, you were gone. Why?" He almost sounds hurt, but that can't be right.

I exhale sharply. "I saw Roman walk in. I knew who he was when you called him by name. He was the man you were talking to that day in the alley. He's the psychopath. *He's the reason you took me.* And here he is, in your house, covered in blood, and you don't even flinch. Then I heard you talk. I heard you agree to step up and start killing people." I swallow hard, my voice raw. "It made me sick. I let a monster touch me. I knew what you were, and I let myself forget it. I won't do it again."

Matty hums. "Hmm. I thought I intercepted Roman before you saw him. I guess I was wrong."

I stare at him, stunned. "You're not even going to deny it?"

"No," he says simply. "I won't insult you by lying. Everything you heard was true. The men in the alley were not the first I'd killed. They won't be the last. I've already killed again since saving you. I burned alive the man who held you down. And I basked in his screams. I didn't look away. I relished every moment. It brought me pleasure to make him suffer for touching you."

His voice is pure evil, and I see the truth of what he's saying in his eyes. He takes delight in the memories of what he did.

I feel nauseous at the confession. At his glee. At the idea of murdering someone so brutally. And enjoying it.

I don't know this man. This sick bastard.

I try to turn my head, unable to look at him for another second. But he doesn't let me off that easily. He grabs my chin and forces me to face him. I squeeze my eyes shut.

He tsks. "You know better. Eyes on me."

I glare at him.

"I'd do it every day for you," he says, low and lethally. "And I've done it for years. For my family. For the Syndicate."

I blink. "The Syndicate?"

"My family runs The Syndicate," he explains. "It's like the Bratva but with no nationality affiliation. We don't answer to anyone. We run many operations in our territory. But for the most part, we keep the streets clean. We make sure those around us follow the rules. And when they don't, we make an example out of them."

I swallow hard.

"All the men I've hurt or killed, they deserved it. Rapists. Murderers. Criminals who would've never faced justice otherwise."

He leans in, his voice a little softer. "You've never had a reason to think about that kind of world. You're not supposed to. That's the point. In your eyes, murder is wrong, and I get that. But take yesterday. If I had let him live after what he almost did to you, do you think he'd stop? I guarantee he's done it before. He would've done it again."

He pauses, letting his words sink in.

"There are rules in what we do. And if we were to break them, we face consequences too. That's what keeps this city safe. People like you don't even know what's lurking in the shadows because men like me are out there keeping it in check."

I shiver.

"I'm sorry you got dragged into this. If the Russians hadn't exposed you, you might've never known. But being mine means you were always going to be involved. It was inevitable."

His hand slides to my jaw, gentler now.

"I'll protect you from the Bratva. I know how they operate. And with the Syndicate behind us, they won't touch you. My brothers and I will keep you safe."

I search his face, desperate to find something good in all of this.

"But to stay safe," he continues, "you have to listen. You have to look past your own moral compass and understand the rules we live by. This world is different. And as *my* woman, you'll live by our rules."

I flinch at the word '*my*', but I don't disagree.

"I usually stay out of the darker side of business. I keep my image clean to run Syndicate Enterprises, the legal front. But now, you're involved. That changes everything."

A sigh leaves him, but there's no regret in it. Only conviction.

"I'll shield you from as much as I can. But you'll see some of it. You need to understand, we are the good guys. We just play by different rules. And if that means hurting bad men to keep innocent people safe? Then we do it. Without hesitation. Without regret."

His words land like a stone on my chest.

Murder is wrong. It always has been. But... if he's doing it to protect people, does that make it acceptable? In a vigilante sort of way?

Even if it is justifiable, can I be with a man who commits such atrocities with a smile on his face?

Yes, babe. You know Matty. He's a good man. And if he has to do bad things for the right reasons, you'll learn to live with it.

He burned a man alive and enjoyed it.

He did it in honor of you. That man was going to rape you. He deserved it. So what if Matty took joy in avenging you?

"So... you're the good guys," I repeat slowly. "You just have to do questionable things to keep people safe?"

"Yes, sweetheart." I hear the sincerity in his voice. "We protect the people. We're feared by our enemies and respected by our allies. We don't hurt people for the sake of hurting. We have a code. It's just not one you're used to. Can you live with that? Can you live knowing that I'll do anything, *anything,* to protect my family? To protect *you?*"

His eyes plead with me to understand.

And I do.

I don't know how, and I don't know why, but I do. I can live with it. He's worth it. And maybe I do believe in justice outside the legal system.

I nod.

"I'm going to keep you safe. You know that, right? Nothing will ever happen to you again."

His promise is absolute. And I believe it.

"I know." My voice wobbles. "Thank you for coming after me. For saving me."

"You're mine. I'll always come after you. But I won't have to again... because you'll never leave me. Isn't that right?"

Despite his gentle tone, there's a threat in his voice.

"Yes," I whisper the promise.

"Good." He leans in, lips brushing my forehead. "Now, time for your punishment."

I freeze.

"You ran away from me. You need to learn your lesson, so you never try again." He smiles, wickedly and beautifully. "Don't you agree?"

"Yes, sir."

I don't know what made me say it. But the way his grin spreads, like I've just handed him the world, tells me he loved hearing it.

"Let's get started."

His grin should scare me. But it doesn't. I trust him.

God help me, I trust him.

I always will.

Chapter 44
Matthias

'Yes, sir.'

Holy fuck. My cock could split a diamond with its hardness. Hearing those words come out of her mouth, hearing her address me with '*sir*', sets something ablaze inside me.

She doesn't realize what she just agreed to.

She doesn't realize this won't be fun for her.

I'll never give her more than she can handle, but this isn't going to be pleasurable, not like eating her out was for her.

I climb off her and sit on the edge of the bed.

"Come here." My voice is sharp with authority.

She hesitates for a second before crawling towards me, settling besides me, wide-eyed and waiting for my next command.

"No. Stand in front of me."

She obeys immediately. *Good girl.*

I give her an approving nod, then deliver the next order. "Strip."

She stills, but only for a moment. I arch an eyebrow, daring her to defy me, while knowing she won't.

Her hesitation crumbles. She heeds the warning, swallows hard, and does as she's told.

She doesn't make a show of it. There's no teasing, no performance. But it's the most provocative thing I've ever seen.

Seeing her in my clothes is one thing. Watching her slowly remove them is another test entirely.

I have to force myself to stay seated.

Punishment first. Then I'll take what's mine.

She pulls my shirt over her head, freeing her perfect, bouncing tits. The sight alone could push a man to madness.

My jaw tightens as rage flashes through me.

No one else will ever see her like this. She is mine.

She shoves down my sweatpants, revealing plush, milky thighs. Her soft curves bouncing slightly as she steps out of them.

I want to sink my teeth into them.

I want to mark her.

She pauses, hesitating when she's left only in my boxer briefs. Her hands twitch as if she wants to cover herself, but she stops.

She remembers my words from the shower.

Her hands fall to her sides.

Her cheeks are flushed adorably. It better not be from embarrassment. Her body is a goddamn masterpiece. *And it belongs to me.*

"All of it off." My voice strains from restraint.

I'm jealous of her hands. Jealous that they get to touch her, to undress her, when it should be me. I'm the one who gave the order, but it should be my hands stripping her bare.

She slides her fingers under the waistband and shimmies them down her legs, bending to push them fully off.

Her tits hang forward so fucking beautifully.

I bite back a groan.

I am in control. She cannot know the power she has over me.

I motion her closer and pat my thigh.

She moves to sit on my lap but I *tsk*, shaking my head.

I guide her into place, laying her on her stomach over my lap until I'm supporting her fully. Her head hangs off my left side. Her hair cascades to the floor like curly silk. Her legs dangle off my right side, her toes barely brushing the ground. And her sexy, plump ass is in the air, waiting for me.

I smooth a hand over the soft curve of her cheeks, gentle at first.

Then I give a light pat.

That's the moment realization dawns on her, and her entire body stiffens.

"No, no," she whispers, then begs.

She's so beautiful when she begs.

She writhes, struggling against me. I grab her wrists in one hand and pin them to her back so she's trapped.

I remember how she moaned when I smacked her thigh in the shower.

She's going to love this.

She just doesn't know it yet.

I lean down, my voice dark and full of promise.

"Bad girls get spanked."

Chapter 45
Margot

Fuck.

I don't know what I expected when he said he'd punish me, but it sure as hell wasn't this.

I don't even realize until he pats my ass. That's when it dawns on me.

I'm naked, bent over his knees, arms restrained behind my back, about to be *spanked.*

This is not okay.

You're going to love it.

No. No, I won't.

You were gushing from those thigh spanks in the shower. This'll be euphoric.

I don't like pain.

Then why aren't you fighting?

"Are you ready, my sweet girl?" His voice is calm, controlled. "I'm only going to do ten today, but next time, I won't be so lenient."

The first smack echoes around the room before I feel it. The sensation blooms. A sharp heat spreads across my skin. And, to my horror, a spark of pleasure shoots up my spine. That wasn't bad at all. I can do this. Easily.

The second hit stings more, but it's still bearable.

The third and fourth come fast and hard. I inhale sharply, not expecting them to hurt so much.

"How are you doing, sweetheart?" His voice is gentle, almost sweet. "Are you sorry for being a bad girl?"

He rubs slow, soothing circles over my ass. The contact overwhelms me. My skin burns now. The break only makes me feel the heat more.

"Answer me, or I'll add to the count." He pinches my right cheek.

"Oh fuck. I'm okay. It's starting to hurt. I'm sorry." The words tumble out breathlessly.

"Good." His voice darkens. "This is a punishment. You won't ever leave me again."

The fifth slap lands right under my right cheek on my upper thigh. Pain explodes through me. A cry rips from my throat.

The sixth lands on the same spot on the left. I wiggle, shifting my legs, trying to escape.

He pinches the already tender skin. "Stay still."

The seventh lands over the exact spot he pinched.

"Please stop, Matty. I've learned my lesson. I promise I won't ever leave."

He chuckles darkly. "Oh, I know you won't. Not after this."

The eighth one is the hardest yet.

My body jolts. A tear slips free.

And yet, you're wet.

Horror slams into me.

No, no, no.

The ninth strike pulls a moan from my lips. Loud. Unmistakable.

I burn with humiliation. I'm so messed up for enjoying this.

No, you're not. You just like it a bit rough.

Matty stills, then exhales a slow, knowing breath. "That didn't sound like it came from pain, sweetheart. Could my bad girl be enjoying her punishment?"

"No! This is horrible!" I squeeze my thighs together, trying to hide the evidence.

He *tsks* then pries my legs apart.

I whimper as cool air brushes over my wet, swollen flesh. I know he can see it. I squeeze my eyes shut, burying my face behind my hair.

"You really are a slut for me." His voice is thick with arousal. "Look at how soaked you are. You're dripping down your thighs."

He drags his fingers through my slick folds, teasing my entrance.

I push against him instinctively, desperate for more.

He *tsks* again.

I hate that fucking sound.

"Not yet. Bad girls don't get pleasure until their punishment is over."

He pinches the same sensitive spot on my right cheek.

White hot pain shoots through me. These pinches are worse than the fucking spankings.

I barely have time to brace before the final smack lands.

It's the hardest of them all.

Tears pool in my eyes. My body throbs.

Pain and relief flood through me in equal measure.

And deep down hidden beneath the ache, buried under the humiliation, there's something else.

Regret that it's over. And arousal from it happening.

Matty rubs soothing circles on my skin, easing the burn.

I exhale shakily, melting into him.

"You took your punishment so well, sweetheart." His voice warms now. Gentle and praising. "Have you learned your lesson?"

I nod, my voice hoarse. "Yes, sir. I won't ever run from you again."

And I won't.

Not because of the spanking.

Not because of the pain.

But because I don't want to.

I want this.

I want him.

I choose Matty.

I choose this life with him.

Chapter 46
Matthias

Her ass glows red from my hand. I've never seen anything so beautiful.

Despite needing to teach her a lesson, it was hard to follow through. If she had cried, my resolve would have cracked. When she started begging, it took everything in me to continue. But I had to. She needs to understand that I'm serious. This isn't just about defiance.

It's about her safety.

If she leaves again, I may not find her in time.

I won't risk that.

But when she moaned, when her pleasure bled into her cries, everything shifted.

Seeing her so wet, soaking from my punishment, sent something dark and primal through me. My cock hardened instantly.

I knew she'd like it.

She's perfect for me.

"My good girl deserves a reward for taking her punishment so well." My voice deepens with approval.

My cock aches, straining against my pants, desperate for a release. But first, I need to feel her.

I slide my fingers through her slick folds, no teasing, no waiting. I thrust two inside her, groaning at the way her cunt sucks them in.

She's so tight.

I start slowly, careful not to hurt her, but she's already lost in the feeling, hips rolling, chasing more, moaning so fucking beautifully.

The view is devastating. Her plump ass in the air, her soaked pussy swallowing my finger, her thick hips fucking my hand.

I have to look away, so I don't come in my pants.

If she saw my face right now, if she saw how gone I am for her, she'd know she owns me.

I add a third finger when she's ready.

She needs to be stretched and prepared. Because I won't hurt her. But I will ruin her.

She's bucking uncontrollably now. I'm grinding my teeth, trying to hold myself together. Then I feel her tighten. Her body climbs toward release. I pull out.

She gasps, twisting in frustration.

"No! Please, Matty. Let me come. I've been a good girl." She pleads in a wrecked voice.

She thinks I'm denying her.

She doesn't understand, the only punishment here is my own.

"Sweet girl, when you come, it'll be on my cock. Don't you want that?" Hunger bleeds into my tone, taking it over.

"Yes, Matty. Please. Please fuck me."

Fuck, her begging. I always knew she'd beg for me.

I can't help the smirk. In the end, she did. Not that it changes anything. Nothing could stop me from taking her.

"Well, since you asked so nicely..." I let the gloat seep in my voice. "Get on the bed."

Before I've finished speaking, she scrambles off my lap. Watching her crawl onto the mattress, hips swaying, has me gripping my cock through my pants just to keep from coming. My girl entices me like no other.

I yank off my slacks and shirt, not giving a fuck where they land.

When I look up, she's eye-fucking me. I slow my movements, teasing her, letting her see what's hers.

Enough waiting.

I prowl onto the mattress, like a predator stalking his prey. But before I take her, I need to taste her.

She's on her back, legs bent at the knees, feet planted on the bed. Spread wide open for me.

I slide down, positioning myself between her thighs. She props herself on her elbows, watching me, holding her breath.

I inhale deeply, savoring her scent. It's sweet. Fruity. Addictive.

I groan, unable to wait another second. I lick her. A flat and slow stroke, dragging my tongue over her clit. We moan in unison. Her taste is lethal.

I don't hold back. I devour her, lap her up, pull her into my mouth. I grab her thighs, spreading her wider, dragging her closer onto my awaiting mouth.

I want her suffocating me.

I want her to be the last thing I ever breathe.

Her moans turn desperate. Her fingers dig in my hair, tugging, pulling me in deeper. She's grinding on my face, chanting my name.

I won't last much longer.

Neither will she.

"Please, Matty." Her desperation overwhelming her.

I smirk against her soaked pussy. "What do you need, sweetheart?"

She shudders, hips jerking at my words. "You. Please. I need to come. I need your cock. Please fuck me."

I can't deny her. Just like she can't disobey me, I can't tell her no. Especially if it's my cock she wants. She'll always get whatever she wants from me. She just hasn't learned her power yet.

"Good girl," I murmur, kissing up her body, trailing my tongue over her flushed skin.

I hover over her face as my cock hangs between her thighs. I can feel her heat against me.

I kiss her, fucking her with my tongue still coated in her juices. She kisses me back, desperate, wild, unrestrained.

By the time we come up for air, she's gasping, wrecked. I take her in. Messy hair. Swollen lips. Flushed cheeks.

I let my gaze drag lower. Jiggling tits. Soft stomach. Smooth pussy. Thick thighs.

"Beautiful." My voice is pure reverence.

As much as I want to draw this out, I physically can't. I can't wait any longer. I need her.

I grab my cock, rub the tip through her slick folds, and coat myself in her wetness. I push inside her. She winces.

I freeze instantly. "Are you okay, sweetheart?"

She nods, but I don't move. Not until she pulls me in deeper.

I push in slowly, inch by inch, until I'm buried inside her to the hilt. Her warmth wraps around me like home. She tenses, squeezing me, and I nearly black out.

Fuck, she's so tight.

"Good job, sweetheart. You took me so well. You're such a good girl." I praise her, meaning every word.

She clenches again at my words, and I groan.

I make a vow to myself, to her, to the universe that I'll be inside her every single day. Not a day will pass where I don't savor her. Claim her. Own her.

There will never be anyone else.

There's only Margot.

Chapter 47
Margot

Full.

I'm so full.

I've never felt this full.

He's huge. I knew it from seeing him in the shower, but fuck, it feels even bigger than it looks. He's stretching me to the point of pain. If I'd said anything, he would've stopped. But I don't want him to. I want this too much. Now that the stretch is bearable, it feels good. He feels so good.

The pinch of pain fades, and I start rolling my hips, desperate for more, but he has me pinned to the mattress.

I can't go a second longer without him fucking me.

"Please, baby. I'm ready. Fuck me."

I know I've been begging. I gave in. He was right. I ended up begging for him. But I don't care right now. All I can think about is how much I need him moving inside of me.

Matty's eyes lock onto mine, checking for hesitation.

Then, he starts moving.

Slowly.

He pulls out until only the tip remains, then pushes back in just as slowly. He does it twice before I snap.

I use my legs to pull him in faster, trying to force his rhythm to quicken.

SMACK!

I gasp as his hand lands hard on my outer thigh.

Fuck! Why does he keep doing that?

Why do you keep liking it?

"I am in control. I set the pace. And we're going to start slow and savor this."

It comes through gritted teeth.

That's when I realize he's on the verge of losing control. He wants to take me just how I need him, rough and hard. But he's holding himself back.

His smirk is pure arrogance. "And I can tell how much you love being spanked. Your perfect cunt squeezed my cock so hard when I smacked your thigh, I was blinded for a minute."

The cocky grin shouldn't be hot. His arrogance shouldn't flood my core.

Oh, but it does.

His slow thrusts continue, but he gradually picks up the pace. It's still torturously slow. Fuck savoring it. I've needed this orgasm for two days, ever since he denied me in the shower.

"Please, Matty. Faster. Harder. Rougher. Please, baby. I need you." I beg, knowing exactly what it does to him.

Bingo.

He snaps.

His rhythm shifts instantly. He slams into me, pounding me into the mattress, driving so deep my freshly spanked ass burns. But the burn just reminds me how hot the spanking was.

I'm moaning, writhing, shaking. I've never felt this good.

You'll never feel this way with anyone else. Only Matty can do this to you.

His breath tickles my ear as he leans down, voice a dark whisper. "My good girl is such a slut for me. You like it rough and dirty, don't you?"

"Yes, I love it."

I can't hold back.

I wrap my arms around his neck, pull him closer, and crush my mouth against his. This kiss is nothing like the one earlier.

That was sweet.

This is fire. This is raw passion and all-consuming need.

Our teeth clash. He bites my bottom lip, then my tongue, so hard I taste blood.

He pulls back. A speck of red stains his lips.

I stare, hypnotized, as he leans down and licks my cut clean.

His gaze is feral, molten. "I've tasted you. Now, you're going to taste me. Open wide, sweetheart. I know how much you love spit."

His voice is unrecognizable. Consumed by lust.

Without thinking, I obey him. Like I always do.

I open my mouth.

And watch as he spits into it.

It's animalistic. Barbaric. Vulgar.

And so damn hot.

I swallow eagerly.

I'll take anything he gives me. Any part of him.

His eyes darken with approval.

"Good girl."

My body ignites. I'd do anything to hear him say that.

He moves lower, trailing down my neck. His kisses are feather light, but his bites are brutal, hard enough to bruise.

You love it. Everyone who sees them will know you're his.

He licks over the marks, soothing the sting, before moving lower.

His teeth clamp down on my nipple, tugging, sending fireworks through my body.

I scream.

"I love these huge tits." His growl is primal, raw. "They're perfect. You're perfect."

All the while, he's still slamming into me.

I reach for my clit, desperate to push myself over the edge, but he slaps my hand away, and pins my wrists above my head.

"My naughty little slut." His smirk is dark amusement. "I control your pleasure. You don't get to touch this needy clit unless I say so. You only come when I tell you to."

His fingers hover, barely brushing my swollen clit. Not enough contact.

"Does my sweet girl want to come?" he taunts.

"Please, Matty." I whimper.

"Not until I give you permission. It'd be a long month with no orgasms."

It's torture.

He's torturing me. With a feather-light touch.

Then, suddenly, pleasure.

"Come for me. Scream my name. NOW!" He commands as he pinches my clit.

Oh. My. Fuck.

"MATTY!" I scream his name until my throat is raw.

The orgasm destroys me.

He keeps thrusting, rubbing, grinding.

"Look. At. Me." He growls.

I do.

His eyes lock onto mine, and it undoes him.

"FUCK! MARGOT!"

His roar shakes me to my core.

Heat floods inside me.

He kisses me tenderly, then collapses on me.

After a few minutes of catching our breaths, he heads to the bathroom. He returns with a washcloth and motions for me to spread my legs.

When I do, our combined juices pour out of me. I'm shocked I didn't even think of using a condom. I've never gone without one.

I look at him, expecting the horror I feel to be reflected in his expression, but instead, his awestruck gaze is locked between my thighs. He looks almost reverently at the mess.

"I have an IUD. And I'm clean. I've never not used a condom." I assure him since he must be in shock.

He frowns at the mention of the IUD. Then his expression darkens as I finish reasoning.

"I'm clean too. And good. We aren't using condoms. I don't want anything between us." I open my mouth to protest, but he interrupts me. "Why would we? We're both clean. And you're protected." He growls the last part in displeasure.

I don't have any argument for that, so I just nod.

He sighs. "Fuck, sweetheart. That was the best thing I've ever experienced. I knew you'd be perfect. My perfect, sweet girl."

I flush, and he kisses the top of my head.

As he goes to the bathroom to rinse off, I get up to follow him.

I accept that things have changed. We can't go back.

And for the first time, I don't want to.

I just want him.

Chapter 48
Matthias

As I towel off, I take a moment to savor what we just did.

That was the best experience of my life.

The sex? Unmatched.

My sweet girl likes it rough. She was made for me. Her body is my personalized heaven. Every curve, every moan, every reaction was perfection.

She's mine. And I will never let her go.

But it wasn't just the sex that made it different. It was her surrender. She gave herself to me. Handed everything over. Not just her body, but her trust too.

She trusted me to take care of her.

And I always will.

I glance at her sleeping form. At her soft and peaceful expression. Even asleep, she's beautiful. She was exhausted after our shower and crashed.

Carefully, I cover her naked body, tucking her in. She's had an exciting morning. She needs her rest.

She also needs to recover. Because there's no way in hell I'm not having her again tonight.

As much as I want to stay, I have work to do.

One last look. One last second of restraint.

Then, I leave our room and head to my office.

I need to find out everything about Koschei Group.

I need to eliminate any threat to her.

Her safety will always be my priority.

I won't let anything happen to her.

The thought of what could happen sends a shiver down my spine.

Because if they so much as look at her the wrong way, I'll make sure they never see anything again.

Chapter 49
Matthias

My phone ringing interrupts my work. I haven't been this focused since Margot got here, but digging into the Koschei Group and the Bratva has my full attention. The fact that they're after her puts a fear running through me I've never known.

Fear for Margot's safety is a hell of a motivator. It's also driving me insane.

I need to know why they're after her. I need to stop them.

I also need to tell my brothers what's going on. Not just because they can help, but because when Roman and I killed those Bratva members, we involved the Syndicate. Hell, I unwittingly involved them the second I killed those first two men who were after Margot in the alley. We just didn't know they were after her at the time.

Dom needs to know what we've dragged the Syndicate into. And Bash can help me dig into this more.

With my lack of tech knowledge, I haven't found much. Just what Margot uncovered. It's frustrating as hell not knowing what's going on, not being able to find anything, not being able to protect her.

From what she told me, those men were going to take her. The idea of Margot in the Bratva's hands, of her as their prisoner, makes me sick.

Even if they figured out she doesn't know anything and hasn't told any authorities, they couldn't just let her go. By then, she'd know too much.

My phone rings again, dragging me out of my thoughts.

Mom.

Fuck. Why is she calling now?

I love her, but this is not a good time. She's been worried about me lately, and I don't have the mental strength to reassure her at the moment.

Still, if I don't answer, she'll just keep calling. She's relentless like that.

So, I pick up the call.

"Hey, Mom. Now's not really a good time–"

"Excuse me, mister. That is *not* how I raised you to answer the phone. Try again." Her disappointment is evident in her tone.

I roll my eyes and start over.

"Sorry." I grumble. Then in a false cheerfulness, I begin again. "Hey, Mom. How are you doing? How can I help you today?" I try to sound upbeat, but even I can hear how tired I am.

"That's better. Now, I would be doing a lot better if my son wasn't hiding his woman from me."

Her anger is evident, but it doesn't fully shield her hurt.

I hate that I hurt her. But how the hell was I supposed to explain my situation with Margot? Sure, she's probably mad she heard about Margot from someone else. But what was I supposed to say? *Hey, Mom, I kidnapped this girl but now I'm hoping she's choosing to stay?*

She's always wanted us to bring home a girl. I know this because she tells us every time we see her. How much we need women. How love will make us happier.

And maybe she's right. I am happier with Margot.

And Mom is definitely outnumbered in the family. A new woman around would be good for her.

"Roman told you about Margot?" There's no point denying my relationship. And I'm not about to lie to my mom, even if I won't tell her everything.

"Yes! He told all of us you have a girlfriend." *Fucking Roman, the gossip.* "You let your poor mother worry while you were happy with a woman. I can't believe you introduced her to Roman before me! Why didn't you tell me? He says she's lovely, so clearly it's not her you're worried about. Are you embarrassed of us?"

Her voice is sharp, but it softens on the last question.

I'm honestly surprised Roman didn't spill more. And I appreciate that he only said good things. 'Lovely,' though? I doubt that was his word of choice, but I'll take it.

"Mom, stop. It's not like that. I didn't want to introduce you guys until I knew it was serious. I'd hate for you to get attached if it didn't work out. I love you guys. I'm not embarrassed of my family. Well, maybe my brothers. They're animals."

"So, it *is* serious!" she says triumphantly. "Because you introduced her to Roman! You're bringing her to family dinner tomorrow afternoon!"

She leaves no room for argument. She totally played me. Sebastian gets his brains from Mom.

She knows how to get us to do what she wants. She plays right into our love for her. And with four sons and a husband, she had to master the art of manipulation.

I can't even argue. If I refuse, she'll know something's up. And maybe this is a good thing.

Maybe meeting my family will help Margot realize how serious I am. And that we're not psychotic murderers. She and my mom will get along well. I'm sure of it. And she needs that right now.

"Matthias, we'll be on our best behavior. Your brothers will behave themselves; I'll make sure of it." She senses my hesitation.

"Ok, Mom, we'll be there at four. What do you want me to bring?" I give in.

Maybe this step will help my girl realize how real we are.

"Just bring Margot! And make that *noon*," she adds.

"Mom, you said dinner!" I'm whining, suddenly twelve years old again.

"Matthias Vincent Montclair, you will listen to your mother! You owe me more than a quick dinner with Margot. I want to get to know her. And once your brothers get here, there won't be a moment of peace."

"Yes, Mom. We'll be there at noon with a bottle of rosé." I concede.

"Perfect! I'm so excited to meet her! I need to go get everything ready."

"I love you."

"I love you too!" she sings then hangs up.

Wait! Get everything ready?

Oh, fuck. This is going to be a disaster.

But despite the chaos brewing in my head, I can't stop the smile that spread across my face at the thought of Margot meeting my family.

Her future family.

Chapter 50
Margot

I wake up to kisses along my shoulder and the sweet smell of coffee.

"Mhmm," is all I manage.

"Good morning to you too, sweetheart. I hate to wake you after keeping you up so late, but we've got plans." I can hear the grin in his voice when he says it.

Once I'd woken up from my nap, I ate brunch and hung out with Benny while Matty worked. We barely made it through dinner before we were sprinting to our room. It's hard to focus on eating with Matty's fingers inside me.

We spent hours fucking until I passed out. At some point, probably around two a.m., I woke to his mouth on my pussy, noisily devouring me like a man starved. After coming again on his tongue, he fucked me once more before we fell back asleep.

Now, my whole body is sore in places I didn't even know had muscles. It just makes me want him again.

But not now. I burrow deeper into the blankets with a low hum. I'm not ready to wake up. Not even the seductive smell of coffee tempts me enough to open my eyes.

He lets out a deep laugh at my refusal to rise, leans in, and gives me another kiss. "Sweetheart, you need to get up."

He starts pulling the blanket down until the cool air hits my bare skin and makes me shiver. I yank the covers back over my head.

"No! Leave me alone." I grunt at him.

He chuckles again, and winning the tug-of-war, pulls the blanket down until my ear is exposed. "Come on, sweet girl. You need to get ready. We're going to family dinner at my parents. My mom wants us there at noon, before the animals that are my brothers show up."

I freeze.

Oh. My. God.

Family dinner. His mom. His brothers.

I can't do this!

Yes, you can. You already met Roman.

"What?" I whisper. Praying he's joking.

"Sweetheart, we have to get ready. We don't have much time." He doesn't sound rushed. Or annoyed. Just calm.

"What time is it?"

"It's ten a.m., so we have a little over an hour before we need to leave."

"WHAT!" I shriek.

I leap out of bed, and bump into him, sending the coffee flying. I don't even care. An hour isn't long enough. I don't have anything to wear. What the hell am I going to do?

This is bad. So, so bad.

I'm going to show up looking like a slouch and his mom is going to hate me. What if his family doesn't approve? What if they think I'm not good enough for him? I mean... am I?

Shut up. He's lucky to have you. Now go get ready.

"Calm down, sweetheart." He sounds amused.

Fuck him. What about this is funny?

"CALM DOWN? How can you just spring this on me!" I'm shouting, full meltdown mode activated.

"I only just found out. My mom invited us yesterday," he says like that helps.

"YESTERDAY!" I screech. "You've known for a whole day, and you're telling me now? An hour before we need to leave?"

He looks at me like I've grown a second head.

"We were a little busy yesterday. I was... distracted." He smirks. Like sex could fix this.

"YOU WERE DISTRACTED? This is a disaster! I don't have anything to wear. Your family is going to hate me, and then you'll hate me and dump me. Are we even dating? Can you dump someone you're not dating? Oh my God. What are we even going to tell them? That you kidnapped me? There's literally no version of this that ends well. I don't think we sh–"

He strides across the room and shuts me up with a kiss. A sweet, soft one.

"No one's going to hate you," he says against my lips. "Honestly, I think my mom is already planning our wedding. Roman told her you're lovely. My brothers will like you too."

I narrow my eyes. "Roman said I'm *lovely*?"

"I don't know what words he actually used, but that's what my mom took from it. Sweetheart, everyone will love you." He leans back, eyes scanning me with something close to awe. "Wear that blue and white striped dress you have. It looks great on you but doesn't show too much. No one gets to see you. And it'll cover my marks. This is the only time I'll let you hide my claim." His voice dips low and dark, and he gestures to my neck. "We'll go shopping later this week. Get you new clothes."

I glance down. Purple hickeys dot my neck like I'm a damn teenager. I look ridiculous.

You look like you're his.

My heart swells at the thought.

He knows what dresses you own. He has a favorite. He's so gone for you.

I smile at my inner tramp's declaration.

I'm just as gone for him.

Chapter 51
Margot

Matty sits beside me in the driver's seat, wearing a blue button-up that perfectly matches my dress. I can't help but think he planned it. He smiled so brightly when he saw I'd taken his suggestion. It makes me want to listen to him more, just to earn those smiles.

After about twenty minutes, we pull through a gate and follow the driveway up to a gorgeous house. Even though it's huge, it doesn't feel cold or empty. It feels like a home.

"Stay," he says once the car is parked.

I stall in my seat, using the time it takes him to walk around the car to collect myself. I give myself a little pep talk.

It's going to be fine. I can do this. It's just his parents. I've never met parents before. Maybe it's not as bad as people say. Plus, Matty's here. He won't let anything go sideways.

Before we reach the front door, it swings open and a stunning woman steps out. I can instantly tell she's his mother. They have the same brown eyes. The same blinding smile. Hers lights up her entire face when she sees me.

She's much taller than me. She carries herself with the confidence her sons do. But hers isn't arrogant. She looks runway-ready in white pressed slacks, a navy button-up rolled at the sleeves, a white sweater tied over her shoulders, and navy pumps. The personification of power and class.

This woman is going to eat you alive.

I try to do that yoga deep breathing thing.

Nope. Still panicking.

"You must be Margot. I'm so glad you could make it!" She bypasses her son entirely and pulls me into a hug. It's warm and comforting and makes me miss my mom.

She pulls back and looks me over. I try not to shrink back at her gaze. I'm praying, begging, for her approval.

"Aren't you just beautiful! Matthias has a great eye. You're far out of his league." Her grin softens the teasing, but the compliment's sincerity shines through. I blush.

"Mom, don't tell her she can do better. She's going to realize it's true and try to leave me," Matty jokes, but there's something almost earnest in his eyes.

He pulls me from his mom's arms and tucks me into his side like he can't go long without touching me.

Good. I'm going to need his comfort to survive this.

A man steps outside. Definitely Mr. Montclair. Matty and Roman clearly get their strong noses and sharp features from him. He's just as tall as Matty, and dressed sharply like he's heading to a meeting, not lounging at home.

He's extremely handsome in a silver fox kind of way. If this is how Matty ages, I'm a lucky woman.

Already picturing growing old together?

"Evelyn, give the girl some space. We don't want to scare her away." He pulls his wife into his side just as Matty did to me and presses a kiss to her temple. Despite his teasing, the way he looks at her... this man adores his wife.

He turns to me and holds out a hand. "I'm Damien, Matthias's father. And this is my beautiful wife, Evelyn. We're so glad to have you over. We would've done so sooner if our son hadn't been monopolizing you." He shoots Matty a glare when he says it.

I shake his hand firmly. They say a weak handshake reflects a weak person, right? The Montclair's exude power. I need to match them. Or at least fake it.

"Thank you for inviting me over. It's so nice to meet both of you." And to my surprise, the smile on my face isn't even forced. They seem kind and welcoming.

"Come in. We have refreshments." Damien gestures inside.

Matty lets go of me so we can walk, but he grabs my hand the second we lose contact. When we get to the sitting room, he pulls me onto the couch beside him and tucks me into his side again.

"Thank you for coming early. We wanted to get to know you a bit before the rest of the boys arrive and chaos ensues." Evelyn smiles like she loves every second of the chaos they bring.

"It's no problem, Mom." Matty says smoothly, like my meltdown this morning didn't happen.

"So, tell us about yourself Margot. Where are you from? What do you do? What's your family like? We're just so excited to meet Matthias's girlfriend. None of our sons have introduced us to anyone before."

Wait, he's never brought anyone to meet his parents? I'm the first?

That has to mean something.

Obviously.

"There isn't much to tell. I'm from here, born and raised in Boston. I work for a shipping company, but I'm looking for something new. My parents retired and have been traveling for the last year."

"She's being modest," Matty cuts in. "She's a financial advisor for Northwestern Hemisphere Cargo. But she doesn't need to work anymore."

"Umm, I do. I need a job to, you know, make money and survive." I say, confused. Does he really think I can just not work? I know I'm done with NHC, but I still need a job.

"Sweetheart, you don't have to work anymore. I have enough to support us. You'll never want for anything." He smiles like he's saying something sweet and leans in to kiss my head.

I jerk back. "Like hell I will! Are you out of your damn mind? We only just started... getting serious. I'm not mooching off you." I correct myself just in time. His parents don't need to know about the whole kidnapping situation.

"We already live together. I'd say that's pretty serious." He looks frustrated, like he expected me to just go along with it.

"I didn't choose–" I catch myself when he coughs. Right. They don't know I was his hostage. I should out him! Make his parents realize what a psycho their son is. *But you won't. You want them to like you and Matty together.* "–to move in permanently. Just while my place is being worked on."

"Maybe this is a conversation for later," he says through a tight smile. But his eyes say it's already over.

He's insane if he thinks that I'm just going to live off him.

But it would be nice. No more spreadsheets. Just audiobooks.

Not the point.

I glance at his parents, bracing myself for judgement, expecting them to think I'm some gold digger.

But they're smiling. What the hell?

"How did you two meet?" Evelyn asks, kindly changing the subject.

I freeze.

No. No. No.

"I was ordering coffee," Matty says smoothly, "but had to step out after paying. Margot, being such a good Samaritan, chased me down with my forgotten credit card. I knew then I had to lock her up and keep her. It took some effort to win her over, but she's finally mine now. She only tried to escape once, but she won't be able to get away from me again."

My heart stops.

Did he just admit to kidnapping me?

Then he winks and all three burst into laughter.

I force a laugh too as relief crashes through me.

"Oh, son. The good ones always make you work for it," Damien says fondly. "It took months for your mother to agree to go on a date with me. But once she did, she fell for that Montclair charm."

"I find the best approach is to not give her a choice," Matty says with a grin.

I dig my nails into his thigh. *Shut. The. Fuck. Up.*

He flexes under my grip.

The smug bastard.

...

After a few hours of small talk, the front door opens. "Mom, Dad, I'm here."

The voice is unfamiliar, but then a younger, dorky version of Matty walks in. His wireframed glasses make him look studious. He's lean, maybe around my age. A little shorter than his brothers, but not by much. He's definitely the youngest.

He kisses his mom on the cheek, then freezes when he sees me. His face pales, and his eyes widen, like he's looking at a ghost.

"Sebastian!" Evelyn hisses. "Introduce yourself to Matthias's girlfriend."

"I'm so sorry, Margot. I'm Sebastian, Matthias's youngest brother. You can call me Bash. I wasn't expecting him to bring you."

Matty's grip on me tightens.

Why are they acting so weird?

"It's nice to meet you." I say awkwardly.

A few minutes later, another man steps into the room. He has to be the oldest, not because he looks old, but because of how he carries himself.

He's not like Roman, who radiated anger and violence.

This man is cold. Controlled. Calculated.

If Roman is fire, this one is ice.

I shrink into Matty when his eyes land on me.

"Who are you?" he asks, voice sharp and demanding.

"Dom, this is Margot. My woman." Matty's voice turns serious. All of his earlier charm gone.

Dom steps closer, looking skeptical. His eyes rake over me. Unlike his brothers, he has Damien's near-black eyes. But on him, they don't look warm. They look cruel.

I press closer to Matty.

Matty stands. Blocking me from Dom.

They're face to face, glaring at each other.

And thankfully, Roman shows up out of nowhere and pulls them apart.

"Not now," he says. When he spots me, he winks. "Looking good, Margot. How're you feeling?"

It would sound sweet, if not for the extra purr in his voice.

Matty decks him. Fist straight to the stomach.

Roman just laughs. Doubled over, clutching his gut.

"It's too easy. This is going to be so fun."

"Boys. Cut it out. You don't act this way in front of ladies." Their father's voice booms. All three glance at either me or Evelyn and mutter apologies.

Evelyn shoots them a warning look, then sighs. "Seems like we only got it right with Sebastian."

She pats Bash's knee and walks out.

Bash throws his brothers a smug grin behind her back. Okay, maybe he's not as innocent as he looks.

I glance back at the three oldest, hoping the tension has dissipated.

Dom meets my gaze, then flicks his eyes at Matty. "We'll discuss this later."

Then he turns to me and flashes a smile.

It transforms him. For a moment, he looks... handsome.

"Nice to meet you, Margot. I look forward to learning more about you."

Matty's jaw clenches at his words, and his glare follows Dom as he leaves.

Roman catches my eyes and raises a brow in question. I give him a thumbs up and a forced smile. He nods and returns to teasing the others.

Maybe I misjudged Roman.

After a few more minutes, the brothers head out, leaving just Matty and me in the sitting room.

"So, that's my family. Roman's an asshole, but he means well. Dom will cool off. He's just slow to trust new people. Bash is not as good as Mom thinks, but he's solid. They're good guys. You'll see."

He leads me towards the dining room.

Evelyn is a saint for putting up with these boys.

I have no idea how I'm going to survive the Montclair bothers.

Chapter 52
Matthias

Dinner went well. My brothers didn't make a fool of themselves, so that's a relief.

Unsurprisingly, Margot hit it off with Bash. He's the most approachable out of us. If you met him on the street, you'd never guess he's involved in criminal activities. He lulls people in with his sweet smile and soft demeanor, but he can be just as ruthless as the rest of us.

If he weren't my brother, I'd be a little jealous of how much of my sweet girl's attention he got tonight.

Her attention should be on me. Only me. She definitely shouldn't be laughing at another man's jokes. Or sharing her smiles with anyone else. Just the sight of it made my blood boil.

Surprisingly, she got along with Roman too. I guess saving her from an attack forms a bond. She doesn't seem scared of him anymore, which is good, since he'll be around more with the Bratva threat looming. They got along like siblings, teasing each other, laughing at my expense. I should be annoyed, but I can't be. Watching her enjoy my family fills me with hope of a happy future.

My parents accepted her like she's already theirs. Mom saw her as family the second she laid eyes on her. You can tell what kind of woman Margot is just by being near her. And Dad's treating her like the daughter he never had.

When Margot and I *disagreed* about how she'll no longer be working, because I *will* be supporting her, my parents were won over. They love that she's not afraid to argue with me. That she's not chasing my money.

But she's out of her goddamn mind if she thinks she's ever moving out of my place.

Fucking Dom. I would've fought him earlier if Roman hadn't stepped in. How dare he make her uncomfortable? And he didn't bother trying to fix it over dinner. He just alternated between interrogating her and ignoring her. That won't fly. No one treats Margot like she's out of place. I won't allow it.

…

"There are things we need to discuss. Brothers, in the study. Now," Dom says, pushing from the table and heading towards Dad's office.

"Please excuse us. We'll be back shortly," Bash says to Margot, with a charming grin on his face that's starting to piss me off.

If he looks at my woman like that again, I swear to God I'll–

Then Roman fucking winks at her, and she laughs like they're in on some inside joke. I don't like it. I don't like it at all.

I lean in and press a kiss to her head. "We'll be back soon, sweetheart. Mom and Dad will keep you company."

She kisses my cheek and flashes me her sweet smile. "Don't worry about me. We'll be just fine. Evelyn wanted to show me a few things."

I shoot Mom a warning look. I trust Mom with my life, but she loves to meddle. And I don't want anyone dissecting what Margot and I have. It's too new. Too fragile.

Also, if Mom finds out I kidnapped her, she'll kill me. Dad and Bash will help.

Fuck, Bash.

He definitely recognized her earlier. He's probably pissed. Hopefully Margot won him over, and he's forgotten what I had him help me do.

We follow Dom into Dad's study. As soon as the door shuts, both he and Bash turn to me, anger in their eyes.

"Who is she? Why is she here?" Dom snaps, just as Bash explodes. "Why is fucking Margot Peterson in our living room? What the fuck did you have me involved in?"

They're both pissed. Dom may sound calm, but I can see it in his eyes. Bash, however, is not hiding anything. He's furious. I don't remember the last time I've seen him this worked up.

Dom turns to Bash. "How do you know her? What did he involve you in?"

Fuck.

This is unraveling faster than I'd hoped.

Roman won't care. He's already covering for me.

Bash's furious, and when he connects the dots, he'll be worse.

Dom is the wildcard. He's done questionable shit. But keeping the truth from him about Margot and the attacks? That might be what sets him off.

Bash's voice cuts through. "You made me run her background. You said it was for the Syndicate. Was that what the phone thing was about too? You had me cut her off from everyone. You swore you wouldn't hurt her. You lied to me. And I helped you do it."

"She isn't hurt. Look at her. She's fine."

Bash isn't buying it.

Dom narrows his eyes. "When did this happen? And what happened? Why did you use Bash to do all that?"

"Look, we can get into the semantics of my relationship later." *More like never.* "Right now, we need to talk about the Bratva. There's a new development."

"Why are you involved with the Bratva?" Dom asks skeptically.

"Dom, let him talk. He'll explain everything." Roman interjects, looking just as frustrated.

I tell them what happened. About the attack. What Margot told me about the Koschei Group. I start from when Roman and I found her at her place but leave out everything prior.

When I finish, Dom is quiet. Processing.

Bash, however, is not.

"Why was Roman with you? And why were you following her to her house? What did they mean about two men disappearing?"

Fuck. He's putting it together. He's too damn smart.

Roman chooses this moment to chip in. "I was at Matthias's place when she ran away. He freaked out, needing to catch her before she disappeared. I was curious about the girl making him lose his fucking mind, so I went with him. And it's a damn good thing I did. This fucker didn't even bring his gun."

I shoot Roman a death glare. Traitor.

"SHE RAN AWAY FROM YOU?" Bash yells, right as Dom says, "You didn't bring a gun?"

I pause, trying to decide which one is safer to answer.

Dom. Definitely Dom.

Guns are more forgiving than kidnapping.

"I left in such a rush, I forgot it. It won't happen again," And it won't. I'll never be unarmed when it comes to protecting Margot.

Dom opens his mouth, but Bash cuts in.

"WHY WAS SHE TRYING TO ESCAPE YOU?"

He's yelling now. He's not letting this go.

I glance at Roman for backup, but he just raises an eyebrow wanting answers too.

"She... may not have been *choosing* to stay at my place at the time," I say slowly. "But she's here now of her own free will, so does it matter?" I shrug. "And keep your voice down. If Mom finds out, I'll destroy every one of your computers."

"Yes, it fucking matters! Why were you forcing her to stay with you? That sounds like you kidnapped her." Bash laughs. It's not a good laugh. It's unhinged.

I go quiet.

They all stare at me.

Dom's voice is low. "Was the girl being kept against her will?"

"She overheard a conversation between me and Roman about interrogating a Bratva guy. Then she witnessed the alley attack. At the time, I thought they were after me. Turns out, they were after her. How ironic. I didn't know that and couldn't risk her going to the cops. So... I took her. I didn't know what else to do. I messed up." I exhale. "But things changed quickly. I didn't expect to care this much. And now we're happy together. So, it's fine."

"You kidnapped a girl! AND I HELPED YOU!"

Bash launches himself at me.

Caught off guard, I lose my balance, and we hit the floor. Before I can react, Roman pulls him off me.

"Get it together," Roman says. "She's happy with him now. Did you see how pathetically in love they are? He even lets her call him Matty." Roman reasons with Bash. He looks at me. "The only way you can get a girl is through kidnapping her? Pathetic."

"Fuck off. I'm sorry for involving you, Bash, but I needed your help. And she's happy now. You can go ask her yourself. Just... don't tell Mom and Dad."

Bash shoots daggers at me with his eyes, clearly still upset.

Dom brings it back around. "We need to talk about this Koschei Group. This might be the missing piece. I want to talk to the girl. Bring her in."

"No. She's not getting dragged into this." My voice sharpens. "And her name is Margot. Stop calling her 'the girl.'"

"She's already involved." Dom says coldly. "*She* brought *us* into this. Now I want to know what she knows. This isn't up for debate."

I grind my teeth hating that he's right.

"Fine," I bite out. "But Dom, get your shit together around Margot. She's it for me. If you make her uncomfortable again, I'll shoot you."

And I mean it.

I won't kill him.

But I'll put him on his ass.

No one disrespects my woman.

Chapter 53
Margot

Matty enters the sitting room, cutting off my conversation with Evelyn. He walks straight to where I'm sitting on the couch, but instead of joining me, he holds out his hand.

"Come on, sweetheart. We need to talk to you about... everything," he says carefully. Understanding, I take his hand and stand.

"Do *not* involve her in Syndicate affairs!" Evelyn snaps, jumping up. Her voice is sharp. Sharper than I've heard all evening. Not even when she scolded her sons did she sound like this.

"Mom, please don't get involved. Dad retired from this life. Enjoy the peace," Matty says, sounding tired. I can tell he doesn't want me involved either.

"No. I will not have you corrupting her or putting her in danger! You listen to me, boy." She's truly upset on my behalf, and as much as I appreciate it, I need to step in.

"Evelyn, it's okay. I've become a target without realizing it. Matty and the Syndicate are helping me."

"Mom, I won't expose her to anything she's not already wrapped up in," Matty promises. Then he turns to me and cups my face in both hands. "I swear I won't let anything happen to you. I will keep you safe." His eyes bare into mine. They're beautiful, steady, and full of so much conviction. It's a promise I know he'll keep.

"I know, Matty. I trust you." I say softly.

Evelyn sighs, breaking the moment. I forgot we had an audience. My cheeks flush.

"I can see how much you love her," she says gently. "I trust that you'll protect her just as your father protected me."

I open my mouth to correct her, to say love is a strong word, but Matty doesn't give me the chance.

"I will, Mom." He nods. "Come on, sweetheart. We need to talk to my brothers."

And just like that, he leads me out of the room.

I'm still spinning from the fact that he didn't correct her, that he didn't deny loving me, when he opens the study door.

The brothers pause their conversation. Roman throws me a flirty wave, which earns him a glare from Matty, and an arm slings tightly around my waist. Dom just stares at me like I'm some kind of puzzle. And Bash won't meet my eyes. His remain glued to the floor.

I probably should've asked Matty how much he told them about our situation.

"Tell me about your connection to the Bratva," Dom demands.

"Back off. I already told you everything she told me," Matty snaps, turning me into his side, shielding me with his body.

"I want to hear it from her." Dom's voice stays cold.

"I didn't even know what the Bratva was until Matty explained it after they attacked me in my house," I say, trying to stay calm. "I think I accidentally found something about their shipments at work. There were some sketchy orders from a company called the Koschei Group. The name is Russian, but the company doesn't seem to exist. I had no idea any of this was real. I didn't know organized crime even existed in Boston."

Dom keeps staring, like he's testing the weight of every word. He's the kind of man you'd be insane to lie to.

"She doesn't know anything. And she sure as shit doesn't work for them." Roman cuts in. I give him a grateful smile.

"I would've found a connection if she was," Bash mutters, still not looking at me.

Damn, he works fast. When did he have time to research me?

Dom quiets pensively. After a long pause, he finally speaks. "I believe you're innocent. You've provided helpful intel. We've noticed some strange behaviors from the Bratva lately. This could all be connected. We'll figure it out. For now, we'll set you up in a safe house with guards. We won't let them get near you."

"She's not going anywhere. She's staying with me," Matty growls. His voice is a low rumble I've never heard before. It's furious and fierce. His grip tightens like he's afraid I'll leave him if he gives me an inch of space.

"Is that what you want?" Bash finally meets my eyes. His stare is intense. "To stay with Matthias? We can keep you safe on your own if you'd rather."

"I want to stay with Matty," I say instantly. I press myself further into him. "Please don't make me go. I only feel safe around him." My voice cracks. I can't help it. It's the truth.

"No one's making you leave," Matty says, dead serious. "And even if they tried, I'd never let them. You're mine. You're staying by my side."

The room falls silent and that's that.

The guys shift back into strategy mode. I don't have anything else to contribute, but I listen, trying to connect the dots. It becomes clear that Dom runs the Syndicate. He's already laying out the next steps. Bash is the hacker. He's going to dig into the Koschei Group. Roman is the muscle. He'll interrogate anyone caught breaking whatever underworld laws exist. They can't just go after people without cause. There's structure, even in this world.

Matty wants to do more. I can tell. But for now, his job is me. Keeping me safe.

After an hour, we head back to the sitting room to say our goodbyes. Both of Matty's parents hug me. Damien tells me the door is always open to me. Evelyn smiles and welcomes me to the family.

Their warmth hits me harder than I expect. I appreciate it. I do.

I just don't have the heart to correct them. To tell them we're not that serious.

Or maybe...

Maybe we crossed that line a long time ago.

Chapter 54
Matthias

I'm lost in thought the entire car ride home. I'm worried about Margot. Furious about the Bratva. And frustrated there's not more I can do.

Sitting tight until Bash finds something or Roman captures a Russian doesn't cut it. I'm usually a patient man, you have to be running a company like mine, but this? This isn't business. This is *my Margot.*

And with Margot in danger, patience feels like a weakness I can't afford. I need answers. I need action. I need this threat gone.

She can sense it. I know she can.

She tried talking to me for the first ten minutes. She got one-word answers at best. Eventually she gave up, and we fell into silence.

I hate that I'm doing this to her. That I'm shutting down. But I don't know how to turn the emotions off.

When we get home, we head upstairs.

"I'm going to take a shower," I tell her. "Need to rinse off the day."

She's quiet for a second.

"Do you want to talk?" she asks, barely above a whisper.

"No, sweetheart."

I walk into the bathroom and close the door behind me.

I feel dirty.

Not from sweat or grime, but from worry.

The kind that sticks to your skin.

Because I still don't know what's coming for Margot.

And that makes me feel helpless.

Chapter 55
Margot

I can feel the anxiety emanating off Matty. It's heavy. Thick in the air between us.

I know it's because of me. Because of my safety. And I feel awful about the position I've put him in.

He gave me such a beautiful day. He doesn't even realize what a gift it was, being around his family. Evelyn's hug? That little moment of softness? It felt like a weight I didn't know I was carrying had been lifted.

I'm happy for my mom, getting to travel. She deserves it. But I miss being someone's daughter. Only a few more months until she and my dad come back. Unless they extend their trip again.

Matty doesn't realize it but today healed something in me.

And I want to return the favor.

He's always there for me, keeping me grounded. Holding me steady when I start to fall apart.

He's been holding the weight of everything for me, and now he's unraveling in silence.

He held me when I fell apart. Now it's my turn.

Chapter 56
Matthias

The shower door opening jolts me out of my thoughts. I didn't even hear Margot enter the bathroom.

Margot steps into the steam, completely naked.

God, she has the most beautiful body I've ever seen.

She doesn't say a word, just picks up my soap and starts to wash me.

It's intimate. Gentle. Reverent. I don't dare speak. I just let her.

My cock reacts instantly. I harden until I'm brushing against her stomach.

She finishes cleaning me, steps back, and lets me rinse off.

When I go to grab her soaps, ready to return the favor, she shakes her head, *then drops to her knees.*

I forget how to breathe.

She wraps her small hand around my cock, and I let out a broken gasp. Her hand doesn't even fit around my girth. She braces herself with the other, pressing it against my thigh.

She leans in, licks the bead of precum from my tip, and moans at the taste. The vibration sends a shiver up my spine.

She licks along my shaft, and it takes everything in me not to grab her hair and fuck her mouth.

She strokes me once, twice, then pauses, sensing the friction is too dry. She looks up, questioning.

"Spit on it." I rasp. Not a command, just desperate need.

She hesitates, then obeys. She spits on my cock and rubs it in.

It's the hottest thing I've ever seen. I much prefer her spit there than on my face.

She finds a rhythm. Stroking me. Tongue flicking against my tip. Licking the precum like it's her favorite treat.

Then she stills.

For a second, I panic.

Don't stop now, sweetheart. Please don't stop.

Then she opens her mouth and starts to slide me in, one inch at a time.

My vision blurs.

Her tongue traces along the underside of my shaft, and I nearly collapse. She starts bobbing her head, slow and steady.

Then she moans. And I lose it.

I grab her hair, holding her in place, and thrust into her throat.

I pause, checking her response.

Her fingers tighten on my thigh, and she leans forward, taking more.

That's all the permission I need.

I grip her hair tighter and thrust deep, hitting the back of her throat. She's not ready for the full length yet, but we'll get there.

I build a rhythm, thrusting deeper each time.

When I think she's ready, I stop at the back of her throat.

"Open for me, sweetheart. Take all of me. You can do it." I coax, my voice thick with desire.

She relaxes her throat enough for me to push in a few more inches until she chokes.

The sound is beautiful, but I won't let her suffer.

"Breathe through your nose, sweet girl. Match it with my thrusts."

I guide her. In and out. Until her nose is pressed to my abs and I'm fully inside.

"That's it, sweetheart. You're doing so well for me."

I speed up, fucking her face faster now. But when I feel myself getting too close, I slow down. Her pussy is heaven, but this mouth? This mouth is pure sin.

I look down. She's watching me. Eyes locked on mine.

I hold her there.

She starts to sputter. Spit dripping down her chin. Her nails dig into my thigh. The sting only pushes me closer to the edge.

She starts to pull away. Fighting for air.

"Just a few more seconds," I promise.

She struggles again, and the vibrations against my cock almost undo me.

I pull out and let her breathe.

She should know I'd never hurt her. I'd never let her suffer more than she's capable of.

She coughs, catching her breath.

Then I do it again.

"You're doing so well, my good girl."

I can't stop my grunts as she takes everything I give her.

And then I see her fingers. Between her thighs. Touching herself.

I groan. "I see your pretty fingers playing with that pretty pussy."

She freezes, caught.

"It's okay, naughty girl. Get off on being used by me. Such a good little slut for me."

She moans in agreement.

"You're going to come when I do. I want to feel you scream my name around my cock. You're going to swallow everything I give you. Not one drop goes to waste. Do you hear me?"

She hums a yes, and I tighten my grip.

I start thrusting harder. Her hand moves faster. She's close, and so am I.

She lets go of my thigh. *And cups my balls.*

"Fuck, sweetheart. Squeeze them. Just like that. Good girl. Are you close?"

She moans.

"Come with me, Margot. NOW!"

I thrust all the way in and hold her there.

I roar her name as I come, spilling down her throat. Her scream vibrates through me. My release goes on and on. My vision sparks. My body shakes. I barely stay standing.

When I come back to myself, she's struggling.

I pull out of her mouth and haul her to her feet, holding her against me. She feels so small. So fragile. I could break her. But I'd die before I ever did. A wave of protectiveness overwhelms me.

"Was that okay?" she whispers. The uncertainty in her voice upsets me. I need her to know she's perfect.

I grip her chin and tilt her face to mine. I kiss her, tasting myself on her tongue.

"Sweetheart," I breathe against her lips. "That was perfect. Don't ever question yourself." I press a kiss to her temple. "If you ever want me, in any way, all you have to do is ask. I will always be ready for you."

She blushes and nods.

I grab her soaps and wash her gently. I savor the feel of her skin under my hands. I memorize every curve, every scar, every perfect imperfection.

This intimacy, it's everything.

...

Later, lying in bed, I reflect on our day. How well she got along with my family. How Mom already sees her as one of us. How even Dom came around by the end. He finally accepted she's not a threat.

My mom saw it first. She saw what I wasn't saying out loud. That I'd do anything to keep Margot safe.

And she was right.

Because seeing Margot with my family? That sealed it.

She's my future.

She's going to be my wife.

She's going to bear my children.

And she's going to belong to me, in every way that matters.

Forever.

Chapter 57
Margot

"Sweetheart, I have a surprise for you," a voice whispers in my ear.

It takes me a moment to realize it's Matty, his smooth voice pulls me from my beauty sleep.

"Huh?" I mumble, still half-asleep.

"Sweet girl, open your eyes. I brought you coffee, and I want to show you something before I start working."

That one word does it.

"Coffee?"

He chuckles. "Here you go, sweetheart. Be careful, it's hot."

He hands me the mug and presses a kiss on the top of my head.

"I'm sorry to wake you, but I have a meeting soon, and they just finished. I couldn't wait another minute to show you." His excitement is adorable.

I take a sip and squint at him. He must read the confusion on my face, because he keeps going.

"I have a surprise for you. I want to give it to you before my meeting starts in–" he glances at his watch "–seventeen minutes. Come on, sweetheart."

Still confused, but now curious too, I slide out of bed. "Lead the way."

He hands me my robe, not wanting me braless around his guards. I put it on, and he nods in approval.

He flashes me a full smile that makes my heart skip, then leads me down the hallway. He takes me to one of the spare rooms Dotty showed me during the tour the first day. *That feels like a lifetime ago.*

"What are we–"

I don't even finish the sentence. I can't.

It isn't a guest bedroom anymore. The bed is gone. In its place are a couch, two comfy armchairs, a wall of books, and a beautiful table in the middle.

But what stops me in my tracks is the recording equipment.

Microphones. Headphones. A band-new laptop.

It's a full studio. My dream studio.

"Surprise," Matty says softly, eyes on me like he's holding his breath.

He looks like a kid on Christmas, except he's the one giving the gift.

"When? How? Why?" I don't even know what to say.

"The day of our... *disagreement*," he says, sheepish, "after the shower, I made a few calls. I had my guys put it together. It took a few days to soundproof the walls properly. The setup turns the space into a professional booth. I wanted you to have the best equipment. If it's missing anything, let me know. I picked out everything with you in mind, but we can change anything. I thought you might want to focus on narrating. If you want to. You don't have to work at all. I can support us–"

He's rambling like I do. I cut him off with a kiss, showing him mercy.

"Matty, it's perfect. I can't thank you enough." I kiss him again. "I've always wanted to narrate full-time but couldn't guarantee I'd make a living from it. This is amazing."

I wander the room in awe. The couch and chairs are cozy. There are even throw pillows and blankets. I check out the bookshelf and notice there's an entire shelf dedicated to books I've narrated. Books I poured myself into with only hopes and dreams.

How did you get this man?

I turn to face him. "I don't understand. What made you change your mind? You were so against it."

"I actually came in to apologize before your god-awful taste in music *distracted* me," he says with a smile. "I saw how much it meant to you. I'm not going to stand in the way of you doing what you love."

My heart clenches.

"Plus," he adds with a grin, "listening to your sexy voice narrate books makes our time apart while I work a little more bearable."

I laugh. "Maybe I'll do a few extra recordings just for you." I wink.

His eyes light up. "Excellent idea! Can it be personalized? Preferably with my name? Maybe moaned a few times."

"I'll consider it... with the right incentive." I try to keep my voice strong, like a boardroom negotiation voice.

"Oh, fuck, sweetheart. I'd make it worth your while." He purrs, hand already gripping himself through his slacks. He's already hard. Just from the idea.

I prowl over to him, swinging my hips. When I reach him, I press against his body, pull him down by his tie with one hand, and palm his hard cock with the other.

He groans sharply and thrusts into my hand. He wraps an arm around me, trapping me against him.

I pull him lower until my lips are brushing his ear.

Then I whisper, in the voice I use to narrate erotic scenes, "Mr. Montclair... don't you have a meeting to get to?"

"Fuck, Margot!" He groans, not nearly as entertained as I am.

I burst out laughing. "Sorry, baby. You're the one who has to work."

I turn to walk toward the couch, but I only get one step before he yanks me back into him.

"That was cruel," he growls. "You're going to pay for it later. Using that sexy voice on me... *Fuck.*"

He swats my ass, gives it a squeeze, then storms out of the room.

Damnit. Now I'm turned on too.

I look around the studio again and smile. I can't believe he did this.

What did I do to deserve this man?

Maybe this is the universe's reward for returning his credit card.

Maybe it is true.

He saved me.

If he hadn't taken me that day, I'd still be targeted. I wouldn't have the Syndicate protecting me.

And you wouldn't have this sexy man.

I heard once that when you do good things for others, it'll come back to you.

Maybe this is what that looks like.

Chapter 58
Matthias

I can't believe that little minx. Playing me like that right after I gave her the studio. And where the hell did that sexy voice come from?

I'm absolutely taking her up on her offer of those personalized recordings.

Just the thought of her voice purring in my ears, saying filthy things meant only for me, has my cock hardening all over again.

And now I'm sitting in this goddamn meeting with a semi. Unbelievable.

Honestly, I can't believe I'm attending this meeting at all. I should be spending every second figuring out how to stop the Bratva from getting anywhere near Margot. This company can survive a few days without me.

But I'm stuck waiting. Waiting for my brothers to dig something up. Waiting until I can be of use.

Helplessness doesn't suit me.

At least the studio worked out. Not just because it makes Margot happy, but because it gives her something to focus on. Something to keep her occupied.

She doesn't realize it yet, but she's on lockdown.

She's not allowed off the property.

Scratch that. She's not allowed out of the house, except the enclosed backyard. And only if Benny is with her. And a guard. No, two guards at least.

That dog surprised me. I underestimated him. He's loyal, and I know he'll defend her.

I've doubled the guards. Every entrance to the property and the house is monitored. Security has eyes everywhere now.

I'm not taking any chances.

The only advantage we have is that no one knows about us. There's no trail connecting Margot to me. No photos. We've never been seen in public together.

And there's no Syndicate connection.

Roman made sure of it. He personally disposed of the bodies and cleaned the scene. He didn't delegate like usual. We kept everything tight. Partly to keep Dom in the dark, but mostly because you can never be too careful.

And I'll never risk Margot.

Not for anything.

Chapter 59
Margot

The days start to blur together.

Not in a bad way. I'm actually enjoying every single one.

I spend most of my time recording. The audiobook's coming along great. I'm about halfway through. As long as I keep up my current pace, I should finish before the deadline. I finally responded to the author, apologizing for my lack of reply, and letting her know I'm in the process of recording.

I'm loving this one. The story is intense. It might end up being one of my favorites.

It's about a guy who becomes instantly obsessed with a woman the first time he sees her. He dates her, but she doesn't realize he's been slowly infiltrating her life until she's completely dependent on him. There's a happily ever after, of course, but the journey is wild.

The guy actually reminds me of Roman, though I doubt Roman would ever be so obsessed with a girl that he'd go this far to keep her. Actually...

The heroine's way too sweet for Roman, anyway. If he ever settles down, it'll have to be with a woman who can put him in his place. Someone strong enough to handle him. Honestly, he'd probably do well with someone who could kick his ass.

Anyway, it's a great book. That's why I've been putting so much extra effort into this narration.

Or it's because you want Matty to like it.

I want all my readers to like it.

You want Matty to enjoy it.

I don't know what you're talking about.

Yes, you do. It's all you think about when you record spicy scenes.

Regardless, it's probably my best work yet.

Aside from recording, my life's fallen back into the rhythm it had before the attack. Matty still wakes me with coffee every morning. We meet for lunch most days, depending on his schedule. We have dinner every evening. And end every night with sex.

I fall asleep in his arms, no longer waiting until I'm asleep to seek him out.

This relationship is real. There's no denying it anymore. I've accepted that. I've stopped fighting it.

And really? If I'd known how much better life would be once I gave in to my feelings for Matty, I would've done so sooner.

I was right!

Okay, fine. You may have been right.

You should've listened to me.

I'm much happier now.

We spend all our free time together. Even Benny has been affected by Matty's presence. He's happier. More energetic.

He just needed a daddy.

Stop.

Don't get me wrong. He still enjoys his daily naps. But he's more playful now. He bounces around more.

I'm enjoying this life too. This little bubble we've built.

But part of me is scared. How much longer will it last? Will he get rid of me once the Bratva issues are resolved?

Because now that I have him...

I don't know if I will survive without him.

Chapter 60
Matthias

"How do we still not know anything useful? It's been weeks! I can't keep her cooped up in this house forever. I won't have her feeling like a prisoner." I can't hide the irritation in my voice.

"Now that she's not your prisoner anymore, you mean," Bash snarks.

"How fucking long is it going to take you to get over it?" I snap back.

"Oh, I don't know. How long should it take someone to get over being tricked into being an accessory to a kidnapping?" he throws back, full of sarcasm.

"Enough," Dom cuts in. His tone shuts us both up. "I'm sorry, Matthias. I know this isn't what you want to hear. None of the men Roman's captured have heard of Margot. And Roman would know if they were lying–"

"They wouldn't dare," Roman interrupts cockily.

Sometimes the way he talks about his more *hands-on* work makes me uneasy. I don't think he enjcys the violence, but I can't say for sure. It might just be brotherly hope clouding my judgment.

"Don't interrupt me," Dom growls. "Bash found a few things. Let him explain."

"I followed the payments from Northern Hemisphere Cargo and the Koschei invoices," Bash begins. "They trace back to a Russian account overseas. I'm working on tracking where those investments come from and what else the account is used for." He pauses, then adds, "I'm sorry, Matthias, but this isn't the only thing on my plate. There are other priorities."

"Fuck that! This is the only priority. What the fuck else could you possibly be working on that matters more? Margot's life could depend on this!" Just the words make my stomach twist. The thought of her in their hands makes me sick.

"No, Matthias. There are other Syndicate concerns Bash has to address," Dom says coolly, which pisses me off more. "I know she means a lot to you, but this isn't our only concern. And Bash's also designing for your company."

"She doesn't 'mean a lot to me,'" I growl. "She means *everything* to me. If anything happens to her, I won't survive. There's no living in a world without Margot. And I don't want to survive in one. So, we're going to fucking figure this out. Bash, scrap everything for Syndicate Enterprise. Focus on Margot. On the Bratva. Nothing else matters."

"That's not a good idea. You have deadlines to meet," Dom reminds me.

"Don't tell me how to run my fucking company. I don't tell you how to run your gang," I hiss.

"Okay, everyone cool off," Roman jumps in. "We're working on it. We'll figure this out, Matthias. Dom, Margot's family now. Try acting like it. And Bash, I'd shut the fuck up if I were you." He sighs. "Now can we get off the damn phone? I have shit to do."

Roman being the voice of reason is unsettling. We don't usually fight like this. And he definitely doesn't usually play peacemaker.

We end the call, but I'm still shaking with fury.

No one's taking this seriously enough. And not being able to help? It's *torture.*

I've always loved my role as the face of the legal side of the family, bringing in the money. But lately I've been wishing I had Dom's power over the Syndicate, Roman's brutality, Bash's tech skills. Anything to help. Anything to protect her.

I've never felt so useless.

And beneath all the anger is something worse.

Fear.

I need to clear my head. There's only one thing that helps.

Margot.

I check my watch and pull up the camera in her studio. She's typically there around this time. I always know where she is. I will always know where she is, even after the threat is gone.

She's in an armchair, talking into the mic. I turn on the speaker connected to the feed and listen in.

Sometimes I do this. Just hearing her voice calms me.

And today? It melts the anger out of me.

"–I'm running from him, knowing what a monster he is. Unfortunately, my body doesn't seem to get the message. I can feel my arousal dripping down my thighs.

'You're not fucking going anywhere,' he growls in my ear.

He throws me on the bed. Before I can move, he's on me. He rips my shirt down the middle, exposing my breasts. My peaked nipples betray my arousal."

She pauses, then mutters to herself, "Come on, Margot. Let's do it again. Get your head in the game."

Her voice switches back to her narrator voice, and she starts over.

I'd think it's adorable, if what she was saying wasn't so fucking hot.

I don't even notice I'm palming my cock until I feel a prick of pain.

I start loosening my belt, ready to jerk off to her voice, to her moans, to the filthy scene she's voicing.

Then I pause as I get a better idea.

I buckle my belt, head out of my office, and start down the hall toward her studio.

All the fury and fear are replaced by a hunger I can't ignore

Sweetheart, I'm coming for you.

She has no idea what's in store.

Chapter 61
Margot

CREAK!

The door opening makes me stop mid-sentence. I pause the recording, surprised. Matty stands at the entrance to my studio.

"Hey, babe. What are you doing in here?" My voice carries clear confusion. He never interrupts me when I'm working.

"Keep going, sweet girl." The cocky grin I wish I didn't love so much curls across his face.

I smile despite myself, turning back toward the mic before his words register. *Keep going? Now? During this chapter?*

"Oh, no, it's okay. Why don't we get some lunch? Dotty can probably whip something up," I offer quickly, hoping to distract him.

"Oh, I intend to eat." His grin turns wolfish. "Now, keep reading. I want to hear."

I blink, confused. If he wants food, why is he telling me to keep narrating?

He strolls to the couch and sprawls out, his head next to the extra mic. I sit frozen in my armchair, staring at him in disbelief.

"Now, Margot. Keep reading." His voice deepens into an order.

I open a different chapter, something cleaner, safer. He sighs.

"No, Margot. The chapter you were on."

I freeze. There's no way he knows what I was reading, right?

"I won't say it again."

A shiver runs down my spine. My hips twitch. I'm aching to rebel.

You are such a slut for him.

I play the recording.

"*He's straddling my hips, not letting me move. His hands hold his aching cock, stroking it slowly, never breaking eye contact. I drop my gaze, unable to withstand the heat, the ownership in his gaze. My eyes land on the head of his member, and I follow a drop of precum.*

'Beg for me, sunshine. We both know you still want me. No matter what I did. You'll always want me–'"

I pause it.

"This isn't necessary. I can continue later." I mumble, face burning. My voice was steady moments ago, but now I can't meet his eyes.

"Look at me."

I hesitate before listening.

"Good girl. Now come here. Bring the mic."

No explanation. Just a command.

Curious and helpless to resist, I move toward him. He points to a spot on the floor in front of him. I go.

Without warning, he grabs my waist and yanks my yoga pants down. Panties too.

"What–"

"Step out. Arms up."

I obey before I've even processed what he's doing. And now I'm standing completely naked in the middle of my studio.

He grips my waist, grunting as he lifts me and places me on his chest, all while lying down.

Damn, he's strong.

My knees press to either side of him, but he slaps my thigh in same spot as always, and I drop onto him, my full weight settling against his chest.

My arousal soaks through his shirt.

"Scoot up and sit on my face."

I snap my gaze to his. His eyes are gleaming with mischief, though the rest of his expression is deadly serious.

I laugh nervously and unsure, but the look he gives me wipes it clean off my face.

"What? No! Absolutely not."

"Do it." His voice sharpens.

"I'm too heavy."

Slap. Same spot.

"Don't say that. You're nowhere near big, and I'm insulted you think I couldn't handle you. I just lifted you off the floor while lying down."

"I'll smother you."

"Death between my sweet girl's thighs, her pussy drowning me, sounds like the perfect way to go."

"But–"

"Now, Margot. Or I'll spank you."

Heat rushes through me.

"My dirty, little slut, already dripping. I can feel it through my shirt. Feel your thick thighs clench around me. I need to find a punishment you don't enjoy... Edging and orgasm denial seemed to work."

He's right.

If he wants to suffocate between my thighs, then so be it.

I crawl up his body, and his hands guide me until my thighs are framing his face. I stay on my knees, hovering just above him.

"Grab the mic. Finish the chapter."

"What?"

"You're finishing the recording. Just like this."

I stare at him, frozen.

Slap.

"Fuck! Stop doing that!"

"I can see, feel, and smell how turned on you are. Don't pretend you hate it. Now read the scene."

I grab the mic and play the track.

"*I can't even deny it. I'll always want him. Nothing he's done, nothing he could do would ever change that. My body knows its master–*"

"You can come when you finish the chapter," he growls then pulls me down.

His mouth pounces instantly. There's no buildup. He's slurping, tongue-fucking, devouring me.

I start grinding against his face. I can't help it.

Slap.

Same. Damn. Spot.

I fumble back into narration, my words broken and breathy. I stumble and stutter. Moans spill between sentences. My volume fluctuates wildly.

Every time I stop reading, he slaps the same spot. When I get into a groove, he triples his effort destroying any composure.

Read. Grind. Pause. Slap. Repeat.

His mouth is a melody of sin beneath me, a wet soundtrack to my humiliation. No editor will ever hear this. It's practically pornographic.

I'm not even processing the chapter anymore. The words are just sounds. I couldn't tell you what I'm saying. I couldn't tell you my name.

But somehow, I finish it.

The last two paragraphs nearly kill me, but I survive. Barely.

And then it ends.

And so do I.

I fall apart screaming. Maybe his name, maybe nonsense. I don't know. I don't care. The orgasm rips through me like a supernova.

My vision whites out, sparks dancing behind my eyes. I drop the mic. My fingers tangle through his hair, holding him to me as he licks me through the aftershock.

When the shaking finally subsides, I slide down his chest and collapse on top of him.

He wraps me in his arms, chin resting on my head, gently rubbing my back.

"Good girl," he murmurs. "You did so well, sweetheart. I'm so proud of you."

I melt. I don't have the strength to reply. I just curl deeper into his warmth.

"Send me that recording. Then delete it. No one hears my woman's pleasure but me." It's a possessive growl.

I nod faintly, too dazed to even feel smug about what he'll do when he listens to it.

He drapes a blanket over us, tucking me against him as my eyelids grow heavy. I'm wrapped in him, buried in his scent, lulled by his steady breathing.

I could get used to this.

Chapter 62
Matthias

I take a few deep breaths and try to calm myself before dinner with Margot.

It's been a few days since the call with my brothers and still no update. The silence is maddening. I'm trapped in a constant state of stress, always on alert, waiting for something to happen to Margot.

I know it's irrational. No one knows she's here. But I can't shake the feeling. There's a target on her back, and I feel it like crosshairs on my own skin.

Once I've reined myself in, I head to the dining room, and instantly, a genuine smile breaks across my face.

She's already seated. Not at the other end of the table like she always insists, but at the chair to the right of my head seat.

My smile widens.

She's finally given in. Every dinner, she would move her setting to the opposite head of the table, and every time, I moved mine to her right. But now... now she's placed herself beside me without prompting. It's such a small gesture, but it means everything.

This is why I do it all. This woman is worth every moment of worry.

I sit down beside her and immediately reach for her hand. Her smaller one disappears inside mine, so delicate and soft. It's a reminder of just how fragile she is, and how fiercely I need to protect her.

"So, what's on the menu tonight?" she asks casually, pretending like her seating choice means nothing.

"Nuh-uh." I squeeze her hand. "Why are we sitting at my head of the table, sweetheart?"

"Oh, we are, aren't we?" she says, glancing around like she didn't pick the seat on purpose. "I didn't even notice."

"Not a chance. Try again." I grin.

She huffs. "I just didn't feel like moving my stuff. My arms are tired from walking Benny earlier."

I arch a brow. "That's funny. Because I distinctly remember *me* being the one holding his leash."

She gives me a half-hearted shrug. "Your legs are longer, and you'll fit better there?"

"Margot," I warn.

"Fine," she relents, eyes rolling. "I wanted to sit next to you. Where we're supposed to. I like you being at the head."

My smile grows so wide it aches.

That's my girl.

"How about a movie tonight. It's been a while."

Her face lights up. "Yes! That sounds great. What do you want to watch?"

"Whatever you'd like."

...

"What the fuck are we watching?"

She giggles, her whole body shaking in my arms. "Matty, just give it a chance."

The way she's curled up against me, so relaxed, so carefree... it soothes something deep inside me.

This is why I keep everything from her. Why I carry the stress alone. She doesn't need to know how close the Bratva is or how dangerous this world can be. She deserves peace. Happiness. She deserves to laugh like this without fear.

I'll take all the darkness so she can stay in the light.

Her laugh pulls me from my spiraling thoughts. I unclench my fists and gently rub her back, grounding myself in the feel of her against me. When she's in my arms, I know she's safe.

"The last date I went on was worse than this," she sighs.

What the fuck?

My entire body stills.

Who? Who the fuck was the last guy? Why is she thinking about another man? Why is she comparing us? I swear to God, I will kill him.

I suck in a sharp breath and exhale slowly, trying and failing to stay calm. Every muscle in my body locks. I'm seething.

"He was a nice guy," she continues, oblivious to my rage. "We'd been seeing each other for about a month. We were ready to take the next step, so after dinner one night, I invited him over. We were making out on my couch, and he took my shirt off, then my bra—"

"Stop! I've heard enough!" I cut her off, my voice louder than I meant. I can't take another word.

She waves me off. "Hush. It gets better."

No, no it fucking does not.

"So, he's holding my boobs, right? Just kind of staring at them."

I feel nauseous.

Why is she doing this to me?

"Then, still holding my tits, he looks me dead in the eyes and says, 'I can't thank you enough. You've helped me come to terms with who I am. I'm gay.'"

What?

"He hugs me. Mind you, my tits are still out. Then kisses my cheek. He starts telling me how hard it's been, and before I know it, he's downloading Grindr and we're scrolling through profiles together. He was so appreciative. Needless to say, I didn't get any that night. It was the straw that broke the camel's back. I stopped dating after that."

The laugh explodes out of me before I can stop it. My whole body shakes so badly that Margot falls off my lap. I'm wheezing, my eyes watering.

"Stop it! It's not funny," she protests, smacking my chest.

"Oh, sweetheart." I'm still gasping. "The man held your glorious tits, and that's what made him realize he was gay? I'm sorry, sweet girl, but that's fucking hilarious."

She huffs but eventually cracks a smile. "Fine, that one's funny. But trust me, I've had way worse dates than what's on the screen right now."

Oh, this should be good.

"There was the guy who insisted on ordering the spiciest ramen on the menu, against both the waiter's and my protests. He made it about three bites before sweating through his shirt, crying actual tears, and I kid you not, pissing himself at the table."

Jesus Christ. What a fucking disgrace. I could down that ramen without blinking. Pathetic.

She grins wider now, clearly enjoying this. "Then there was the one who wanted to 'share his passion' with me... He brought me to his workshop and had me watch him taxidermy a beaver."

That's not just disgusting, it's deranged. Who the fuck thinks dead animal stuffing is first-date material?

"Oh! The second date with another guy? He brought me to his uncle's funeral. Introduced me to his entire family as his 'future baby mama'"

My jaw clenches. Future baby mama? *No. She's only having my babies.*

She shrugs like it's nothing. "One guy tried to recruit me into joining his pyramid scheme. Called it a 'business opportunity for entrepreneurial spirits.' I said no, obviously."

My smart girl. But still, he pitches a Ponzi scheme instead of asking how her day was?

"Another one told me we should go to the gym for our next date because I 'clearly need it.'"

I nearly black out. The audacity. The fucking corpse of a man is lucky he didn't leave with his jaw broken. Margot is perfect. He should've been grateful to breathe the same air as her.

"And then," she says with a laugh, "there was the guy who brought two other women on our first date. Claimed he didn't have time to waste and wanted to speed up the search for his wife."

"What the fuck," I mutter.

She smirks. "He got three drinks in his face."

Damn right he did. Any man who even thinks about another woman while in Margot's presence deserve a beating.

Not that another man will ever have her.

She's mine.

"Okay," I say, forcing calmness in my voice. "You've had some bad dates. I'll give you that."

I'll replace each one. I'll fly her across the world, take her to every five-star restaurant, give her everything she's ever wanted. I'll treat her like the princess she is.

"I'm so glad that's over," she says. "I never have to go on another first date now that I have you. Wait! Not that I think this is permanent. I mean, I know we're just waiting out the Bratva thing. I'm not trying to lock you down or anything. I'm not planning our wedding or naming our babies or–"

I am.

"Margot, stop," I say gently. I lift her off the floor and place her back on my lap where she belongs.

"You're never going on another first date. There will never be another man for you. Just as there will never be another woman for me. There are no other women. There's only you, sweetheart."

She opens her mouth, but I stop her with a finger on her lips.

"This isn't temporary. I'm handling the Bratva, and when that's done, I'm taking you on so many dates they'll erase every single one before me. And yes, we're getting married. We're going to have a house full of kids. A home full of laughter and love. We won't ever be apart. You will never run from me again. And no one will take you from me."

I tilt her chin up to meet my eyes. "You are mine."

I see the hesitation in her gaze, the disbelief. The way her eyes widened at the mention of kids. She starts to respond, but I silence her with a kiss.

She melts into it. It starts soft, then turns deep, and ends with me buried inside her.

Later, as we lie together, her body curled into mine, I stare at the ceiling.

I have a date to plan.

Chapter 63
Margot

Today has not been a good day. I've been in a bad mood since I opened my eyes. Even Benny noticed and started avoiding me. I can't even pin down why.

Is it because Matty wasn't there when you woke up? That he had Dotty deliver you your coffee?

Ok, maybe that's it.

I just don't get it. Last night felt perfect. We were laughing at my disaster of a dating life. He looked me dead in the eyes and said what we have is real. He talked about marriage and kids like he meant it. He couldn't have been lying, right? Why would he lie?

Calm down. He probably just had a busy day.

But even my inner hussy doesn't sound convinced.

We didn't meet up for lunch or to walk Benny. Which isn't unheard of, but it makes me question us. I needed to see him. Just to reassure myself everything's okay.

I head to dinner with one goal: confirmation. I'll see him. He'll say something charming. And I'll feel ridiculous for worrying.

But the second I open the dining room door, all hope vanishes.

There are no place settings.

My heart stops. A tear slips down my cheek. Then another. I break without making a sound.

What did I do wrong? Why is he changing his mind?

I thought everything was going well. I ignored all the signs today, clinging to hope. I should've known better. I do know better. I knew not to get involved with him.

How did I let it get this far? When did he take my heart?

"There you are, dear! I was looking all over for you. Matthias–" Dotty cuts off when she sees me. "Oh, goodness. What is going on with you, girl?"

Her voice is the perfect blend of soothing and scolding, that only Dotty can manage.

I didn't even hear her come in. I probably look like a wreck. It takes a second to find my voice.

"There's no place setting," I whisper. Any louder and I'll cry again.

"Well of course there isn't. You two are having dinner on the terrace. Matthias set the whole thing up. Woke up early just to tell me exactly what he wanted. He was very particular. Said he wanted everything perfect. And I quote, 'This will be the first date of many to erase all her *shitty* ones before me.'" She shoots me a look that says I'm being absurd. "It looks beautiful up there. Dinner will be ready soon, so wipe those tears, and off you go."

Well, how the hell was I supposed to know?

Drama Queen. You're in here bawling your eyes out while he's upstairs setting up your date.

I don't even try to play it cool. I thank Dotty and take off. I'm running up the stairs like my life depends on it—

For five steps before you got out of breath, lazy.

I stop at the terrace door, suddenly realizing I should've taken a minute to compose myself. I'm still a mess. But now I'm a sweaty mess. A wheezing, flushed mess. God, I hope I don't smell.

Wait. She said date.

Date.

I need to change. And shower.

I take a step back and immediately trip.

I fall with a loud thump. With zero grace.

I let out a startled scream as I smack the ground.

Perfect.

Before I can recover, the door swings open. Matty appears, and his smile crumbles the second he sees me.

"Sweetheart, what happened? Are you okay?"

He crouches in front of me, eyes scanning for injuries. I checked myself too. I'm fine, just embarrassed.

"Sweet girl, please don't cry. Tell me what hurts."

"I'm okay, Matty. I just tripped." I mumble.

His brows furrow. "Sweetheart, you've been crying. What's wrong? Do you need a doctor? I can have the Syndicate doctor here in thirty minutes."

He's already reaching for his phone.

"No, baby. Don't call the doctor. I'm not crying from the fall."

He pauses. "Then why are you crying?"

"It's stupid. I was overreacting. Just forget it."

"Margot."

The use of my first name makes me crack.

"You didn't bring me coffee. Then we didn't eat lunch or walk Benny together. Then I get to the dining room, and there aren't any place settings. I thought... I thought you changed your mind. That you were done with me. I thought I messed up."

A tear slips out. He catches it before I can.

Then he pulls me into his arms and tucks my head against his chest like he never wants to let go.

"Sweetheart, I'm so sorry. I wish you would've told me. I got up early to plan this evening and worked through lunch just so I'd have time to set it all up. I'm so sorry. I didn't think you'd notice, and I definitely didn't think you'd think I was ending things." His voice goes soft. "There is no ending things. This is forever. I could never be done with you. And if you still doubt that, then I clearly haven't done enough to show you. Tonight is my next step."

He pulls back just enough for me to see his eyes.

"Margot Peterson, one day Margot Montclair, would you do me the honor of going on a date with me?"

He bows dramatically. Then kisses my hand.

My heart melts.

"I'd love to," I whisper.

He helps me up and opens the doors to the terrace.

And I freeze.

It's stunning.

Strings of warm light hang from the ceiling. Soft music flows throughout the room. A table covered with candles, crystal glasses, real silverware, and folded napkins makes it look like we're at some five-star rooftop restaurant.

I turn, and he's holding roses. Beautiful, deep red ones.

He's in a navy suit and a white button-up. Crisp, clean-shaven. Polished in a way he never is by this time of day... and I'm in yoga pants.

He smiles, waiting for my reaction.

"Matty, I don't even know what to say. This is amazing. It's too much."

"No. Nothing will ever be enough for my sweet girl. But I'll damn well try."

He pulls out my chair, waits until I sit, then slides in across from me.

His legs find mine under the table and wrap around me. As if even now, he needs the contact.

It's perfect.

He's perfect.

Chapter 64
Matthias

Margot can't stop looking around. Her face glows with awe. Pride swells in my chest. I did a damn good job. I wanted to give her the perfect date, even if we had to stay on the property. She'll never have a bad date again. I'll treat her like the princess she is.

She's still soaking it all in when David, the gate guard who let her leave and got her attacked, steps onto the terrace with a bottle of wine. He looked confused when I told him he'd be our server tonight. But considering I let him live after what happened to her, he'll do any job I assign. Including this one. Dotty's cooking. He's serving.

"Good evening. I have a cabernet for you tonight." His voice is bright, too bright. He avoids eye contact, clearly ashamed. If he knew what had happened to her, he'd be on his knees begging for her forgiveness.

He pours a taste into my glass. I swirl it, sniff it, and taste it, then nod once in approval. Not at him. At the wine. I don't approve of him.

He fills Margot's glass, then mine, and sets the bottle on the table.

"Dinner will be ready shortly." He disappears quickly.

"Was that–" She starts.

"Yes. That's the man who almost cost me you. He's lucky to be alive. He'll do whatever job I give him, including server. And he'll do a damn good job. He's fucking lucky I'm showing him mercy."

My sweet girl, sensing my rising anger, slides her hand into mine on the table and squeezes gently. One smile from her, and the anger vanishes.

"Well, he's doing a good job," she says, teasing.

"I'm sure Dotty drilled etiquette into him. She rules that kitchen like a dictator."

"I believe it. She's hounded me during breakfasts more than once." She winks.

"She's the only one I trust in my kitchen."

"That's because she babies you. She adores you so much. It's sickening."

"That was before you came along and stole her from me."

"Wrong. You should've heard her the first day. She went on and on about how 'sweet Matthias is' and how 'his brothers need to seek the Lord's forgiveness.'"

I laugh loudly.

"Where did you even find her?"

"She's good friends with my parents. After her husband passed, she needed income but refused charity. She demanded to earn her keep. She didn't want to work for her friends, and with her opinions about my brothers, I was the only option. She's been with me eleven years. I've offered to let her retire with full pay, but she refuses every time. I think she's lonely. Not that I mind. I wouldn't know what to do without her."

"That's really sweet of you. I'll try to spend more time with her. I used to, but with how much I've been recording lately, I haven't been around as much."

"No, sweetheart. Do what you need to do."

After a pause, I ask, "Why audiobooks? You had a good job. You didn't need the money. It's such a niche thing to do."

"I'm a hopeless romantic. I love rom-coms, love stories, romance book, even trashy ones. Happy endings are my weakness. I've read over six hundred romance books since college. One of my favorite series didn't have an audiobook, so I offered to narrate it for free. That turned into a demo. And the rest is history."

She lights up talking about it. Her passion practically hums.

"You're great at it. You bring your characters to life. And your voice... God, your voice."

She blushes.

"Did you actually listen to my last book, or just the sex scenes?" she asks innocently.

"I listened to the whole thing. I'm not a pervert, despite what you said. I only have one of your books left. I listen to them while I work. It's the only way to get my Margot fix without dragging you into my office. I've even delayed meetings to finish chapters. But honestly? It's your voice. You could narrate a commercial for geriatric erectile dysfunction, and I'd enjoy it. The erotic scenes are just a bonus."

She hides behind her wine glass, face blazing.

"I have a confession," she mumbles, avoiding eye contact. My curiosity spikes. "I've been picturing you in every *scene* I've recorded. Sometimes I mess up and call the character 'Matty' and have to redo a scene."

"Fuck." I groan, tipping my head back and pinch the bridge of my nose. "Sweetheart, you can't tell me something like that during dinner. I'm trying to be a gentleman."

I discretely adjust myself under the table. My cock rages, but I am trying to be a gentleman.

When I glance at her, she's biting her lip and staring at where my lap is hidden under the table.

"Margot," I warn.

She keeps staring.

"If you don't stop looking at me like that, dinner won't happen. I'll break this damn table fucking you on it. Then I'll spank you for ruining dinner. And Dotty spent all day preparing it."

She's still staring.

"Margot!"

She weighs her options. Defy me and get fucked *and* spanked. Or behave. Eat. Then get fucked afterwards.

She finally looks up and smiles sweetly.

"Sorry, Matty. What were we talking about?"

My cock twitches, but I force myself to answer.

"Audiobooks. Was it just a hobby, or do you want to do it long term?"

"If I could make a living off of it, I would, but I need something stable. My parents always pushed for that. It's why I went into finance, so I could take care of myself. Never have to rely on a man."

"But your heart wasn't in finance."

"Not at all. I hated it. What about you? What's your five-year plan?"

You. You're my five-year plan. And every year after. You, me, and a house full of kids. 'Til death do us part. And even after that.

"I'll keep expanding Syndicate Enterprise. But once my family starts to grow, I'll step back. Become a silent partner."

She catches it. *My family starts to grow.*

With her.

"That's nice," she says softly. I can tell she's picturing the same future as I am.

"So, what's on your bucket list?"

I want to know what dreams I need to make come true. What we'll do before kids. And what we'll do with them.

"I've never really made one. I just want a storybook love. Someone to be everything. Someone who holds me through the bad times and is beside me in all the good memories. A best friend. Kissing, crying, fighting. All of it."

Sweet girl, you already have it. You already have me.

Our love will make every fictional one look pathetic. You'll never go without anything. Not for a second.

I'll drown you in love.

And I'm honored to do it.

Chapter 65
Margot

We're both leaning back in our seats, full and satisfied. The steaks were perfect. He really planned the perfect date, but it's not just the food or the ambiance. It's him. It's our conversation. I feel closer to him, like we truly see each other now. He's such a good man.

You lucky bitch.

"Tell me about your childhood," he asks.

I blink, caught off guard at the request. "Oh. There's not much to tell. I'm an only child, but I always wanted siblings. My parents barely had time for one, though. Not that they were bad parents. They loved me. They just worked a lot. My dad was a high school math teacher, and my mom an ICU nurse. They loved what they did, but it meant tight schedules and tighter paychecks. That's why they pushed me to choose something lucrative. We didn't vacation much, so now that they're retired, they're traveling the world. I'm really happy for them, but I miss them. I hope they come home soon. They'll love you. My dad's been teasing me about becoming a spinster since I never leave my house. He'll be relieved. I think he just doesn't want me to be alone anymore. And they want grandchildren. Not that... I mean, not that I'm saying... I mean..." I start rambling, trying to correct myself. I don't want him to think I'm thinking about our children.

But you are.

"They sound great. I can't wait to meet them," he says easily. Then adds, "and we'll give them as many grandchildren as you'd like. The more the merrier."

I laugh, thinking he's joking, but when I meet his gaze, I realize he isn't. Should that concern me?

No. He's made it clear how he feels. He wants babies with you just as much as you do.

"So, what about you? How did your mom survive a house full of boys?" I redirect quickly. We are not talking about our kids.

"She's a dictator. Don't let her sweet face fool you. She ruled with an iron fist. She had to. Dom was bossy from birth, being the eldest. Always ordering Roman and me around. Which, of course, made Roman furious, and he'd take a swing at Dom. Roman spoke with his fists. I'd either heckle or join the fight. Bash was too young to be in the mix. Dom's a year older than me at thirty-five. Roman's a year younger at thirty-three. I'm in the middle. Bash's only twenty-six. A 'happy surprise,' as Mom says."

He smiles.

"He definitely got more of her attention. We were terrible influences. One time, when we were around seven, eight, and nine, we wanted pellet guns. We'd seen Dad's real ones and wanted to be like him. Mom said no, so we decided to get them ourselves. The only problem? We had no money. So, we started a business. We told the kids at school we were campaigning to improve the cafeteria food and needed to 'interview chefs,' which obviously required funding. With my charms, Dom's leader aura, and Roman's intimidation, classmates were happy to invest."

My jaw dropped.

"I basically created a Ponzi Scheme. The day Mom came home to find us bloodied and bruised, with black eyes and broken nose, she had some questions."

"The other kids beat you up?" I gasp.

He scoffs, offended. "Of course not. No one could touch us. We were big for our age, and we stuck together. We got the guns and took them out to test, but a few stray pellets hit us. I couldn't tell you who shot first, nor who was hit first. Some *altercations* followed. The whole story came out, and she was livid. She made us return the guns, give back the money, publicly apologize, and even write letters about how bad we were. It was mortifying, but effective."

I double over, laughing.

"She's amazing. I'll have to take notes."

"She knew what she was doing," he says fondly.

"What about Bash? Was he as bad?"

"Worse. He was too behind us to fight with us, but he was smart. Manipulative, even. Especially with Mom. He was her golden boy. We protected him at first. He was nerdier and a few classmates caused him some trouble. We taught them their place. No one messes with a Montclair. But then he started playing chess while we were still learning checkers. He learned to hack around age eight. He used it to his advantage. I won't say we were scared of him, but...Freshman year of high school a kid kissed Bash's girlfriend. Bash exposed *everything* about him. Texts, therapist's notes, his parent's divorce, even his fucking porn preferences. The kid had to change schools."

My mouth drops. "He seems too nice. I can't picture him doing that."

"Oh, sweetheart. That's just the tip of the iceberg. Bash's lethal with a computer. I'm lucky to have him at Syndicate Enterprise."

"Why did you start that instead of just working for the Syndicate?"

"Dom was always meant to run the Syndicate. He's powerful. He can lead an army. Roman's too hotheaded. Bash's intelligence would be wasted in boardrooms and galas. We wanted a legal front to clean up the family name. And I love what I do. I'm good at it. Charming clients. Building the company. It's so successful, most of our net worth comes from it now." He says with pride.

"I'm impressed. I'm sure all that money and power has won over many women." I wink teasingly, but the energy shifts.

His grin drops.

"There are no other women."

I scoff. "Please. You're thirty-four. You've been doing this for over a decade. There've probably been hundreds. Come on, I told you all my dating horror stories."

He sighs. "I won't lie and say I've never been with anyone else. But it was never emotional. Strictly physical. If they caught feelings, it ended. I don't even remember their names. They were nothing. They weren't *you.*"

His eyes are sincere, but my doubts crawl in.

"How can you expect me to believe that? That you'd pick *me* over models and heiresses? I love myself, but let's be real."

"Because I do! I'd pick you every time. You're everything, Margot. My life revolves around you. I don't measure my days by time anymore; I measure them to you. It isn't morning until I've brought you your coffee. It isn't night until I'm back beside you. If I don't know where you are, I can't function. I listen to your narrations at work just to have a piece of you. I can't eat dinner if you're not with me. I can't sleep unless you're pressed against me. I need you. Maybe more than I need air. You consume me. Margot, you are my future. I won't even consider any future where you're not by my side. There's no version of life without you. You will be my wife. We will have as many children as you want. We will grow old together. And we'll even die together, because if you go first, I'll follow. I won't spend one second of this life without you. Don't you get that?"

His voice is loving and frustrated and raw.

I sit in stunned silence, my heart racing, trying to process what he's telling me. He said we are real last night, but this? This is undeniable.

Do I feel the same?

Yes, you dumb girl. You love him.

Love him?

I don't... I couldn't...

But don't I?

He's my whole world. I'm my happiest when I'm with him. I count the minutes when we're apart. I only feel safe with him nearby. He brings me joy. Real joy.

The sound of his chair scraping back jolts me. He must misread my silence as rejection. His chair crashes behind him as he shoots to his feet.

Is he leaving?

I open my mouth to stop him, but instead of walking away, he circles the table, pulls my chair out to face him, and drops to his knees.

He cups my face, his palms warm on my cheeks. He leans in until we're only a breath apart.

"Damn it, Margot! I love you. With everything I am, I love you. I've known for so long, but I held back because I didn't want to scare you. But all that did was give you room to doubt us. So, no more holding back. I love you. And you're going to get every ounce of that love whether you want it or not. You may not love me yet, but I'll earn it. And once I have it, I'll work every damn day to deserve it. Do you understand, sweet girl? I love you."

His voice shifts from stormy to soft, from desperate to devoted.

And just like that, I know.

With every fiber of my being, I know.

"I love you too, Matty."

Chapter 66
Matthias

"What?" It's barely audible. I whisper it, afraid that if I'm too loud, she'll vanish. That I'll wake up, and this moment will be gone.

"I love you," she repeats, and I swear I hear it in her voice.

"Please don't say it if you don't mean it, sweetheart. There's no rush. I will earn your love," I manage to say, even as I silently beg her not to take it back.

"Matthias Montclair, I love you. I love the way—"

She doesn't get any further, because I can't hold myself back. I pull her in and kiss her. It's hard, deep, and unrelenting.

I kiss her like a man possessed, like I've never kissed before. It's love and desperation and need. Raw and wordless. There's no space between us now. There never will be again.

I lift her out of her seat and place her on the table. One hand cups the back of her head, anchoring her to me. The other presses into her spine, molding her body to mine.

She pulls back, her eyes locking with mine.

"I love you, Matty."

I groan.

Then she yanks me forward by my hair, pulling me right back in.

My cock hardens impossibly so. Beyond hard. Forget a two-by-four, I could split a diamond right now. She grinds against me, and I groan, deep and guttural.

I trail kisses down her throat, behind her ear, across her chest. Biting. Marking. Worshipping. Whispering my love against her skin with every kiss.

Her moans harmonize with the soft music in the background.

"Matty, fuck me," she breathes.

"Sweetheart, I need to get you ready." I whisper, apologetically.

"No, baby. I am ready."

I tug her yoga pants down, letting them bunch around her ankles. Her panties stay up. I don't even have the patience to take them off. I shove them to the side and slide my fingers over her soaked slit. She's dripping, ready and needy for me.

"My love does this to you?" My voice is hoarse. My love does to her what her love does to me. I've never been harder. Never needed a woman as much as I need her. My cock needs its home in her.

I slide one finger in. Then another. She clenches around them and nods, gasping.

She's ready for me.

"My sweet girl–"

She cuts me off by unbuckling my belt. I step closer so she can free me. She shoves my boxer briefs down just enough for my cock to spring out.

She groans at the sight.

"Please–"

I don't let her finish. I thrust into her in one hard, desperate motion.

It's fast. Frantic. Every thrust chasing something deeper.

I bite her neck. Her shoulders. Her ear. My fingers find her clit and circle, adding to the chaos.

"I'm so close, Matty!" she cries out.

"I know, sweetheart. Come for me."

It's not an order. It's a plea.

"I love you, Matty!"

That's what breaks me.

She comes, shaking around me. I follow, thrusting as deep as I can and holding her, filling her with everything I have. My seed. My love. My entire fucking soul.

Her walls pulse around me. I keep pressure on her clit, drawing out her pleasure. Letting it pull mine deeper.

When we finally still, I collapse against her, my forehead resting in the crook of her neck. Her fingers weave through my hair. My cock twitches, still inside her, not ready to leave.

I hold her upright, being her support. Being her protector. Like I always will.

"I love you," she whispers into my hair.

I lift my head, eyes meeting hers. "Say it again, sweetheart."

"I love you, Matty. I love being with you. I love our life together. I love the future we'll have. The children we'll make. I love it all. I love you."

She cradles my face in her hands, mirroring what I did to her earlier. I close my eyes and just breathe her in.

I will never feel anything greater than this.

After a long moment, I pull out and tuck myself away, watching our combined releases pour from her. It's the hottest thing I've ever seen.

She starts to fix herself, but I beat her to it, pushing her panties over and pulling up her pants. She's still messy. Still mine.

She wraps her legs around my waist and pulls me close. Her lips part to say something, but the door creaks open.

"Would you like dessert now?" David's godawful voice breaks the spell.

"No." I growl.

"Be nice," Margot whispers.

"Would you like dessert in ten minutes?"

"No. Fuck off. You're done for the night. Leave."

Sorry, sweetheart, I don't have nice in me for this jackass.

"Where should I–"

"I don't fucking care. Just leave. Now!"

"Yes sir."

His retreating footsteps bring me peace.

"That wasn't very nice. What if I wanted dessert?" My sweet girl teases.

I pause, torn. I don't want her to miss out on something, but I don't think I can wait any longer to be inside her again.

She smirks. My spitfire as always.

"I thought I already gave you dessert," I say, flashing her a cocky grin.

She laughs. I want to bottle the sound.

I tighten her legs around my waist and pull her off the table, her arms winding around my neck.

"Now," I whisper, carrying her back inside, "I need to show my sweet girl just how much I love her."

Chapter 67

Margot

When we reach our room, Matty sets me gently on the edge of the bed.

He steps back and kneels, lifting my right foot to his knee and removing my shoe. Then the left. He rises and steps closer again, guiding my arms with soft touches. He peels off my shirt, then unclasps my bra. His movements aren't rushed. Nothing like the frenzy we just came from.

When I'm bare, he stares at my breasts in awe. He holds their weight in his palms reverently.

Needing to see him, I lean forward and slide off his jacket, then unfasten the top button of his shirt. When he realizes what I'm doing, he steps closer, letting me undress him slowly.

We take our time. No words. Just looks. Just touches. Each layer removed with care. Each breath shared.

We're fully exposed to one another, not only our bodies bared, but also our feelings, laid at each other's feet. Nothing hidden. No barriers. I can see his soul, and it's calling to mine.

He lifts me, and I wrap around him instinctively. He climbs onto the bed and lays me down, my head resting on our pillows.

Then he kisses me tenderly. I can taste his love.

I open for him.

He breaks the kiss only to ease himself inside me. He sets a gentle rhythm, and I match it, our bodies moving together like they've always belonged.

There's no urgency. No rush. Only reverence.

It's never been like this before. He touches me like I'm sacred. Worships my body as if I'm his altar. Like I'm the most precious thing in his world. And all the while, he stares into my eyes, making wordless promises I believe with every beat of my heart.

The only forever I've ever dared believe in.

Chapter 68
Matthias

I'm done sitting around. Done waiting. Done playing it safe. I'm Matthias Montclair, damn it!

They should fear me. They should flinch at my name. No one should ever feel comfortable enough to come after what's mine.

Margot is safe because she's mine, but they don't know. Not yet. I need to claim her. Publicly. Once the world knows she belongs to me, she'll be protected by more than just security. She'll have the full force of the Syndicate behind her.

I grab my phone and call Dom.

"I'm not hiding anymore. I'm taking Margot out. Once people see she's mine, they'll back off. She'll be protected."

"That's not a good idea. Rom–"

"Fuck that! I'm doing it. I'm done waiting. Margot deserves more than being locked away."

He sighs. "Matthias, Roman caught one. He got some info out of him. It's bad."

He quiets.

My whole body stills. "Spit it out."

"There's a bounty on Margot. A big one. They think she's responsible for the men who disappeared. Her name and picture are being passed around. Anyone who sees her will try to take her."

No.

No.

"We killed those men. She's innocent," I rasp. My vision narrows. A fucking bounty. *On my sweet girl.*

Dom hesitates. "It's not dead or alive. They want her breathing."

My stomach drops.

"Don't say it like that's better. You and I both know what they'd do to her. If they got their hands on her..."

I can't finish the sentence. I won't give that nightmare life.

"As long as she stays on your property, she's safe. Your security is airtight. And no one knows you're connected."

"That's the problem. They don't know she's mine. That's why we need to be seen together. If she's claimed, they'll back off."

"You think that'll be enough? Do you really want to risk it?"

"I would never put her in danger." I grind the words out, insulted he even implied it.

"I know. It needs to be somewhere secure. Controlled. What were you thinking?"

I start to answer when my computer chimes with a message from my assistant, asking if I'm attending this weekend's event.

Perfect.

"A charity gala. Saturday night."

Dom snorts. "Don't you hate those things?"

"Not when my sweet girl is by my side."

Showing her off. Making it clear she belongs to me. Every man in the room will know she's mine. And every woman will know I'm taken.

"Fine. I'll place my men at the entrance. Only vetted guests will enter. I assume there's no need for inside detail if she's glued to your side."

"Exactly. No one will get to her."

Relief floods through me. This is the beginning of the end. Once she's seen on my arm, this entire situation will shift. She'll be protected. She'll be safe.

"Don't forget your gun this time."

He ends the call before I can reply.

I turn to the feed. Margot sits in Benny's room, playing with him, arms flailing as she laughs. Her whole body lights up when she does.

My lips twitch into a smile.

Now, I have some shopping to do.

Chapter 69
Margot

"Good morning, sweetheart. I have some coffee for you."

My eyes crack open at the bribery.

I must be moving too slowly because he adds, "Wake up, sweet girl. I have a surprise for you."

Never one to turn down a present, I sit up and reach for the mug. I take a sip, then a few more, and once the caffeine hits my bloodstream, I ask, "What's my surprise?"

He's grinning widely, clearly excited. "I'm taking you to a gala. We're leaving the house."

"That's great! So, you guys figured out the Bratva situation?" My relief is immediate.

His grin falters. "Not exactly. We're hoping that being seen together, staking my claim, will show them you're under Syndicate protection. It'll be okay." His voice is strong, confident.

"I believe you. You wouldn't put me in danger."

"Margot, I won't *ever* let you get hurt. You are my everything. This will help things get back to normal."

"This is great! When is it?" I'm smiling now, buzzing with excitement at the idea of fresh air. I love this house, but I'm starting to crave the outside world.

"It's tonight!" he says brightly.

I freeze and slowly place the mug on his nightstand with more restraint than I feel. I turn to him, eyes narrowed.

"The gala is *tonight?*" I repeat, my voice falsely calm.

"Yes?" he answers, wary now.

"And you're just telling me. This morning." Still that same even tone.

"I wanted to surprise you," he says carefully.

"I see. Do you remember this exact scene happening before the family dinner?"

"Oh."

"Did you enjoy how that played out?"

"But this is different! You have all day to get ready. I–"

"How long have you known?"

"... A few days."

"Argh!" I throw my hands up. "Why would you do this to me again? You suck! I have nothing to wear!"

I nearly hurl the mug at him, then reconsider. No need to waste perfectly good coffee. Instead, I grab a pillow and launch it at his smug head.

The asshole shamelessly catches it without flinching. Ugh. Fuck him.

I fly out of bed and storm into the closet, rifling through clothes even though I know I don't own anything gala-worthy.

"I can't go! I have nothing to wear!" I yell.

His arms wrap around me from behind. I struggle to free myself, but he's too damn strong.

You love his strength when he's throwing you around.

Well, I don't love it now.

"Get off me!"

He just holds me tighter.

"Calm down, sweet girl. I–"

"DON'T TELL ME TO CALM DOWN!"

"Shhh. I got you a dress. And shoes. And jewelry. I have everything figured out. I hope you like it. But if you don't, we'll find something else. I picked it all just for you."

He gently turns me toward the end of the closet. Hanging front and center is the most beautiful dress I've ever seen.

A floor-length, jade green gown. Green, gold, and crystal beads radiate from the center like a starburst. Sharp shoulders glimmer with intricate gems. A sheer beaded cape draws from the back, curling around the arms like delicate sleeves. It's surprisingly conservative, except for the plunging neckline. It's elegant. Ethereal.

All I can do is stare.

It's breathtaking. Fit for a queen.

"I knew it was the one the moment I saw it," he murmurs. "Green looks great on you. The shimmery stuff reminds me of you, spitfire. Also, your tits are going to look amazing in it. I mean, you'd look gorgeous in anything, but this'll make you shine."

His lips brush against my ears, sending shivers down my spine.

"It's beautiful," I whisper.

"Try it on." His command is soft and paired with a gentle nudge.

That's when I realize I'm still naked from last night. It's not exactly rare for me to wake up naked after nights where Matty fucks me to sleep.

I grab a green lace thong. Even though panty lines won't show under the flowy skirt, a dress like this deserves something decadent. I can feel his scalding gaze on me as I slip it on.

I run my fingers over the fabric. It's softer than anything I've worn before and probably worth more than my yearly salary, pre-tax.

I lift the cape, spot the hidden zipper, and step into the gown. I'm tugging it up when a warm hand catches mine.

"Allow me." His voice is husky.

He drapes the cape over my shoulder, fastens the hook-and-eye, and slowly pulls the zipper up. His fingers graze my spine, shooting sparks through me. He adjusts the cape and gently lets my curls fall down my back.

Then he turns me to face him. His eyes sweep over me.

"It's perfect. Only a dress this stunning could do you justice."

He doesn't sound cocky, just in awe. Like he can't believe *I'm* standing in front of him.

He spins me toward the mirror. "Look at yourself, sweetheart. You look like a goddess."

I stare.

He's right.

The green compliments my porcelain skin. The deep neckline highlights my curves. The gown hugs me in all the right places. I've never felt more beautiful.

"How did you get my size right?" I ask, dazed.

"I looked at the tags of the outfits you wear most, the ones that fit best. I know you like fitted tops and looser bottoms." He rolls his eyes, like it's obvious. Like all men do this. Like it's normal.

This isn't the man who kidnapped me. This man cherishes me, adores me.

"Thank you, Matty. It's beautiful."

I lift my hair and the cape, gesturing to the zipper. "Will you help me take it off?"

He frowns. "Why are you taking it off?"

"Baby, I need to eat, shower, and do my hair and makeup. Then I'll wear the dress." I laugh at his utter lack of knowledge about what it takes for a woman to get ready.

"Huh. That makes sense."

He helps me out of the gown and carefully returns it to its hanger.

Attending a gala in that dress, with Matty as my date, will be to be unforgettable.

Tonight is going to be perfect.

Chapter 70
Matthias

I'm waiting at the base of the stairs for Margot, fully dressed and ready to go. I don't care what time we arrive. She can take all the time in the world. I'm Matthias Montclair. I show up when I want.

The click of heels on marble draws my attention upward, and my heart stops.

No, it races.

My pulse hammers. My chest tightens. My breath catches in my lungs. My world tilts.

She isn't real. Can't be. No woman born of this earth could look like that. Could stop time with merely her presence.

She lifts the side of her dress to descend the stairs, and the movement jolts me into action. I climb the stairs to meet her and offer her my arm. My mom raised me with manners, and right now, my girl deserves nothing less than worshipping.

At the bottom of the stairs, I let her go and circle her slowly.

"Sweetheart," I breathe, "there are no words. There's never been a sight more beautiful."

She smirks. "You don't look so bad yourself, hot stuff."

Even through her makeup, I catch the blush blooming across her cheeks.

I'm in a custom tux. Usually, this feels like a chore, the layers and stiff bowtie. But tonight? With the way she's eyeing me? I may never take it off.

Well... not until I rip it off to fuck her.

I lean in for a kiss, but she dodges at the last second.

What the fuck?

"You'll ruin my lipstick," she says matter-of-factly.

I grunt in protest, tempted to kiss her anyway. I want people to see the smudge. I want them to know she's mine, all marked and claimed. But she catches the look in my eyes and points a warning finger.

"Don't even think about it."

I don't answer. I'm too busy drinking her in.

From the elegant twist of her hair to the way the dress grazes the floor, she's a vision. When my gaze lands on her bare neck, I remember what's in my pocket.

"I have something for you."

I pull out the velvet box and open it. Inside is the necklace I picked for her, one of many to come. I want her draped in jewels, wrapped in elegance, reflecting the beauty within.

Her eyes widen, and she lets out a soft gasp.

A row of diamonds glisten in the box, dipping into a delicate V. At the center, a large teardrop diamond hangs from a smaller one, perfectly matching the earrings I left out for her. Luxurious, but not loud. Elegant, yet commanding.

"Matty," she whispers, "it's beautiful."

I step behind her, fasten the necklace, and smooth it against her skin. When I return to face her, I nearly lose my breath again.

"You should always be encrusted in diamonds."

She gapes at me. "Wait, these aren't real diamonds, right?" Then she laughs as if it's absurd.

I scoff, offended. "Of course they're real. I'd never insult you with anything less. Only the best for my sweet girl. Pure diamonds. Genuine stones." I scowl at the insinuation that I'd give my woman anything other than genuine diamonds.

The diamond I really want to give her belongs in a ring. One that ties her to me. Forever.

"I can't wear these!" she panics. She reaches behind her and tries to unclasp the necklace.

I catch her hands and pull them between us. "You're not taking them off. These are yours. You'll accept them, wear them, and love them. Get used to it. There'll be more."

"But what if I lose them? Or break them?"

"Then I'll buy you more." And I'll keep covering her in beautiful things, until she starts believing she's one of them. I press a kiss to her knuckles. "Now come on. The limo's waiting."

"Limo?"

"Of course." I place her hand on my arm. "Let's go."

I lead her outside, trying to focus on the moment. On what's supposed to be a calculated outing to stake my claim and ward off enemies.

But all I can think about is how long I'll last before I ruin her lipstick. *Or that tiny green thong.*

The thought alone has me hard.

I'm already counting the hours until the gala ends, and I get to take her home.

Chapter 71
Margot

We pull up to one of the nicest hotels in town. The driver circles around the limo and opens the door. Matty steps out first and, brushing the driver off with a wave, offers me his hand. Ever the gentleman.

His palm rests on the small of my back as he leads me through the front doors. The man at the entrance doesn't even bother asking for Matty's name like he does with the other guests. I guess he's more important than I realized.

Matty gives a small nod to two men behind the bouncer. Both wear suits but clearly aren't staff. There's a coldness in their eyes, a sharpness that reminds me of Dom.

We step into the ballroom, and everything else disappears to its beauty.

The massive chandelier casts a warm, golden glow across the space. The white ceiling is trimmed in intricate gold crown molding. Everything gleams. Tables are scattered around the room, draped in white linen, but most people stand in the center, drinking and mingling. The air hums with soft music and money.

I must be gawking there too long, because Matty nudges me gently toward the bar and presses a kiss to my forehead.

"This is beautiful," I whisper.

"Not as beautiful as you," he replies with a wink.

"That was so cheesy." I laugh and swat his chest.

He catches my hand and kisses it. "Cheesy but true."

"Do you come to these things often?"

"I used to when I had to. But I think I'll be attending more in the future."

"Why the change of heart?"

He leans in, voice low. "If galas mean showing you off, then I'm all for them. I never liked these events before. There wasn't good company."

We order drinks, champagne for me, whiskey on the rocks for him, and start to drift toward the crowd. I spot a tray of something fancy nearby, and Matty leans down to whisper.

"Let's try these. One of the only good things about these events is the food."

He grabs one for each of us. Matty pops his in whole, but I try to be ladylike and take a small bite.

I moan. Out loud.

The flavor melts on my tongue and before I can even blush, Matty pulls me closer, his eyes dark.

"Make that noise again and–" He gets cut off by a shrill voice cutting through the air.

"Matthias, darling! I didn't know you'd be here. If you'd told me, I would've cleared my evening." She curls her voice around his name like a leash

I turn to see a tall, skinny blonde in a gaudy, hot pink dress so low-cut I'm shocked her nipples aren't showing. She leans in to kiss him on the cheek despite his obvious hold on me.

He doesn't move. He just freezes.

I stare at her while trying to swallow the rest of my appetizer. She obviously knows him. That much is clear. But how?

It doesn't matter. She's nobody. You're the one he brought here.

She giggles, and the hairs on my neck raise. "But of course, I'll always make time for my Matthias."

Okay. She's fucked him.

But she was just a fuck. He said you're the only woman he's ever felt anything for.

I cough to draw her attention. She glances at me, then dismissively turns back to Matty like I don't exist. And then she tries to wedge herself between us.

Hell no!

Put her in her place!

I step closer to him, with my fake smile in place. "Hello, I'm Margot. And you are?"

She turns and looks me over. It feels like she's peeling my skin off as her eyes crawl from my head to toe, searching for flaws. Then she flashes me the fakest smile I've ever seen.

"I'm Adrienne. Matthias and I are... *good friends.* We always enjoy each other's company at these events. And sometimes after." She smirks.

Anger flashes through me.

"That's funny. He's never mentioned you before."

Ooh, catty.

"Oh, I wouldn't expect him to talk about his lover to his... I'm sorry, are you his sister or something?"

This fucking bitch.

"Actually, I'm his girlfriend–"

"Soon-to-be wife," Matty interrupts, voice firm as he pulls me in front of him, wrapping his arms around me from behind. "As soon as I can convince her to say yes."

He kisses the top of my head and rests his chin there like a crown.

Adrienne lets out a shrill laugh and reaches out like she's going to touch him. He flinches, pulls me in tighter, using my body as a shield.

I can tell she's not done by the gleam in her eyes.

"Don't be silly. Drop the girl and meet me in the coat closet. I'll show you a good time."

I open my mouth to tell her off, but Matty beats me to it.

"Adrienne, there's nothing I'd rather *not* do. Why would I want *you* when I have my sweet, perfect girl right here? Why would I even look at other women when I have the love of my life in my arms?"

She gasps. "You're not serious. You'd pick *this pig* over me? Look at her, darling. You could do so much better. You could have *me.*" She gestures at her body that's been on a surgeon's table one too many times.

Matty stills behind me. His grip on me tightens.

His voice is calm, but there's venom laced in every word. "Listen closely, Adrienne. If you ever talk about Margot like that again, if you ever so much as look at her again, I'll ruin your life. No man will want you. You'll be blacklisted from every circle that matters. You were nothing more than a warm body. Margot is my everything. You will never compare. So, go find some pathetic man desperate enough to fuck you tonight. You'll never be more than the whore that warms their bed."

The disgust in his voice is sharp and unapologetic. And while I don't condone slut shaming, this bitch deserves it.

Adrienne lets out a screech, stomps her heels like a child, and storms off into the crowd.

I turn and lean into Matty, a smirk curling on my lips.

Chapter 72
Matthias

Now that the Wicked Witch of the West is gone, I can finally appreciate the beauty of what just happened.

"You were jealous." I can't hide the glee in my voice. My spitfire was jealous over *me*. She was possessive. She staked her claim. Watching her do it had me hard. I had to lean my hips back so she wouldn't get the wrong idea. But, holy fuck, her ownership of me was so hot.

"No, I wasn't. She's just a bitch," Margot grumbles.

"Oh yeah, she's a bitch. But you were possessive of me."

"I was protecting you from the snake. What did you even see in her? Was it just her hot body?"

"You were claiming me and fuck me if it wasn't the hottest thing ever. The way you did it... It's exactly how I want to claim you." I press my hips into her ass, letting her feel just how much I enjoyed it. "And no. She's not even close to your league. She was just easy."

"Don't lie to me. I know what I look like. I can't compete with someone like her."

I spin her around and stare into her eyes. "You can't compete with anyone, because no one comes close. You are my fantasy come to life, Margot. You're the girl I love. And I'll keep showing you that every damn day until you believe it."

"No, Matty. I know that. I just can't help it when my insecurities take over," she whispers.

"It's okay, sweetheart. I won't stop until every insecurity disintegrates. And even then, I'll keep telling you how perfect you are, every day, for the rest of my life."

Her eyes brim with unshed tears, and she nods.

I pull her into my arms and rest my chin on her head. One hand cradles her head while the other rubs soothing circles along her spine.

"Sweetheart," I murmur, "there are far too many hors d'oeuvres to waste time on tears. I think I saw brie bites."

I say it teasingly, hoping food will pull her from her spiral. After all our dinners together, I know her tastes, and I know those brie bites will make her moan in that way that makes my blood burn.

She laughs and leans back. "Let's go."

...

After what must be an hour of way too much mingling and not enough snacking, I realize I haven't checked my watch once, haven't felt the usual itch to leave.

Aside from the part of me dying to fuck Margot in that sexy dress.

When I finally glance at the time, I'm shocked. Three hours have passed since we arrived. I guess time really does fly when you're having fun. And I've definitely enjoyed showing her off.

Even the schmoozers haven't annoyed me as much as usual. But the way some of them looked at Margot? Yeah, that got under my skin. There were moments I was seconds away from throwing a punch. She always seemed to sense it. She'd grab my arm and pull us away before I exploded.

My phone rings, cutting off my stewing.

Dom.

I hesitate. Do I answer and step away from Margot, not willing to risk her overhearing something I don't want her to. Or ignore it and possibly miss something crucial about the Bratva?

Fuck.

"I have to take this, sweetheart. Stay right here." My voice leaves no room for argument. She cannot move from this spot.

Once she promises to stay put, I step out of the ballroom and answer the call.

I'll only be gone a few minutes. But I can't shake the foreboding in my chest.

Chapter 73
Margot

Matty's only been gone about a minute when the need to pee hits me. I know he told me to stay put, but surely going to the bathroom is fine, right? No one's going to hurt me here.

Still, he did seem serious.

It's fine. I'll be back before he's even off the phone. He'll never know.

I scan the ballroom and spot a hallway on the far side. That must be where the bathrooms are. I head down it and turn the corner, only to find this stretch of hallway dark and quiet. There isn't a bathroom. Just an exit door.

I turn around to head back to the main area and nearly scream when a figure appears behind me.

"God, I'm sorry. You scared me." I let out a nervous laugh.

"Margot Peterson. How odd to see you here. How odd to see you at all."

The voice slithers through the dark like smoke, and my blood runs cold.

My old boss steps into the faint red glow of the EXIT sign.

"Hi, Ronald. It's been a while," I say, relief flooding me that it's someone I know, but it doesn't last long. There's something off about his eyes. They're too hard. Too cold.

"It has," he replies. "What have you been up to?" His casual tone contrasts his hard eyes.

"Oh, you know... this and that. Nothing to write home about." I keep it vague, not wanting to remind him that what I have *not* been up to is working for the company.

"We agreed to meet up for coffee, and then you disappeared without a trace. I almost filed a missing person's report." His voice remains friendly.

He says it like a joke, but it doesn't feel like one.

"Right... I'm really sorry about that. Something came up." I laugh awkwardly. I don't have a good excuse for ghosting him and my job.

"But you're not the only one who's gone missing, I hear." He tilts his head, still smiling.

What?

My skin prickles. Something's wrong.

I glance around. My back is to the exit door, and he's blocking my only way out. Trapping me in this dark hallway.

"Um... I should get back. My boyfriend's probably looking for me."

It's not a lie. Matty could be done with his call by now. I should've stayed where I was. I should've listened.

"You're not going anywhere, Margot," he says calmly. "Some important people are looking for you. They're offering a high finder's fee. I saw you when you walked in and called them. They want answers."

His smile warps into something vicious. It sends a bolt of ice down my spine.

And then it clicks.

The Bratva.

He was the inside man. The coffee meeting wasn't casual. It was a setup. He must've told them I figured it out. That's why they're after me.

Fuck. I have to get out of here.

I lunge forward and try to shove past him, but he grabs me. I struggle, but he's stronger than he looks, and I'm just a short, plump girl with zero self-defense training.

For the second time since this nightmare started, I'm overpowered by a man with evil intentions in his eyes.

"Let me through," I growl through gritted teeth.

I claw at his face and manage to scratch him. He howls, then a fist soars at me.

Pain explodes across my cheek and stars burst in my vision.

"I'm sorry, Margot," he sneers. "But you knew too much. Then men started going missing. You made this too easy when you left your date."

He lets out a full, deranged, gleeful laugh.

There's a ringing in my ears. I barely register the sound of the exit door opening.

Heavy footsteps echo down the hall. Then, a rough voice, thick with a Russian accent asks, "Is this Margot Peterson?"

"Matty will kill you for this!" I gasp out, continuing to struggle.

"Yes. Grab her. I can't hold her much longer," Ronald pants like the weak bitch he is.

I feel a sharp prick at the base of my neck. My limbs become heavy. My knees buckle. My vision dims.

My last thought before the darkness swallows me is,

I'm sorry, Matty.

I never should have left.

Chapter 74
Matthias

"Dom, I need to get back to Margot. Make it quick," I snap.

"Roman caught another one. He was loitering outside of one of the clubs. Security called him before the guy could approach anyone," Dom's sharp tone betrays his frustration. They're getting bolder encroaching on our territory like that. It's blatant disrespect.

"What did he want?"

"Same as the others. Roman got him to talk. He was tasked with spreading a new product. Wouldn't say what it is."

"Did he say anything about Margot?"

It's the only part I care about. I know I should be focused on the Syndicate, but right now, Margot consumes my thoughts.

There's a long pause. I check my phone to make sure the call hasn't dropped. It hasn't. His silence means it's something bad.

"Just tell me."

"The bounty's gone up. They still want her brought in alive."

"Fuck."

"That's better than the alternative." Dom offers, but he doesn't believe it.

"You and I both know that's not true. They can't have her. She won't survive that."

"They won't get their grimy hands on her. You won't let that happen."

"I won't let them take her."

I've made a lot of promises in my life, but this one is sacred. I'd rather die than let them touch my sweet girl.

Dom starts to give me more updates, but I cut him off.

"I need to get back to her. I'll call you in the morning for the rest."

"You're too busy after the gala tonight to call?" He smirks through the line.

"With the dress Margot's wearing, I won't be available until morning." I hang up, grinning as I head back into the ballroom.

A man I vaguely know from business steps in front of me.

"Mr. Montclair, I didn't expect to see you here. I'd love to catch up–"

"Apologies, I need to get back to my date. Can't risk someone else stealing her from me. Let's talk Monday."

I don't wait for a response, already walking away.

I get to the spot where I left her, but she's not there.

I scan the area. Nothing.

My eyes sweep the ballroom, looking for that sparkling green dress.

Still nothing.

My pulse starts to race.

I move through the crowd. A flash of jade catches my eye, and I exhale in relief, until I get closer. Too tall. Not her.

The bathroom!

Of course. She's been sipping champagne all night.

I make my way to the ladies' room and catch an older woman heading in.

"Excuse me, I seem to have lost my date. Would you mind checking for me? Her name's Margot. Green dress." I try to suppress my stress, but it shines through.

"Sure, honey." She disappears.

I wait.

Five minutes that feel like five hours pass.

She finally comes back out but gives me a small frown. "I'm sorry, boy. She's not in there."

"Thanks," I mutter, barely holding it together. My body's frozen but my brain is spiraling. I pull out my phone and call Dom.

"So soon? I–"

"She's gone." I cut him off. "Check with your guys at the entrance. Have they seen Margot or anyone suspicious?"

"You lost her?"

Dom doesn't *do* worry, so the worry in his tone makes this so much worse.

"No. She's not where I left her. Not in the ballroom. Not the restroom."

"Got it."

He hangs up.

I stand still, trying to breathe. I'm overreacting. She's here. She just wandered off, looking for me.

Seconds feel like eternity. My phone rings.

"She hasn't left. And no one unapproved entered."

I exhale in relief. Just a false alarm.

"I'll keep looking."

"If you don't find her soon, call Bash. He'll pull camera footage." Dom hesitates. Then, quieter. "I hope you find her. Call me when you do."

"I will."

I hang up and leave the ballroom.

I comb through the hotel lobby, checking the bar, even asking the concierge. Nothing. No one's seen her.

Twenty minutes pass.

She promised she'd stay put. Where is she?

I dial Bash. No answer.

I call again. Still nothing.

The third call he picks up on the first ring.

"What the fuck, Matthias? You're cockblocking me right now. Literally. My dick is in my hand and... Caroline, right?"

A feminine voice corrects him.

Classy.

"You're at the gala, right?"

That snaps me out of it.

"Pick up your fucking phone when one of us calls. Especially at this hour."

I pause. I don't want to say it. I don't want it to be true.

"Margot's missing."

It comes out a whisper.

He goes silent. "Fuck, I'm sorry. Tell me everything."

I hear rustling, then the woman arguing. He tells her to leave in a cold, sharp tone I've never heard from him before.

He's moving. His office door opens. His keyboard clicking sounds through the phone.

"We're still at the gala. I stepped out to take a call from Dom. Maybe five minutes, max. When I got back, she was gone. I checked everywhere. Dom said no one left or came in."

"How long ago?"

I check my watch. "Thirty-two minutes."

He inhales sharply.

It's been too long. She could be anywhere.

"Okay, I'm in their system. Where did you leave her and what was she wearing?"

"Northwest corner of the ballroom. Jade green dress, some sparkly shit on it."

"I see her. She's debating something. Looks like she needs to pee. She does this little wiggle."

God, I love that wiggle.

"She starts walking. Enters a hallway on the southeast side. She reaches the EXIT sign. There's a man behind her. She startles. They talk. She knows him, I think. Her body language changes. She tries to get past him and... *Fuck.*"

He pauses.

"Bash. What?"

"He grabs her. She scratches his face. He... he punches her."

Red.

That's all I see.

He hit her.

"Two men enter from the exit door. Definitely not guests. They speak to the guy holding her. Then..."

He growls. An ugly, animalistic sound.

"I'm sorry, Matthias. They took her."

Chapter 75
Matthias

"Stop pacing and sit down. We're figuring this out," Dom snaps.

"No, we're *not* figuring this out. We haven't figured shit out. She's been gone for four hours, and we have *nothing.*"

I'm shaking with rage. It's easier to hold onto the anger than face the all-consuming fear. The worst thing that could've happened to my sweet girl has happened, and we're empty-handed.

"Matthias, it's only been four hours. These things take time. We're working on it," he exhales like I'm being a burden.

"You don't even fucking care!" I yell.

His calm, detached tone is the last straw.

I get in his face and shove him. His eyes flash. Finally, a fucking reaction. He's been a cold, calculated bastard this whole time, and it's driving me insane. He should care. It's *Margot.*

"You know that's not true," he growls. "I'm staying level-headed, so someone in this room can make decisions. Unlike *you.*"

He shoves me back.

"Fuck you! This is your fucking fault! If you hadn't called with bullshit, I wouldn't have left her. She'd be safe beside me!"

"No. It's your fault. *You* left her. *You* walked away. It was *your* duty to protect her. Do you even care–"

I don't let him finish.

I roar and lunge. He sees it coming, but I'm faster and angrier. I slam my fist into his jaw. He reels back, winding up to hit me.

"Enough!" Roman's voice breaks through the room as he grabs me. Bash grabs Dom, and pulls him back just as hard.

"Matthias, we're doing what we can. Dom, give a shit. This is Margot. And this is both of your faults." Roman doesn't sugarcoat it. His voice is harsh. Barely controlled fury. "Dom, you shouldn't have called unless it was urgent. You knew he'd answer. We always pick up for each other. Matthias, you walked away. You left her. You know better. And you're furious at yourself for it. Don't take it out on each other."

We stand in silence, chest to chest, breathing like animals.

Dom slowly holds out a hand.

"I'm sorry. I do care. She's family now. I feel like shit for calling. I just wanted to give you a heads-up. Getting her back is my top priority."

I look him in the eyes and take his hand. We shake then step back.

"Roman's right. I'm fucking furious at myself. If I hadn't left her, she'd be safe. It was stupid, and now she's the one paying for it." My voice cracks. "I broke my promise. I swore I'd protect her. And the first time we go out, I leave her. And now she's gone. I'll never forgive myself."

Silence.

No one argues. No one defends me.

Because it's true.

"Dom..." I whisper. "What are they doing to her right now?"

He looks at me, and something breaks in his expression. I've never seen that kind of sorrow in his eyes.

"If they used a basic sedative, it'll be wearing off any minute. She'll be held somewhere overnight. It won't be clean. The Bratva doesn't care about comfort. If it were winter, she'd risk hypothermia." He pauses.

She's probably so scared.

My chest tightens.

"Tomorrow or Monday, Viktor will meet with her. He'll demand answers. What she knows, who she told, where his men are. It's in her best interest to tell him that she's yours. That she's protected by the Syndicate. Maybe it buys her time. But even if he believes her, it won't be enough."

He meets my eyes.

"When we get her back... she won't be the same. They don't have a line, Matthias. They won't be kind."

My heart shatters.

My girl.

My sweet, beautiful girl.

She doesn't deserve this. No one does.

I would take every second of her pain if I could.

I whisper a prayer to a God I don't know. *Spare her. Please.*

We sit in silence.

Hearing it out loud makes it real. Too real.

Dom clears his throat. "Bash. Anything on the men who took her?"

Good. Back to business.

Sitting in grief won't find her.

Bash sighs. "They faced away from the cameras the whole time. The only way I knew it was Bratva was from the tattoos. I followed their car through street cams, but they turned down alleys with no coverage. I lost them. Their plates were fake."

His voice is heavy. He's taking this hard. Since learning how I got her, he's taken on a quiet, protective role. Like a brother.

"Keep digging," Dom orders. Then he turns to Roman. "Anything from the guy you interrogated?"

"No." Roman's jaw clenches. "He didn't know who called in the bounty. He didn't even know we were connected to her."

"Can you get more out of him?"

"No." He doesn't flinch. "I killed him. He started bragging, and I snapped. I strangled him with my bare hand." His fists tighten. His whole body shakes with fury. "He was filth. He was laughing at what they'll do to her. I couldn't let him keep breathing."

I nod. I understand.

We needed him alive. But I still get it.

Then, "I have something!" Bash exclaims.

We all snap to attention.

"I identified the man who cornered her in the hall. It's her boss from the shipping company. That's why she seemed to know him."

He pauses, typing.

"I have his current location."

I stand.

"Let's go."

Chapter 76
Margot

My head is pounding. My eyes feel heavy. I crack them open, then slam them shut as vertigo takes over.

Wait. What did I just see?

I open them again, slower this time, and blink against the blur.

This isn't our bedroom.

I manage three seconds before I lean over the side of the cot and throw up.

Again. And again.

Five full minutes of vomiting.

Once it's over, I breathe through the nausea and force myself to look around.

The room is small. Windowless. There's a single door across from me, with a window placed too high for me to see through. I'm lying on some shitty excuse for a cot, barely more than a slab of foam on metal. The floor's covered in grime. There's a metal toilet on the far wall. The room smells like metal and mildew.

Where the fuck am I?

Why am I in a cell?

Then it hits me.

The gala.

My boss.

The hallway.

The needle.

The men.

They have me.

The Bratva has me.

And Ronald. That bastard. He's the one who sold me out. My own boss.

Fuck. This is bad. This is so fucking bad.

I jump off the cot and rush toward the door. I trip on the hem of my dress but don't stop. I reach the handle and, of course, it's locked.

I whirl around to head back to the cot and trip again.

"Ugh, fuck this," I mutter.

I grab the bottom of the dress and rip off ten inches of fabric, freeing my legs. Then I yank the cloak from my shoulder, tearing it off completely. It'll have to serve as my blanket now.

My breathing is ragged. My head is spinning.

Whatever they injected me with must've been strong. My body's screaming to shut down. My limbs feel like concrete. My thoughts flicker and fade.

But I fight it. I can't sleep. I don't know what they'll do while I'm out. I have to stay awake. I have to.

My body doesn't listen.

But I'm not afraid. I know Matty's coming. He'll find me. He always does.

I let the darkness take me, whispering one promise to myself.

He'll save me.

He'll be here soon.

Chapter 77
Matthias

I watch Roman shimmy the lock like a professional, silent except for the soft click as it gives way. Ronald Ward's front door swings open. The cocky bastard didn't even lock the deadbolt.

It's just after three a.m. He'll be in bed.

Perfect.

I refused to wait. Grabbing him at night also lessens the chance of witnesses. And no one else is home. His wife left him and took the kids. Good. They deserve better than this piece of shit. Hopefully he has life insurance. They'll get it after tonight.

Bash showed us the floor plan before we left. His bedroom's upstairs. We creep up the stairs, and I'm both impressed and annoyed by how light on his feet Roman is.

Then I remember. He's the Syndicate enforcer. Of course, he's good at this.

We enter the bedroom and stop at the foot of his bed.

I'm shaking with fury at the sight of him sleeping soundly, while Margot is God-knows-where because of him.

Focus.

"Ronald Ward," Roman bellows. "Get the fuck up!"

We stay cloaked in darkness. He doesn't need to know who we are yet.

Not that it matters if he did. He'll be dead before the sun rises.

Ronald jolts upright, clutching the covers like they'll protect him.

They won't.

"Who... who are you? How did you get in?" His voice trembles.

"I'm Matthias Montclair."

Recognition hits him fast. His eyes widen, then his brows furrow. Confusion flickers across his face.

He knows the name. From Syndicate Enterprises. Not the real Syndicate.

For the first time, I regret turning our name from crime lords into businessmen.

"Mr. Montclair, what are you doing here?"

"And this is my brother, Roman Montclair."

At Roman's name, he pales. I guess he knows of him from his Bratva connections.

"Your... brother?" His voice cracks. "Take whatever you want."

Roman growls, "We want *you.*"

"Please. I didn't do anything. I don't know anything!"

I step into the light.

"I think you know exactly what you did."

His eyes widen again.

"You're the one who was with Margot." He whispers, white as a ghost.

"She's mine," I say softly. Calmly. Steadily. "She's my everything. And you took her from me."

I get closer. Roman moves around the other side of the bed, boxing him in.

"Please. I didn't know she was connected to the Syndicate. I didn't know!"

"You took my woman and handed her over to murderers. Rapists. How much did you get for her?"

"I didn't know–"

"*How much?*"

His voice shakes. "Fifty thousand."

He actually has the nerve to look ashamed.

"I need the money. I had a few bad runs... I thought I'd get lucky again."

He sold my sweet girl to feed his gambling addiction.

I roar an inhuman sound and launch myself on him.

"You fucking hit my Margot." My voice cracks on her name.

My fists crash into his face. Over and over. I hear a *pop,* then a *crunch.* Blood sprays on the bed. His teeth shatter under my knuckles. I don't stop. Not even after he does.

Eventually, Roman grips my shoulder.

"We need him alive. For now."

Reluctantly, I pull back. Roman slings a limp Roland over his shoulder like a sack of garbage and leaves the room. As I follow, I look down at myself.

My white dress shirt is soaked red. As well as my knucks and all visible skin. I look like a monster.

It reflects the beast within.

...

We're in a Syndicate warehouse.

Ronald's wrists are chained to the ceiling. His body hangs limp and wrecked. He looks just as pathetic as he is.

Roman splashes cold water on him.

He sputters awake, eyes darting around the room.

"Ready to talk?" Roman asks with a grin.

"Yes. I'll tell you everything if you let me go."

Coward.

Not even trying to hold out. Greater men have suffered in here for days before breaking.

Roman tilts his head. "What would you trade your life for? Would you give us your wife and kids?"

"Yes! You can have them!" The bastard doesn't even hesitate.

Roman sneers. "You're lower than filth. Now, you're going to answer some questions."

He nods frantically. "Anything."

"What do you know about the Koschei Group?"

I drift behind him and scan the tools on the table.

"They're a front for the Bratva," he blurts. "They use Northern Hemisphere Cargo to smuggle whatever they're moving. Pay us big money to look the other way."

"Us or you?" Roman demands.

"Me." He whispers in shame.

"What product are they moving?"

"I don't know. They give me the container numbers, and I arrange the pickups. We drop them at lot X in the northern dock, and the money shows up."

Roman's voice turns friendly. "Where's the money?"

"I lost it. Cards. I've had some bad luck, bad hands. You know how it is."

We both stare.

"No," I growl. *"I don't"*

Roman chuckles. The bastard doesn't even notice it's fake.

"That's why you sold out my Margot." I'm behind him now, whispering in his ear.

I light the blowtorch and hold it just shy of his spine.

He starts shaking.

"No... Yes. But I didn't know–"

The flame licks his skin.

He screams, but I don't stop until I'm satisfied.

Roman continues the interrogation. His voice remains smoother than honey.

"How much have they been paying?"

"Ten grand per shipment. Every other Saturday. It's been about a year."

"How'd it start?"

"A Russian guy approached me. I declined at first, but he knew about my debt. He raised his offer. I needed the money. My wife had just left me. I thought I could win her back."

I lean in and let the heat brush over his fresh burn.

Bullshit. He never said no.

"But she didn't come back, did she?" Roman mocks.

He shakes his head. "No."

"And what about Margot Peterson?"

He stiffens.

"She found the holes in the paperwork. She dug into the Koschei Group and realized it doesn't exist. She threatened to go to the authorities. I panicked and told my contact. He said to set up a meeting and let him know when."

He swallows.

"I set up coffee with her, but she didn't show. He had men waiting and... they didn't come back. He was furious. Cut my pay. Said to find her."

My fists curl.

"I started looking for her. Went to her house. Asked neighbors. Nothing. More men disappeared. He put a bounty on her. Then last night at the gala, I saw her. I called him immediately. I waited until I could get her alone. Led her to the exit."

He looks down.

"They took her. He paid me. I went home."

And Margot didn't.

"Who's your contact?"

"I don't know his name. He goes by Koschei. I have a burner phone. I keep it in my nightstand. There's no password. You can have it."

Roman's jaw tightens.

"What are they doing to her?"

"I don't know. They just said... she wouldn't be a problem anymore." He pauses. "And that she'd pay for his men."

I roar and burn his back again.

His screams fill the room.

"Please! I swear I don't know anything else!"

I circle around to face him.

"Is that everything?"

"Yes," he sobs. "Please. Let me go."

"Good."

I raise the torch and begin writing.

M

A

R

G

O

T

Burned into his chest.

His howls echo, but I don't stop.

"Now that you've punished me, you'll let me go?" He begs.

Roman steps forward.

"No, you piece of shit. You hurt Margot. You fucking *sold* her."

He punches the center of the burn. I hear ribs snap.

Roman walks behind him and returns with a tub of gasoline. Ronald sees it and starts begging again. Sobbing. Roman pours it over him like a baptism.

"I figured this is your new M.O. Do the honors." He nods.

I step forward, inches from Ronald's face.

And inhale the pungent smell of gasoline.

A scent I've come to love when it's turning to ash those who stand between me and Margot.

"Enjoy hell."

I bring the torch to his face and squeeze the trigger.

Flames engulf him.

His screams fill the warehouse.

But they don't soothe me.

Not yet.

Not until Margot is back in my arms.

I'm coming, sweetheart.

I promise.

Chapter 78
Margot

The sound of the door creaking open jolts me awake, but I don't move. I keep my eyes shut and focus on breathing evenly. If they think I'm asleep, I might catch them off guard.

I hear heavy footsteps approaching. The second he's beside the cot, I strike, jamming my elbow into his gut. He doubles over with a Russian curse, and I bolt. I don't know where I'm going, but I know one thing.

I've been here too long. I have to get out.

I hit the hallway at full speed, the darkness pressing in as I run. I push myself harder, faster. Adrenaline drowns the ache in my underused muscles. I hear him behind me, gaining ground. At the end of the hall, I take a sharp turn and pray it's the right way. I see it, an ascending staircase. I must be in a basement. *No windows, no light, that tracks.*

I make it two steps before he yanks me back by my hair.

"Stupid girl. You have nowhere to run," he spits in my ear as he hauls me down.

Pain explodes across my scalp and tears burn behind my eyes, but I won't let him see them. I won't let him win.

He spins me to face him and slaps me so hard I hit the floor. "Try that again, and it'll be worse," he snarls.

He drags me by my hair and forces me up the stairs on all fours. My hands scramble to keep pace, so I don't get slammed against the steps. The door at the top opens and light pours in, blinding me. I squint, blinking fast. I've been in the dark too long, at least a full day. Maybe more.

We move through the house, and when my vision adjusts, I'm stunned.

This isn't a shack.

It's a mansion.

A gaudy, overdone mansion, like somebody bought every expensive item they could find and threw them all together without a second thought.

Oil paintings hang beside photographs of street art. The furniture clashes with the rugs, which clash with the wallpaper. It's messy. Flashy. Tacky. Ugly. The Bratva has no taste.

He pulls me up another flight of stairs and down another hallway. We stop at a door, and he knocks.

I finally take a good look at him. He's more put together than the other Bratva goons I've encountered. For one, he's bathed recently. He's in a leather jacket and has all his limbs intact. He must outrank the others.

A muffled Russian command comes from inside, and we're let in.

The office matches the rest of the house in its hideousness. An ornate Persian rug sits under an ugly, modern metal desk. Nothing matches. It's disgusting.

Behind the desk sits a man old enough to be my father. His full head of hair, expensive suit, and friendly smile almost make him look distinguished.

Almost.

But I know better.

"Hello, Margot Peterson. I'm Viktor. Welcome to my home. I apologize for the method of your travel. I hope the accommodations have been acceptable," he says in a smooth accent.

"I wasn't a fan of the method, seeing as you *kidnapped* and *drugged* me," I reply, keeping my tone light. Non-confrontational.

"I do apologize. My men weren't supposed to harm you. Those who did will be punished accordingly. Why don't you take a seat." I don't believe him.

He gestures to the leather chairs in front of his desk.

I hesitate, and the man beside me shoves me forward.

Viktor shoots him a glare, but it's gone in a blink.

I sit.

He smiles again. "You've been difficult to find, Miss Peterson. All I've wanted is a simple conversation. There've been odd things happening around you."

Bullshit he just wanted to talk.

"I'm not sure what you mean." I keep my voice even. Play dumb. That's my move.

"It came to my attention that you stumbled onto some shipments you shouldn't have. You know what they say, 'curiosity killed the cat.' I don't think you have a death wish, so I figured I owed you a talk."

"'But satisfaction brought it back,'" I shoot back.

He blinks. "Excuse me?"

"That's the full saying. Most people don't know it. It means curiosity is risky, but having the answer makes it worth it." I smirk, just a little. One point for me.

"Clever. You remind me of my daughter, Katerina." He raises a brow. "Has your snooping been worth it, considering it landed you here? Considering you've been in hiding for months?"

Point revoked.

"Where have you been? You vanished from work and left your home. My men stopped by multiple times to retrieve you. Some never came back. Then, out of nowhere, you appear at a gala far above your pay grade. It's puzzling."

"I've been here and there. I moved," I say vaguely.

"Hmm. Well, back to the matter at hand. You stuck your nose where it didn't belong and caused us all kinds of trouble. What exactly did you find?"

"I don't know what you're talking about."

"Don't play dumb. It doesn't suit someone as intelligent as yourself. What did you uncover about the Koschei Group and the shipments coming through your company?" His smile falters for a second.

"All I saw were some shipments at weird hours without full invoices. I looked into the company, and they didn't seem real. I told my boss."

"Who else?"

"No one." I lie. The Syndicate knows.

"It would be unwise to lie to me. Did you go to the authorities?"

"No! I swear I didn't." At least that's true.

"Hmm. I believe you. Now tell me, what happened to my men? The ones who went looking for you? Two disappeared. Then three more. That's a problem."

"I have no idea." Another lie.

He glares. "What did I say about lying? Where are they?"

"I really don't know. Maybe they ran away. I hope you find them." I try to come across as innocent.

"WHERE ARE MY MEN?" he shouts.

"WHY DON'T YOU ASK MATTHIAS AND ROMAN MONTCLAIR!" I shout back.

So much for innocent.

He freezes. Shock, then suspicion overtake his expression.

"What do you know about them?"

"I know you pissed them off by taking me."

"You don't have a connection to the Syndicate. We researched you. You're lying," he hisses, but there's unease in his eyes.

"I'm Matthias Montclair's fiancée."

His gaze flicks to my bare ring finger, then back to my eyes and he raises a brow.

"The ring didn't go with my gown."

"That's your story? The mafia CEO has chosen to marry the finance girl and is sending the Syndicate to rescue her?" His voice drips with disbelief, but I see it. I see his worry.

"It's the truth. They saved me from the attackers."

"Take her back to her cell," he snaps. "She can come out when she's ready to be honest. And if that doesn't work... maybe she needs a visit to the docks." His face and voice are so dark, I don't even recognize the handsome man from minutes ago.

The mention of the 'docks' makes my blood run cold. I don't know what goes on there, but I know I don't want to find out.

"It has *not* been a pleasure meeting you," I spit over my shoulder as I'm dragged away.

He chuckles darkly.

I send up a silent prayer.

Please, let my bluff be true.

Please, come for me, Matty.

Chapter 79
Matthias

I walk into my office, and Benny perks up. He trots over to meet me at the door, head craning to look past me searching for Margot. Nose lifted, he sniffs the air, trying to catch her scent.

But he won't.

She's not here.

She hasn't been here for days.

It's been so long, I can't even smell her on our sheets anymore. I stopped visiting our room shortly after. I hadn't been sleeping there anyway. I couldn't stand lying there, not knowing what she's enduring, only knowing it's bad.

Benny lets out a low whine. His tail drops as he slinks back to his bed and curls into a tight ball. He's been just as wrecked by her disappearance. He refuses to sleep alone. He stays in my office with me, at my feet.

Neither of us can stand the silence.

The house is too quiet without her. It used to echo with her laughter. Loud, wild, and free. The kind that filled a room and pulled you in, whether you wanted to be a part of it or not. She'd throw her head back with bright eyes and body shaking.

I could never stop myself from joining in. Even when I didn't get the joke. Even when I was pissed. I'd end up laughing too. Just because she was.

Now there's nothing. No sound. No warmth. No security feed to check. I can't see her. I can't hear her. I don't even have that.

Just silence.

And I swear to God, I'd burn the world down just to hear the sound again.

I can hardly look at him. His eyes are too knowing, too full of a grief I caused. He misses her. I can see it. I can feel it. If he knew who took her, he'd tear me apart. I'll let him if...

Don't go there.

Some nights, I pray she's no longer suffering.

And then I hate myself for it.

Because the only fate worse than her suffering, is a world without her in it.

If she's gone, I won't stay.

I can't.

The thought of what they could be doing to her makes me physically ill.

My poor girl.

My sweet, brave girl.

I glance at the whiskey on my shelf, my fingers twitching toward the decanter. But I turn away.

If she doesn't get to dull her pain, then I don't get to either.

When we get her back, I don't know how I'll ever earn her forgiveness. I'll spend the rest of my life on my knees, begging. Groveling. Worshipping the ground she walks on, and still, it won't be enough.

Tomorrow is Saturday.

A full week since she vanished.

A week of madness.

A week without sleep. Without food.

Everything I eat comes right back up. I stopped trying days ago.

Roman's been on a warpath, tearing through every Bratva member he can find. But there haven't been any in our territory. I suspect Margot told them who she's connect to, told them about us. And now they're lying low.

Part of me hopes that means they're keeping her alive. That they haven't hurt her. But I know better than to hope.

Dom mobilized every soldier we have. When we find her, we're sending everyone, no hesitation, no holding back.

Her rescue is the only priority. All other Syndicate activity has been frozen.

That's never happened before.

It means something.

It means Dom finally sees her as one of us. *As family.*

Bash has been glued to his screens, digging into every inch of Bratva activity. We've uncovered a lot, but we're ignoring anything that doesn't lead to Margot. I don't care what's being smuggled. I don't care about business.

I only care about one thing.

Margot.

RING!

The sudden blare of my phone snaps me out of my thoughts.

Sebastian.

My heart stops as I snatch the phone.

Before I can say a word, he speaks, fast and breathless.

"I found her. We're heading your way."

For the first time in a week, I can breathe.

Relief crashes over me like a wave.

Hold on, sweetheart. I'm coming for you.

Chapter 80
Margot

The door to my cell creaks open, but I don't even lift my head to see who it is. It can't be good, and I don't have the energy to care.

I've refused every meal they've brought me. Partly out of fear of being drugged again, but mostly out of spite. It's the only thing I can control. The only way I can defy them and fight back.

They don't care. But still, I rebel.

The only problem? I'm weak. So weak.

I don't know how long it's been since I ate at the gala. The days have blurred together. I'm lost to the darkness. With no windows, time doesn't exist.

At first, I tried to keep track, sleeping in intervals, listening to my body's circadian rhythm. But now, I can barely stay awake long enough to form coherent thoughts. I sleep most of the time. It's easier.

I thought I knew what it meant to be kidnapped when Matty took me.

I thought I knew fear.

But now I understand, I was never really his prisoner. And he never truly scared me.

Back then, I was in silks and satins, falling in love in a gilded cage. Now I'm wasting away in a concrete cell.

I've been dragged by my hair. Slapped. Kicked. Punched. I've been hauled in front of Viktor more times than I care to count.

At first, I fought. Even knowing I couldn't escape, I still fought.

Even when it ended in bruises.

Even when it left me hurting.

But eventually, I ran out of fight.

Ran out of strength.

Ran out of hope.

Now, I just exist. Succumbed to my captivity. A shell. A shadow.

Every time I faced Viktor, I gave him the same answers. But last time, he said something that struck.

"If Montclair cares so much, why hasn't he come for you yet?"

That hit me harder than any punch.

Why hasn't he come?

Maybe he's still looking.

Maybe you're hard to find.

But he knows who took me. Knows what they are.

Could I really be this impossible to track down?

Or did he cut his losses?

No. He loves you. He's coming. You just have to believe.

A voice I recognize breaks through my spiral. The same man who dragged me upstairs on the first day.

"Tonight, you go to the docks. The Pakhan has no more use of you, but you must be punished for the men we lost. A shipment arrives tonight. You will join it. Be grateful he has shown mercy and spared you."

I stare at the wall, unmoving. Unwilling to give him the satisfaction of a response.

He waits. Then huffs and storms out, slamming the door behind him.

Silence returns.

But his words linger.

The docks.

I know whatever happens there will be worse than this.

Worse than hunger.

Worse than beatings.

Worse than silence.

I've grown numb in this cell, learned how to endure. But where they're sending me... I know it won't offer that comfort.

I wonder what hell waits on the other side.

Matty will save you. Just hold on a little longer.

But even as my inner voice echoes through my mind, I don't believe it anymore.

If he were coming, he'd be here by now.

I've lost hope.

Lost hope in him.

And now... it's too late.

When I get to the docks, everything will change.

I can feel it in my bones.

The nightmare they have waiting for me, I don't know if I'll survive it.

Or if I'll even want to.

...

I jolt awake. My arms give out beneath me as I try to push myself up. I groan, dazed and dizzy. I blink fast, trying to understand what woke me.

There's no one in my cell.

Then I hear it.

Commotion upstairs.

A loud *boom* rattles the floor.

Russian shouts. Chaos ensues. And then, gunshots.

Beautiful, blessed gunshots.

For the first time in forever, I feel something close to joy.

My eyes try to form tears, but I'm too dehydrated. My body has nothing left to give. Even the headache that comes doesn't register.

I try to sit up again, but I can't. My body won't cooperate.

That's okay. He's strong enough for both of you.

I know it's him.

I know he's here.

I can feel him.

Like my heart knows its other half is near.

He's here.

He kept his promise.

I feel myself slipping, darkness tugging me under.

But I'm not afraid.

Because this time, as I fall asleep, I know he'll be here when I wake up.

Chapter 81
Matthias

BOOM!

The front gate explodes, blasting open a path to Viktor Sokolov's estate. Bombs are one of Bash's specialties. I don't know where he learned it. I don't ask questions I don't want the answers to. All I know is, I've never been more grateful for one of his odd hobbies.

BOOM!

A second blast tears through the front door. Dom leads the charge, abandoning all stealth now that our cover's blown. Fifty Syndicate men flood through the front while another fifty, led by Roman, enter from the back, as Bash's third bomb clears that entrance.

Bash and I bring up the rear, guns raised, moving fast down the hallway.

A Russian rounds the corner. Without any hesitation, I fire a headshot.

Down he goes.

Dom wants to minimize casualties. Says we need to preserve our relationship with the Bratva as much as possible. That we need to avoid a war.

That's fine.

But if anyone gets between me and Margot, they're dead.

Even though Bash and I don't usually fight on the front line, we're just as trained. And there was no chance in hell we were sitting this one out.

We move fast, crouching low. Bash got us the floor plan, so we know the layout. We're betting she's in the basement. I doubt she got the luxury of a guest room.

I force myself not to think about what I'll find down there. Not yet. First, I have to get to her.

A Russian ambushes us, grabbing Bash in a chokehold. Bash doesn't miss a beat. He flips the guy over his shoulder and takes him down like it's nothing. Pressure points, or some ninja shit knocks him out cold.

We leave him. Bash's apparently honoring Dom's 'don't kill unless necessary' order. I'm not sure I would've.

Finally, we reach the basement door, but it flies open. Another man lunges at us. Bash moves to take him, and I push past them.

"I'm going down. Hold the stairs," I snap. "Don't let anyone follow. I'll take care of whoever's left down here."

I charge down the steps.

The basement splits. Left or right.

I pause for half a second.

Then go left.

My gut never lies about her.

Doors line the hallway, each with a tiny, grimy window.

The first room: a filthy cot, a metal toilet, and floors stained with God-knows-what. My stomach twists. These are cells. This is where they've kept her.

Second room: empty.

Third: a man. *Not my problem.*

Fourth: empty.

Fifth: my heart stops.

She's curled on the cot in fetal position. Her back to the door.

Brown curls, once bouncy and vibrant, now lie limp and lifeless. The once jade dress from the gala is now ripped, stained, and barely clinging to her frail frame. Her skin, once glowing, is now sickly pale.

Margot.

Relief surges through me, slamming into my chest like a wrecking ball.

She's here.

After seven goddamn days, she's here.

I try the handle, and it gives. I fling the door and let it hang open. These doors lock automatically. I won't let it trap us.

I step inside.

Relief morphs into heartbreak.

She's thin, too thin. Like she hasn't eaten once. Her curves are gone. Her bones are visible beneath her grimy skin. Bruises mark her face, arms, and neck. Cuts and filth do too. Bags hang under her eyes so dark they match the bruises.

My chest aches. My girl, my spitfire, lies broken.

I move toward her but freeze.

She hasn't moved.

She should have heard me.

She should have stirred.

But she remains perfectly still.

Fear. Pure, blinding fear rips through me.

She's just unconscious.

She has to be.

Then, her chest rises. Barely.

She's breathing.

Relief rushes in again.

I drop to my knees and gently cup her cheek. My fingers graze a lock of her hair. It doesn't even bounce, too stiff with grease and dirt.

I shake her shoulder carefully, terrified she'll break under my touch.

"Sweetheart, it's me," I whisper. "Please wake up. Please open those beautiful eyes."

She stirs.

Her lashes flutter.

Then, those eyes find me. Dazed and distant, but there.

"Matty?" Her voice is hoarse, barely audible.

But it's her. It's really her.

Tears sting my eyes.

I lift her into my arms as gently as I can. She's too light. Too frail. A feather in my arm. I clutch her tightly. Too tightly.

I realize it must be painful for her, so I let go a little.

"No." She whispers.

I freeze as my heart shatters.

She doesn't want me to hold her.

I start to lay her back on the cot, but she lets out a weak sound of protest and wiggles closer.

My breath catches.

She meant 'no, don't let go.'

I pull her back to me, tighter than before. I bury my face into the crook of her neck. Her sweet scent is gone, replaced by dirt and blood and fear, but it's still her. It's still my Margot.

She lets me hold her.

And I cry. One tear. Then another.

I glance down. Her eyes are slipping closed again.

She's losing consciousness. My heart squeezes. She's been through too much.

I don't know everything they did to her, but I will. I'll have to ask. One day. And when I do, it'll gut me.

"Thank you," she murmurs.

My throat tightens.

Thank you?

No. I don't deserve her gratitude. I don't deserve anything from her. I don't deserve her.

I failed her.

I left. And that's why she was taken. That's why she suffered.

I will spend the rest of my days trying to earn her forgiveness. And still, it won't be enough.

We wait in silence. Me holding her, her body soft against mine, until the gunfire ceases.

Bash appears in the doorway.

"We're clear. Let's go. We–" He stops when he sees her. His eyes well up as he lets out a gasp of horror. "Matthias... is she...?"

I shake my head. "She's alive."

He exhales. "Thank God. She's going to be okay. But we have to go now, before Viktor gets back."

We waited until the house was empty. His wife is dead, his daughter is at college, and his son lives elsewhere. Only guards were home.

It's one thing to rescue my woman. It's another to storm in while Viktor's there. That would be war.

Dom's betting everything on framing this as a retrieval of Syndicate personnel. A rescue, not an attack.

Bash turns and disappears down the hall.

I rise with Margot in my arms. She's light enough to carry one-handed, but I cradle her with both. One hand on her back. One pressing her head to my heart.

Her soft breaths warm my chest. I need it to know she's still with me.

We exit the basement. For the first time, I take in the house.

It's hideous. Tacky as hell. It looks like someone vomited money all over it. I'd expect nothing less from Viktor.

I'm glad to leave it behind.

The whole ride, I don't let go of her.

I can't.

I won't.

She's safe now.

She's coming home.

And I will never let her go again.

Chapter 82
Margot

Jostling wakes me up. Panic claws at me until I hear a voice I never thought I'd hear again.

"It's okay, sweetheart. It's just me, your Matty. We're home." His voice cracks.

"Hey," I whisper, giving him the softest smile I can manage, and nestle into his chest. He lets out a choked sound and tightens his hold on me.

The door opens, and relief fills me as my eyes land on the mansion.

Our mansion.

This is real. I'm really home.

Inside, the sound of claws clacking against marble echoes through the house. Benny barrels around the corner, tries to stop, but skids straight into the wall.

I let out a breathy laugh.

Light. I feel light for the first time in forever.

"Hey, buddy," I say, and he's by my side in a heartbeat.

Matty lowers, still cradling me, so Benny can sniff me over. He starts at head, working his way down to my toes. I must reek, but he doesn't seem to care. He circles around us, inspecting every inch of me, and finally settles with his head on my lap.

I lift a shaky hand and place it on his head. He closes his eyes contently.

"He's been waiting for you," Matty murmurs. "Checked the door every time it opened. He was just as destroyed as I was. We kept each other company, but... nothing filled the void."

"You were destroyed?" My voice is barely a whisper. I'm not even sure he hears it.

But after a few moments, I look up and see his eyes brimmed with tears.

"Margot... my sweet girl. You were gone. *Taken.* Because of me. I knew you were suffering. I couldn't eat. Couldn't sleep. I was a wreck. All we did was search. Every second you were gone we were looking for you. I'm sorry it took so long. I'm sorry they took you. I'm so fucking sorry."

"We?" I ask.

"My brothers and I. The whole fucking Syndicate."

Benny's low whine interrupts us, and Matty stands.

"Let's get you in bed. The doctor's on his way."

"No. Shower first." I whisper. "Please."

I can't relax. Not until I wash all of it away. I need to feel clean, human.

Matty hesitates, but when he meets my eyes, he sighs and nods. He heads for our bathroom.

He shuts Benny out, but my poor puppy lets out a whimper and scratches the door.

Matty opens the door wide enough to tell him, "Stand guard." I laugh at the absurdity, until Benny actually does, sitting tall and alert, watching the hallway like a soldier.

Matty carries me into the bathroom and lowers me gently on the rug, leaning against the tub.

He undresses quickly, his tactical gear off in seconds, and I can't help but notice how good he looks in it. Even after everything, I still see him. Still want him.

He kneels and carefully helps me out of the shredded, ruined gown. I stare brokenheartedly at it on the floor. It was once a symbol of our freedom, our magic night. Now it's just a reminder of everything we lost.

Matty's eyes scan me, but there's no lust in them. Only sorrow.

I glance down at myself. My body is a map of damages. Bruises. Dried blood. Dirt. Pale, thin, wasted skin. My bones jut where curves used to be.

"Oh, my sweet girl. I'm so, so sorry." He whispers, lost in his thoughts.

I don't respond. Not because I'm angry, but because I know anything I say will be brushed off. He needs to see I don't blame him.

"Can you stand, sweetheart?" he asks.

I try, but my legs buckle instantly.

He catches me. "Okay. I'm going to hold you in the shower. You won't have to stand at all. Does that work?"

I nod.

He carries me into the shower cradled in his arms and turns on the water. He waits until it's warm before stepping under the spray.

With one arm wrapped tightly around me, he detaches the sprayer with the other and rinses me. Then he replaces the sprayer with my shampoo and pours a generous amount on my head. He massages my hair, carefully working it into my scalp. I almost drift off under the warmth of his touch.

He rinses and repeats, then conditions just as I taught him.

He lathers a loofah and begins to wash my body, slowly and tenderly.

"Again," I murmur when he stops.

"Of course, sweetheart." He kisses the top of my head and begins again. And again. And again.

On what must be the sixth round, I give him a small nod.

I finally feel clean.

He steps out, dries me off, and dresses me in a pair of his boxer briefs. They hang loosely on my hips, and I hear him sigh in defeat.

He wraps me in his thick robe and lays me on his side of the bed.

After dressing quickly, he returns to my side.

"What do you need? What can I get you? The doctor will be here soon."

I pat the mattress beside me.

He climbs in without hesitation and pulls me into his lap.

I fall asleep in his arms.

...

The door opens, waking me.

Matty's voice is soft as he whispers in my ear, "The doctor's here, sweetheart."

A throat clearing draws my gaze. An older man with white hair and kind eyes steps into the room.

"Hello, Margot. I'm Dr. Anderson. I'm the doctor for the Syndicate. I'm here to check you over." His voice is full of warmth. I instantly trust him.

An idea pops into my head. I glance at his ring finger. Empty.

Maybe he and Dotty would hit it off...

"Hi," I greet softly.

"I briefed him on what I knew," Matty says. "We don't know what she's been through. She'll tell us when she's ready. I want every inch of her examined. I want her healthy. Healed."

"Matthias, boy, I've been doing this longer than you've been alive," Dr. Anderson replies, gently but firmly. "Now step out so I can examine her."

"No!" We say in unison.

My heart races. He can't leave.

I just got him back.

If he goes... I won't be safe.

"I won't leave her side," Matty says, steel in his voice.

"You don't want to hear this conversation," the doctor warns. Then he turns to me. "Margot, if you'd prefer privacy, I'll make him leave. Your comfort is my priority."

"No. Please don't make him go. I need him. He keeps me safe," I plead.

"Some exams will be intrusive," he warns. "You'll need to be honest. If there's anything–"

"No one raped me," I whisper.

Matty exhales. "Oh, thank fuck."

He presses a firm kiss to my hair and pulls me in closer.

"Matty, please don't leave me." I beg.

"Never, sweetheart. I'm never leaving you again. Fucking never."

The exam is thorough. The results are just as I expected.

Everything will heal. I'll be fine.

But I know Matty needed to hear it from a professional. He needed that confirmation.

He only lets go of me when absolutely necessary and picks me back up the second he can.

"When's the last time you ate, dear?" Dr. Anderson asks.

"The gala," I admit.

"Fuck! That long ago? It's been a week!" Matty curses.

"A week?" I blink. I hadn't realized.

"Yes, sweetheart. It's Saturday." He's right. That explains why I'm so weak.

"They starved you," he growls.

"No. They gave me food. One meal a day. I just refused to eat. It was all I could do to fight." At the time, it felt brave. Now it feels foolish.

"My stubborn girl," he murmurs with a slight upturn of his lips. It's the closest thing to a smile I've seen from him since the gala. "Even in hell, you're still a spitfire. I love you, sweetheart."

"I love you too," I whisper back.

He exhales and kisses my hair again, resting his lips there like a promise.

"Start her off with crackers and electrolytes," Dr. Anderson says. "We'll use an IV to start hydration. Food too fast could shock her system. She'll gain the weight back in four to six weeks. Patience, it's a slow road."

"I understand. Leave the list with Dotty," Matty says.

"You'll be okay, dear," Dr. Anderson tells me after he hooks up the IV. Matty flinched when the needle was inserted in me. "Call me if you need anything." Then he leaves.

I let myself drift off again, but Matty gently shakes me.

"Sweetheart, do you think you can eat some crackers before you doze off?"

I shake my head. Even the thought of food makes me nauseous.

"Okay, but next time you wake up, you need to eat a little something. You'll feel better after the fluids replenish you."

"Please don't leave," I murmur.

"Never. I swear to you, Margot. Never again."

His arms wrap tighter around me.

And I fall asleep in the safest place in the world.

Chapter 83
Matthias

My phone vibrates, pulling my attention from Margot curled next to me in our bed.

I've been watching her sleep for hours. She looks so serene, so peaceful, like none of it ever happened. I'm beyond relieved she can even sleep after the week she's had.

Since I got her back, I haven't been able to tear my eyes from her. I can't put space between us, and I know she feels the same. She hasn't let me leave her side. This shared need, this tether between us... it gives me hope. Maybe she doesn't hate me. Maybe she'll forgive me. I don't deserve her love anymore, I don't deserve *her*, but I'll spend every second proving how sorry I am. Proving how much I love her.

When she told the doctor she wasn't safe without me in the room, it broke me.

Because I want to be that for her, be her safety. Her sanctuary.

But it also gutted me.

Because she only felt safe with me after a week of hell without me.

The phone buzzes again. I grab it quickly, not wanting to wake her.

Dom.

I answer but stay silent. My sweet girl is asleep. I'm not breaking the quiet for him.

"Matthias, we're in your office. We figured you wouldn't want to leave your house for this meeting. Come downstairs." Dom says it like he's doing me a favor

He's lost his goddamn mind if he thinks I'm leaving this bed.

"No. Go away. I'm not leaving her side," I whisper-yell.

"Matthias, get your ass down here. We need to debrief. I'm meeting with Viktor tomorrow."

That's the only thing he could've said to make me move.

"Go get Benny and meet me upstairs."

"Who the fuck is Benny?"

"My dog. Dotty will bring you to him."

"Fuck. Fine. I'm not holding this meeting in your bedroom with Margot in there. She doesn't get to hear Syndicate issues."

"You bet your ass you're not coming into our bedroom," I growl. "Especially not while she's sleeping."

"Fine. We'll grab the dog and meet you upstairs," he mutters, then hangs up.

We. Of course they're all here.

I should be more grateful. They spent the past week doing everything they could to get her back. But I'm not. I don't want anything Syndicate-related near her ever again.

I hear Benny's footsteps approaching and sigh as I slip from bed, careful not to wake her.

I open the door to see Benny alert and ready, and Dom holding his bed with a scowl.

"When the fuck did you get this monster? I didn't even know you liked dogs."

"Who doesn't like dogs? And don't call him a monster. He's just a puppy."

Dom snorts while I take Benny's bed and set it up beside Margot.

"Watch her," I tell him. Benny sits like a sentry, eyes locked on the door.

I leave the room but crack the door just enough to keep her in view. I turn to face my three brothers.

"Alright. What's going on?"

"You're kidding, right?" Dom snaps. "We're not doing this in a hallway."

He wouldn't get it. Dom doesn't have a heart to give someone. He's a frigid bastard with no emotions.

"Leave him alone," Roman says, surprisingly the voice of reason. "They've been through hell. Let's just get started."

I blink. Empathy is a strange look on Roman.

Dom rolls his eyes but starts, "I'm meeting with Viktor to explain that today's break-in was a rescue mission. That Margot is a Montclair woman and therefore off limits. We're not escalating this to a war. Viktor didn't know. But I need to know what she told him. How much he knows. We'll be backing off tracking shipments for now. Peace takes priority."

I glance through the crack in the door again. Margot's still sleeping. I exhale and close it a bit more.

"I'll keep looking," Bash chimes in. "But nothing that can be traced."

Dom nods. "Roman?"

"I'll only touch Bratva men who cross into our territory. It's still Syndicate law, even during peace."

Dom turns to me.

"No," I say immediately. "I'm not forcing her to relive what happened. We know what we need to know. They took her. They hurt her. Now she's home."

"Matthias, be sensible. They lost four of their men in this raid. Two of ours were injured. I need the full context for negotiations and to get the bounty off Margot."

I curse under my breath. He's right. And that pisses me off even more.

"Fine. I'll talk to her when she's ready and get back to you."

"Tomorrow."

"No."

"Matthias, tomorrow morning. I have to meet with Viktor in the afternoon. We can't give him time to assume the worst."

I glance toward the door again. Margot hasn't moved. I grit my teeth.

"Fine. In the morning. Then I'm out. I want nothing to do with the Syndicate."

"You don't get to opt out, Matthias. We're not a fucking email list. You're a Montclair. You're in it whether you like it or not."

"I have to protect my woman. And the Syndicate isn't safe for her. She's done with it. I'm done with it. I won't risk her again."

I step into his space, toe-to-toe.

Roman shoves between us. "Matthias will step up when necessary. But give him some space, Dom. He just got his girl back." He glances between us. "Figure your shit out. I'm sick of playing referee."

I step back and take another peek into our room. She's still sleeping. Dom's fucking lucky he didn't wake her.

Dom exhales. "Fine. Get me the info in the morning. I'll let you know what Viktor says."

"I will. Now leave. I need to get back to her."

Dom gives me a look, his *don't screw this up* look, then heads out.

Roman and Bash linger. I glare at them.

"How is she?" Bash asks. Roman actually looks like he cares. Dom's footsteps stall on the stairs.

"She's going to be okay," I say softly. "Everything will heal. It'll take a few weeks for her to get her strength back. She hadn't eaten since the gala. Her silent rebellion. Actually, not silent, I'm sure. Not my spitfire." I smile. "The doctor gave her fluids. We'll keep doing that. She's bruised, bloody, and banged up, but she wasn't raped."

Three audible sighs.

"Good," Roman says, voice gruff. "Take care of her, man. Let us know if you need anything."

He pulls me in and slaps my back once before turning. Bash does the same.

When I hear them reach the stairs, I slip back into our room.

They can see themselves out.

I can't be away from her another second.

I crawl back into bed and pull Margot into my arms.

And for the first time in a week, I sleep.

Chapter 84
Margot

The door creaking open wakes me, and for a second, panic grips me.

Then I remember I'm home, and the fear dissolves.

But when I see Matty opening the bedroom door like he's about to leave, a new kind of fear creeps in.

"Thanks. Did you make it just how I said?"

"Boy, I know how to make coffee. Now let me in to see her." I hear Dotty demand.

"No. She's sleeping. You can see her when she comes down for breakfast. Stick to the meal plan from the doctor."

I hear her grumble and stomp away, clearly unimpressed.

"You could've let her in," I say lightly once the door closes.

"Hey sweetheart. I didn't know you were awake," Matty turns with a warm smile. "I have your coffee."

"Thanks, baby." He crosses the room and hands me the cup. I take a sip and let out a soft moan.

He shifts slightly, and I notice the way he adjusts his sweatpants.

I hide my grin behind the mug, blushing.

"Why didn't you make it?" I tease.

"I'm not leaving your side," he says simply. "Not even to make your coffee."

My heart swells. I don't know if he's doing it for me, or for him, but either way, it makes me feel loved.

I can't be alone right now.

He knows that.

He sits on the edge of the bed, watching me as I drink. I know what's coming and start the conversation, so he doesn't have to. Listening will be hard enough. I don't need him to feel guilty for forcing the conversation.

"You want to know what happened."

"Not want. Need. Sweetheart, it's going to kill me to hear it. I hate myself for making you relive it. But we have to know, so we can move forward with the Bratva." He looks pained at having to have the conversation.

He looks miserable just saying it.

"It's okay, Matty. I knew this was coming." I reach for his hand, and he immediately puts both of his around mine.

So, I start.

When I reach the part where my boss grabs me, Matty's face twists in rage. I pause and squeeze his hand.

"Baby, it gets worse. You need to calm down."

He pulls me into his lap and moves so his back rests against the headboard, and I'm lying across him.

"I know. It's just hard to hear. Keep going, sweetheart."

So, I do.

Every time someone hurt me, he holds me tighter.

When I relay running through the basement, he curses.

When I repeat my conversation with Viktor, he sneers.

"You told him you were mine? That you're Syndicate?"

"Yes, but he didn't believe me." I lower my gaze.

"That's okay, sweet girl. You did the right thing. This gives us enough to justify what we did. You did so well." He presses a kiss to the top of my head.

"Actually, I think he believed me at first. He was worried. But when you didn't come... he started to doubt me. He said if I were really yours, you would've come by now."

My voice quiets at the end. Shame creeps in. Because I believed Viktor.

Matty hears it. Hears the doubt I carried.

"Sweetheart, we never stopped looking for you. You were our top priority. You have to know that. I'm sorry it took so long. I'm sorry I gave you time to doubt me."

"You saved me. That's what matters." I kiss his cheek, and he pulls me in tighter.

When I get to the final interaction, the man telling me I'd be sent to the docks, Matty stills.

"Tell me exactly what he said."

I repeat it verbatim.

His mouth moves in a string of curses, but his voice stays low.

"Thank you, sweatheart. You did so well. That's all I need. I'm so proud of you, my strong girl. You never have to talk about it again. Not unless you want to. I'll always listen." He assures me and sprinkles my head with kisses.

We lie there for a while longer. I feel safe in his arms. But eventually, I start to stir.

"Where do you think you're going?" he murmurs, pulling me back in.

"Downstairs. I need some breakfast."

"If you're ready to eat, let's go. But you're not going anywhere without me." He pops up and scoops me into his arms.

"Matty! I can walk." I laugh as he carries me toward the stairs.

"Absolutely not."

We enter the kitchen and are immediately ambushed by Dotty. It's almost a mirror image of Benny's reaction yesterday.

"Give her space," Matty growls, shielding me.

Dotty huffs and backs off as he sets me on a stool at the island. He stands behind me, arms caging me in like a protective wall.

"You're nothing but skin and bones," Dotty mutters. "I'm cooking feasts until you're back to normal."

"No. You're following Dr. Anderson's meal plan," Matty snaps. "She'll get sick if she eats too much."

Dotty grumbles, but I think it's agreement.

That reminds me.

"Dotty, have you met Dr. Anderson?" I ask casually.

Her cheeks flush instantly.

I jump out of my seat in excitement, but Matty catches me mid-motion and lightly forces me back into place. "Sit still, sweetheart."

"I have," Dotty says while pretending to focus on the stove. I know better.

"What do you think of him?" I say in the most innocent tone I can muster.

"What are you doing?" Matty leans down and whispers in my ear.

I ignore him.

"I was thinking maybe you two could coordinate my meal plan together. I think he'll be over more often to do checkups. He seems like a really nice man."

"Such a naughty girl," Matty murmurs, but there's a grin in his voice. He loves this.

"Oh. I didn't realize he'd be over again," Dotty says, scrambling eggs with more focus than necessary.

"Neither did I," Matty whispers sarcastically.

"Yes. And since he's not married, he probably has a lot of time on his hands."

"I didn't know he was single," she muses.

"There seems to be a lot you don't know about him," I tease. "Maybe you should spend some time together. He seems lonely."

It's bold. I hold my breath, waiting for her to snap at me.

But instead, "Maybe I'll reach out to him," she answers, her voice soft.

I grin.

It's damn good to be home.

Chapter 85
Matthias

She hasn't left my side all day, but I also haven't given her a chance. I won't let her out of my sight. I'm not sure which one of us has worse separation anxiety. Even Benny seems affected.

He's perched nearby, standing guard over Margot as she sleeps on the couch in my office. I had some catching up to do. Syndicate Enterprise hasn't seen a flicker of my attention in the past week. Nothing mattered except finding her. But now that I have her, I have to pull the rest of my life back together.

She followed me in here earlier with her Kindle, but she didn't last long. Her body's been through hell. Honestly, I'm surprised she didn't crash sooner. She's already recovering. She's been eating and taking fluids. I've never had a problem handling needles, but sticking one in her? That hurt.

Not her, of course. My strong girl barely flinched.

But me? Yeah, it gutted me.

I sigh and pick up my phone. I know what I have to do if I want to put this behind us.

"Did you talk to her?" Dom's voice cuts through the quiet.

"Yes," I grit out. "She told me everything. In detail."

My jaw clenches as the memory resurfaces, rage tightening every muscle. I force myself to relax before I crush the phone in my hand. The volcano of fury in me borders on rupturing. She went through all of it alone... and still survived. My strong girl.

"What does Viktor know?" Dom skips the sympathy. I'm grateful. I don't want to repeat her words. Don't want to relive them.

"She told him the first time they spoke that she's mine. That the Syndicate would come for her. She thinks he believed her at first, but after a while... he doubted it. He figured we weren't coming. That puts this on him, right?"

"Yes. That helps us. What else?"

"She said the men who attacked her were the reason Viktor wanted revenge. She told him I stepped in to protect her. I think he bought that and realized she wasn't the one who took out Bratva men."

Dom hums in approval. "You defending your woman, especially on our territory, is justified. And the shipments?"

"She told him she didn't know anything. Said she noticed a discrepancy, told her boss, and that was it. She never leaked anything. She said he didn't believe her at first... but by Saturday, he didn't seem to care anymore."

"What do you mean?"

"She said one of the men told her they were 'done with her' and 'taking her to the docks to join the new shipment'. What the fuck does that mean?"

Dom's quiet for a beat, then, "Nothing good. We'll figure it out."

He's angry. I can hear it.

"So, what now?"

"I'll talk to Viktor. Smooth it over. You've claimed Margot, so she's under Syndicate protection. We'll deny any knowledge of their shipments and keep ourselves out of a war."

His calm is reassuring. I let myself breathe.

This is it.

Margot is safe.

"Good. Now keep us out of it. I don't want anything of your Syndicate bullshit to touch her again." My voice hardens to steel.

"Matthias... you know how this works. I'll give you space, but when you're needed, you'll have to step up."

I see Margot start to stir. She doesn't need to hear any of this. She's safe now. That's all that matters.

"Fine. I have to go." I hang up before he can respond.

I watch the rise and fall of her chest. Every breath she takes soothes the fire in me. I can't bear to let her out of my sight. I don't know how long this'll last.

I love her. God, I love her. And all I want to do is be close to her. To be with her in every way.

But she's still healing. Still climbing out of this nightmare. So, I'll keep my distance.

As much as it kills me...

I won't touch you, sweetheart.

Not until you're whole again.

Chapter 86
Margot

I've been home a week now. I'm getting stronger every day, slowly coming back to life. My curves have started to return thanks to Dotty cheating the meal plan. Much to Matty's chagrin.

Everything's getting better...

Except one thing.

He won't touch me.

I mean, he does, just not in the way I want him to. Not in the way I need him to. I get a chaste kiss, a morning cuddle, a short embrace. But every time I try to take it further, he pulls away.

It's not because he doesn't want me. I see the proof of his need every time I press up against him. He just won't act on it. Not while I'm still 'healing.' Not when he's drowning in guilt.

If he won't touch me out of guilt, then maybe he needs a reminder that I'm not fragile. That I'm his.

Instead of letting the rejection embarrass me, I let it fuel me.

Because today? Today, I'm getting my man.

I slip into the blue sundress that I know he likes. The one he's ripped off me more than once, and a couple times, didn't even finish getting off. No bra. I want to tease him a little. Show him how much I need him.

We're finally at the point where I'm allowed in a different room. For small stretches, anyway. But that's enough.

"Come here, Benny."

He trots to me like the perfect accomplice, tail wagging. I turn and skip down the hall toward the front door.

"Where are you going, sweetheart?" Matty calls lightly from behind me in his office.

That light tone won't last much longer.

I keep walking.

I hear his chair scrape back. His footsteps follow, quickening when he sees where I'm headed.

"Margot, don't you dare open that door. Get your cute ass back here. One of the guards can walk Benny," he growls, his voice sharp now.

He hasn't let me outside once all week. He acts like there's a sniper camped across the lawn just waiting to take me out. It's ridiculous.

I reach the front door and unlock it.

"Not another fucking step! I swear to God, Margot. I'll spank your ass raw!" he bellows, and I hear him start to run.

That's all the encouragement I need.

I swing the door open and bolt. I make it to the bottom step before his arms wrap around me.

"What the fuck, Margot? You can't be out here. It's not safe." His voice is tight with fear, but I don't stop.

"Ow!" I fake a cry, sagging against him.

He freezes in panic and drops me immediately

I twist out of his arms and run, laughing as I race through the garden.

"Margot, get back here! I'm not kidding!" he shouts, angry and scared in equal measures.

"No," I call back, spinning in the sun. "I'm fine. I'm safe. I'm on our property. Nothing can get me here!"

Sunlight kisses my skin. My pores soak up the vitamin D.

Naughty girl. We all know you're after a different D.

"Margot, get back here, right now! You're going inside and staying there. I'll lock you up if I have to. I've done it before, and I sure as fuck will do it again," he threatens.

I shoot him a wink, then sprint around the house toward the garage. There are no guards stationed over here.

Perfect.

I wait for him to round the corner, and when his eyes lock on mine, I slip the straps of my dress off. It falls easily, pooling at my feet.

The only thing left is my black lace panties. The one from that first day.

Matty freezes, his eyes locked on my bare check. His cock hardens visibly. He curses under his breath, tilts his head up, and pinches the bridge of his nose like he's praying for patience.

"What the fuck are you doing, Margot? Put your goddamn dress on," he grits out, eyes locked on the sky. He refuses to look at me.

"Nope." I turn slightly, feigning a step toward the backyard where there definitely are guards.

It snaps him out of his little fit.

He lunges, grabbing me by the waist and hauls me to the wall of the house. One hand grips my hip, while the other braces the wall beside my head, caging me in.

"You're going to put that dress back on and march yourself inside, or I will throw you over my shoulder and lock you in our bedroom for a month. Do not test me."

"No. I want to be outside. I want to be free. I want you. Touch me, baby. Please, Matty. Fuck me."

I press my breasts against his chest, and grind against the solid length I can feel through his slacks.

He groans, tortured.

"No. I can't. You're not healed yet." His voice is hoarse, begging me to understand.

Too bad for him, I don't.

And today, I'm getting what I want. So, I go for my ace.

I spit in his face.

His pupils blow wide.

Rage. Lust. Hunger.

"You want to play that game?" he snarls. "Fine, spitfire. Let's play."

He wipes my spit with his fingers, then smears it on my cheek. He grips my face, pinching my chin to force my eyes up.

"I'll give you one chance to apologize."

"Fuck you."

I go to spit again, but he covers my mouth with his palm, finally learning his lesson.

He laughs darkly. "Have it your way."

He spins me around, so I'm facing the wall.

RRRRIP!

The sound alone sends a shiver down my spine. Then the cool air hits my soaked core.

He *ripped* my panties off.

"You're being a naughty girl. Looks like someone needs a spanking to remember her place."

And then his palm lands hard on my ass.

Once.

Twice.

Three times.

By the fourth, I'm moaning and arching into him.

"Fuck, sweetheart. You love this, don't you?"

"Mhmm," I moan.

"Fuck it." he curses.

I hear his belt come undone.

"You drive me insane. You know that? You don't listen. You don't behave, and I still can't fucking breathe without you."

I hear his zipper lower.

"Spread your legs."

When I hesitate, he kicks them apart. He pulls my hips out and presses my chest against the brick.

"Arch your back."

The rough texture scraped my nipples, and pain and pleasure merge.

"Please, Matty. Please, fuck me. I need you."

"Fuck, spitfire."

He thrusts in hard and deep, and I cry out. It's been too long.

He fucks me with long, punishing strokes. Pulling almost all the way out, then slamming back in. Over and over again.

I push back into him, chasing every thrust.

"You're fucking mine," he growls. "And when I make rules to keep you safe, you listen."

And then, he pulls out.

"No!"

Before I can protest further, he spins me around and lifts me into his arms. His eyes are wild and unhinged. It's enchanting.

He slams back into me as I cling to his shoulders, my legs locked around him. He moves one hand to my cheek and kisses me so fiercely I forget how to breathe.

He breaks the kiss, and trails his lips down my neck, biting and marking me.

When he reaches under my ear, I clench, and he groans, doubling his pace.

He tweaks my nipples, then drops his fingers to my clit, rubbing just the way I need.

I'm a mess. A pleading, shaking mess.

"I... I need to come," I gasp, knowing I should wait for permission.

He doesn't hesitate.

"Do it. Choke the cum out of me. Take my seed like a good girl."

I come instantly, screaming as stars burst behind my eyes.

He follows with a roar, pumping into me as I feel him fill me. It's hot and heavy and endless. It's him. It's perfect.

He drops his head to my shoulder. We breathe together, our heartbeats syncing.

Then he lifts his head.

"Don't break my rules, sweetheart. They're to keep you safe."

"Matty, they're *ridiculous*!" I whine.

"I might tweak them since you're healing but promise me you'll let me protect you."

"Yes, sir."

He groans, and I clench around him. The groan turns into a growl.

"You're such a naughty girl," he rasps. "Coming out here with no bra. Did you plan this? Did you plan to be a little slut for me? To strip in our yard and beg for my cock?"

I moan in answer, resting my head back against the bricks.

"Look at me."

I obey instantly. He smirks, loving it.

He unbuttons his shirt, finally shredding a layer. I blush at being naked while he's fully dressed.

He pulls his shirt off and wraps it around me, then takes my weight from the wall, and cradles me.

"Let's go, spitfire. I have two weeks to make up for."

Epilogue I
Margot

I wake up to the smell of coffee, and the sexiest man on earth bringing it to me. My smile breaks out.

"Morning, sweetheart. I brought you coffee," he says, voice still rough with sleep.

"Thanks, Matty," I murmur, sitting up.

He hands me the mug, and I melt into the warmth. One sip, and I sigh. Perfect. Like always.

"After you finish drinking, get ready. We have plans," he says excitedly.

I set the cup down slowly. "I will kill you."

His smile falters. "What?"

"Matthias Vincent Montclair. I'm not fucking around. If we have somewhere to be today and you're only just telling–"

His shoulders drop in relief. "No, no. It's not like that. It's just the two of us. I swear."

I narrow my eyes, but the anger's already fading. "Okay... what are we doing?"

"Just breakfast on the terrace. I wanted to get you up before it starts raining."

"What should I wear?"

"Whatever you'd like."

I roll my eyes. "Ugh. That's not helpful. You're back on thin ice, mister!"

He just winks and walks out of the room like he didn't give me whiplash. I grumble, but my feet are already moving. I reach for the blue dress I know he loves.

...

We start the morning off with breakfast on the terrace. Then we take Benny out to play, and after that... well, a shared shower ends with me screaming his name so loudly, the guards outside probably heard.

Now, we're in the dining room. I sit beside him at his head of the table. Dotty walks in and places plates of eggplant parmesan in front of us.

Something shifts.

Once she's gone, I turn to Matty slowly.

"Our first dinner, we had eggplant parmesan. Dotty said it wasn't a usual meal of yours, but you demanded it." I hesitate. "Did you... did you know it was my favorite?"

I can't bring myself to look at him.

But he never lets me hide. He tilts my chin up, forcing me to meet his gaze.

"Of course I did. I had Bash run a background check on you. It was very thorough," he smirks. "He didn't know I was keeping you here. He was furious when he found out he'd helped."

I don't even process that last bit. I'm too caught up with the former part.

"But why?" I whisper. "Why would you go through the trouble? I was just some girl who saw too much."

He shakes his head. "You were never *just some girl*. From the second I took you, I knew I wasn't letting you go. And not because of what you saw. You were mine far before I ever said it out loud. I just had to convince you." A small smile plays on his lips. "I thought starting with your favorite meal might help."

I let out a snort. "Look how that turned out."

"It brought us here," he says softly. "To right now. I wouldn't change a thing."

"Not even how difficult I was?"

"*Especially* that. Being a spitfire is what drew me in. The more you fought, the harder I fell."

My cheeks flush, and I focus on eating. His hand rests on my thigh. Not teasing, not inching higher. Just holding. It's warm. Grounding.

When we finish eating, he clears his throat.

"Do you want to go to the theater? There's something I want to put on."

It's not a demand; it's a question. That alone makes me blink.

"Sure…" I say slowly, watching him fidget with his napkin.

He leads me to the theater and sits me beside him. Not *on* him. I try to climb into his lap anyway, but he shifts me off. I try not to take it personally, but he senses my hurt.

"I ate too much. I just need a few minutes, then I'll hold you," he murmurs, brushing my cheek. "I promise."

I nod and lean into his side.

"What are we watching?"

"Hush, sweetheart."

He grabs the remote. The lights dim but not all the way. I can still make him out.

Words appear on the screen:

Once Upon a Time.

"*Once upon a time…*" he begins.

Except it's not him. Not live at least.

It's a recording. Playing through the theater's speakers.

"*A man went out for coffee but never got his drink. Instead, he got the love of his life.*"

I freeze.

"*Well… not got. Took. He took the love of his life.*"

My heart stops. He's narrating our story.

"*When she witnessed something she shouldn't have seen, he had no choice. But deep down, even if she hadn't, he still would've kept her. She was his other half. The part of him he hadn't known was missing.*"

I can feel his eyes on me.

"*So, he took her. And to this day, he still doesn't regret it. He never will.*

She fought. Of course she did. Every sassy comment, every act of rebellion, every ounce of resistance, they just made him fall harder for his spitfire."

I laugh through the lump in my throat.

"*He learned everything about her. When he found her hidden passion, her audiobooks, he was brought to his knees. He came like a teenager the first time he heard her voice whispering sin in his ears.*"

My face burns.

"*He saw her sleeping in his bed and knew it wasn't his anymore. It was theirs. Their room. Their home. Their life.*

Even her lazy, sorry excuse for a guard dog stole his heart.

Hell, he was even jealous of that damn dog. Because the dog made her smile in ways he couldn't. Not yet."

The dog and she were a mischievous pair. He saw when they would run his guards around, making them fetch balls purely for her amusement.”

I cover my mouth, eyes wide. How did he even know that?

“He couldn't help himself. Couldn't stay away. He watched her constantly. Security feeds on every screen. He still does. He can't concentrate if he can't see her.”

“What–” I whisper.

“Shhh,” he murmurs.

“She barged into his life like a hurricane. Spit on him. Defied him. Seduced him with every step, even though she didn't mean to.

He did everything he could to get her to choose to stay. To choose him. To choose them. He changed for her. Became better for her.

And when he professed his love to her, he didn't know how she'd react. But he couldn't contain it. He wouldn't hide it any longer. He loved her, and she needed to accept it.

When she told him she loved him too, it was the greatest moment of his life.

Her love is his most prized possession.”

Tears well in my eyes.

“Then, he lost her. He lost his everything. He'd never been so scared. He would've burned the world to ash to get her back. And once she was back where she belonged, beside him, he swore he'd earn her forgiveness. Earn her love. Earn her.”

I reach for his hand and grip it tightly.

“Now? Now, he's her whole world. She was always his. She just didn't know it then. But she'll never forget it now, he'll never let her.”

The screen fades. Soft music begins to play.

I turn to him. “Matty, I–”

“Shhh,” he whispers.

Then he stands.

Reaches into his pocket.

Drops to one knee.

Clears his throat.

"Margot, sweetheart... I remember when you told me you wanted a storybook love on our first dinner date. Someone to be your everything. Someone to hold you through the bad times and be by your side during the good ones. A best friend. Kissing, crying, fighting, all of it."

He takes my hand.

"I want to be all of that for you. I am all of that for you. Just as you are for me."

He pulls out the ring.

"I made this narration of our story to remind you how far we've come. Of every moment that led us here. I'll never hide how I feel again. I promise."

His eyes glisten.

"It's our anniversary. A year ago today, we both went to get coffee. We didn't get our drinks, but we did get each other."

He swallows.

"Please let me be your forever. Let me be yours in every way."

He takes a shaky breath.

"Margot Peterson, will you marry me?"

Full-body sobs break out of me in waves. I fling myself into his arms.

"Yes! Yes, Matty. *Yes!*"

He slips the ring on. I glance down at the round diamond in a delicate halo, set in white gold. Simple. Timeless. Perfect.

"Oh Matty..." I whisper. "It's beautiful."

"I made it for you," he says softly.

He cups my face and kisses me like I'm the center of his universe. Like there's no one else in the world.

Then he sweeps me into his arms, stands, and lowers me onto the cushions like I'm made of glass.

He hovers above me, eyes filled with wonder.

"Finally," he breathes, "my Margot Montclair."

And it sounds like home.

Epilogue II
Matthias

"So, Margot, have you guys decided when the wedding will be?" Mom asks.

We're all gathered at my parent's house for family dinner. Well, everyone except Roman. He's running late, so we went ahead and started without him.

"We're thinking between six months to a year," Margot replies. "We're not stressing too much about it."

"That's the way to do it," Mom nods. "We're here for anything you need."

"We appreciate it, Mom," I tell her with a warm smile.

"Who all will be in the wedding?"

"Bash, Dom, and Roman will be the groomsmen," Margot says, then hesitates. Her cheeks flush. "And I figured their dates could be the bridesmaids."

She's embarrassed. I know she feels self-conscious about not having any close girlfriends.

"I won't be taking a date," Dom cuts in, his voice flat.

"Nor will I," Bash spits out, arms crossed, as though the idea of a date to my wedding disgusts him.

What the hell?

I'd expected it from Dom, but it's surprising from Bash. The man has dozens of women on speed dial.

"Why not? It's not like you don't have a long list of options," I ask Bash.

"I'm not seeing any of them anymore."

"Since when?" I ask, eyebrows raised.

"They don't interest me."

Before anyone can follow up, the dining room door swings open and Roman walks in.

A beautiful woman trails behind him.

Tall and graceful. Long, dark waves framing her soft features. Her skin is tanned, her brown eyes vivid and wide. She's wearing a floor-length skirt and a flowy blouse.

Who the hell is this?

"Hey guys. This is Cecilia, my girlfriend." Roman delivers it casually, like he didn't just drop a grenade in the room.

We all stare, stunned. She looks way too soft for Roman. He's going to eat her alive.

Margot recovers first.

"Welcome! It's such a pleasure to have you. I'm Margot, and this is my fiancé, Matthias." She flashes Cecilia one of her warm, radiant smiles.

For a second, I'm jealous that someone else gets to be on the receiving end of it. Then Margot squeezes my hand beneath the table, and I pull her close.

"It's so nice to meet you," Cecilia beams. "Roman's told me so much about you guys. Mr. and Mrs. Montclair, your home is absolutely lovely. Thank you for having me."

"Of course, dear," Mom responds smoothly. "We're so glad to finally meet you. Please, sit down." She stands abruptly, realizing there's no place set. "I'm sorry. We'll have a spot made right away. Please, sit."

Cecilia's smile doesn't waver. "I'm so sorry for intruding. I can leave if this was meant to be just family. Roman must've forgotten to mention it." She turns to him with teasing eyes. "Héroe, how silly of you."

I brace myself for it. Waiting for Roman to snap. To bark at her. To correct her.

For teasing him.

For reprimanding him.

For calling him *hero.*

What the fuck was that? Roman's the villain.

But instead, he pulls her into a hug.

"I'm sorry, sunshine. I thought it'd be a nice surprise. And maybe we'd avoid the interrogation they put Margot through."

That snaps Mom back into hostess mode. "No, dear, you're absolutely welcome. We're so excited to meet you. You'll have to stay later so we can chat more."

"We'd love to," Cecilia chirps just as Roman mutters, "We don't have time."

She turns to him, smiling up sweetly. "Hero, please. I want to get to know your family."

And just like that, the beast melts. "Of course, Celia."

Dinner continues not as usual. Roman's acting charming. Saying please and thank you. He's cooing at her. It's unsettling.

Bash and I keep trading glances. Dom's just glaring at Roman, taking breaks only to flick skeptical looks at Cecilia like she's a puzzle he can't solve.

"Did you know about her?" Margot breathes out under her breath for only me to hear.

"No. I have no idea what's going on." I whisper back.

"So, Celia, when did this start?" Dom asks bluntly.

"It's Cecilia to you." Roman corrects lightly, but shoots daggers at Dom. The calm voice is unsettling against his glare that his woman can't see. *Cecilia* giggles, thinking Roman's joking.

"A few months ago," Cecilia answers, her gaze fond. "He saved me. He's my personal hero. He's rescued me more than once since then. My life has been unexpectedly chaotic these past few months, and he's always there when I need him. It's like he just knows."

Saved her?

Roman beams at her. "Of course. I'll always be there to protect you, Celia. I'll always be here to keep you safe. You'll never get rid of me."

There's warmth in his voice, but something sharp flickers in his eyes.

"It makes sense," Cecilia continues, completely oblivious. "Since his job is saving people. It's amazing that you guys run Syndicate Enterprise. You keep people safe. That's incredible."

A heavy silence crashes over the table.

Margot drops her fork with a *clank*. Dom stiffens. Mom and Dad share a sharp glance. Bash pales.

And Roman.

He's staring us down.

A silent warning.

A threat.

I've never seen him so terrifying.

"Yes," I reply, my voice clipped. "It's great to have him on the team."

The conversation carries on, but we're all off kilter.

With every sweet word this naïve girl says, one thing becomes terrifyingly clear.

She has no idea who Roman really is.

After months together, she doesn't know him at all.

The ruthless killer.

The angry beast.

The man the underworld fears.

She's none the wiser to the man.

Cecilia has no idea he's lying to her. And he's doing it with a smile. She thinks he saved her. But he's the one she needs saving from.

She's falling in love with a mask.

God help her when it slips.

Dear Reader

Thank you for reading *Innocent Intentions*.

This is my debut novel, and it's surreal that it made it out of my head and into your hands. Every reader who finishes this book is helping my dream come true. I appreciate you more than you know. This journey has been incredible, and now, you're a part of it.

If you enjoyed this story, I'd be truly grateful if you left a review on your favorite platform(s). Reviews are one of the best ways to support an author. Each one makes a difference.

Roman's not done yet... and neither am I.

Next up: *Deceptive Desires.*

Much love,
Ellie

Acknowledgements

There are so many people who have supported me and helped make this dream a reality. *Innocent Intentions* would still be sitting in my mind if it weren't for you. From the bottom of my heart, thank you.

Katelyn, my best friend and biggest supporter, thank you. This book would never exist without you. I'll never forget pitching the idea to you in that booth, and you encouraging me to go for it. You've been here from the very beginning, not only as my alpha reader, but as my ride-or-die. Thank you for believing in me.

Maggie, you have always been my guiding light, recently as my beta reader, but for my whole life as my older sister. I look up to you so much. Your support of me and this book means everything. I'm so glad I could pull you into new genre! Thank you for always picking up my calls, even if it's just me singing poorly or rambling about plot ideas.

Ashley, thank you for being by my side through so many years of shenanigans. You were an incredible beta reader and even better best friend. I'm honored you read and edited my novel, and I'm so grateful you didn't judge me for the, uh... graphic scenes.

Parker Drue, thank you for being a stellar beta reader. Your feedback had me giggling and kicking my feet. Every email I got from you was the highlight of my day. No one loves Benny more than you, and that's saying something, considering I created him as my dream dog. Thank you for your amazing notes and unwavering support.

Haleigh, thank you beta reader and book bestie. What started in the Circle of Trust took flight thanks to you. I'm beyond grateful you encouraged me to chase this dream, and I'm honored you deemed *Innocent Intentions* as a genuinely great read.

Andie, my baby sister (and kind of beta reader), thank you for always being in my corner. You've listened to my endless story rants, cheered me on through every new idea, and supported me without hesitation. I hope you love this book, because there's truly no one whose opinion I treasure more or try harder to impress. I love you so much.

Kenzie, my beautiful best friend. Even though you're not a reader, you've supported me in every way that matters. Thank you for listening to hours (and hours) of plot ramblings and scene breakdowns. Talking things out with you always helps me more than you know. Your constant support and excitement for me and my writing mean the world to me. I'm lucky to have you in my corner.

Mom, thank you for being excited for my book, and for supporting me not just with writing, but through every challenge I've faced. You have always been my biggest cheerleader. I'm sorry I hid this from you for so long, but once you read this book... you'll understand why. I'm still debating whether you're getting the full version or a heavily redacted one.

If you get the real one, please know most of this was not based on experience, and please don't drop me off at a psych ward.

Mimi, my dearest Mimi. Thank you for encouraging me to chase my dreams and try writing. I loved telling you the wild plot of *Innocent Intentions* and thank you for not judging me. I'm not if sure you'll ever get a copy, but if you do… please don't send me to Fr. Cleo.

Dad, thank you for cheering me on and always listening to my writing updates. You congratulate me on even the smallest accomplishments. You most certainly are not getting a copy of this book.

Mrs. Katrina, thank you. Your support started decades ago when you tutored me in English. I owe so much to you, from my ACT score, my degree, and now this book. You were like a second mom to me back then, and I was so excited to share this milestone with you. Thank you.

Mrs. Douet, thank you for sharing that unforgettable story you told senior year, about a student who was caught writing a spicy scene. You told us you disagreed with the teacher who reported her, and said she was simply being creative. That moment stuck with me. Thank you for supporting art in all its forms.

To my ARC readers, and even those who applied but couldn't be selected, thank you! Your support has helped me share my book and my dream with the world. I couldn't be more grateful for every review, every post, every word. It means more than I can say.

To all my book besties on BookTok and Bookstagram, I was blown away by your support. Before my book even launched, you made me feel seen and encouraged. Thank you for welcoming me into this community.

And finally, to all my family and friends, thank you. I am eternally grateful for every person who helped me along this journey. I love each and every one of you.

About the Author

Ellie Hallaron is an author and lifelong storyteller, always turning ordinary moments into something worth retelling.

She fell in love with books early on, and growing up, the only punishment that ever stuck was having them taken away. Novels have always felt like home, first as a reader, now as a writer.

Ellie writes emotionally charged romance with depth, intensity, and heroes you probably shouldn't fall for... but absolutely will.

When she's not writing, she's usually with friends and family who patiently endure her spirals over fictional characters, or she's dreaming up the next story.

She's thrilled to finally share her words with readers.

And she's just getting started.

Let's Stay in Touch

If you fell in love with *Innocent Intentions* and want more of the Montclair brothers, come hang out with me online.

I share exclusive updates, upcoming releases, spicy teasers, unreleased scenes, and more!

You can find me here:

TikTok: @EllieHallaron.Author
Instagram: @EllieHallaron.Author
Goodreads: Goodreads.com/EllieHallaron